MISS HAZEL

and the

ROSA PARKS

LEAGUE

MISS HAZEL

and the

ROSA PARKS

LEAGUE

a novel

by

JONATHAN ODELL

MAIDEN LANE
PRESS

Interior and jacket design by Laura Klynstra
Photograph of young women courtesy of Arlene Beard Norton
Photograph of Hazel and Jonathan courtesy of the author

First Edition

Distributed by Ingram Publisher Services

10 9 8 7 6 5 4 3 2 1

To my parents, Faye and Odell Johnson

Your stories have mattered

PROLOGUE

It was up to Vida to save her boy. With Nate in her arms, she fled through the back door and toward the darkened field behind the house. If she could get Nate to the bayou beyond, into the dark stand of cypress, he would be safe.

The two white men must have heard the back screen slap shut, because the lights of their truck were now cutting across the field. She turned. It roared toward her, plowing through rows of cotton, the bumper mowing down plants half as tall as men. They were almost upon her. There was no way she could make it to the bayou. Vida dropped down between two rows, cradling Nate beneath her.

The truck braked and she heard a door open. She peeked above the row. They stood only a few yards away, listening to the night, the headlights throwing their shadows long across the field.

Nate whimpered and one stumbled off in the direction of the sound.

The old man lurched after him. "Don't!" he shouted. "You don't want to kill nobody, son. Specially not no little baby. Specially not yore..."

"Shut your goddamned mouth! He ain't my nothing," the other one slurred. "That boy lives, I lose it all!"

The old man called out in a panic, "Gal! Stay down. You hear me? Don't raise up." He reached out and tugged at the barrel of the gun.

Vida leaped up and started off again.

Moments later came the first blast, followed quickly by the second. With blinding force, the searing spray of buckshot sent Vida and her child tumbling into darkness.

As the explosions echoed throughout the quarter, the lanterns in the shanties dimmed as quickly as they had come on.

BOOK ONE

HAZEL AND VIDA

Chapter One

A MAN WHO

TAKES CARE OF HIS OWN

Hazel was busy arranging a display of Tangee beauty products at the Rexall where she had been working in Tupelo when a tall handsome man right off the bus, fresh from the Navy and still wearing his summer whites, strode confidently into the drugstore. His eyes were two dark stars.

He grinned at her and tilted his head in a way that set the butterflies in her stomach to fluttering. "Is the druggist in? I need to get me a prescription filled for a root beer float." He spoke in a voice like a country love song, tender and true. At first Hazel couldn't answer, she could only stare wide-mouthed at him as if she were waiting for the second verse. "Now, you wouldn't happen to know the formula for one, would you?"

Blushing, she could only stammer, "I sure do. . .can. . .will." By the time she got behind the fountain, she had calmed herself enough to joke, "I won't even ask to see your doctor's note."

That made him laugh. It was a good laugh, gentle, seemingly incapable of meanness. Setting the glass before him, she warned with a wink, "Don't eat it too fast or you'll freeze your goozle."

He said, "I'm sure not in any hurry now."

It was his eyes that really got her attention. Like dark mirrors of polished iron, they were beautiful to look at, but they wouldn't let Hazel in. His eyes seemed to push back on her, which made her want to come all the closer. She told him, "I bet you could stare a buzzard out of a tree."

He blushed and said, "You got the best posture of any girl I've ever met."

Hazel could tell he wanted to say more, but he didn't need to. In his mirrored eyes she saw herself as pretty, as pretty as she'd felt the day that traveling photographer had snapped her picture.

Hazel had been twelve years old when the slick-haired, sugar-talking man arrived one hot summer afternoon with the mysterious black box he swore would show her to be as pretty as anybody in the movies. Up until then, she had never seen a photograph of herself. While he set up his camera and posed each one of her brothers and sisters, she flirted with him, tossing back her hair and licking her lips the way she had seen Jean Harlow do. Standing out in the yard as the man took her picture, she felt her skin burn at the thought of escaping the Tombigbee Hills.

Her mother never had any patience for this full-of-feelings girl. Each time Hazel asked if the pictures had arrived, she was warned about getting her hopes up. "Hope does the plowing in Misery's field," her mother said. But the delicious anticipation of things hoped for had to be the best sensation Hazel knew of. She didn't know how she could live without thinking something good was about to happen, not in the sweet by-and-by but tomorrow, if not today.

When the photographs finally arrived two months later, her hands trembled as she opened the envelope. The first was of her momma and daddy sitting stiffly next to each other, the way strangers share a bench at the dentist's office. The next was of her daddy with his arm around his mule's neck. How much more at ease he appeared posing with a plow mule!

Finally she came to the family portrait, twelve of them in front of the paintless barn. On one end was her daddy in his white starched shirt and overalls, and on the other end was her momma, tired and worn, holding baby Jewel. Bunched between them was the brood of wooden-faced children, not a size missing between knee-high and full grown, with two spaces left empty for the boys still off to war in the Pacific.

Something wasn't right! Hazel touched her finger to each face in the picture. She could identify her brothers and sisters, yet her own face was missing. Had the camera skipped over her?

"No!" she gasped. That photographer had played an awful trick on Hazel! In her place he had put a half-starved orphan, neglected and bound to die soon. The poor little girl was stoop-shouldered and had hair the texture of broom straw. A dingy, hand-me-down dress swallowed the rail-thin body. The face was gaunt and hollow-eyed. She had the haggard look of a woman of fifty, not of a girl of twelve.

Hazel's shock gave way to tears. It was no trick. She should have known. Her older sisters had told her often enough. Hazel Ishee was as homely as a wart-headed chicken. No fancy man with a magic black box or a head full of hope was going to change that fact of life.

Baby Ishee noticed how her daughter moped, and tried to comfort her. "You're pretty enough."

Hazel was doubtful. "Enough for what?"

"Enough for any man from these parts."

"Were you ever pretty, Momma?" Hazel asked, not meaning to offend, and biting her lip when she noticed the quick tensing of her mother's face.

For the first time, Hazel beheld her mother clearly instead of through the clouded lens of a child's familiarity. The hump that rose from her mother's back. The tiny foot that had not grown since her mother was a child and had turned inward, causing the hobble Hazel had accepted as being as natural as hair color. Before this, Hazel hadn't thought of her mother in terms of "pretty" or "not pretty." Now the hump appeared freakish and the crippled foot grotesque.

She became aware of other things, too. Her mother's nickname,

Baby, had not been given to her out of affection or devotion, but because of a deformed foot, like one would call a person Stump or Gimp. Hazel was suddenly ashamed for her mother.

As if reading her daughter's thoughts, Baby scowled at herself in the mirror. Then she wiped a trickle of snuff from her chin with the corner of her apron. "Pretty don't mean much. Men are like hawgs," she said. "Ever seen an ol' hawg wearing spectacles?"

"No ma'am," Hazel answered, running her toe along a crack in the floor.

"Course not." Her mother spit into the Calumet can she always carried. "Old hawg don't care what he gobbling up. Pretty ain't worth doodly squat to no hawg." With that, Baby Ishee turned and left the room, her little foot sweeping the floor as she walked.

Hazel told herself that her mother had been right. She was a fool to hope. She tried resigning herself to her ugliness, taking to her fate like a Christian martyr. As her mother had done, she would become the wife of some man who didn't care how she looked and who was more flattered at having his picture taken with a mule than with her. She would have a brood of children, each year pushing the last baby out of her lap to make room for the next.

Her older sister, the pretty one, had little patience for Hazel's sulking. "What's the matter with you?" Onareen asked as she poured a bucket of water into the horse trough.

"I'm ugly!" Hazel snapped. "Ain't you noticed?"

Her sister's face softened to pity. "You know, Hazel, having beauty to lose is much worse a burden than never having it to begin with. God was looking out for you by making you plain."

Hazel's mouth dropped. "You saying He did it on purpose? You saying me being homely is God's will?"

"That's right, Hazel. Take it as a blessing. "

Hazel pushed Onareen into the horse trough.

Then and there Hazel decided to come down whole hog on the side of hope. She was going to be pretty if it killed her.

By thirteen, she was well on her way to becoming a self-made expert on beauty. She began by relentlessly working to change her appearance. At the risk of getting a whipping, she snatched eggs from under laying hens and concocted a hair remedy of fresh yolks and mineral oil. After everyone had gone to bed, she boiled a flour sack and wrapped it around her treated hair. In a few weeks, the texture softened.

For her arms, which were as spotted as turkey eggs, she stole pennies from the collection plate and sent away for jars of freckle cream advertised in the almanac.

The toughest challenge was her stooped shoulders. The effects of dragging a cotton sack from the time she was six, and years of hunching so as not to tower over the boys at school, could not be fixed with cosmetics. After much deliberation, Hazel hit upon the solution. Salvaging a discarded mule harness from the barn, she constructed a halter to wear. Though the straps bit into her skin, it forced her shoulders back. For hours she practiced walking like Jean Harlow, one foot directly in front of the other.

It took her a few years, but Hazel's looks began to take a slow turn for the better. Her hair turned a lustrous auburn, her eyes blued brighter than robins' eggs, and she had grown lovely, round breasts, finer even than Onareen's. Still she wasn't satisfied. Hazel decided she needed cosmetic assistance. Knowing of only one person who used makeup, she cornered the undertaker at church and begged a supply of lipstick, rouge, and powder.

After a week of clandestine practice, the day came when she was ready to surprise her family with the new, made-up Hazel. The reaction was swift. Her brothers called her Little Miss Sow's Ear. Her sisters called her worse. Her father made her go wash her face in the horse trough. She might have given up out of pure humiliation if not for the dark, brooding look she caught on her mother's face. That's when Hazel knew she was onto something good.

It wasn't long before Hazel discovered there were other types of men in the world besides farmers and sons of farmers. There were men with routes—men who drove automobiles from farm to farm, never getting their hands dirty on any of them, who looked you directly in the eyes and weren't afraid to laugh at nothing at all. These were men who talked for the same reason other people sang, for the pure, simple sound of it. They looked at her with smiling eyes and told her she belonged in California. Or Jackson, maybe.

Hazel thought nothing of skipping school to make day trips into Tupelo with the Watkins Flavoring man and into Corinth with the Standard Coffee man and into Iuka with the man who had the rolling store. Hazel would catch a ride from any man with a route who was going her way.

They would drop her off and she would spend the day at the soda fountain counter studying the fashions and poses of those picture-perfect women in the movie magazines. Poring over the color photographs, enveloped by the smells emanating from the cosmetics displays, she felt more at home than she ever did on the farm. She spent so much time at the Rexall in Tupelo, the druggist took a shine to her and offered her a job. She right away took her own room in town, the first she didn't have to share with five siblings.

From all the romance stories she had been reading in the movie magazines, Hazel gathered that finding the right man and living off true love was the key to everlasting happiness. Yet she was not foolish enough to believe that just any man would do. You needed someone special, a man you could lay your best hopes on, one who would love you enough to see you got everything you wanted, even before you knew you wanted it yourself. If you had to ask, it didn't count. What worried Hazel the most was the impermanence of good feelings in general. From what she could tell, they tended to melt away as surely as ice cream in the bottom of a Dixie cup. Was love going to be the same way? The magazines didn't tell her that. When she asked her mother, Baby said, "Feelings come and go like morning dew on a pasture. They ain't anything to build a future on."

Hazel frowned, yet her mother went on. "Hazelene, there ain't but two kind of men in the world. Them that take care of their own, and them that don't. Now, the first kind of man will stay on out of duty. The other?" Her mother flicked her wrist as if she were shooing a noisome insect. "Why, as soon as there's a dry spell, the other kind has jumped the fence and is looking for fresh dew. If you know what I mean."

Hazel hadn't been partial to the dewy part, but she did like the piece about a man taking care of his own. That sure sounded right enough. Hazel took her mother's advice to heart, never forgetting her words, using them to measure all comers.

And there was a host of them. Men dropped by the drugstore all the time, flirting and asking her out. Their hungry eyes and grinning, greedy mouths frightened her, and she remembered what her mother had said. Hazel could tell that all they had an appetite for was the dewy part.

But the minute Floyd walked into the store, she began hoping he was the one she'd been waiting for. She wondered, is this how true love shows itself? Can a complete stranger walk into your life on a fine Indian summer afternoon while you are stacking tubes of lipstick, and then, just like that—in the twinkle of a mirrored eye and the flash of a toothy smile—all your hoping suddenly pays off, and life is never the same? Is that the way it's supposed to work? Can something that happens so quickly be counted on to last a lifetime?

Chapter Two

THE VIEW

FROM DELPHI

They had been dating a few weeks and were seated in their usual booth at Donna's Dairy Bar. Hazel could tell something was on his mind by the way Floyd attacked his butter pecan as if it were a chore to be got out of the way.

Then he took a deep breath. "Ain't no reason to go on doing something just 'cause it was done before us," he firmly asserted. "There's plenty of other ways for a man to make a living than farming. Don't you agree, Hazel?"

Hazel was taken aback, not at what he said. It was the way he said it, as if he had rehearsed the words beforehand in a mirror, and now he was acting out his little speech just for her. While she studied him curiously, he tilted his head to the side and smiled the way he did when he wanted her to answer a certain way. The idea that her response was so important caused Hazel's heart to pound like the drum in the homecoming parade. She said, "You right about that, Floyd. Why, they's many a man who get themselves a good route and never look back."

When Floyd's face lit up, Hazel knew she had said the right thing.

"Selling! You reading my mind. That's exactly what I'm talking about." He leaned in over the table and let her in on his secret.

"You see, I read a book while I was off in the Pacific." His tone was reverential. "It was called *There's No Future in Looking Back: The Science of Controlled Thinking*. Writ by a preacher who ciphered out a hidden code in the Bible. The 'knock and ye shall receive' part. He went on to make a fortune selling soap door-to-door."

"I swan."

"I'll let you read it one day, but it all comes down to this. You are what you think. And your mind can be trained like any other muscle. Say your leg or your arm muscle."

Floyd's eyes were shining, and he was speaking with such authority Hazel felt chill bumps on her arms.

"Hazel, an untrained mind spends all its time looking back on things it can't do nothing about. This preacher says if you keep your mind focused on what you want and think positive thoughts, you bound to get what you after. He says it's right from the Savior's own mouth. To cut the tail off the dog, it's changed my life."

"Already?"

He smiled shyly. "Met you, didn't I?"

"Floyd."

"Plus, the other day I got a letter from this ol' boy that was on my ship at Pearl Harbor. He said he could get me a job selling these mechanical cotton pickers to the big Delta planters."

"The Delta? I heard of that."

"Sure. That's where all the money is. Clear on the other side of the state from here. Cotton as high as a man and stretching as far as the eye can see. All being handpicked by a million niggers."

"A million? I swan."

"As soon as I get Daddy's crop put in, I'm buying my bus passage to Delphi, all the way over in Hopalachie County. You never gonna catch me looking at the south end of a mule again."

"Nothing I hate worse than seeing a man married to a mule." Then she blushed, afraid she might have mentioned marriage too soon, even if it was in reference to a mule.

"Hazel, you and me think the same." Floyd reached for her hand. "When I go on out to the Delta, would you wait for me—till I got some money saved up?"

He grinned, but he didn't need to coax. Floyd's plan was so big with hope, Hazel believed she could live off the anticipation for years. By the time he sent for her, maybe she would be ready to give whatever it was a wife was supposed to give up to a man.

"Hazel. . ." he said, and she felt the squeeze of his hand, "would you. . .I mean. . ."

She looked into his eyes to find herself, and she liked what she saw. "Floyd Graham, I ain't budging till you come and get me."

⌒

Floyd hadn't lied one bit.

On a coolish spring day, Hazel said good-bye to her landlady and stepped onto her broad green porch, a cardboard suitcase in her hand. Her makeup was careful, and she wore bright red earbobs and a cotton print dress splashed with roses so big they threatened to bloom right off the cloth. Her toenails, which were on view for the world to see in a pair of fancy strapped shoes, were like ten rose petals fallen from her dress. When Floyd took her arm to lead her to his car, she noticed he squeezed a little tighter than necessary, seeing as how she wasn't the least bit inclined to go anyplace but where he led.

After a stop at the justice of the peace, they headed straight west, the Tombigbee Hills to their backs and the Delta in their sights. They were man and wife, muleless, betting their futures on an easy smile and an irresistible tilt of the head.

The farther they drove, the more the geography began to straighten out and lose its rocky ruggedness. "Is this the Delta?" she asked every time she believed things couldn't get any flatter.

"Not by a long shot," Floyd kept saying. "Wait till we get to Hopalachie County. That's where God invented flat."

When the terrain began to lift once more, Hazel became confused. "Looks like the hills are taking over again." There was disappointment in her voice. "Did we miss the Delta?"

This time Floyd didn't say anything. No way he could explain that what they were driving on was not a mountain of rock but a gigantic rim of river silt, windblown and piled over millions of years, and that these fragile bluffs contained the great floodplain like the cliffs contain the ocean. So instead of telling her, Floyd waited for her to see it for herself.

Finally, drawing the car into a shallow curve, Floyd cut the engine. "Let's go for a little walk. I got something to show you."

Hazel followed Floyd across a shallow ditch to a locust-post fence entwined with Carolina jasmine. After pulling up one wire strand with his hand and stepping on the bottom one with his foot, Floyd waited patiently for Hazel to gather her skirt and squeeze through. He led her up a rise crowded with oak and hickory, and then told her to shut her eyes. When she did, he reached for her arm and guided her to the top of the bluff. Again Hazel noticed how tight his grip was. Did he think she was going to bolt down the hill without him?

"Now open," he said.

The sight made Hazel shudder. Spread out below her was the Delta, miles and miles of flatness stretching relentlessly to some foreign horizon, China perhaps. Nothing was hidden from sight. She saw vast open fields of black earth ready for planting and green ribbons of cypress swamps snaking through the terrain and lakes strewn about like pieces of a giant's broken mirror, and not a single rising or falling to ease the unyielding openness of it all.

The spectacle drew Hazel forward, and she momentarily leaned into it, like someone tempted to step into a painting. Home to Hazel had been a place where nature provided plenty of places to hide. Ridges and hollows and bends. Yet out there the world was laid bare for all to see. "What a wondrous thing," she whispered reverently, as if God had just finished making it. "You can see everything at once." Had that revival preacher been right when he said the earth was really as flat as somebody's front porch? If he was, then the falling-off place must be out there on that very horizon. "How far does this Delta reach, Floyd?"

He pointed. "See where the sun is sinking?"

Hazel shaded her eyes with her hand and looked into the sunset.

"That's where the mighty Mississippi runs. The sun beds down in the river for the night. In a few minutes, when the sun slips between the levees, you can hear the river sizzle."

Hazel looked up at Floyd, half believing. "Don't fun me."

"For true. At sundown, the river water gets so hot, catfish jump out on the banks already fried and ready to eat. All you need is the hushpuppies."

"Floyd, you could make me believe about anything." Hazel reached her arm around her husband. "We going to have us a house down there somewhere and live off catfish and hushpuppies?"

"Nope. We going to live up here in the bluffs with the rich people." Waving his arm over the vast river basin, he said, "Down there is where the money is made. Nothing but cotton and mules and niggers. More niggers than you can shake a stick at. They outnumber white people four to one."

Hazel's gaze swept once more over the landscape. "I swan," was all she could say, still trying to imagine such a thing as a whole world of niggers, living on the flatbed bottom of the earth.

"I want to see it. Take me down there, Floyd."

He smiled, pleased at how excited she was getting. They got in the car and Floyd happily aimed it down Redeemer's Hill. The decline was sharp, and Floyd drove so roller-coaster fast, it made Hazel's stomach drop. Then all at once the road went as flat as a pancake and straight as the finger of God. With Floyd smiling confidently at the wheel, Hazel gazed out the window, pointing to each new sight. She saw all manner of wondrous things. Mules by the hundreds and work gangs from the penitentiary in striped uniforms and towering cypresses rising from dark and foreboding swamps, and even an alligator staring up at her from a roadside slough. Things that gave her chill bumps. Not to mention all the coloreds. Floyd was right, there were millions of them, working the fields, filing down dirt roads, and crowding plantation stores. And not all looking dirt poor and raggedy as she had expected. When they pulled up for soft drinks at a crossroads grocery, Hazel spotted a colored girl outfitted in an all-white costume, gaily prancing around on the gallery twirling a parasol as snowy white as her shoes. Hazel had never in her life seen anybody dressed so fine, especially not a colored person. She guessed maybe the girl was passing through with a minstrel show or was part of a high-wire circus act. There were countless riddles out there that left Hazel mystified and wanting more.

"Time to take you home now, Hazel," Floyd said as the dark began to creep up on them.

"Home," Hazel said, trying out the word, putting an old name to a new world.

∽

Winding back through the bluffs, Floyd topped a ridge and there, nestled in the soft rolling terrain, was Delphi. The town was old even by Mississippi standards, settled long before the giant flood-plain below had been tamed from bears and Indians and malaria.

Hazel was struck speechless. Stately homes with expansive lawns and ancient live oaks crowned the hills of Delphi. Homesites were laid out without rhyme or reason, each fine house oriented without consideration of any other. To Hazel, each house gleamed brighter than the next. Until she was eight, she hadn't known you could put paint on a house. About that time she saw a picture in her history book of Mount Vernon.

"My Lord," she gasped. "If it don't look like George Washington went on a tear and built hisself a town."

Floyd turned onto a down-sloping gravel lane that led up to a little house sitting in the shadow of one of the grander homes. After turning off the car, he got real quiet. He looked up at the cottage and said almost apologetically, "It used to be a slave cabin to the house up on the hill. But it's been fixed up real nice."

Hazel beamed, and without waiting for Floyd to get her door, hurried out of the car and ran up to the house. The front door was unlocked. Before Floyd had made it up the walk, Hazel was running from room to room. He was right. It had been fixed up nice, and already furnished to boot. There was an indoor bathroom, floors that were smoothed and varnished, and rugs throughout. A wringer washing machine sat right out on the back porch. There were two bedrooms and brown iron beds with roses painted on the posts. It even had a little parlor with a couch and two stuffed chairs.

Then Floyd took her into the kitchen. "Look, Hazel, a stove that don't need wood." He turned a knob and a blue flame snapped to attention. As soon as she saw it she began to cry.

Floyd's face fell. "Don't worry, Hazel. One day I'll put you in one of them houses up on a hill. I promise."

"Oh! No! It ain't that. I love the house." She sobbed louder.

"Then what is it?"

"Oh, Floyd." She blew her nose into a tissue. "I ain't been honest with you. I can't cook. I can't sew. I don't even know how to change a diaper or burp a baby. My sisters done all that. All I learned to do was pick cotton and strip cane and dig taters. I ain't no good to you!"

Floyd smiled at her. "It don't matter, don't you see? We're starting fresh. You and me are through with them old-timey ways. I don't care if you can't cook. You're my wife. You don't have to earn your keep. And we going to have children 'cause we want children, not farmhands. I'll take care of my family."

Hazel looked up to find herself reflected in his eyes. My God, she thought, he still wants me. She leaned her head against his chest and started to cry again. Today she was a brand-new wife to a new kind of man, living in a storybook town overlooking a mysterious flattened-out world. Her future was as wide open as that view from the bluffs, without a single familiar landmark. She felt lost and found all at the same time.

Chapter Three

A DEAL
WITH THE DEVIL

Billy Dean Brister was chugging to the top of Redeemer's Hill, and he wanted it all to himself. After honking twice, he butted his rattletrap Ford up against the tailgate of a gin wagon that was hogging the gravel road. The colored driver swung about, but when he saw the two white men, he smiled weakly, touched his hat, and popped his mules smartly with the ends of the reins.

Nothing was going to hold Billy Dean back. He was determined to have clear sailing on the downslope. Though blind to oncoming traffic, he swerved the car toward the far ditch and held his ground.

"Wait on it, you hear?" his uncle said. "They ain't enough road for you to pass."

Billy Dean grinned. He drove the left tires into the ditch and straddled the road ledge.

"Dammit to hell," his uncle muttered.

Billy Dean had no doubts. Good luck had finally shifted to his side of the road. Billy Dean Brister, once destined to take his place in a long line of white-trash Bristers, was going to break from family tradition. Come fall, Hopalachie County would be his for the taking, and nobody could keep him from grabbing ahold of it with both hands and a knee to the throat. No matter if he did have to make a deal with the devil to get it.

With two tires on the road and two in the ditch, dirt and rock slinging out from the rear, he drowned the wagon, its colored driver, and his two brown mules in a storm of dust.

Billy Dean jammed the Stetson tight on his head, reared back in his seat, and mashed the accelerator flat to the floor. The truck, propelled as much by gravity as by gasoline, sailed down Redeemer's Hill, the final belly-dropping descent from the bluffs to the flatter-than-flat Delta. There was nothing ahead now but miles and miles of cotton plants studded with pink-and-white blossoms.

Billy Dean's uncle pulled up in his seat again. Furman was a big man with a nose that resembled raw hamburger. "You driving like a blue-assed fly," he said, "Ain't gone live long enough to win no 'lection." He reached down to the floorboard for the fruit jar.

Billy Dean tipped back his Stetson with his thumb. He knew better. The bargain had already been struck. That primary was his for the taking. Senator told him that it didn't matter that Billy Dean hadn't yet had his twenty-first birthday: "In this county, I decide how old folks are. Why, when it comes to the voting, I get to decide if they're dead are not." Even the election flyers they were posting today were a waste of time, yet the Senator had insisted they make a good show of it.

"Where's the next stop at?"

With two fingers pressed against his lips, the old man turned to the window and spit, finessing a brown trail of tobacco juice clear of the rear fender. "You gone take a right about a mile up ahead." Furman unscrewed the top of the jar, took a sip, and swallowed hard. "Hodamighty!"

Billy Dean took his turn at the jar while keeping an eye on a horizon that never seemed to get any closer no matter how fast he went. He hadn't known how big Hopalachie County was until he decided he was going to be sheriff over all of it. Then it got mighty big.

There was this, the Delta part, with its thousands of look-alike acres of nothing but cotton hiding tiny crossroads settlements built around gins and country stores. Farther west there were the swamps and bayous with little clusters of cabins and fishing shacks raised up on stilts. At their backs, where Billy Dean and his uncle had just come from, were the bluffs.

Perched up there in those bluffs was the uppity little town of Delphi, looking down like an old powdered woman on the whole shebang. That's where Billy Dean was going to settle when the devil paid him his due. He was going to be high sheriff and move to town and live in a big white house with the rich folks. The same ones that had shamed his daddy and their kind ever since Noah. They'd soon be calling him "sir." All he had to do to make that happen was to marry the ugliest girl in Hopalachie County. Billy Dean took another drink.

The gravel had nearly given out, and the road became like a ribbed washboard. They were coming up on the Hopalachie River. Shaking wildly, the truck began to drift off in a sideways direction. Uncle Furman reached down for where a door handle once was and then crossed his arms over his face instead. "Boy, what's got into you?" he shouted with a mouth full of chambray. "You tempting the devil?"

Maybe he was. But at that moment, Billy Dean's future seemed to be laid out before him as sure and straight as one of these Delta plantation roads.

The Senator and him had shook on it. The next day Billy Dean went to Delphi and bought himself a Stetson and a pair of hand-tooled cowboy boots, the kind he had dreamed about since he was a barefooted boy of ten.

Pointing on down the road, Uncle Furman shouted over the rattle of the truck, "There it is. Slow down, you hear?"

The general store sat on a bare island of packed dirt surrounded by cotton plants that lapped right up to the back door. According to the thermometer nailed to the front of the store, the temperature had already hit ninety-three in the shade, and it was still early morning.

As the dust settled around the truck, Billy Dean opened his door and turned himself sideways in the seat, giving his legs an extra-long stretch. The place was dead quiet. Looking around, he began to recollect where he was. He had bought shine here one time. After dark. It had been a couple of years. He was starting to remember.

Off in the distance a silent cloud of dust was rising above the green horizon, heading their way. As it neared, Billy Dean could make out the deep-throated hum of a car with a substantial engine. Finally a dark green Buick, old but well tended to, came into sight, drawing the cloud behind it. The car turned off into the yard and rolled to a careful stop.

The colored man who got out was taller even than Billy Dean and all dressed up in an old-fashioned baggy suit with a gold watch chained across his stomach. He leaned down to the open window and said a word to the three children who remained in the car, a boy in the back and a young girl clutching a baby in the front. Then the man headed toward the store.

Coming up on Billy Dean and his uncle, the colored man removed his felt hat, nodded respectfully, and said, "How do, sirs?"

After he had gone into the store, Uncle Furman got out of the truck and shambled over to the Buick. "Boy, that chaps my ass!" he said. "How many white folks you know got a car this good?" He aimed a stream of tobacco juice at a shiny hubcap with expert precision.

The boy who sat in the backseat glared at Furman with all the ferocity a child could muster. He wore a red straw cowboy hat with a yellow star painted on the crown, the drawstring pulled tight under his chin.

Billy Dean clenched his cigarette in one side of his mouth and spoke out the other. "Them nigger preachers sure know how to spend the Lord's money."

"Sho!" Furman said. "That's what he was, awright. Wearing a painted tie as wide as your Aunt Beulah's butt. And did you see that watch chain on his belly? Looked a hunnurd percent karat gold."

The girl in the front seat didn't look old enough to be a mother, just a little older than the boy in the back. She was studying Billy Dean's face hard, and when she saw him looking back, she swung her head toward the store again, whipping her plaits over her shoulder. Even though it was boiling hot, she pulled the baby closer.

Furman noticed the girl, too. With his hands behind his back, he crouched down and peered through the front window at her. She was dressed in white from head to toe—a white ruffled dress, white shiny shoes and cotton socks, white satin ribbons tied to the end of her plaits. "Hey, Billy Dean, looks like we got the Cotton Queen in here!"

The girl didn't flinch. Instead she kept looking straight ahead, into the smug face painted on the shiny new screen door. Little Miss Sally Sunbeam, with her cornsilk hair and baby-doll blue eyes, seemed to be smiling back at her, all the time holding a slice of light bread up to her mouth. Miss Sally didn't appear to be worried about a thing.

Gripping the back of the front seat, the boy in the straw hat pulled himself forward. He gave Furman a steely look that defied the old man to touch his sister. "Lookie here, Billy Dean." Furman pointed to the star on the boy's hat. "This'n wants to be sheriff, too. Think you can beat a nigger boy come the primary?"

Billy Dean grinned. "Might be close."

Furman's gaze shifted to the baby in the front seat holding tight to the girl's plait. "Gal, who's that baby belong to? Ain't yours, is it?"

"Yessuh," the girl answered, squinting hard at the screen door as if willing her father's return.

Furman studied the baby for a moment. "That don't look like no colored boy to me. Pass for Eye-talian. I reckon some white boy been sneaking around her woodpile late at night." Turning back to his nephew, Furman asked, "Who you think he takes after?"

Billy Dean examined his boots, but sneaked a look at the baby when his uncle turned back to the car.

"How old are you, girl?" asked Furman.

"Fo'teen, suh."

"You hear that, Billy Dean? Her baby can't be but a year. Maybe two. Jesus! They born to breed, ain't they?"

Billy Dean did the math. "Shit," he muttered. He fixed his eyes on the baby. "Get me that ball-peen hammer out of the back of the truck," he told Furman.

The girl's eyes grew big again. She put her hand on the window crank, thought better of it, and tightened her grip on her baby instead.

While Furman rattled around in the truck bed, Billy Dean pushed back his Stetson and leaned into the girl's window. "You—"

"I ain't said nothing about what happened."

"Shut up!" Billy Dean spat, low and harsh. He studied the child next to her. She wouldn't have to tell nobody. The baby's face would tell the deed.

Billy Dean took the cigarette from his mouth and flicked it into the car. The girl sat stock-still, clutching the boy, while the smell of scorched cloth filled the car. In the backseat, her brother made a move for the cigarette. Without turning around the girl said in a panicked voice, "Willie! Leave it be. Don't do nothing."

He slowly eased back in the seat, his eyes not breaking from Billy Dean's.

When Furman returned with the hammer, Billy Dean took it and slapped the head into the palm of his hand. The baby started to whimper, yet his mother resisted looking down at him.

Just then the screen creaked open and the girl's father stepped onto the gallery carrying his sack of groceries. Seeing the two white men over by his daughter, he moved hurriedly toward the car. "Yes, Lord! Going to be a hot one, ain't it?"

The colored man opened the rear door and put the groceries in the backseat. "Too hot to be out of the shade for long," he went on. "Nosuh. Maybe the good Lord send a little shower thisa way. Look like it's coming up a cloud down off yonder." He nodded toward the distant north, but didn't take his eyes off the ball-peen hammer.

"Yessuh. Be nice to get a little rain to cool things down. Settle the dust some." He opened the door on the driver's side and casually brushed the smoldering cigarette onto the ground. Then he removed his handkerchief from his coat pocket and laid it out over the burn.

"Well, I best be getting on to home. You sirs have a fine day, now." Tipping his hat to the men, the preacher pulled out into the road, departing faster than he had come.

Furman spit. "Crazy preacher." He grabbed a handful of flyers from off the truck seat and joined his nephew up on the gallery. He held one of the flyers flat against the gray weathered wood, right between a faded war bonds poster and the Garrett Snuff sign. Billy Dean hammered a nail into each of the four corners.

Furman took a step back and said, "Looks just like you."

Billy Dean spun around. "Who looks like me?"

His uncle nodded at the flyer. "Yore picture there. Good likeness, don't you think?"

He studied Furman for a moment and then turned back toward the flyer. "Yeah," he said. "Reckon they caught me."

"Odds say you gone win that primary easy, Billy Dean."

"Better," Billy Dean said darkly. "The Senator done had all my competition paid off or scared off."

"Aw, hit's OK," Furman reassured him. "The Senator only doing what's best for his little girl. She gone be the wife of the next high sheriff if it costs him half his plantation." Furman spit over the railing. "Boy, howdy, are you a lucky shit."

"Yeah, well," Billy Dean said. "Everything's got its price."

Furman put his hand on his nephew's shoulder. "Don't worry, son. She ain't that ugly. Anyway, you and Hertha's young'uns probably take after our side of the family. Brister blood always wins out when it comes to looks."

"Seems to," Billy Dean said under his breath, staring down the road.

Chapter Four

THE WAY OF THE MULE

That morning up in Delphi, Hazel eased a plate down in front of Floyd. She took a step back.

Her husband stared silent and unblinking at his fried eggs, goopy with the uncooked whites shimmering in the morning light, the bacon in ashes, and the toast soggy with butter in the center and burnt black around the edges.

"You don't have to eat it," Hazel offered. "I'll bury it in the backyard with last night's supper."

"No, honey," he stammered, "there might be something here I can—"

"Just let me fix you anothern." What she didn't say was this was already her second halfhearted attempt this morning. The first had made her own stomach queasy, which was happening almost every time she cooked now.

Floyd managed a weak smile and pushed the plate away. "Don't worry about it, sugar. Slept too late. I'm in a hurry."

Her face clouded up. "On a Saturday? I thought you was going to take me driving today." Hazel lived all week for their drives, just the two of them. She wouldn't say so, but it took her back to those hope-filled days of catching rides with the route men.

"Can't. Big customer out in the Delta." He looked at her hopefully. "Maybe you can have something fixed for me by suppertime."

She squeezed out a smile, yet inside Hazel bridled at the suggestion. Not that she would ever say it, but she couldn't bear another minute in front of that stove. It was like somebody trying to hitch her up to a mule on plowing day. If she got good at it, she might never break out of her harness. She knew she should be ashamed of herself for thinking such thoughts. Floyd had saved her from all that.

Her husband casually turned away from her and cast his gaze out the window, staring off into space again. Look at him, she thought. Already he was a million miles away from this kitchen and his bumbling housewife. Maybe he thought her ineptness cute, proud of being able to afford a wife who couldn't keep a house.

"Floyd? Sure I can't fix you something?" she asked him. "Maybe some Cheerios or...Floyd!"

He beamed a surprised smile and rose up from the table to give Hazel a hug. "You sure are pretty. Takes my hunger for food clean away."

She sighed in his arms. Exactly what she thought he would say. She remembered that day back in the hills when Hazel had asked her mother about "pretty." "Forget about pretty," she had told her daughter flatly. "Pretty can't keep a husband. 'Cause pretty can't cook and pretty can't clean and pretty can't raise children. And, girl, the biggest thing pretty can't do is last."

"Floyd, what kind of wife am I to send you off to work without a decent breakfast?" she said, waiting for him to ease her guilt a bit more.

"It don't matter," he assured her. "I love you anyway."

She knew he would say that, too. There had been a lot of those "anyways" lately. Like when she got up the courage to use the washing machine and then cracked most of his buttons feeding his shirts through the wringer. As he held her, she asked, "Floyd, how many 'anyways' reckon you got left in you?"

"As many as the stars you got left in your eyes."

With all her heart she wanted to believe him, that he loved her no matter what and that his love would be enough to get them through a lifetime of bad cooking. But it still left her wondering, what did he want from her?

Floyd must have been reading her mind. "We living in modern times. It's nearly 1950 and you ain't some farm wife who works herself into an ugly, wore-out nubbin of a woman. Anyhow, you don't see any other white women around here doing for themselves. Just study on how to keep yourself the pretty and pampered wife of Delphi's next rich man."

"We going to be rich?" Hazel asked, again knowing what he would say next, word for word.

"If you can see it, you can be it," Floyd said, reciting his favorite verse from the book of success sayings he kept by his side of the bed. "The way things are going, won't be long before I can get you some regular colored help. It's about time we took a step up."

She smiled sadly. "Floyd, you stepping so high now, I get a nosebleed looking up at you."

"Well, get used to it," he said with a grin. "You know where I'm off to this morning?"

"Where to?" she asked. "Where you going without me?"

"To talk face-to-face with one of the biggest men in the Delta. You heard me tell about him. They call him the Senator. He asked me to come by this morning personal to look over his place. To get the lay of the land, so to speak."

"That's real nice, Floyd." Her voice was resigned.

"He's a real old-time planter. Lives down in the Delta amongst his tenants and the skeeters. Got him a mansion they call the Columns. Everybody swore he would be the last to buy mechanical cotton pickers to replace his hands with. Why, the first time I called on him he told me I was wasting my breath and his time. Remember what I told you I said to turn him around?"

"It's just that if you and me could spend some time—"

"What got him was when I told him, 'Senator, do you want to

spend your time studying the mysterious habits of niggers, or do you want to make money?' " Floyd shook his head at himself for saying such a thing. "Then I told him, 'Are you a planter or a dad-blamed anthropologist?' You should have heard him laughing at that one."

Again Hazel smiled weakly, ashamed to ask him what an anthropologist was, even though this was the third time she had heard the story. "Floyd, it's only that I've been feeling—"

"You just wait," he said. "If he sticks with me he'll go from messing with six hundred niggers to only a handful of drivers. After the Senator buys in, everybody will get on board."

Hazel noticed a sudden pang of sympathy for the displaced. Was her husband becoming that important, where he could get rid of a whole world of coloreds because they had outlived their usefulness? And the little circus girl all dressed in white? Would she be gone as well, before Hazel could figure out her riddle?

"Where they all going to go to?"

"Who?" Floyd asked.

"The niggers. You know, if nobody needs 'em no more, where they all going to go to?"

Floyd shrugged. "Oh. Somewhere, I reckon." He said, "Ain't no stopping us, Hazel. We done put the mule behind us for good." He playfully patted her on the rear on his way to the door.

"Nope. You right about that," she said, taking the frying pan to the sink to scrub. "Not a mule in sight nowhere."

Floyd pushed open the screen and turned to say good-bye, then stood there for a long moment, staring at Hazel with a curious look on his face.

"What?" she yelped, afraid she had gone ugly in his eyes.

He rushed back to Hazel and laid the flat of his hand on her stomach. "If I'm not wrong, looks like you might better go see the doctor."

Hazel's heart sank. "You want me to go to the doctor 'cause I'm getting fat?"

He only grinned bigger.

Hazel thought for a moment and then her face burned. "You think I'm going to have a baby! That's what you're saying! Ain't it?"

He gave her a few seconds and then asked carefully, "Well, what do you think, honey? You the one it's happening to."

She should have known. Her sister Onareen told her the only way not to get pregnant was to do it standing up, and she sure wasn't going to suggest that to Floyd.

Hazel sat down, all of a sudden feeling woozy. Oh, Lord, she thought, the only thing worse than being pregnant would be Floyd knowing about it before me. "No, I can't be preg—you got to be wrong about it."

Floyd knelt down by Hazel and slipped his arm around her, placing his hand on her belly again. As if knowing her thoughts, he said, "Don't worry. You gonna be a good mother. Remember that little saying I taught you, 'If you can see it, you can be it.' "

Her smile was pained. Well, that was just it, Hazel was thinking, I can't see it. How was a "good mother" supposed to look? Back in the hills where Hazel came from, there wasn't talk about good ones or bad ones—only live ones and dead ones, sturdy ones and sickly ones, fertile ones and ones who had dried up early. Yet now with this good–bad difference, she was convinced she would end up being a naturally bad one. Another thing Floyd would have to love her anyway for.

She looked into his face. Floyd gazed at her with so much faith and hope, it made her heart ache. "I'm scared, Floyd. I don't know how to care for a baby. I seen it done, but I ain't never done it myself."

"Oh, that ain't no problem. We can ask some of the women from church to help. Maybe your sister Onareen can come stay."

"Get Momma," Hazel whimpered, for the first time in years finding a kind of comfort in that particular word. She couldn't help saying it again. "Momma. I want my momma." Hazel needed somebody who knew her, somebody who wouldn't expect too much from her. Somebody who would be surprised at how far she had come.

"You sure? You know she don't take to me since I stole you from the hills."

"No, I want to show her how wrong she was about hoping. I want her to see how good you done. How good you been to me."

Floyd blushed. "Well, then," he said with a snappy nod of his head, "I'll go fetch her when the time comes."

She raised her eyes and looked into Floyd's face again. He was so confident. The sense of dread returned.

Why should that be? she wondered. Why should her husband's rock-hard certainty scare her so, making her feel so small and lost? What had happened to her own feelings of hope?

Hazel remembered the day Floyd had come home and found her crying, sitting by the new oven she was sure she had broken. Growing up, the only cookstoves she had ever seen burned wood. Floyd simply struck a match and lit it back up. And she knew it wasn't just the oven. Somehow, it was as if the rush of Floyd's success had blown out her own little pilot light.

Chapter Five

SNOWFLAKE BABY

L ater in the day, Vida's baby boy played on the parlor rug with his collection of wooden spools as she and her father, sitting on opposite sides of the room, worked hard to avoid each other's eyes. Vida, on the sofa, stared down at the satin bows on the toes of her baby-doll shoes, and her father, in his armchair, studied his light-skinned grandson as the child stacked one spool on top of another, toppled them over, and began again.

They often found themselves embarrassed in each other's presence, but it had not always been this way between them.

After his wife died birthing Willie, Levi had doted on Vida. He called Vida his Snowflake Baby. Not because her last name was Snow, which it was. And not because her skin was white, which it wasn't. Vida had the same coffee-with-cream complexion as her father. Vida became his Snowflake Baby because he always dressed her in white.

For her eleventh birthday, Levi even sent to Memphis for a parasol of white satin, which he said would keep his Snowflake Baby from melting in the Delta sun. The day it arrived, Vida had excitedly snatched the package from the mail rider and torn away the brown paper wrapping. She twirled the pretty parasol over her head in the bright noonday sun. Her father had laughed with delight and proclaimed, "Now my Snowflake Baby can carry shade everwhere she goes." He raised her up in his strong arms. "No sir! Nothing never going to hurt my Snowflake Baby." Levi proudly pranced Vida around the yard, twirling her in half circles, while she giggled.

And then there were the music lessons. Vida was the only colored girl in all of Hopalachie County able to take piano. Her father had personally gone to Miss Josephine Folks, the white lady music teacher, and arranged it. That's how important her father was. He could get things other colored people couldn't even think about. Of course, Miss Josephine charged Levi a dollar a lesson, twice as much as her white students, and she insisted that Vida come only after last dark. That didn't spoil it for Vida. She enthusiastically memorized choruses straight from the Broadman Hymnal to serenade her father when he picked her up in the Buick.

Except for one night when he didn't. Her father was conferencing late with his deacons, and Vida had to walk the two miles to her house, alone in the dark. Yet she wasn't scared. Vida had walked the road hundreds of times with Willie.

Mr. Bobber's general store sat midway between Miss Josephine's and Vida's house, and when she passed, she saw the lights were still on. She had often gone inside the store by herself, but her father had solemnly warned her to never venture in there after dark, refusing to say more. Tonight she put the warning aside. With a robust Baptist refrain coursing through her blood, Vida marched right in to get herself an Orange Crush.

The screen door slapped behind her, and the music fled from Vida's head. The light was dim, and smoke floated thick and eerie. From the back of the store came the sounds of laughter, yet not the free and easy laughter of daytime. This was hard and coarse.

Even the odors were different. No longer the clean bright scents of hoop cheese and mule feed and honey-cured hams and yard goods. The night smells were stale and rancid and clotted at the back of her throat when she tried to swallow.

Leaning with one arm against the counter, holding himself at a tipsy angle, stood the young white man, his dark eyes swimming drunkenly in pools shot with red. He smiled. It wasn't at her. His sideways grin was meant for the squat man behind the counter who was placing a Mason jar in a paper sack.

Mr. Bobber frowned at his customer and said, "Boy, next time come around to the back, you hear?" He pushed the sack across the countertop.

Several men sitting in ladder-back chairs in the rear of the store under a swirling haze of smoke made coughing sounds and moved about uneasily in their seats. They kept their eyes cut toward the business up front.

"That'll be three bits," Mr. Bobber said to the man.

Eyeing Vida, the man sniggered. "She come with it?"

More laughing, hoarse and ragged, came from the back of the store.

Mr. Bobber wasn't laughing. "You got it or you don't, boy?" He looked down at Vida and said, not unkindly with a firm warning in his voice, "You better get on home now, Vida. You know better than to come 'round here past dark." He glanced warily at the customer and then at Vida again. "Now git, do you hear?"

Vida found her legs and took two steps backward, bumped the screen, and fled the store, running through the yard for the dark of the roadbed. Her stomach had gone queasy from the way the man had looked at her.

Vida raced down the road toward home. She needed her father to promise that nobody would ever dare hurt Levi Snow's little girl. Then the headlights fell upon her.

☙

Nate tired of the spools and with his eyes narrowed and his bottom lip pooched out was pointing in the direction of his grandfather. Vida knew what he wanted—for her to fetch Levi's watch chain. The boy loved gripping the two miniature praying hands that dangled from the chain. He couldn't get to sleep at night unless he was gripping tightly to that gold chain.

"Hands, Momma. Hands," he pleaded.

Vida didn't move. She was waiting for her father to speak his mind. Waiting for him to say his first word since they had left the store.

Her father finally broke the silence. "That was the one who got you bigged up. That white man at the store be Nate's daddy." Levi Snow wasn't asking, he was telling, speaking with the same certitude as when he told his congregations that Jesus was coming to total up their books and they'd best settle their accounts today.

These were not the words she wanted from her father, harsh and accusing. Trying to pretend she hadn't heard him, Vida stretched out her legs so that the white baby-doll shoes caught the late-afternoon light streaming through the open window. The patent leather finish shone like the icing on a coconut cake.

"I said, that be the man. He be Nate's daddy," her father repeated.

Sweat had darkened the top of Levi's white collar. Taking a hand-kerchief from his back pocket, he mopped his face. "Looka here, girl, and tell me the truth."

Tears welled up in Vida's eyes. Why was he asking her to say the truth, now that he knew it? The night her father came home to find her crying and her dress torn, he had gotten quiet when she told him it was a white man who had done it. That had been enough truth for him then. He hadn't even asked which white man it was.

She wouldn't have told him anyway. The man said he would kill her whole family if she told. For a while she made believe her daddy was protecting her by not asking, and that she was protecting them all by not telling.

"Yessuh," Vida answered finally. "He be the one."

"Oh, my sweet Jesus!" he said as she knew he would. "And now that man running for high sheriff. You know what that means?"

Vida wouldn't look up, yet from his angry voice, she figured it meant something about his standing as the Reach Out Man. That's what they called him and what he was most proud of. If you needed something from the white man, Levi Snow was the one to go to. People bragged that he sure enough knew how to tickle the white man's ear. Colored folks were always coming to her father for a favor. Mothers who wanted to visit their sons in jail, or sharecroppers who got cheated at settlement time, or families who lost their credit at the plantation commissary. Very seldom did Levi get what he asked for, but sometimes he got something, and in the coloreds' eyes that was a pretty good record. Two years ago he even got the Senator to let Statia Collins put a little pea patch on her place to help feed her ten children, the first time the Senator had let any sharecropper raise something besides cotton and field corn for the mules. And the people knew that when the Senator's wife died with a bad heart, it was Levi the big white man went to for consolation. Levi had made sure everybody knew that. Levi was favored above all coloreds.

"I'll tell you what it means." Levi struck the tops of his legs with his fists. "If that peckerwood get voted high sheriff, it be the end of everything."

He bolted to his feet. "Let's go. We got to go warn the Senator." Calling to the back of the house, he cried, "Willie! Get out here."

Vida's brother bounded into the parlor and did a marching step up to where his father stood, giving his father what he called his Texas Ranger salute. "Yes! Sir!"

"Stop actin' a fool. Go wipe down the car. I got to conference with the Senator."

"Can I go too, Daddy?" Willie begged, no longer a Texas Ranger, but a boy of eleven. "Let me drive y'all out there. I can drive good. I can reach the pedals now. You let *Vida* drive."

"This me and your sister's business. Now hurry on up." He turned to Vida. "Get my hat and brush it off. Need to look my best for the conference."

Vida finally looked up at her father, her expression pleading. Since she was a child she had heard stories about the Senator and how bad niggers disappeared into secret dungeons and how he ate colored babies for breakfast. "Daddy, don't make me go," she begged. "I ain't got nothing to say to the Senator."

Nate toddled over to Vida and looked up at her with searching eyes. When she picked him up and held him close, he grabbed hold of her plait and with his other arm reached out toward Levi, opening and closing his fist, signaling for the gold chain. "Momma! Hands!" he cried.

"You my baby," she whispered to him. "You my baby and that's the onliest thing that anybody need to know."

Levi turned his back to both of them and straightened his tie in the looking glass. He talked at his reflection. "You tell the Senator how that white man got you bigged up. When he hear that, he'll show that cracker the fastest road out the county."

"He say he kill us all, Daddy!" she cried. "He say he burn us up alive!"

Levi didn't turn from the glass. "Hush up, now. The Senator always done the right thing by us. You explain it to him how it wasn't your fault."

Without thinking, and still holding Nate, Vida ran across the room and flung her loose arm around her father. She began sobbing into his boiled white shirt.

"What's got into you, girl? What you carrying on for?"

"'Cause you say it wasn't my fault," she sobbed. "You ain't never said that."

Levi tenderly patted the back of Vida's head until his eyes fell upon his light-colored grandson.

"I 'spect you better bring the baby on to the conference, too," her father said with a sigh, watching the boy cram the golden hands into his mouth. "He can tell the story without speaking a word."

Chapter Six

THE COLUMNS

The sun was setting scarlet by the time Levi drove past the last cluster of tenant shacks and turned onto the generously graveled lane leading up to the Columns. Like emerald-suited soldiers, house-tall cedars lined both sides of the quarter-mile entrance. The Buick slipped between the last pair of trees and Levi slowed, proceeding at a crawl as if in reverence to the white mansion that rose up before them. Vida was forever in awe that something that gleaming bright had been plopped down in a heat-distorted world of mules and shanties and sweating field hands.

Tonight half a dozen cars were already parked in the circular drive. Instead of joining them, Levi pulled off the lane onto a rough track used by mules and tractors, and drove carefully around to the rear of the house, bringing the Buick to a stop at the back gate. He got out and walked over to the cast-iron bell that sat atop a cedar post. He pulled the rope three times. The bell clanged loudly.

The kitchen door was flung open and Vida was relieved to see that it was Lillie Dee Prophet, the Senator's cook, who came out, limping across the yard up to the fence.

"That you, Brother Pastor?" she asked, squinting hard into his face.

"Hello, Sister Prophet." He formally tipped his hat to the wizened woman. "How you this evening?"

"Ain't jumpin' no stumps, Rev'rund."

Vida's father laughed and shook his head in the way that made you feel like you were really something for saying what you did.

Lillie Dee bent her head down and strained to make out the shadows inside the car, her toothless gums working without pause. "But it's like I told my last boy over there," Lillie Dee said, nodding her head toward the woodshed in back of the house, "like I told Rezel, ever day I can get out of bed, I count it as a blessing from the Lord."

Hearing Rezel's name, Vida crooked her head to see around Lillie Dee. She spied him standing in the shadows, hard-muscled, wearing overalls and a ripped cotton shirt, gathering an armload of stove wood. She tried to catch his eye. Sullen, he stubbornly kept his gaze away from the place where people were bandying his name about. Vida'd heard stories about him singing the blues at the juke joints in a way that could turn sisters one against the other. Yet the Rezel she knew was gentle and shy-mannered, sometimes stopping by her house when her father was away with flowers or pears stolen from the Senator's own trees. And he was good to Nate. They never talked about it, but maybe Rezel would take her and Nate in. He would be a good daddy. He could protect her, and, maybe love her enough to kill the man who wanted to hurt her child.

Her father said to the old cook, "Well, Lillie Dee, you certainly blessed to have your boy staying on with you. That bound to be a comfort."

"Rezel?" Lillie Dee shook her head sadly. She looked back at the boy, throwing her voice loud enough for him to hear. "He the same as all the rest of them. Talking about going up North. Say people up there pay him money to sing that devil's music. Pardon my snuff, Rev'rund." Lillie Dee spit juice on the ground and continued, "Why, you think it be the Promised Land, the way they all heading off up thataway."

For a moment the news saddened Vida. Then her spirits lifted.

Maybe Rezel was planning to ask her to go with him to this Promised Land! Out of the reach of the white man. And if he was too shy to ask, then she would certainly ask him.

"I'm sorry to hear about it, Sister Prophet," her father said. "They still plenty of good life left in Mississippi for the upright colored man. 'Cause of you, Rezel got him good work here with the Senator. Too bad he can't see that."

"That's the truth, Rev'rund." Lillie Dee grinned slyly at Levi. "Carrying my wood never did *you* no harm, did it?"

Vida saw that Lillie Dee's comment brought a rare expression of bashfulness to her father's face, and for a moment Lillie Dee was no longer a member of his flock. This was the woman who had overseen his chores when he was the houseboy for the Senator's father.

He cleared his throat and removed his hat. "Lillie, will you tell the Senator that I need to conference with him on something weighty?"

"Senator's got company tonight, Rev'rund. Why don't you come back in the morning after breakfast?"

"It can't wait. Tell him it's about the election. He going to want to see me and my girl."

The old woman worked her gums thoughtfully for a moment. "Well," she said, "y'all drive on up in the yard and I'll tell him." As she unlatched the gate, she said, "I'm warning you, now, he ain't going to 'preshate it. They been drinking most the afternoon and just commenced they supper."

While Vida, Nate, and Levi waited in the car, the Senator's bird dogs sniffed around the Buick and, one by one, hiked their legs and relieved themselves on the tires. Field hands drove tractors and led mules in through the gate and put them away in the barn for the evening. White people's laughter, cold and brittle, broke over the darkening yard. For over an hour, Levi sat sweating behind the wheel, mopping his face and jumping in his seat every time the door opened. But each time the screen swung back, it was only Lillie Dee announcing the start of another course.

This was not how Vida had imagined the "conferences" her father talked about so proudly. She had expected the Senator to welcome her father on the front gallery under those grand columns and make him comfortable in a room fit for Solomon while her daddy advised the Senator on important matters.

The smells from the Senator's supper drifted into the car, and Nate began to whimper and tug on Vida's braids. She tried to comfort him by stroking his soft black hair, but her own fingers trembled.

"It's a ways past Nate's suppertime, Daddy. Maybe we ought to do like Lillie Dee says and come back again."

Her father gripped the steering wheel tightly, staring through the windshield into a grove of pecan trees rapidly disappearing in the dark. "Can't. The Senator know we out here. Anyway, he be glad we come with a warning. He going to thank us. You wait and see."

There was something missing from her father's words.

"He'll show that peckerwood which road leads out the county. I know he will. You wait and see if he don't."

At last Lillie Dee poked her head out of the door and called, "I just served them they cake and coffee. Won't be too long now."

Levi turned to Vida, his eyes pleading through the darkness. She had never seen her father fearful, and the sight jerked at her stomach.

"Now, Vida, you pay respect to the Senator. Say 'yessuh' and 'nosuh.' Don't look him in his eyes. Don't shame me, girl."

"I'm scared, Daddy. What he going to do to Nate?"

Her father didn't seem to hear Vida's question. "The Senator been good to me. He raised up my first church. He believed in me when I told him about seeing the shining face of God in a mighty whirlpool of churning water, calling me to be a preacher of the Word. He believe me then. He'll believe me now."

Like a cannon, the voice of the Senator came booming from the kitchen. "All right now, Lillie Dee. Tell Levi to come on in."

⁓

They entered through the back door, and Vida saw the Senator up close for the first time. His frame rose before her like a cypress trunk, dense and broad. He had one massive arm propped against a marble biscuit block while the other held out an empty whiskey glass to Lillie Dee, who took it and left the room. Other colored servants scurried in and out of the kitchen carrying silver trays of tinkling china.

"Now, what's so important that it can't wait, Levi? And why you got the young'uns with you?" The Senator wiped his hand his on linen suit coat. "Hurry up, now, I got company."

Levi kneaded the brim of his hat with both hands. "Yessuh. I know you do. I just thought, see'n as you and me go way back...well, suh...what I gots to say..."

Vida's heart dipped down past her stomach. This was not how it was supposed to be at all! This was her father, the man whose words made people shout with joy and dance in the aisles. Who stood up to the white man. She found herself taking a step backward toward the door.

The Senator's face colored. "Stop beating the devil around the stump, Levi. Spit it out."

"Yessuh. Well, my girl here...well, she got something to say."

Vida could feel the Senator's bleary gaze fall upon her. No words would come. The only sound was the pulsing of her blood pounding in her ears. She took yet another step backward.

When things didn't seem as if they could get any worse, her father's shoulders fell like a cord of wood had been dropped on his back.

Looking up, Vida saw that Billy Dean had stepped into the room. His eyes, as dark and cold as the iron pots that hung on the wall behind him, bored into Vida through mean little slits.

"Go on ahead, girl," he said. "What you got to tell the Senator?"

Vida's knees went soft as Nate grew impossibly heavy in her arms. She backed against the warming oven to keep from crumpling to the floor. Even though she wasn't supposed to look a white man in the eyes, in Billy Dean's she had seen murder.

"Billy Dean," the Senator said, not bothering to turn around. "I'm glad you were able to tear yourself away from Delia. She ain't yours." His voice was full of scorn. "You know, it's getting hard to tell which of my daughters you got engaged to. I hope I don't have to point Hertha out to you."

"Only being sociable, Senator. Don't you worry about me none. I ain't letting Miss Hertha out of my sights." Then Billy Dean stepped up beside the Senator and smiled a sideways grin. He slapped the Senator on the back. "I'm a man of my word. Just like you."

The Senator wasn't amused. Billy Dean quickly removed his hand and then waved his drink at the callers. "You having yourself some kind of high-level meeting back here with all these fancy-dressed niggers?"

The Senator scowled at Billy Dean. "This here's the colored preacher I was telling you about. You take care of ol' Levi and he'll tell you what the nigruhs are up to."

The Senator smiled fondly at the preacher. "Ain't that right, Levi?"

"Yessuh. That sure is right," Levi mumbled, looking at his shoes.

"Why do I care what the niggers are up to?" Billy Dean scoffed.

The Senator spun toward Billy Dean. "I'll tell you why you better care. If you going to be my sheriff, looking out for my five thousand acres, you sure as hell better know what the nigruhs and everybody else is up to. I want to know about Yankee labor agents trying to steal my tenants, and croppers lying about gin weights, and the federal government trying to agitate. That goes double for the Klan scaring off my coloreds. And I better know about trouble a day before trouble happens. You got that, Billy Dean?" The Senator kept up his glare until Billy Dean dropped his eyes. He focused instead on Levi's chain, glowering at the praying hands.

"Whatever you say," Billy Dean grumbled, looking as if he had more to add but jiggling the ice in his drink instead.

The Senator turned back to Levi. "Now, what you got to tell me about the election?"

Vida prayed for her father to say something. He stood there motionless, bent like a willow after an ice storm. There was only silence. Finally Lillie Dee returned with a tray of fresh drinks for the Senator and Billy Dean.

Billy Dean tossed back half his drink and wiped his mouth. He sniggered. "I bet I know what Levi wants. He wants to vote for me come the election. That right, boy?"

Levi looked as if he had been slapped. "Nosuh!" he said quickly, the sound of alarm ringing in his voice. "Voting is the white man's business. You won't catch me messing with none a that."

"I don't know," Billy Dean said. "Could be I heard talk about you and that secret nigger club. What y'all call it? The Double-A-C-P?"

The Senator looked at Billy Dean as if he were an idiot. "Levi?" He gave a sharp laugh. "Levi cares as much about voting as a horse cares about Christmas. Besides, he knows which side his bread is buttered on." This time it was the Senator who slapped Billy Dean on the back. "Just like you, boy."

Billy Dean's face reddened again, but his angry scowl was directed toward Levi.

The inside kitchen door swung open and a plump, well-dressed white woman about the Senator's age poked her head in. "What are you men doing in here?" she asked, holding a lacy handkerchief up to a neck whiter than the china on the countertops. "You are entertaining guests, Hugh. Did you forget?"

When her brother didn't answer at once, she looked carefully around a kitchen filled with tense expressions. Without speaking another word, she touched the handkerchief to her lips and eased back through the door.

Straightening his jacket, the Senator started after his sister. "Billy Dean," he said on his way through the door, "you find out what Levi wants. Then come tell me. Get some practice at being my sheriff."

Left alone in the kitchen with the preacher and his family, and his face still flushed from having been told off, Billy Dean motioned toward the back door. Through clenched teeth he said, "Let's go outside and have us a little powwow."

Vida hurried Nate down the steps first. Before her father could take the first step, Billy Dean shoved Levi hard, causing him to topple down from the porch and land sprawled on the ground at Vida's feet.

Looking up, she saw the crazy smile on Billy Dean's face. His eyes cut toward the boy in her arms and at last Vida found her voice. "Lillie Dee!" she screamed.

The old cook was at the door in a flash. "Merciful Jesus! What's going on out here? Levi, what you doing spraddled out in the dirt? You hurt yourself?" Without waiting for an answer she yelled out into the yard, "Rezel! Where you? Get here and help the Rev'rund on his feet."

Her boy emerged out of the dark of the yard. From his fierce expression Vida could tell Rezel had been watching the whole thing. After helping Levi up, he went to Vida's side.

"You and Nate all right?" he whispered.

She nodded, thinking about begging Rezel to run away with her that very minute

Just then the Senator's younger daughter, Delia, the one they called "the pretty one," joined Lillie Dee on the back porch. "Billy Dean," she cooed, "what on earth are you-all doing out here? You were in the middle of telling me an amusing story, remember?"

Then she saw Levi brushing himself off. "My goodness, Levi, are you all right?" She shot Billy Dean a pouty look. "What have you done to Levi?"

"The old man fell down's, all," Billy Dean said gruffly. "I'll take care of it. Everybody get on back in the house."

Lillie Dee did as she was told, and when Rezel hesitated, his mother ordered him inside. He reluctantly obeyed.

Yet Delia remained behind. "Levi, you tell me to stay and I will.

I won't let anything happen to you."

The woman's tone confused Vida. It sounded kind, but the way you would be kind to your pet dog. Nothing to hang your hopes on.

"No, ma'am, Miss Delia," Levi insisted. "Nothing going on out here to worry you about. I was just giving my best to Mr. Billy Dean on his election."

She looked back at Billy Dean. "You!" she laughed tipsily. "Our next sheriff. How low has our democracy sunk?" Delia shook her head, teasingly. "Hurry on back in, Billy Dean. Your fiancée is getting—*oops!*" she said, covering her mouth in mock embarrassment, "I mean, your *food* is getting cold." She gave out a giggle and went back into the kitchen.

The screen door shut behind her, and Vida felt their last hope had left with her. She could hear Billy Dean's breathing, fast and furious. In a voice bled dry of emotion, he said, "This ain't over," and then stomped back into the house.

During the ride home, the car was thick with things not said. Vida could tell from her father's clenched jaw that he was figuring hard, considering and then discarding one option after another. As for herself, she could only come up with one, and she was doing it, holding tight to her baby until the nightmare passed.

Levi parked the car next to their house, switched off the motor. He left the lights burning. He sat there motionless, looking off into the distance where the headlights cut a ghostly path across the field.

Without looking at Vida, he said, "The boy ain't safe here with us. And we ain't safe with the boy."

Nate was trying to tickle Vida's neck with her plait. She stilled his hand, struggling with her father's words. "What you saying, Daddy?"

"You heard the man. He say it ain't over. Nate make that man crazy." Then he said, almost to himself, "Your momma got kin in Alabama."

Grasping his meaning, Vida cried, "I ain't letting go of Nate,

Daddy. You can't make me do that."

"We ain't got no choice, Vida."

Then she remembered. "Rezel's going to the Promised Land! Me and Nate can go with him!"

"No, daughter. You know better. Rezel can't take care of you and a baby. Rezel can't take care of hisself. I promise, you pray on it and you'll see it my way. God going to show us the righteous path."

Chapter Seven

MOTHER AND CHILD

Floyd made it to the hospital in Greenwood in less than thirty minutes.

"Now, everything is going to be OK," he said, striding confidently beside Hazel as they rolled her down the corridor on a gurney. "All you got to do is lay back and let nature take its course. Do everything the doctor says, do you hear?"

"Yes," she said, feeling a spark of irritation at her husband.

"And remember to push. That's always a good thing."

"Yes, I will," she said. Yet what she wanted to say was, "How do you know? How many babies have you birthed between cotton picker deals?"

Mercifully, the nurse told Floyd he had to stop at the delivery room door. Hazel was more than relieved when she heard the sound of his footsteps retreating toward the waiting room.

With or without Floyd, Hazel could never have been ready for what came next. The pain was unlike anything she had ever imagined. Nothing anybody could possibly live through. And that wasn't the scariest part. As she lay spread open and vulnerable on that table, pinned down and surrounded by a doctor and nurses who were demanding so much of her, her own body turning on her, with only her elbows to support her, the worst part was that this time there was no escape. No back door. No place to run. It had been put squarely on her shoulders. At eighteen she was expected to see it through all alone.

The bright lights that caromed off the sterile white walls were indifferent to her pain. The faceless doctor yelled at her, telling her to bear down. She didn't think she could. Hazel shut her eyes against it and prayed to die.

"She's crowning!" the doctor shouted. His tone was now jubilant, conveying to Hazel that she was doing something right. No, that they were doing it right—her and her baby, together. With the doctor's words, from the center of her pitch-black world of hurt, flashed the most glorious realization. She could read it like lightning across the night sky. This baby was coming to save her, not to harm her.

Hazel gave in to the pain, no longer afraid, and thrilled by the prospect that somebody was arriving who, no matter what, would always be on her side. She welcomed her son into the world with a cry of joy.

Back in her room, Hazel held her baby, whispering softly to the newcomer in her arms, "My baby. My baby," over and over, trying to get her ears used to the words. The nurse patted Hazel's hand and said right there in front of Floyd, "You did a real good job, honey. Your son is healthy, whole, and one of the best-looking things ever to come out of the Greenwood Leflore Hospital."

Hazel smiled at the baby. "He knew what he was doing, all right. I couldn't a done it without him."

"Well, little momma," the nurse said after a short silence, "I guess I never looked at it that way. What y'all going to name him?"

Without batting an eye, Floyd announced his decision. "Johnny Earl Graham."

"After who?" asked the nurse.

"After nobody," he said proudly. "From neither side. Our boy ain't gonna owe his future to nobody's past."

Hazel smiled, liking the sound of that. Maybe it was true. She hoped it was—that she and Floyd and Johnny Earl had been cut loose and were traveling free, floating high above all the doubts and fears that prowled the past. Maybe there was nothing ahead of them but a blue-sky future.

෮

Five days later, as Floyd drove, neither he nor Hazel could take their eyes off the baby, which put Floyd all over the road. Peeking at the child in his wife's arms for about the hundredth time, Floyd asked, "How's my little monkey doing?"

"Floyd," Hazel said, "I hate it when you call him that. He don't look anything like a monkey."

He patted Hazel on the knee. "That's not what I mean by it. He's just so cute and all."

Narrowing her eyes at the baby, she said, "Floyd, he's got your black hair. Your dark eyes. He even got them wide moccasin jaws. I swan, I don't see me anywhere. Looks like you did the whole thing on your own."

Floyd laughed, and without bothering to look he said, "He's got your cute pug nose. Don't you see?"

Hazel didn't, but she figured Floyd was giving her the nose to be nice, which was perfectly fine. Right now she needed him to be real nice. Without a whole hospital of nurses backing her up, she was already struggling to keep on top of her fears. She was returning to Floyd's world, and she was not going alone. She had a baby to keep alive. Here was this living, squirming, kicking, crying, puking, pee-ing, wordless ball of needs. Everything depended on her being able to decipher what he wanted quick enough to keep him breathing, so that he would grow up and love her enough to be grateful. Until then, she hoped Johnny Earl gave good directions.

"I'm so glad you went to get Momma," she said. "I got a million questions to ask her about babies."

Hazel's mother brought little comfort the whole time she was there, insisting that there was nothing special to raising a child. "It's only your first, Hazelene," Baby Ishee said more than once. "I had fourteen. Twelve lived. Some make it and some don't. It's mostly up to them, I reckon."

After her mother left, Hazel spent one sleepless night after the other, repeatedly getting up out of bed to check on Johnny in his crib. In the beginning she was afraid to touch him. Later, she was afraid to set him down. She studied him frantically for signs of intelligence, of hunger, of thirst, of infestation and blight, trying to read him like she would a field of corn, pleading with him to tell her what it was he wanted of her.

"What would a good mother be doing now?" she asked him over and over. He stared back silently with those big, dark, Indian eyes, not so much looking at her, she thought, as considering her, like he was sizing her up.

⌒

Floyd watched anxiously from the sidelines, hoping Hazel would find her gait and come around to the job. "Hazel," he called to her one night, gently shaking her arm. "Honey, you're doing it again. Wake up."

Awake now, she continued to cry. "Oh, Floyd! It was awful," she sobbed. "I was trapped in Daddy's storm pit and I couldn't find the door. I knew it was there somewhere and it was so dark and I heard Johnny crying on the other side and I couldn't get a match lit and he...and..."

Floyd pulled her to him and soothed her with his words, letting her cry until she was all cried out. He said all the right things. That they were in it together. He would always be there for her. They had come a long way and had a wonderful life still ahead. He said even he had his doubts sometimes.

"You, Floyd?" she asked, feeling an immense comfort in his confession.

"Uh-huh. Everybody does."

"Tell 'em to me, Floyd." She anxiously waited to hear what they were. Maybe she could comfort him for a change.

Floyd switched on the light and smiled at her sympathetically. At first she thought he was going to say that he loved her. Maybe without the "anyway"—his expression was just that tender.

"Hazel, honey?" he said,

"Yes, sweetheart," she answered, feeling comforted. "I'm listening." She nuzzled up to his neck.

"Hazel, honey," he said again, "I think it's time you learned about the Science of Controlled Thinking."

"Wha—?"

"Now, hear me out," Floyd said, taking her hand. "Controlled Thinking is the way to get rid of all the second-guessing you been doing. It's the reason why I'm selling more equipment than any John Deere salesman in the Delta."

"Floyd, what has that got to do—"

"Now, I've been considering it for a while, and I don't think raising a baby is no different. Sure, you're having a little problem adjusting to it all," Floyd said. "Any change is hard. But change is also opportunity. If you let me help, I promise you'll come around."

Floyd reached beside him on the nightstand and brought his book into bed with them. "Like I was reading last night, 'Enthusiasm is contagious.' And Hazel," he said with a grin, "probably nobody around is more catching than me."

He began flipping through the pages and pointing out his favorite little sayings. "Listen to this," he said excitedly. '…To a controlled thinker, every problem is an opportunity.' "

"And here's a good 'un: 'Attitude determines altitude.' And, 'If life serves you a bum steer, eat steaks.' How about this one: 'If you get a raw deal—' ' "

By then she had stopped listening. Those things didn't make any sense to her at all, and she sure didn't see what they had to do with Johnny Earl. So instead of looking at the book as he pointed out the words, she stared at the purple burn scars on his fingers and remembered the story he had told her when they were still getting to know each other. She had finally got up the nerve to ask about his mother. Without blinking, he said, "Died when I was six months old."

Hazel didn't know what to say. She must have looked sad because Floyd quickly tried to reassure her. "It's not like I knew her or anything."

"How'd she die?" Hazel asked, sounding a lot more sorrowful about the loss than he.

Floyd looked down at his hands and began to rub the little purple blotches on his fingers that Hazel had always assumed were birthmarks. "Well, what they tell me is Momma was holding me in her arms, warming herself in front of the fireplace, when she had a stroke and fell out." He held out his hands for her to see. "Daddy said I got these scars when I grabbed aholt of a burning log."

Hazel's eyes had welled up with tears, not knowing what it would do to a person to reach out for his mother and touch fire instead. Yet Floyd told it as if it had happened to somebody else, somebody he had little patience for.

Now she wondered why he wasn't the one having nightmares, too. What was wrong with her that she couldn't get past it all?

✣

Over the next few months, the more fearful she became, the more Floyd preached his religion of success at her. He told her in every failure is a seed for the next victory; it's all in a person's thinking. Then he began to write the sayings down on tablet paper and hung them around the house for her to find.

"DON'T SPEND A SECOND OF TODAY FRETTING TOMORROW OR REGRETTING YESTERDAY," the bathroom mirror warned her. The Philco greeted her with, "IT'S A MATTER OF MENTAL MAGNETISM: WHAT ARE YOUR THOUGHTS ATTRACTING TODAY?" "BE A CONTROLLED THINKER!" the hall closet door hollered.

The last words she heard at night were from the lamp by her bed. The paper taped to its shade chided, "HOW FAST YOU TRAVEL

ON THE TRACK TO SUCCESS IS DETERMINED BY YOUR TRAIN OF THOUGHT," and to hear Floyd tell it, they were still only in slow motion. He had big plans for his family and was keeping a positive mind on the future, and she needed to be there with him.

Hazel tried to live by his words, wanting desperately to be a good wife and a good mother, yet couldn't gain that Floyd-Graham-rock-solid certainty. She watched with a mixture of wonderment and trepidation as Johnny ate regular, never got sick, learned to walk, and grew like he was supposed to. Best of all, he loved his mother and knew how to show it. That especially was a comfort. Of course Hazel loved him, too, but love took its toll. Hazel's stabbing anxiety dulled to a constant dread.

Not long after Johnny's first birthday, Floyd talked her into getting pregnant again. He figured that with two children she wouldn't have time to fret over things that didn't matter. Another child would help prioritize her thinking, he advised.

Hazel did as Floyd asked. She got pregnant and had another boy, Davie. She memorized more sayings. She recited them to her children like nursery rhymes. As much as she tried changing her thinking, she couldn't get over feeling that she had only the loosest of handholds on the caboose of Floyd's speeding train of success.

❦ 1955 ❦

Chapter Eight

UP TO THE BIG HOUSE

E ven though she couldn't find her voice to say it, Hazel figured their entire cottage could easily fit into this one room, and she was not alone in reverential silence. She and Floyd turned slowly in the middle of the empty parlor and neither spoke, as if a house this grand might not want to carry voices as common as their own. That the house was now theirs may have been a reality on paper, yet this minute, as they gawked openmouthed, that truth felt as hollow as the cavernous rooms themselves.

"Well, punkin," Floyd said, whispering for a reason unknown to him, "it took me six years to keep my promise. But I did it. I got you out of that slave cabin and put you up on the hill."

He looked at her with that sweet expression she remembered from before they married. It was the way he looked at her over ice cream during that magical month of planning their escape.

"You proud of me?" he asked.

The question comforted Hazel. He still cared what she thought. "I'm real proud,

Floyd," she whispered back. "It's a dream come true."

Floyd stood a little straighter. "Like I always say," his voice stronger now, "success is a dream with sweat on it." He spoke the last part loud enough to send the saying echoing lightly off the walls. He must have approved of the way it sounded, because he said it again, louder. "Success is a dream with sweat on it," he shouted, and smiled at Hazel proudly as his voice rang throughout the house.

Hazel smiled weakly. There was no doubt about it. Floyd had been sweating big time. He broke all records selling farm implements, single-handedly putting enough machinery into operation to free up thousands of field hands. He had been such a standout that the Senator convinced his brother-in-law, the president of the bank, to loan Floyd the money to start Delphi Motors. The Senator had taken a liking to Floyd.

On one occasion, the Senator had slapped Floyd on the back and said that already, with nothing more than a few well-turned phrases and that shit-eating grin of his, Floyd had changed the Delta landscape more than Ulysses Grant had during the invasion. Floyd had replaced the primitive hollers of the coloreds with the smooth hum of machinery. The Senator said there was no telling how far Floyd could go if he was his own boss. Now, thanks to the Senator—plus Floyd's positive thinking, of course—he was selling Mercurys and Lincolns and Ford trucks out of a business he ran himself.

While the boys scampered through the house, making their bare feet screech against the slick hardwood floors, Hazel stood there holding fast to Floyd, the same way she had that late afternoon when he showed her what lay beyond the bluffs and she struggled to make sense of it all.

The walls around her were the pinkish color of mimosa blossoms, and all along their length were the empty, lighter spaces where portraits of the previous owner's ancestors had hung. It occurred to Hazel that it might be easier living with the ghosts of slaves than of rich people.

"How we going to fill it up, just the four of us?" she asked. "This house got rooms I don't even know the names of."

"That's why I'm taking you to Greenwood. So you can outfit this house with the grandest things you can find. Like I always say, 'If you want to attract money, you got to smell like money.' "

Choosing the curtains for the little slave cabin had stretched Hazel's imagination to the limit, but this assignment made her head swim. She had no idea how rich folks went about filling up their homes, never having been inside a house this grand before.

"Now, I mean it," Floyd said. "When we go to Greenwood, buy only deluxe. We got an image now." His eyes narrowed. "Oh, that reminds me."

Hazel braced herself. She could feel one of Floyd's "lists for success" coming on.

"You got to stop tussling with Johnny and Davie in the yard right out in plain view. I'll find you a colored girl to watch them. And another thing, don't let the boys go out the house looking like Indians. Put shirts and shoes on them. Even in summertime. We ain't in the hills no more. People are going to be watching us close now."

Stamping like horses, Johnny and Davie, half naked and already brown as berries, their feet stained green with spring grass, giddyupped into the sitting room. Hazel got that old sinking feeling again in her chest. A good mother would have known better. This was supposed to be getting easier, she thought. Lurleen and Onareen turned out children like canned tomatoes and never seemed to give being a mother a second thought.

With his arms outstretched, his frail blue eyes pleading, Davie bounced up and down at his father's feet, calling out, "Catch me! Catch me!"

Floyd lifted his son off the ground and threw him into the air, making Davie gurgle with laughter. At the peak of his rise, Davie yelled out, "Catch me!"

Hazel clutched herself. She hated this game.

Johnny noticed his mother's dread. "Daddy, you be careful. Don't drop Davie on his head."

Hazel smiled sadly at Johnny, relieved yet at the same time a little ashamed that he had been the one to speak out.

"We just having some fun. No harm done." Floyd set Davie down on the floor and then turned to Johnny. "Hey, Little Monkey. You wanna go next?" he asked, holding out his arms. Johnny took two steps backward.

Rebuffed, Floyd returned his attention to his wife. "Now, like I was saying, you got to help me, Hazel. We're building us up a reputation. This house is only the start of it."

Nodding her agreement, she looked up into his confident face. Floyd was already acting as if he had been born and bred in this house, when only a few minutes ago he was asking like a child if she was proud of him. It amazed her how things came so natural to him, in the way raising babies came natural to her sisters.

Floyd unveiled the next item on his list. "I think it's time you learned to drive."

Hazel's mouth dropped open. "You gonna teach me, Floyd?" she asked, not believing her ears. She had always assumed that driving was beyond her, mainly because Floyd had never suggested it before.

"That and more. I'm going to get you your very own car. Brand-new Lincoln. Columbia blue. Special-ordered it."

"My own car? For me?" Hazel began to tear up.

"Yep. That way you can be a rolling advertisement for Delphi Motors. I'll put the trucks under the men, and you can help me put Lincolns under their wives." He winked at her. "We can be a team."

"A team," she repeated. Yes, she thought, that was it! Exactly what she had wanted and didn't know how to say until Floyd put it into words. He was so smart. Hazel wanted to be a team with him. The idea thrilled her as nothing had in years. Leave it to Floyd to find a way for her to catch up and travel by his side.

⁓

To her delight and Floyd's amazement, Hazel took to driving like a duck to water. Two weeks with her new Lincoln and she was backing up the big car, passing on the left, even parallel parking. Her stops became feather light and her turns as smooth as butter.

After all those hours riding around with the route men, she fig-ured something must have rubbed off. Hazel didn't mention that to Floyd. She let him assume that at long last there was something she took to natural. Others might be good cooks and good moth-ers or good salesmen, but driving a car was going to be Hazel's special calling.

In no time she was confident enough to do the furniture shop-ping all by herself. She got behind the wheel and powered the mighty machine west on 84, taking the highway straight on into Greenwood. Once there she negotiated big-city traffic, insisted on her rightful turn at intersections, and competed for parking places with the most aggressive of men drivers. The Lincoln was making her into a new woman.

Floyd was nearly as excited about her success as she was. After the furniture started arriving and they began to get settled into the house, he lost no time setting the next phase of his team plan into motion. He told Hazel her team goal was to put at least ten miles a day on the Lincoln and to do it in public view. "You can be an inspiration to all the women in Delphi," he told her. "Nowadays ever woman ought to have her own independent means of transpor-tation. It's the way the world is going."

One evening he brought home a brochure and dramatically spread it out on the kitchen table. "Looka here," he said.

What Hazel saw was the full-color picture of a very happy woman driving down the road in her Lincoln. "Try to look like her," he said reverently. "She's the sign of things to come."

The beautiful woman wore a large off-the-face hat with a mile-long ribbon rippling out the window, a matching scarf, and white gloves just to the wrist. At first Hazel felt a little strange about the idea, hoping that Floyd wasn't trying to trade her up into something that she wasn't. Yet when she saw the look of respect with which he regarded the woman in the picture, she knew she had to do it. Taking the advertisement to Gooseberry's Department Store, she suited herself up as close as she could come to the happy woman.

Hazel put shirts and shoes and bow ties on the boys, loaded them up, and in her new picture hat with a blue satin ribbon, silk chiffon scarf, and white gloves, backed away from their beautiful home and drove up and down Gallatin Street, from the bridge to the church and around the courthouse, looking happy, six times a day.

Chapter Nine

THE TROIS
ARTS LEAGUE

Hazel stepped back from the hall mirror and tugged at her skirt, evening the hemline. The dress was the most beautiful thing she had ever bought, an ice-blue shirtwaist made of silk shantung, which the salesman swore set her eyes to dancing like the sunlight on lake water. She took a tissue from the hostess pocket and, leaning in close to the glass, carefully dabbed at the lipstick in the corner of her mouth. Next she fussed expertly with the collar, smoothing the tips down flat.

Well, the clothes and the makeup were certainly up to muster. Everything shaded, highlighted, smoothed down and lined up. However, what Hazel couldn't see was the person between the lines. Touching her cheek gently, she longed for Floyd and wished he was there to tell her how beautiful she looked. A glimmer in his eye would do. But he wasn't there, and she needed to do this on her own. Floyd was counting on her to be a team with him.

At his insistence, she had invited some of the neighbor ladies over for punch and to show them what she had done with the house. More than three months had passed since they had moved in, and not a single person had come calling. Floyd had told her, "Hazel, you can't wait for success to come knocking. You have to find out where it lives and then go hunt it down with a stick."

"Floyd, I don't know what to say to women like that. What do they talk about?" Whatever it was, she was sure it wasn't mules, heel flies, and ringworm.

The women reigning in the houses around her were formidable-looking creatures, skin untouched by the sun and white as alabaster, with rouged cheeks, severe as Delta sunsets, their shoulders pulled back and chests puffed out, dripping with brooches and breastpins and cameos like generals on inspection. They were proper in ways that were foreign to Hazel, having cultivated curious manners that pushed you away rather than pulled you closer. When met on the street they could use a smile like an extended arm as if to say, "OK, that's near enough."

Hazel stood there at the mirror waiting for the bourbon to kick in. To make it through more and more days, she had been relying on the Jim Beam in the pretty decanters that Floyd received from the Senator each Christmas and kept lined up on the counter. She knew she shouldn't, but sometimes it was the only way to muster the hope she needed to keep on going.

She remembered her first drink. As a girl, wandering the outcroppings, she came upon one of the places where her father hid his shine under a rock ledge. When Hazel unscrewed the top and brought the bottle up to her nose, the smell cut her breath and made her eyes burn. Should she? The preacher said it was a sin. Her mother called it a curse. However, that didn't stop her daddy from devoting a good portion of his life to it.

Hazel took a drink. The clear liquid breathed its fiery breath deep down into her and caused her to tear up and cough. She took another.

The sensation was like nothing she had expected, like two warm hands clasping her face. Her spirits soared higher than the chinquapin oaks before her, higher than the Appalachian foothills that surrounded her. She now understood why her father drank. He missed hope, too. When she couldn't find hope in Floyd's eyes, sometimes a sip or two of bourbon would hold her over the dry spells.

Hazel heard Johnny yelling from the backyard. "Momma! She's here! She's here!"

At last! The maid Floyd had promised for the day. A day was probably as long as she would last. Maids came and went with such regularity, Hazel barely got to know their names, because usually by the end of their first day on the job Floyd had found some reason to suspect them of stealing from him.

Hazel waited to hear the confirming slap of the back door and then called out, "Bring her on in here!" She quickly drained the bourbon from the tumbler she kept hidden behind the flour sack and popped a peppermint in her mouth.

A husky voice sang out, "Whoo-ee!" When Hazel turned, the first thing that caught her eye was a stretch of white fabric showcasing a prominent rear end. At that moment the colored woman it was attached to was gazing into the parlor, her hands planted on her well-rounded hips.

"Look at all them pretty colors," the woman said, apparently to the boys who stood on either flank. "More tints than One Wing Hannah's jukebox."

Davie yelped and then took off in the direction of the green vinyl sectional, undoubtedly with the aim of scaling up the back of the couch and jumping off. A split second later, Johnny was in hot pursuit.

The woman turned again toward Hazel. She was wearing the snuggest maid's uniform Hazel had ever seen. Her breasts pooched out the top of her dress, reaching for daylight. Her smile involved at least two gold teeth. "Hidey. My name's Sweet Pea. You Miss Hazel?"

"Glad to know you," Hazel said hesitantly. Where did Floyd find this one? she wondered. He was surely scraping the bottom of the barrel now.

Sweet Pea turned back around and surveyed the room again. "Where you get all them nice things, Miss Hazel? I never seen nothing like it in Delphi."

That definitely tipped the scales in the maid's favor. She gave Sweet Pea a big grin and crossed the hall to stand next to the woman. "And you won't see nothing like it in the whole state of Mississippi, neither," she said excitedly. She had been wanting so badly to brag on herself. "I had to order all the way to Chicago. The salesman says this stuff is just catching on. Colors nobody ever heard of before. Just invented. Parakeet green. Flamingo pink. Peacock blue. I tried to get some of each."

Sweet Pea laughed. "Um-hum! I can see that. Look like a big flock of zoo birds done shedded all over your company room." She took a moment to admire the yellow Formica coffee table in the shape of a prize banana, the plastic end tables with gleaming enameled metal legs, and the aluminum pole lamp with pink, blue, and green bullet shades. "Yo furniture shinier than the front end of a Cadillac. And not a stick of wood to be seen."

"You're mighty gracious to say so," Hazel said delightedly. "When that salesman showed me all those pretty pictures, I said to myself, why be old-fashioned when nowadays you can get everything in plastic, chrome, and vinyl?"

Sweet Pea waggled her head appreciatively. "Must be a joy to sit here in this room when the morning sun hits it. You probably need to put you on some sunglasses to do your dusting."

The maid's opinion, even though it was a colored one, was doing wonders to boost Hazel's confidence. For the first time since Floyd suggested the party, she almost looked forward to the ladies coming over. If they were only half as struck as Sweet Pea, Hazel would do Floyd proud.

After Johnny had successfully fussed his brother down from the couch, Hazel told him, "Take Davie outside and finish that quiet game y'all were playing, OK honey? We got to get things ready for company."

Sweet Pea asked, "What we going to feed these womens, Miss

Hazel?"

Hazel pulled the newspaper article from her waist pocket. It was titled *Entertaining: Elegant and Easy.* "Now here's some new recipes they say everybody just loves. I thought between the two of us we could figure out how to put it together. I bought all the ingredients."

"What you want me to do?"

"Well, I ain't much in the kitchen," Hazel said, "so you do the cooking part and I'll do the opening and stirring. And you can serve it, if you don't mind."

This took Sweet Pea back for a moment. "No'm, I don't mind," she said, half smiling, amused at the thought that her minding had something to do with anything.

The doorbell rang as Sweet Pea finished spooning the crushed pineapple around the chunks of ham. "They's just in time," she said, looking up at Hazel. When she saw the blood drain from Hazel's face, she comforted her, "Don't you fret none, Miss Hazel. Everything going to come off jest fine." She headed for the door.

Hazel checked herself for a final time in the hall mirror, once more wishing Floyd were there to tell her how pretty she looked. The bourbon didn't seem to be working. She breathed deeply and tried to act the way she imagined the happy woman in the Lincoln advertisement would if she had to get out of her car and entertain. Straightening her shoulders, she prepared her smile and followed Sweet Pea airily to the door to meet the women.

Sweet Pea flung open the door to see that three women had arrived at once, looking like a posse. "How y'all doin' today?" Sweet Pea bawled happily. "Come on in out the heat!"

The women stepped into the entryway and Hazel said the words she had practiced. "How good of y'all to visit me today." Her voice was shaky yet the words clearly enunciated.

Miss Pearl, the Senator's sister, smiled warmly and brought her handkerchiefed hand up to her delicately wattled neck. In a rush of breath she said, "Hazel, you are so kind to have us over. When Hayes told me about your new home, I felt terrible that I hadn't stopped by before and properly welcomed you to the neighborhood. And me living across the lane from y'all. Will you forgive me, dear?"

With all those kind words having been spent on Hazel, and with so much feeling backing them up, Hazel felt her stomach settling a bit. "That's mighty gracious of you to say. I'm just proud y'all could come today's all."

"Well, better late than never. Isn't that what the sage professed, Hazel?" she smiled sweetly again.

Pearl Alcorn was an older woman with kind, misty blue eyes and an understanding smile. Her silver-blue hair looked like it was still warm from the beauty parlor. Hazel thought she was quite lovely, even if she did have a crippled hand. It was said that when Miss Pearl was a little girl living at the Columns, she was out riding and her horse stumbled, threw her off, and then rolled over on her hand, crushing the bones. From that time on, she was never seen without a lace handkerchief carefully arranged among the fingers to make the hand look useful. It gave her an air of tragic elegance Hazel couldn't help but admire.

Miss Pearl waved her handkerchief at an unpleasant, horsy-looking woman at her side. "Hazel, I want you to meet my nieces. Hertha." The frightful woman she pointed out emitted a little snort. "She's your next-door neighbor. You've undoubted met her husband, the sheriff."

"How do you do?" Hazel said, slow and careful. Hazel knew she shouldn't take comfort in another woman's ugliness, yet it did boost her confidence a bit. Couldn't even get a man on her own, Floyd said. The rumor was that the Senator had agreed to make Billy Dean sheriff if he took the eldest daughter off his hands. At least Hazel had fought fair and square to get Floyd.

"And my other niece, Delia."

Delia was another story entirely. She was a beautiful younger woman with lustrous blond curls and blue eyes that seemed to be laughing at something, Hazel could only wonder what. She had heard the stories from Floyd. Delia married twice before she turned twenty and had boyfriends flung as far as St. Louis.

"So you two is sisters?" Hazel blurted. "I swan, you don't look nothing like each—"

Pearl coughed once and said, "Isn't this nice, Hazel? I hope you will consider us your new best friends."

Realizing she had been saved from something terrible, Hazel nodded. "Best friends. Oh, yes, ma'am. I would love that more than I can say."

The sisters met the suggestion of friendship with blank expressions, but Pearl seemed sincere. Hazel found herself surprised she hadn't noticed this kindness when they had occasionally passed on the street. That was back when they lived in the slave cabin, before she had officially moved up the hill into Delphi proper. Maybe now things would be different after all.

Hazel sucked in a deep breath. It was time to show them her new room. Gesturing with a wide sweep of her arm, she said, "Will y'all please come into my company room?"

Miss Pearl led the way and the other two followed dutifully behind, but upon entering the parlor the trio stopped cold, apparently stunned simultaneously. The women put Sweet Pea in mind of a herd of fainting goats her uncle used to have. When startled, their joints locked up and they toppled over, rigid as boards. Sweet Pea smiled, picturing all three white ladies dressed in voile and crinoline, lying about Miss Hazel's new rubberized floor, stiff as a load of lumber.

As for Hazel, at first she smiled proudly, judging their reaction to be positive, yet as the seconds ticked by without a word, her stomach began to grow queasy again. She didn't know what to say. She would have fled through the door had she not been in her own home.

"Y'all sit yourselves down," Sweet Pea said, taking charge. "Miss

Hazel done got some fine eating planned."

"Yes, yes," Hazel stammered. "Y'all sit down. Anywhere."

Still standing in a bunch, the women swiveled their heads around the room as if determined to find a place to roost as a group. Finally, Miss Pearl and Miss Hertha chose the Stratoloungers and Delia settled on the vinyl couch. When her guests were seated Hazel eased herself into a plastic shell chair. There was a period of uncomfortable silence when Sweet Pea disappeared into the kitchen.

Hazel's mind raced furiously, trying to think of something to say. When she looked over at Miss Pearl the woman smiled pleasantly, dismissing any awkwardness from the room. Pearl leaned in toward Hazel. "I'm so sorry. We can't possibly stay but a few minutes. Our little club meeting went longer than we planned, and the rest of the ladies are at this very moment finishing up without us."

"What kind of club y'all got?" Hazel blurted, excited that she had thought of something to say.

"Why, we call it the Trois Arts League."

"It's French," Delia explained, her eyes still laughing. "For 'three arts.' "

"I swan."

"Exactly," said Miss Pearl. "Every month we consider the life of a painter, a composer, and an author."

"Ain't that nice! Sounds so smart of y'all."

"Why, thank you, Hazel," Pearl said. "And of course we do our part for the community. Our busiest time is coming up, and we have a host of events to plan for." Pearl touched her handkerchief to her heart and whispered, "Charity season, you know," as if the poor people might be listening. "So we can only stay for a chat. I hope you don't mind."

"Don't think nothing of it," Hazel said to Pearl. "I'm just glad y'all could show." Hazel knew she should be disappointed, but she wasn't. These three ladies had only been there under five minutes and they had already overloaded her wagon.

Of course Pearl wasn't being bad at all. It was Hertha who sent shivers through Hazel. The sheriff's wife was sitting straight-backed and wooden in her lounger. Hazel couldn't help noticing that her front teeth bucked worse than a rodeo horse and her brow hung like a fireplace mantel over eyes the color of cold ashes. She may well have been the most disagreeable-looking person Hazel had ever seen. It was she who spoke next. "Well, you certainly have a unique decorating style, Hazel." There was something about the way the word "unique" splintered in Hertha's throat that made Hazel judge the observation not at all complimentary. "What do you call it?" she asked. Even though Hertha was asking Hazel, she was looking sidelong at Delia. There was a slight curl to Hertha's lip.

Thinking of how to answer a question she didn't understand, Hazel noticed how warm it had become. She heard something that resembled the tinkling bells on a faraway hill. Or maybe, she thought, like laughter right before it breaks out into sound.

She looked again to Miss Pearl, who smiled at her sympathetically, encouraging her on. "Well, I don't call it nothing by name," Hazel said haltingly. "Just furniture, I suppose. Things I thought was pretty."

The woman nodded and the corners of her mouth twitched and her nose scrunched up, as if she could burst into ugly hysterical snorts at any moment. "It's certainly...what's the word? Intense."

The tinkling of the bells grew louder, and Hazel checked Miss Pearl's expression. She was still smiling reassuringly.

Delia spoke up. "It all looks so...new."

"Brand new. Just been bought," Hazel said hopefully.

"Didn't you bring any family pieces with you from home?" Hertha asked, wincing as if something hurt.

"No. My folks is still sitting in 'em, I reckon," Hazel answered.

Little coughs were exchanged between Hertha and Delia, a cold was catching. To keep from crying, Hazel bit her lip and again looked over at Miss Pearl, her eyes pleading.

Pearl nodded agreeably and said, "It must be nice not to have to bother with dusty old hand-me-downs and start fresh." She raised her lace handkerchief to her creamy throat and lowered her voice, as if she were confessing a deep dark secret. "Why, many a day I want to throw out the old and begin anew. Just because we saved them from the Yankees, we feel we have to display our pieces as if they were monuments. Now, *that's* what I call silly. We should all be more sensible like Hazel here."

The other ladies nodded, agreeing that they were the foolish ones after all. The bells were silenced and Hazel breathed easier.

"Where did your people distinguish themselves during the war, Hazel?" It was Hertha asking.

Hazel was confused. She snatched at the collar of her dress and said timidly, "War?"

"Well, for instance, my great-great-uncle served with Lee. And my great-grandfather was the drummer boy at Chickamauga. In fact, all the Trois Arts women belong to the United Daughters of the Confederacy."

"Chicka—oh *that* war!" Hazel said, very relieved to be catching on. "We got a funny story about that."

"Do tell it, Hazel," Miss Pearl urged.

"Well, my great-great-granddaddy didn't own no slaves, so he didn't figure he should have to fight no war to keep them. He spent the whole time up a sycamore tree hiding from both sides. The only general we got in my family is my daddy, Major General Ishee, and that's because he got to name hisself."

The laughter Hazel evoked with her story was different from what she was aiming for. It was sharp and jagged like broken glass. Miss Pearl shot the two women daggers and the laughter ceased.

Then into the deathly silence clattered Sweet Pea with a large serving tray, bellowing, "Y'all surely going to love this here." She set the tray on the banana table next to the punch bowl and backed away to let the women gaze at the feast of potato chips and onion dip, Vienna sausages smothered in barbecue sauce, and boiled ham bits floating in a bowl of crushed pineapple.

No one moved. Figuring that the women may not have read the *Hopalachie Courier* and therefore were not up-to-date on their delicacies, Sweet Pea decided to instruct them, bending down so low over the tray that everyone's eyes went nervously to her tightly bound breasts, which looked ready to discharge themselves into the dip like cannonballs.

Sweet Pea held up a toothpick. "You git you a little stick here and poke yourself one of these little Veener sausages." She pointed at the dip, "Or you can drag your tater chip through this here mess. Go on now and get you some." Sweet Pea smiled at them wide, her gold teeth gleaming as brightly as the furniture.

Miss Pearl squirmed a little in her vinyl recliner. "It certainly looks delicious, Hazel. Though I have to confess that the club lunched at my house earlier, and I'm sure I forced too much food on them. Only finger sandwiches and such, nothing as hearty as what you offer." Miss Pearl dabbed the corner of her mouth with her handkerchief.

Sweet Pea shrugged as if there was no accounting for taste and ladled the punch, making sure everyone got a marshmallow, except for Hazel, who got two and a sympathetic wink. Then she made her hip-rolling exit from the room.

There followed another long silence. Her face hot with shame, Hazel seized the opportunity to steer the subject away from the food. "What y'all studying in your club?" she asked Miss Pearl desperately. She was the only one Hazel dared to look at now.

"Well, we are presently up to the *p*'s. Puccini, Proust, and Picasso. Hertha here has been leading us in an animated discussion of *Remembrance of Things Past*." When Hazel only stared blankly at Miss Pearl, she asked, "Have you ever read it, Hazel?"

"No. It don't sound familiar. I know a good book, though," Hazel ventured. "Have you ever heard of *David Copperfield*?"

"Why, yes! By Mister Charles Dickens! Are you familiar with that work?" Miss Pearl asked, pleasantly surprised. The other women leaned forward greedily, gawking like customers at a sideshow promising a French-speaking pig.

"I sure do!" Hazel said, relieved to be talking about something she knew. "When I was a girl they playacted that story on the radio. We never had a radio before. Just when it got good, Daddy said I had to go milk the cows. Well, I thought when you turned the thing off and then come back later, you could pick up right where you left it. Lord, was I disappointed to find out my program done went on without me." Hazel shook her head sadly and then looked up at Miss Pearl. "I never did find out how that boy turned out. Do you happen to know?" Miss Pearl smiled tenderly. "He turned out just fine, Hazel. Just fine." She began to edge herself out of the recliner. "Hazel, I'm afraid I really must be going. Hayes will be back from the bank anytime now and I've still got the meeting to adjourn."

Hertha and Delia followed suit and began their ascents. They made little sucking sounds as they peeled themselves from the furniture.

After the other two ladies had filed out the front door, Miss Pearl lingered behind for a moment. "Hazel, thank you so much. I think it went fine, don't you, dear?"

"Well, I hope it did."

"We'll do it again real soon, all right? Next time we'll have you and Floyd over."

Miss Pearl left, trailing agreeable beauty parlor smells. Though Hazel wasn't so sure things had gone as well as Miss Pearl said, she was delighted that she had made at least one new friend. Floyd would be proud.

◦○◦

Sweet Pea looked down at the untouched tray. "It's a shame they done ate. Sure is some purty food. Shoulda sent a plate home with them."

Hazel beamed. "That's a good idea!" she said and wrapped up some Fancy Franks and filled an orange Fiestaware bowl with Hula Ham. She headed off for Miss Pearl's house, thinking maybe she could serve them to Mr. Hayes with his supper.

As she came up the steps, she was met by gales of laughter pouring through the Irish lace curtains and unshuttered windows. The Trois Arts League must not have adjourned yet.

"Thank heavens you didn't touch the food!" someone was saying. "What did you say she called them? Fancy Franks?"

"And did you see the wallpaper?" That was Miss Hertha's voice. "Am I wrong or were those actually bird dogs with pheasants in their mouths?"

"You've got to hand it to her," Delia said. "Most people choose their wallpaper as background. Not Hazel. Hers screams out 'Hey, y'all! We got *wallpaper!*' "

"How could you keep from bursting out laughing?"

"And the colors!" Delia went on. "I couldn't hear myself think, they were in such a riot."

Hazel didn't stand and listen because she wanted to. She stood there because she was too shamed to move.

"Now, that's enough!" Miss Pearl was speaking. Hazel waited for her new friend to set them straight about her. Miss Pearl knew who Hazel really was. Hazel had seen it in the woman's kindly eyes.

"You can't blame her, girls," she said in the same sad whisper in which she'd spoken earlier about charity. "Now, put yourself in her place for a moment. Being poor and from the hills, you're probably thankful to get a new spread for the bed. You can't be terribly concerned if it goes with your curtains. Or if your curtains go with the rug on the floor. It's only natural that Hazel missed out on the concept of 'goes with.' " That brought on another burst of laughter.

"I wasn't trying to be humorous. Y'all are being too hard on her, now." Miss Pearl was sounding flustered. "After all, she has learned to dress nicely. You saw that. Very tasteful. And she's pretty. Maybe interior decorating is her next conquest. Give her time."

The women stopped to consider Miss Pearl's point for a moment and then sped right past it. Hertha said, "And that sassy colored girl she found. Sweet Pea. A real Saturday-night brawler. She might as well have been serving drinks in a barrel house." Miss Hertha lowered her voice. "Billy Dean has that girl in jail more times than I can say. Why, every time I see my husband, he's got her in the back of his cruiser. For soliciting, you know."

There was a chorus of clucks and gasps.

"And speaking of soliciting," Miss Hertha said, "Hazel seems to have her own route. Have y'all seen her peddling Lincolns for her husband up and down Gallatin? And with those poor children in tow. A sorry spectacle. What *will* become of them with a mother such as that?"

"Really!" Miss Pearl said. "That's uncalled-for. You are being *much* too hard on that poor woman."

༄

By the time Floyd came home, Hazel had stopped her crying and pulled herself together. When he asked how things had gone, she didn't answer. She went to the sink and began scrubbing a clean pot.

"Do you think they'll invite you to join their club?" he asked. "That sure would be good for business."

"Well, I'm not sure," she said with her eyes closed, keeping her back to him. "I don't think they have any openings."

She dried her hands on her apron. "And besides, I might not be their kind of people, Floyd." Hazel's breathing was labored, and she began to feel a little wobbly. It was another one of those sinking spells she had been having lately. She leaned against the counter for a moment and then turned to look at her husband, hoping he might reach out and steady her. That would feel real nice about now.

"Nonsense," he said. "You've got to stop thinking that way. If you want something bad enough, you can have it. Ain't I proved that to you? Quit dwelling on the negative. Some right thinking would do you wonders," he said.

Hazel looked up at the man who stood before her. Sure and certain. She really did wish she could think like him, as clear and positive as the slogans he was always spouting. "Winners never quit and quitters never win." "Can't never could." "Failures find excuses and controlled thinkers find a way." To him it was all a matter of knowing where you want to go, setting your jaw, and moving on in a straight line, without any time-wasting detours. To Floyd, life ought to be the straightest road between birth and death.

But Hazel felt she was living her life in an ever-widening curve, blind at both ends. Not only had she lost sight of where she had come from, she could no longer see where Floyd was taking her. Back in the hills she had had hope. At least she thought it was hope, that vague whispering in her ear that there was something grand up ahead. The whiskey in her daddy's jug always confirmed it when she had any doubts.

Floyd kissed her lightly on the cheek. "Your attitude determines your altitude," he said. Then he fixed a plate of Vienna sausages and pineapple ham and took it with him into his den to read the news. A moment later she heard him call out, "I think that colored girl made off with my paper!"

Hazel reached for the Jim Beam bottle in the shape of a pheasant and poured a small bit into her special tumbler. After returning an equivalent amount of tap water to the decanter and grabbing a couple of peppermints from the drawer, she went out to the back porch.

As the shadows lengthened across the yard, she watched two fat mourning doves wobble like a drunken couple under a nearby oak. It was obvious they belonged together. Staggering around in no particular hurry to get anywhere, not caring one bit if they were traveling in a straight line or not. She envied them their tipsy little dance full of stops and starts and unbalanced strides, and how, in all their separate, uncoordinated motions, they remained together.

The doves lifted in flight, breaking her reverie. Davie came toddling around the corner of the house, with Johnny screaming after him.

"Get that rock out of your mouth, Davie. You gonna swallow it and die!"

Should I do something? she wondered. No, Johnny could handle it. Barely five years old and he could do it better than me.

Down below, at the foot of the stairs, Johnny caught up with Davie and grabbed him by the shoulders. Johnny shook Davie firmly, yelling for him to spit. Instead, Davie swallowed hard, then grinned. Did he swallow the rock? Seeing the look of panic on Johnny's face, Hazel almost cried out.

Before she could utter a sound, Davie, with his face beaming, opened his hand to reveal the rock. He began to laugh. He had fooled his brother, and he was proud of it. Hazel smiled.

Instead of being relieved, Johnny's face darkened. He reared back and slapped his brother. Hazel could hear the sharp whack from where she sat on the porch, stunned.

She opened her mouth to call out, and again she was checked, this time by the look on Davie's face. It was one of pure bewilderment, as if he were still trying to connect the sting of the slap with any action on his brother's part.

Both boys appeared to have suspended their breathing. It was like they were waiting for the weight of what had just occurred to settle, so they would know how it had changed their world.

From Davie's confused expression, it was obvious that this was the first time his brother had ever hit him. As the younger boy's eyes brimmed with tears, Hazel could see that reality was slowly setting in. Something inside Davie was beginning to break. She felt it was perhaps a thing so fragile that when it did break, it would crumble into pieces as fine as powder.

She knew she should hurry down the steps and comfort Davie. To hold him. To tell him his brother hadn't meant it. Tell him it wasn't important. Lie to him. Anything to keep the pieces together for a little while longer. Yet still she sat there, her limbs heavy, because she knew the truth. Things do break, and there's nothing a person can do about it.

Davie began to sniffle, and Johnny looked on worriedly, as if he were considering a favorite toy he had thrown in a fit of anger, frantically hoping it would fix itself and go back to the way it was before.

It was Johnny she pitied now. She knew he would never be able to take it back. That some things never could be put like they were before. That you can disappoint people and they really do lose faith in you and there is not a damned thing in the world you could do about it. Before she could decide which one was in need of comforting the most, Johnny did a strange thing. Still with an expression of fear tinged with sorrow, he pushed Davie squarely on the shoulder.

Davie dried his tears. "Stobbit, bubba," he whined, covering an eye with the back of his hand.

Johnny shoved him again, a little harder this time. "Stobbit!" Davie yelled, angry now.

Johnny shoved Davie harder still. This time Davie pushed back.

Clumsily and purposely, Johnny fell to the ground and his brother climbed on top of him and began flailing away with his tiny fists. Johnny let his brother hit him again and again, on the chest, in the face, refusing to make the slightest gesture to defend himself.

Chapter Ten

BABY MOSES

Vida stood among the fieldworkers who crowded the shade of the general store gallery, drinking her Orange Crush and glaring at the white woman as she veered her big fancy car sharply into the yard. She braked to a stop and Vida noticed she even sported white gloves and a hat as big-round as hubcap.

This was the kind of car her father might have driven, Vida thought, before the world got turned upside down, back when she herself wore starched petticoats and satin ribbons in her hair instead of the sweaty rags of a fieldworker.

This wasn't the first Vida had seen of the woman. Several times over that summer, upon hearing the approach of the big engine Vida would look up from her row of cotton or behind her as she walked the road to see the woman barreling toward her, going eighty and blanketing everybody in a layer of dust. And always with the little bow-tied boys hanging out the windows, hands wagging in the wind. Once the woman flew by so fast Vida had to dive for the ditch. The woman carelessly tossed an empty pint of whiskey out her window, barely missing Vida's head.

The white woman might have been drunk, but she never looked happy, not as happy as she should be, with her fancy car and fine clothes and two alive-and-well sons. Spoiled, Vida figured. All white women were. Never knowing when they had enough, and always wanting more. Usually somebody else's. All the time flaunting their good fortune, speeding carelessly through life, making everybody else eat their dust.

As for Vida, she would be happy if she could just get back what white people had stolen from her. If He did that, she told God, she would never ask for another thing.

Her father used to promise Vida that nothing bad would happen to his Snowflake Baby. After all, Levi Snow had a reputation as the man who could read the mind of God. Yet now Vida often wondered—if her father had truly known how things were going to turn out, might he have done things differently? For instance, if he had known that his sermon that long-ago Sunday was to be his last, would he have perhaps preached on some other text?

If her father, the most revered colored preacher in Hopalachie County, a man favored by God with the largest of churches, had known that before that day was out he would be pleading for his life, he might have chosen to preach on Daniel in the lion's den. Or Jesus being tempted in the desert. Or God's taking everything away from Job for no other reason than to show Satan what a righteous man he was. A story that would move his people to see how the good and the upright suffer for their faith and need to be stood by in dangerous times. If he had, maybe his people would not have been deaf to his cries in his time of desolation. Perhaps then, someone would have been there when he himself needed saving.

But on that bright Sunday morning nearly six years ago, her father, the Reach Out Man, didn't know any of this as the choir fell back breathless in their seats and he strode majestically up to the pulpit, on his way glancing down at the gold watch cupped in the palm of his hand and then slipping it back into its pocket. As if time was nobody's business except his.

Vida remembered how her father towered over the congregation that day, how he searched every sweating face in the church, letting the tension mount as a hundred hand-held funeral fans flashed the face of Jesus back at him.

The rigid benches were jam-packed with field hands transformed for the day into baggy-suited deacons and white-clad mothers of the church and royally robed choristers. Fine white cotton gloves kept their secrets, disguising the field-wrecked hands of men as well as women.

Except for Vida, of course, who sat clutching her gloves, revealing smooth, delicate fingers that had never picked a boll of cotton in all her privileged life as the daughter of Reverend Snow.

Every eye was riveted upon Levi, watching for him to cut loose and tear up the pulpit. Every eye including Vida's, who waited more anxiously than most.

Her father had promised her an answer that day. The awful night they drove out to the Senator's, the night Billy Dean Brister shoved her father off the porch and threatened to kill her child, Levi told her that God would find a way to keep them safe.

What story would her father tell today? she wondered. What story could he possibly preach to put everything back in its place? She prayed he would be able to create a story with a happy ending, big enough to hold them all. With the right story she had heard her father turn losses into victories, slaves into masters, pain and suffering into glory.

What about her boy, wanted dead by a white man? How would her father weave Nate safely into their lives again?

Levi Snow's silence weighed heavily on the congregation, and they began to stir.

"Tell, it, brother!" a bald-headed deacon called out in a voice frail with age.

Hooking his thumbs up under his arms and rocking back and forth on his heels, Levi Snow stared up into the rafters and shook his head like he was conferencing with God himself about whether or not to go ahead and preach today. Reverend Snow nodded solemnly, as if the Lord had whispered something that the preacher couldn't argue with, and then glared down again on the congregation.

He began, "Next to God's love there is no love like a mother's love."

Heads nodded. A few said "Amen," and others "That's right."

"The Lord said, even though a mother's love is mighty, His is mightier. Isaiah say, even if a mother forgets the babe at her breast, God will never forget you. Ain't that right?"

"That's right!"

"But a mother ain't likely to forget the babe at her breast, is she?"

"No, Lord!"

Then he looked down at his daughter and smiled, as if to put flesh and blood on his story.

Vida swelled with pride. Her father was bragging on her in front of the whole church. Putting her arm around the boy, she pulled him close. She should have known her father would find a way.

Levi Snow continued. "We like to hear about Moses and how he stood up to ol' Pharaoh and said, 'Let my people go.' Ain't that right?"

"That's God's truth!"

"About how he marched the slaves out of Egypt and split the Red Sea wide open and then led the people to the Promised Land. Yes, Lord! We all know the story about Moses. Moses indeed was a great man. God surely loved Moses."

"Sure did!"

"But there was somebody else who loved Moses."

Levi let this new information settle in between the benches before he sang out again. "Moses had a momma. How mighty was his mother's love?"

"Tell it, preacher!"

"When Moses was a baby at his momma's breast, the Pharaoh wanted to snatch him up and drown him in the River Nile. How mighty was his mother's love?"

"Go on!"

"Did his momma forget about that baby at her breast?"

"No, Lord."

"Did she want to keep her baby close at her breast? Like any momma would? Course she did. But...how mighty was his mother's love?"

"How mighty?"

"The love she had for her baby was bigger than her own selfishness. She had a love so mighty she laid her baby in a basket and put him in the bulrushes and let the river take him. Now I ask you, how mighty was his mother's love?" His eyes burned hot and bright. "How mighty, Lord?"

He dropped his gaze onto Vida, like the question was for her. Then he answered it himself in a loud crackling whisper, "Mighty enough to let him go."

At first she wasn't sure she had heard him right. Holding on to Nate, she kept her eyes glued on her father, struggling with the divine revelation.

Levi turned back to his congregation. "Next to God's love...there is no love...like a mother's love. Before Moses could grow up and tell the Pharaoh, 'You got to let my people go,' his momma had to pull her own child from her breast and say, 'I got to let my baby go.' Now, I ask you again. How mighty was his mother's love?"

The shouting now was deafening, and some rose to their feet.

"Her love was mighty!" a deacon called at the top of his voice.

Levi looked down at his daughter again as if giving her this final chance to give her answer, and then he raised his arms over his head and sang out to the rafters, "Mighty enough to let that baby go!"

That day six years earlier, her father's words had whipped up a roiling sea of emotion through the church. All around her, people were standing with their palms toward heaven, others rocking side to side on their benches and clapping their hands. Vida was caught up in a mighty current that promised to pull her and her son under.

Chapter Eleven

FISHERS OF MEN

"What you think *you're* staring at?" Hazel asked.

She sat parked in her Lincoln, gazing through the windshield at the country store. On the front gallery stood a group of colored fieldworkers gathered for their noontime meal. They were pretending to ignore Hazel, all except one, a sullen girl about Hazel's age who was at that moment trying her best to burn a hole in her freshly made face with a scalding look.

Hazel didn't take any notice of the girl. It was someone else who held her attention.

"Look at you," Hazel fussed. "Natural blond hair with a little blue ribbon to match your eyes. Good teeth. Probably never knew an ugly day in your life. Everything handed to you on a silver platter, like that slice of light bread you're eating. You the kind everybody wants to have in *their* club, ain't you, little girl?"

Little Miss Sally Sunbeam, whose face stared back from the bread advertisement attached to the store's battered screen door, didn't answer. She just smiled, acting innocent. Yet Hazel knew this girl was doing more than selling bread. She was taunting Hazel. Her eyes, still baby blue after years of weather and dust, said, "Pretty is as pretty does."

"What the hell does that mean, anyway?" Hazel said back. "Sounds like something Floyd would come up with."

Floyd's slogans never made much sense to Hazel, but beneath the snappy phrases she could hear his scolding voice: "Catch up! Catch up! You're dragging your end of it." Just where was it they were going in such a hurry? That's what she wanted to know. Hazel drained the last of the bottle.

From off in the distance she thought she could hear the gnarling and rumbling of what could have been a herd of ferocious animals closing in on her and her boys. When she turned toward the field she saw one of Floyd's hulking green machines, growling greedily, eating its way through the impossibly white cotton.

Hazel glanced down at her two boys drowsing next to her on the front seat, Johnny leaning against the door and Davie nuzzled under his brother's arm. After riding through the country with Hazel for hours, they were tuckered out.

Since her humiliation at the hands of her neighbors, Hazel had abandoned her town route and taken to driving down from the bluffs and out into the Delta. Each morning she drove the endless depression for miles, along desolate dirt roads where the only people who would see her were field hands or work gangs from the state penitentiary—nobody she expected Floyd was out to impress. Driving the earth's flattened-down places, Hazel could yell and cuss and cry to her heart's content. Nothing could creep up on her. Everything could be seen at once and for what it was. Out here was where the bare-bones truth lived, plain and simple and absolute. No silly childish dreams or false hopes or wishful thinking could survive. It was like looking God square in the eye and speaking your name and daring him to strike you dead.

Hazel usually drove until her half-pint ran out. Then she went home and spent the rest of the afternoon sobering up for Floyd. Lately, however, a half-pint hadn't done the trick. Hope couldn't be roused from its sickbed. So Hazel blew her horn twice and a colored boy sitting on the gallery saw her and then ducked into the store.

Her children had begun to stir with the honking, but Hazel

didn't notice. She had locked her eyes on Miss Sally again. The girl was still holding the bread up to her mouth, as if she had all the time in the world. No sense in gobbling it down. Sally knew there was more where that slice came from. Didn't know what it was to make do with nothing.

"Yeah, Little Miss Sunbeam," Hazel said, feeling good and sorry for herself now, "you don't know what life can do to people like me. Make-do people. That's what I am." She hiccupped.

The screen door swung open and shut again. Otherwise, Sally Sunbeam remained unmoved. Hazel let a tear trickle unimpeded down her cheek. "My husband done put me behind the wheel of a Lincoln like Daddy put me behind Jawbone. I guess I'll be plowing somebody else's fields till the day I die."

The door flew open again and the colored boy came running up to Hazel's window with a paper sack in his hand. Hazel began to dig through her purse.

"Momma, I'm hungry," Davie said, having just awakened.

"When we going to eat dinner?" Johnny called out.

While the colored boy waited with his thumbs hooked in the straps of his raggedy overalls, he watched the two white children with matching bow ties, dressed nice enough for Sunday.

"Here," Hazel said as she handed the boy a little extra, "go on back in the store and get me a couple of banana moon pies and two Nehi grapes."

The boy took off, leaving Hazel to feel Sally's eyes looking disapprovingly at her. "Well, what do you expect, Little Miss Perfect? I'm a make-do momma, making do the best I can."

⁓

Hazel sped along, the wind in her hair, sipping from her bottle. After a few miles she slowed the Lincoln and edged the car right up to the lip of a rickety one-lane bridge suspended between the two high riverbanks. When she'd passed this way earlier she thought she'd seen some colored people fishing down on the bank, and she wanted to make sure they were still there.

Getting out of the car, she walked unsteadily onto the bridge, her high-heeled pumps tapping hollow against the planks. Hazel tried to decide if the swaying she felt was due to the movement of the bridge or her present condition. Either way, she somehow made it safely halfway across.

Lacking any railing, the bridge offered an unimpeded twenty-foot drop into the dark, snaky water below. Hazel walked right up to the edge and still didn't see the colored people. Leaning forward to get a look underneath, she tottered, frantically thrashed her arms in the air, and, a moment before toppling over the side, caught her balance. She dropped to her hands and knees to view the river through the cracks between the boards.

Just as she had hoped! The people were still up under there. From where she knelt, she could see a man who was standing up to his knees in the water throw a heavy line deep into the river and then drag it back toward the bank. A few other colored people, both men and women, stood by on the bank, watching intently. Never having seen this kind of fishing before, she rushed back to the car and her children and then carefully maneuvered the massive Lincoln over the creaking bridge, off the road, and into the shade of an old beech tree.

This was not unusual for Hazel. When she drove out into the Delta, she often stopped to observe coloreds at work, with the same fascination she'd had as a child observing a colony of ants or a nest of wasps. She thought there was a sad kind of beauty in the way their motions would blend into a shared dance, transcending their earthly lot. It was like something from the Bible. Or maybe a Carter Family gospel song.

Once she'd sat for over an hour watching a gang of colored convicts from Parchman work with their scythes in a weedy ditch. Garbed in black and white stripes, they moved in unison, their blades glinting into a single instrument under the eye of the fierce white sun. And how they could holler out!

Goin' up to Memphis,
I'll be able when I die.
Load my body on the freight car,
Send my soul on by and by.

The whiskey having shrunk any distinction between a white housewife's melancholy and the woes of a dozen colored convicts, Hazel had hollered with them, with the boys joining in.
Uptomemphis,
Uptomemphis.
These colored people by the riverbank weren't singing, yet they did appear very solemn about their fishing, so Hazel hoped for a good show. Maybe, she thought, if they caught something they would burst out into an old gospel song.

Hazel led the children to a shady place closer to the river where they all could sit and observe without being noticed. She then spread out a pallet she kept in the car trunk for such occasions as this. While she busied herself, smoothing out the lumps in the quilt, Johnny called out urgently. Hazel turned to see Davie scurrying up toward the road, no doubt returning to the altitude of the bridge.

Johnny saw the bewildered look on his mother's face and broke after Davie. Just as he reached the bridge Davie stumbled in the road, and before he could right himself Johnny had him by the ankle. As Hazel stood there paralyzed, her heart pounding, she watched as Johnny led Davie back to safety, on the way inventing for his brother cautionary tales about drowning.

Like a brilliant flare, a single thought shone through the fog that had enveloped Hazel, the thought that all this she was witnessing, the way things were playing out before her that very minute, was how it had to be. The three of them were trains barreling down separate tracks, and none of them had a voice about direction. They might could slow, and they might could speed up. But they could not choose what it was they were bearing down on. Or what was bearing down on them. God had fixed it.

She knelt down and clutched her boys to her chest. She told them she loved them, over and over again. Still in a state of wonder, she distributed the moon pies and soft drinks as solemnly as if it were the Last Supper. She tenderly kissed each child on the cheek, and with her mind clouded with whiskey and shadowy revelation, Hazel leaned against a hickory tree with her half-pint firmly clasped to her chest.

⚬

Her attention returned to the spectacle unfolding in the river. Down below them, the man standing in the water and doing the fishing had moved a little farther upstream, like he was trying to find the perfect spot. Hazel was a little disappointed in him. A real fisherman would have more patience.

The water was the color of strong tea and very deep by the bridge, and Hazel was unable to see what was tied to the massive fishing line that, now that she studied it, resembled a rope. As she watched, the fisherman carefully pulled in the line and hauled a shapeless, dark mass up on the bank. A couple of other men gathered around and snatched away what had been grabbed from the river bottom— leaves and branches and snag roots and such. That's when Hazel saw what they were using for a hook. Attached to the rope was what appeared to be a lead pipe with spurs on the end. No wonder they hadn't caught anything! All they would catch with that contraption was more bottom trash. Amateurs!

Without even bothering to bait his line, the man doing the casting waded to yet another spot in the river and once more threw his rope into the water. This time when the man pulled on the rope he yelled something to the others on the bank. Two more men joined the fisherman in the water and began tugging at what looked like a big haul.

"Look, boys," Hazel said, rising up wobbly to her feet to get a better view, "they done caught them something. Must be a big 'un."

Lifting Davie in her arms, Hazel moved closer to watch as they dragged a giant black catfish onto the shore. She heard one of the women on the bank scream.

Johnny bounced on his tiptoes to see the fish. "Momma, what's that woman yelling for? Did she get bit by the fishie?"

Hazel's eyes tried to focus in on the catch. It was about four or five feet long and was wrapped in barbed wire. There was a big piece of machinery tied around its neck. *My God,* she thought, *the thing's got a neck!* She made out the bloated face, with one eye beaten closed and one hanging from its socket. She heard the woman call the fish by name.

"Emmett! Lawd, lawd!" the woman screamed. "My baby, Emmett!"

Then Hazel heard herself scream.

⁂

The Lincoln was all over the road, from ditch to ditch, all three crying their hearts out. Hazel didn't know where she was heading, nor did she care. Speed and distance were all she wanted from the car now.

An hour later, when the black-and-white cruiser with the big star on the door happened upon Hazel and her boys, she had sunk the two left tires deep into a sandy ditch and was hunched over the wheel sobbing. Johnny was patting his mother gently on the arm. Then she heard a man's voice at her ear. "That you, Missus Graham? You all right in there?"

Hazel raised her eyes to see the sheriff. He was watching her with a kind of detached, wary look, as if she might be a stray dog with a touch of foam around the mouth. "Oh, Sheriff!" she cried. "I'm so glad you come along. Back there...in the river...they's a dead boy."

His eyes narrowed. For a moment the sheriff seemed concerned. "A white one?"

"No, a colored one. I watched them pull him off the river bottom. He was all bound up and weighted down. Somebody killed him for sure."

The sheriff's eyes warmed a little. He took off his hat and bent down to the window. "Now, don't you worry none. I'll check into it, Miss Hazel." His voice was reassuring. "You know how they always knifing one another. Come Saturday night ever creek in Hopalachie County'll have coloreds floating in it." He shook his head sadly. "I'm only sorry you had to see it, is all."

Hazel thought he really did look sorry. What a kind, thoughtful man. He was treating her with so much politeness. More than she could say for that wife of his. Right then Hazel's heart went out to the sheriff for being saddled with a horse like Hertha. He was such a nice-looking man, too.

"Let's see if we can't get you out of this ditch," he said. "I got a chain in the turtle hull."

When he motioned to his cruiser, Hazel was surprised to see somebody waving at her from the backseat. Why, it was that whore-for-a-maid, Sweet Pea, grinning to beat the band, her gold teeth gleaming in the afternoon light through the sheriff's back window.

The sheriff saw the curious look on Hazel's face. "Got me a prisoner," he said quickly. "Just hauling her in for questioning."

Nodding back at Sweet Pea, Hazel couldn't help but think she seemed mighty happy to be a prisoner.

Chapter Twelve

LATE NIGHT VISITATION

Vida Snow had heard about the boy they fished out of the river.
Everybody had. It's all anybody talked about when the white
folks weren't listening. Vida had seen the boy once, walking to the
store with his Uncle Mose. Down from Chicago and only fourteen,
they say. Mississippi was dangerous enough for the colored brought
up to know the nasty unpredictability of white folks. That boy's
momma should have never sent her son down to Mississippi by
himself.

Vida laughed darkly at the thought. Who was she to talk about
mommas keeping their children safe?

She wished she could forget. Of course, she couldn't. She remembered too well the night after her father preached on the Baby Moses,
how she was unable to sleep. She had been lying awake with her own
child nestled to her side, fretting over her father's meaning, when
her room exploded in light. Outside her window, a truck revved its
engine.

Her father's feet hit the floor and Vida saw him flee past her room
in his nightshirt and no shoes. He was heading out onto the porch.

"Who that?" Levi called into the light. "What business you got
here?" Vida lifted Nate and moved to the window.

She saw a man stumble from his truck. She couldn't see his face for
the light, but she knew who it was. Billy Dean weaved around to the

rear, and pulled out his shotgun. He staggered back again and propped himself against the hood, between the glaring headlights. "Get that little rat out here," he slurred. "That little albino piece of shit."

Vida instinctively pulled Nate closer.

"Mr. Billy Dean, sir," her father stammered, falling back toward the door. "We don't mean you no harm. I sure didn't know about you and Miss Hertha." He took another step back, his arm reaching behind him for the door. "I hope you two be real happy," he said. "And I sure sorry for that little misunderstanding."

Lights began to come on throughout the quarter. Maybe, Vida prayed, someone would come to their rescue. Maybe it would be Rezel!

With one arm Billy Dean steadied himself against the hood of the truck and with the other he raised the shotgun to his hip. It was aimed at her father's midsection. "Not as sorry as you gonna be. I told you what I wanted. Get that boy out here. Now!"

The door flew open and Willie came charging out past his father with a baseball bat. He took the porch in two leaps and was halfway down the steps before Billy Dean got both barrels aimed at the boy's head.

"Stop right there, boy. I'll blow it off. I swear I will."

Willie froze.

Billy Dean's uncle, who had been standing there frantically rubbing the back of his neck, spoke up. "Billy Dean, this old preacher ain't going to tell the Senator about that baby. We already torched his church. You ain't going to tell, is you, Preacher?"

Levi didn't answer. His eyes turned toward the distance, at a lit-up place on the horizon where his church stood.

Furman put a hand on his nephew's shoulder. "Let's get turned around and go on to the house. Tomorrow's another day."

His uncle's words hadn't softened the vicious expression on Billy Dean's face.

That's when Vida knew it for certain. The man wasn't there to scare them. He was there to kill her son. No one could save Nate but her. She took her son up in her arms and ran. Trying to make it across the field and into the bayou had been the only way.

She remembered the shotgun blasts, the spray of buckshot that sent her reeling into the dark. But what else could she have done? Hadn't she done all a mother could do?

༄

The funeral had been a small, pitiful affair. Most people were too afraid to be seen in public with Levi. A preacher from Holmes County, an old friend of Levi's, had traveled in by night to hold the service. Nobody cried except for Vida, her wounds bandaged but still raw. Everybody else, including her father, sat dry-eyed before the little pine coffin as the preacher spoke mournfully about how the innocence of children was a sure ticket to the Promised Land.

As the preacher droned on, Vida's body ached more from her loss of Nate than from the lead pellets that remained in her leg, embedded in muscle, so close to the bone. She tried to sooth herself by thinking of the Promised Land. She had never noticed before how often her people spoke of it. That made three the number of times that very week she had heard about the Promised Land. Once was from Lillie Dee. She had complained that Rezel was following the rest of her sons up North, to the Promised Land. Another time was from her father's pulpit. It was where Moses was headed to.

Now this preacher was praying for Nate's safe journey, saying Nate was gone off to the Promised Land, as if it might be a good thing she had lost her baby. Vida couldn't believe that Moses's momma would agree.

༄

Even as a grown woman of twenty, Vida still didn't believe it. Yet what she did believe with all her heart, what she thought about every day in the fields, what she lay awake at night promising Nate, what she swore to Jesus in every prayer she breathed, was that one day soon she would balance her books with the sheriff.

Chapter Thirteen

JESUS IN THE
GRAVEYARD

Today up in Delphi at the white cemetery, Jesus weighed heavily
on Johnny's mind. He had listened carefully as Brother Dear
talked to Jesus about keeping Davie safe and watched as they
lowered his brother down into the hole. Johnny wanted to ask his
mother how long Jesus was going to keep his brother down there,
but she wouldn't look at Johnny. She sat next to him stone-faced,
smelling one minute of Gardenia Paradise and the other of the
medicine she had been taking from half-pint bottles.

It seemed everybody around him was calling on Jesus except his
mother, who grimaced every time somebody said his name. The biggest part of the town was there, sitting in rows and rows of straight-
back funeral chairs, men sniffling and bashfully brushing their noses
with the tops of their knuckles while offering their pocket handkerchiefs to their wives. Even his father wiped away tears as big as
summer raindrops. Every now and then, from directly behind him,
he heard the sobs of his aunt Onareen, the only one from Hazel's
family to attend.

"How long is Davie going to have to stay with Jesus, Momma?"
Johnny finally whispered.

She acted as if she hadn't heard him. Her dry stare was focused on Brother Dear, who shone brighter than sun on snow in his white suit. The preacher was now saying something about Jesus's master plan and about never, never, never asking why.

Still staring at Brother Dear, Hazel shredded her tissue until there was nothing but a mound of white bits on the lap of her black silk dress. Floyd reached over and brushed her off and then rested his hand over hers, stilling them.

⁓

Returning from the funeral, Johnny asked his momma from the backseat how Davie was going to find his way back to the house. "Will Jesus set him loose at night? Oughten we come back in the car and get him so he don't get lost?"

His mother swung her head around in the seat. "What are you going on about?" she shouted. "Davie ain't coming home. Never! Do you understand me? Jesus don't let nobody go once he gets aholt of them!"

Johnny sat stone still in the backseat. He was too startled to cry.

Floyd turned to Hazel. "Why are you yelling at the boy? Why are you yelling at all? Why ain't you crying? Everybody else is. It ain't right, you being dry-eyed at your own son's funeral."

Hazel looked accusingly at her husband. "Ain't you the one always saying we can't go back and change the past? That spilt milk ain't worth crying over?"

After taking a deep breath and slowly letting it out, Floyd shifted to his low serious voice, the one he used when he felt he was getting to the nub of the matter. "I'll tell you why you ain't crying, Hazel. It's because you're stinking drunk. It ain't cute no more. You get mean when you drink. Just like your daddy. And I'm sure everybody at the funeral smelt it."

"I ain't drunk, and don't you talk about my daddy." Hazel gritted her teeth. "And I'll cry whenever somebody tells me why Davie is gone." She shot Floyd a look that accused him of holding back the answer from her all along.

"Well…" Floyd said, not appearing so sure of himself. Finally he ventured, "Now Jesus tells us we got to—"

Hazel flew hot again. "I done heard enough about what Jesus tells us! Jesus and his many mansions. Jesus and his big ol' everlasting arms. If His arms is so big and strong, how come they didn't catch Davie? Tell me that!"

Floyd didn't offer an answer. When Davie had died, Floyd and his big ol' arms had been there, too. Floyd had been working on the lawn mower when Davie decided he wanted to play "Catch me" from the porch. Certain as always that his daddy was watching, Davie stepped to the rail edge and stretched out his arms.

Only Johnny had been watching. It was he who had heard his brother's voice call out "Catch me," sounding more like the chirp of a bird, and only Johnny who saw Davie drop off the man-tall porch. It wasn't until his father heard the soft thud on the grass and then something resembling the sound of a twig snapping that he glanced up from the mower to see Davie lying in front of him motionless, his arms akimbo, neck broken, facing Floyd with only the slightest look of surprise.

In the autumn that followed the funeral, Hazel's unshed tears hung dark and heavy on the family's horizon like an approaching Delta storm. The drinking continued. Hazel said if she couldn't drink, she would surely suffocate. She said, "Drinking is like breaking open a window to yell out of."

Floyd said he was trying to understand, but all he thought her drinking did was make her mad. He said every time he looked at her, all he saw in her eyes was a fight ready to happen, and he couldn't afford being around somebody that negative all the time. Not with everything they had riding on his positive attitude. Finally, he moved into a separate bedroom.

They left Davie's bed and toys and clothes untouched, strengthening Johnny's belief that his brother was coming back. Several times a week he awoke to his father silhouetted in the doorway, looking toward Davie's bed for minutes at a time. One night, after a particularly loud fight between his parents, Floyd came to the doorway and stood there as usual, staring. This time, Johnny thought he heard a sniffling sound.

"Hey, Big Monkey," Johnny called out to him.

"Hey, Little Monkey," his father whispered, in a way that made Johnny's heart hurt.

"He's not back yet, Daddy," he said, trying to comfort him. "I'll holler at you when he gets home."

Later, after his father had gone to bed, Johnny woke to the touch of a hand running through his hair. As his mother knelt by his bedside, smelling strongly of medicine, she whispered the oddest question in his ear.

"Who do you love the most? Me or your daddy?"

Certain of the answer she wanted, he said, "You, Momma."

She bent over and kissed him on his forehead and said before leaving, "Don't tell your daddy. You're on my side. Do you hear?"

His mother's question tore the world in two for Johnny. It was like the day he had seen the setting sun and the rising moon in the sky at the same time, opposite each other. Until that moment, he believed they were the same entity, the silver moon being the soft evening face of the hot, laboring sun. Yet when his mother asked him that question and made him choose between his parents, Johnny grasped how separate his parents really were. They traveled in their own orbits. And most terrifying of all, there could be one without the other.

Chapter Fourteen

ONE WING HANNAH'S

Vida reckoned that if the woman who plopped down uninvited at her table wasn't drunk, she was within hollering distance of it. She called herself Sweet Pea, and her shiny black hair, greased down and hot-combed, hugged a plump face glistening with sweat. She grinned at Vida like they were best friends.

"You ought to get out of them fields, honey," the woman lost no time advising. "What are you? Nineteen? Twenty? You wasting yourself. Gal, you do a lot better in town. The mens like your type."

Sweet Pea smiled brightly at Vida with a mouth full of gold teeth and then winked. Motioning toward Vida's chest with an empty Mason jar, she said, "You young and pretty, even with that head of drawed-up hair. And you probably toting some nice boobies in that sack you wearing."

Shifting self-consciously in her chair, Vida yanked at her loose calico dress, trying to pull out some of the slack. Then she stuck her ragged hands under the table and out of sight. It vexed her to think a looped-up stranger could tell straightaway that she had been reduced to being a fieldworker. Especially in a smoke-crowded juke lit by two dim bulbs dangling from a tar-paper ceiling.

Vida made a show of searching the room, partly to defy the busy-body stare of her table companion and partly to locate her brother.

All around her couples were close-dancing in the cigarette haze to a blues-scarred voice rising from the Seeburg.

She didn't have any business among these people. If she could find Willie, she would fuss at him good. Coming to One Wing Hannah's had been her brother's idea, and now he had disappeared, saddling her with some looped-up gal whose nature had obviously gone to her head. Knowing Willie, he was probably outside skylarking with the no-account men in the yard, throwing dice and passing bottles.

As she watched the door, a tall honey-skinned man with a purplish red shirt and green pointed shoes sauntered into the shack. Almost instinctively, the gold-toothed woman spun around and caught his eye. He shot Sweet Pea a wolfish smile. Sweet Pea leaned into Vida and said confidentially, "Look see? Three dollars right there. Five if he was white. How many pounds of cotton you got to pick for five dollars?"

"You do it with *white* men?" She couldn't imagine somebody doing it with a white man if they didn't have to. The thought sent a million little bug feet traipsing over her skin.

"Now, don't look at me thataway. It don't rub off. You tell me which sounds smarter, picking the white man's cotton for two dollars a day or laying on it for five? And that's an hour. I'm talking year-round." She winked at Vida. "I didn't pass through the eighth grade for nothing. I got that deal figgered."

Sweet Pea could figger all she wanted. White people scared Vida to death, the white man with his face as sharp as the steel head of a hatchet and eyes that cut to the bone like the wind on a wet winter day, swaggering around the countryside, unthinking as a cocked pistol. But it was the white woman that vexed Vida the most. Her nose poked in the air like she was all the time smelling dog doo. Acting all soft and breakable when her man was around and conniving and fish-blooded when he wasn't. She had learned the story behind what happened to Mose Wright's nephew, Emmett, only a few weeks ago. White woman claimed the boy was cutting his eyes at her. Said he wolf-whistled at her. That woman cried to anybody who would listen that a real man would do something about it and went on sniveling until last week they pulled that poor boy out of the Hopalachie dressed in barbed wire weighted down with gin parts. His own momma couldn't recognize him.

While Vida was having her thoughts about white people, the jukers around her hushed all at once and the room went still. Vida looked up and froze. There stood Satan himself. For years, Vida and Willie argued over who would kill him first. As she often did when she thought of the man, she reached down and through her dress fingered the buckshot still lodged in her thigh from that night long ago, so as to never forget the pain he brought into her life.

Billy Dean Brister was surveying the shack like he was trying to see if there were any butts that needed kicking tonight. Then he strode over to the owner with his hand out.

One Wing Hannah, her hefty bulk propped up on a stool behind the wood plank that passed for a bar, handed him an envelope with her remaining arm. Vida watched as Hannah, with the armpit of her stump, got a grip on a bottle from the shelf behind her. The sheriff gave her a nasty look, then took it anyway.

He scanned the room again, and when his eyes got to Vida's table, they came to a dead stop. Vida did her best to keep up her stare, wanting him to know she wasn't the least bit afraid, yet avoiding the eyes of a white man was a hard habit to break. Her eyes dropped to the table. She didn't need to look at him, The face of Billy Dean Brister was clearly engraved in her mind. For so long he had been a constant presence.

The sheriff had been a regular visitor to her family's house. Late at night, he pulled his car up close and sat there, his lights illuminating the inside of her bedroom, while she waited for him to kill her or leave. It was a warning to Vida that she had better keep their secret from the Senator.

When she peeked up again, she saw it wasn't her that the sheriff was studying. He probably didn't recognize the poor sharecropper's daughter Vida had become. Instead, he settled his eyes on her table companion, his face devoid of any expression except the usual contempt. He took his loot and walked out as abruptly as he'd come in, like a man with a route to make.

Sweet Pea nodded at the door. "And girl, there goes seven dollars. And he pay in advance."

"You done it with—?"

"Mess a times," she said. "We go to his daddy's old burned-out shack up in the woods."

Vida let go such a look of loathing it would have sobered the woman up if the light had been better.

Sweet Pea squared her shoulders. "Well, it ain't like we do it all that much," she said. "And some days we don't do it at all. They times he just wants somebody to drink with and talk to. Then he go to sleep." She shrugged. "On or off, still cost him seven dollars."

"Y'all talk? Both of you?" Vida asked, not able to imagine the sheriff having a conversation with this woman.

"I don't talk, hon. He do the talking. I listens. Sometimes."

Vida leaned in and lifted her brows. "Yeah? What he say?"

Sweet Pea became animated. "Girl, one time he got some drunk and started talking out of his head about his momma and daddy. About the night that old shack got set afire. Talked like it was happening right then and there! How his daddy gets crazy and throws the kerosene lamp in the window with his momma still inside. Then how he passes out in the dirt yard. How the whole place explodes and his momma comes out screaming to Jesus, running off the porch lit like a torch, dropping dead to the side of her husband. And him scrambling off on all fours trying to get away from his wife before he catches afire. The sheriff still a boy and watching it all happen, froze up with fright. Can't make hisself go to neither of them. And he just a-screaming, 'Momma! Daddy!' Big drops of sweat on his face like he's seeing it all over again. I tell you, honey, I was crying right along with him. Nearly broke my heart."

The amount of pity Sweet Pea was wasting on the man disgusted Vida. Yet she knew she'd better act interested. "Ain't that something? What else he talk about?"

"Well," Sweet Pea said, "one night he give his wife a real bad-mouthing. Cried about how ugly she was and how she as cold as an outhouse in an ice storm. How she turned his two pishy little daughters against him. How his own family don't think he ain't nothing but po' white trash. I figger mostly he go out to that old shack just to be rid of them." The woman leaned in toward Vida, so close Vida could smell the rotten sweet smell of shine on her breath. "Girl, then he passes out and he talk some mo. Mostly babbles."

"He talk in his sleep?"

Sweet Pea eyed Vida suspiciously. "What you care for, anyway? You ain't trying to steal my trade, is you?"

Vida lowered her eyes. "I wondered if sometime he didn't talk about a boy."

"A boy? What boy?"

"Any boy," Vida said.

Sweet Pea began tapping the bottom of her empty jar against the tabletop. "Like I done told you," she said, sounding done with the conversation. "He ain't got no boy. Only them two pishy girls."

The woman cast her gaze over the room like she was ready for new company, yet Vida took no notice. A hundred thoughts swarmed at once.

Sweet Pea made a great show of raising the empty fruit jar to her lips, throwing back her head, and thumping the jar on the bottom to loosen any remaining drops clinging to the sides. She rimmed the mouth of the glass with a long pink tongue.

Before Vida could ask any more questions, the honey-skinned man with the green pointed shoes came over to the table. "You look thirsty tonight, girl! You as hot as me?"

Sweet Pea smiled gold at him, and then glanced back at Vida as if to say, "Watch this."

The man began to rub his thigh into her shoulder to the rhythm of the music. Bending down, he moaned into her ear, loud enough for Vida to hear through the din.

"Umm. Umm. Sweet Pea. You feeling good tonight. How about you and me doing the drag, sugar? Then I put some more shinny in your jar."

Sweet Pea began rubbing on him, gyrating her shoulder into his crotch yet talking to Vida at the same time. "Honey, if you don't want a white man, then least find you a white woman."

Sweet Pea snapped her fingers. "And Lordy, do I have the right one for you! I done a little piece of work for her few months back. She live in a big ol' house in Delphi. That white lady needed somebody bad. Maybe still does. She be a piteous mess. Hazel Graham her name."

Sweet Pea shook her head sadly. "Heard she just lost her boy. Must sure nuff be a wreck now."

"Lost him?" Vida asked, still thinking about Nate. "Where she lose him at?"

"I don't mean she sat him down and forgot him, girl. You crazy? I mean he be dead."

Vida scowled at Sweet. "What that be to me? I ain't got no tears for no white woman."

"Whoo-ee!" Sweet Pea exclaimed, and then looked up at the man with a wink. "Ain't she a hard-hearted one?"

The man grinned at Vida.

"All I'm saying," Sweet Pea confided, "is play your cards right and you be the boss in that house. She don't know her shit from Shinola." Then she rose from the table in her tight dress of white satin, traveling up the man like a curl of smoke.

Vida had a thought. "She live anywhere near the sheriff?"

"Uh-huh. That's right," the woman said, not turning from the man as he led her away. "All them rich people live over there bunched up together like a wad of money."

Vida shook her head disdainfully. No, she told herself, I ain't studying on being no maid for no white woman. Yet, she argued, if it gets me within striking distance of the sheriff...

All at once One Wing Hannah started cussing like a mule skinner, grabbed her pistol from behind the bar, and hauled her two hundred and fifty pounds toward the door as if she were mounted on freshly greased wheels. "Where is that good-for-nothing devil-ish-eyed scound? That pretty boy about to have him two assholes to shit out of."

"Willie!" Vida gasped. She watched as Hannah disappeared through the door. A second later a shot rang out.

In a flash Vida was on her feet and flying. She got to the gallery in time to see people in the yard scattering behind trees and diving under cars. The sweet smell of cordite still hung heavy in the thick summer air. In the middle of the yard One Wing Hannah was flapping her stump and pointing the gun with her good arm at Willie.

Vida grabbed a pool stick from one of the gawkers standing next to her, ready to break it on Hannah's head. But Willie seemed unfazed. He stood there grinning like a child caught sneaking candy. That boy had nerves of steel.

"Nigger, I told you don't you come 'round my place selling no hooch."

Hannah had bolted down the steps so fast her wig slipped over to one side of her head. Her chest was heaving like two pigs crowding a trough.

"Yes, ma'am, Miss Hannah. You sure got a right to be mad." Willie talked as if he had a mouth full of butter. Now Vida knew why Willie had insisted on coming tonight. That rascal must have taken up bootlegging! Probably had him a supply stashed close by.

"Boy, you might be fine to look at, but I'm a mean ol' biddy. You see this here stump?" Hannah waved it proudly in the air. "Know how I got it? Got my arm chewed off by one of them damnedable cotton pickers."

"Yes, ma'am." Willie said, his voice smooth with admiration. "And the Senator let you open this here place 'cause of it."

"You damned right. And I do whatever it takes to keep it. I'll knock heads, bust knees, and pull your pecker out by the root if you get in my way. No matter how sweet-looking you be."

"Yes, ma'am. You surely a rare woman. Rare as one of the blue hen's chickens." Willie gave her his devil's grin. "And you sexy when you riled."

Now smiling like a schoolgirl, Hannah straightened her wig with the pistol-toting hand and waved it back in Willie's general direction. Her voice sweetened considerably. "Now, baby, you listen to me. I be the one who pays the sheriff, so I be the one who sells the whiskey—at least in this cotton patch. That be the nub of it. I'd hate to sick Sheriff Billy Dean on you. Be a waste of some fine-looking ass. Now, you behave from here on out."

"I surely will, Miss Hannah. You a generous woman to be so understandable. You sure something special."

Hannah shook her head and chuckled as if she knew she was the kind of woman destined to be done in by a pretty face every time. "Baby, if you bound and determined to sell hooch, you come see me. Maybe we can work something out."

Vida couldn't see into her own future, yet she could see Willie's. And working a plot of land with her was not part of it. He wasn't even eighteen, but as she had, he grew up fast. He learned early to think and act like a man. And now he had found a man's way to make some traveling cash.

She disapproved of his bootlegging, yet she couldn't help wondering if her brother might be generous enough with his ill-gotten gains to pay off their account with the Senator and let her travel with him, at least as far as Delphi. By foul or by fair, Vida had to get close to the sheriff.

She hoped the crazy Hazel woman could hang on that long.

Chapter Fifteen

A MANGER SCENE

As he did during most of his parents' fights, Johnny retreated to his and Davie's secret listening place in the dark behind the couch. Besides letting him overhear his parents, the position offered an excellent view of the tree. The motorized wheel of tinted cellophane rotated before a bare bulb, turning the aluminum tree from red to blue to green and back to red again. Tomorrow his mother and father would feel better. Surely Davie wouldn't miss Christmas!

His parents continued the argument that had begun over supper. As usual, his father had been complaining about Hazel's drinking and driving. Floyd said it wasn't a family secret anymore. He claimed Hazel was on her way to becoming a legend across the county. Bigger even than the colored girl over in Montgomery they'd had to drag off the bus.

On several occasions the sheriff had personally driven Hazel and Johnny home, leaving the Lincoln behind, straddling ditches or sunk deep in muddy fields. A few weeks after Davie's funeral, she had run a school bus off the road. Floyd said Hayes Alcorn had made a joke about it in a city council meeting. He cracked that instead of spending money on a siren for when the Russians attacked, Delphi should have an early-warning system for when Hazel pulled out of her driveway.

Johnny then heard his father say something about his mother trying harder. "Maybe go see Brother Dear," he suggested.

Hazel had exploded. "That jackleg preacher? He told me Jesus took Davie to teach me a lesson! Said Jesus did it cause He *loved* me!"

"Well, maybe there's some truth to it, Hazel. Maybe, on the upside, it can make you a better mother to—"

That's when Johnny heard the back door slam. Even he knew not to bring up Jesus around his mother.

When he ventured into the kitchen he found his father sitting at the table studying his hands.

"Where's Momma?"

Floyd looked up with weary eyes. "Out driving."

The house went graveyard quiet. Floyd sat at the table casting about for a plan to save his business from his wife, and Johnny fell asleep worrying about the whereabouts of both Santa Claus and his mother.

A little past one a.m., Floyd grabbed the phone after the first ring. It was the sheriff. It seemed that Hazel had driven through his yard, smashed into Hertha's life-sized nativity scene, and sent one of the sheep crashing through her parlor room window. Hazel had come to a stop in a clump of nandina bushes.

The sheriff sounded groggy. "I think she's OK. A little too much...well, driving. She must of really put on some miles tonight."

When Floyd said he would be right over to get Hazel, the sheriff told him not to bother himself. "Everything's under control," he assured him. "I'm getting some black coffee down your wife and a sleeping pill down mine. Didn't even wake the girls. I'll carry Hazel over directly."

⌒⌒

Hazel smiled at the sheriff as he came back into the kitchen. Then she wondered if she was smiling at all, her face being as numb as it was. So she tried harder.

The sheriff looked at her expectantly, as if he were waiting for her to say what was so funny. Then he smiled back. She felt sorry for him, the way Hertha had gone on like she did. Probably embarrassed the poor man to death. Her shouting and carrying on over that silly old sheep. Nothing worse than a woman that can't control herself. Hazel pulled her shoulders up.

Leaning back with his hands propped against the counter and his boots crossed at the ankles, the sheriff smoked his cigarette without removing it from his mouth, the cloud curling up into his face, his eyes squinting against it. Hazel figured he could finish an entire cigarette without laying a hand on it. To her he had the look of a cowboy star. But not the old kind that wore a white hat and drank milk. Not a Goody Two-Shoes. He was the new sexy kind of cowboy. The outsider who had a dark secret in his past and could go either way and kept you guessing till the very end.

"I'll take you home when you ready," he said. "I think we can get the car out this time no problem."

What was he saying? The car? Oh, yes, the Lincoln parked in the manger with the cows and the remaining sheep. And she was alone in the kitchen with the sheriff. That's right. He had sent Hertha upstairs. It was all clear to her again. She had a handle on things.

Hazel knew she needed to say something, though her tongue felt as stiff as a sausage. Determined to sound sober, she weighed and measured each word as she said it. "You...make...'lishhuss...coffee. Shurff. I'd like anothern, don't mind."

"Well, I just poured you that one."

Hazel giggled and said he was right, she remembered him doing that, now that he mentioned it. The sheriff stood there smiling at her. Hazel wondered again what he saw in Hertha. He was such a nice-looking man. Almost pretty, in a dangerous kind of way. Long black wavy hair. Sulking eyes with lashes a woman would envy. A face that looked hurt and angry and starved for love all at the same time. Hazel knew that look. She had grown up with it. Billy Dean Brister was one of her kind, the kind well-bred folks would just as soon throw out with the trash.

She felt alive around the sheriff. As if something were about to happen that could change everything. Something that could knock the world off its dead-center butt. It was the feeling she used to get riding with those route men in the hills. Like when Floyd first swaggered into the drugstore in tight-fitting bell-bottoms fresh from the war. Full of plans and hope and room for her.

"You finish that one up and I'll pour you anothern. OK?"

Hazel thought she might have just winked at him. She hoped not. Sober, Hazel couldn't look the sheriff in the eye, yet after she had been drinking, she could feel the thrill that lay beneath the fear. It was worth getting stuck in the mud to have him come rescue her. Being with him was like riding danger piggyback.

She wished she could tell him about the dream she had been having about Jesus. How He tells her to walk with Him across the Hopalachie River. She tells Him she doesn't think she's up to walking on water. Jesus tells her all she needs is a little faith, hope, and charity. When they get to the middle of the river, she realizes that she is all bound up with barbed wire, and the engine to the Lincoln is tied around her neck. She begins to sink to the bottom.

What she wanted to tell the sheriff was, it's not so bad. The water is dark and warm, and the current caresses her as a lover would. It's kind of peaceful down there where the only thing you can hear is the water rushing in your ears. She wanted to ask him what he thought it meant. And what it means that in the dream he's standing on the shore watching, smiling knowingly, as if he has seen it all before. But she couldn't tell him any of this. She knew her tongue was not up to all the words.

The sheriff reached up into the cabinet, pulled down a bottle of bonded whiskey, and poured himself a shot. "Merry Christmas," he said, lifting the glass at Hazel.

"Happy Yew Near!" Hazel said, returning the toast by sloshing coffee over the side of her cup. It took a moment for her to realize that she had said the wrong thing. She laughed at her mistake to let him know she wasn't all that drunk. "I mean, Happy Near Yew." No, that didn't sound right either.

"Happy Near You, too." The sheriff winked at Hazel. Then he grinned and tossed back his drink. Hazel returned his wink and grin, not feeling at all as if he were laughing at her. No, he liked her, she could tell. The sheriff was on her side.

⁂

Floyd was waiting in the doorway when the sheriff led Hazel up the walk, his arm around her waist pulling her tightly to him for balance. Lost in the aroma of cigarettes and Old Spice, she was disappointed when the porch steps came into focus. She could have strolled with him all the way down the bluffs and clear out into the Delta night.

"Hazel! Are you all right?" Floyd took over from the sheriff, but his handling wasn't as gentle. After he got her in the house, he grabbed Hazel by her shoulders and shook her once. "You could have killed somebody!" His eyes widened at the thought. "She didn't, did she, Sheriff?"

"Nope. Not that we know of. You didn't kill nobody, did you, Miss Hazel?"

Hazel turned and saw her friend grinning by her side, and she grinned back. "Only in self-defense." She winked at the sheriff, thinking he understood what she meant. He shrugged it off with a grin and said his good-night.

Floyd called after him as he cut through the yard, "Sheriff, we're awful sorry. I'm sure she didn't mean nothing by it. Since Davie and all..." He stopped. "She's not responsible for it right now."

Hazel's face lit up. "You think you know me so good, don't you? Well, I am responsible. I *did* do it on purpose," she announced proudly.

"Hazel!" Floyd shook her again. "You're still drunk as Cooter Brown."

"Maybe, but I still did it on purpose. When I saw that tiny baby in that manger, I knew I had to kill it. Had to get it before it grew up and made my life hell. I aimed the car right for that little crib. I think I got him."

"You tried to kill Jesus?" Floyd said, incredulous. "You can't kill Jesus, Hazel, honey. That's a simple fact. Jesus going to live forever, whether we like it or not."

"Not in my house, He ain't. If He can't be nice, then out He goes." Hazel flung her arm so hard showing Jesus the way out, she toppled over. Floyd caught her. She looked up into his face. It seemed frozen in disbelief. Didn't he understand? Everything was so clear to her now. Life could go ahead and roar past them like a freight train. She had everything under control. She had won.

Only Hazel wished Floyd would stop staring! What was he looking at? Then she turned and peered into the mirror that hung in the entryway. There she saw a madwoman, her hair in wild tangles and long black fingers of mascara reaching for her throat. Lipstick smeared almost to her ears, like a circus clown gone mad. A pair of dead eyes peered back at her from the farthest reaches of hell. This was what the sheriff had been grinning at.

Floyd spoke softly, carefully. "Hazel, it ain't Jesus's fault."

For a long time she stared blankly at him. When Hazel spoke, it was as a small girl. "Then whose fault is it, Floyd?"

His eyes offered her nothing.

"Tell me," she asked, "when is somebody going to be on my side?" Without expecting an answer, she dropped her head on her husband's chest and he led her off to bed.

Chapter Sixteen

BROKEN THINGS

"**G**it!" Johnny yelled from up on the porch. "And don't neither one of y'all stupid girls come back in my yard. I'll shoot you both." Nobody was going to get away with saying that about *his* mother.

He watched LaNelle and LouAnne Brister retreat, and didn't take his eyes off them until he saw the sisters disappear through their own back door. It was early February, and his mother had been gone for a week. Johnny had yet to understand why, and the girls' answer had only infuriated him. It was true that his father had left his mother at a hospital called Whitfield, down in Jackson, but the girls were calling it a nuthouse.

Still indignant, he tramped inside to look for his father, who he found sitting on the kitchen floor. "Daddy! What's a drunk?"

Floyd glanced up from the vacuum cleaner, the motor in pieces all around him. "Why? Who's been talking about drunk?"

"LaNelle said Momma was a drunk."

Floyd frowned. "That right?"

Billy Dean Brister's little girl had wasted no time in telling every person she saw about what had happened in her front yard Christmas Eve. The evening that, thanks to Brother Dear's ad-libbed quip to a packed house, became better known as "the night shepherds kept watch over their flocks in flight."

"LaNelle said Momma got sent to Whitfield with the crazy people for being a drunk and for running down Baby Jesus."

"Um-hmm. Hand me that belt before you step on it."

Cautiously, Johnny picked up the greasy thing by his foot, clutching it between his thumb and index finger and handing it to his father like a bait worm. Floyd inspected the belt and then looked up at Johnny again.

"Son, your momma might drink some, but she's not your average drunk. Your average drunk drinks to get drunk. For no better reason than that. Pure and simple. Now your momma, she's different. She drinks when she gets mad."

"In fact," Floyd said thoughtfully, as if the conclusion was at that moment congealing in his mind, "you might say your mother drinks *at* people." He smiled at Johnny. "So when she comes home, we got to make sure we don't get her riled up. You hear?"

"LaNelle said Momma was getting lettercooted."

"Electrocuted." Floyd put the belt down and picked up the vacuum cleaner hose. "Girl knows a lot for a six-year-old, don't she?"

"It's this way," Floyd explained. "Your momma's got all these thoughts backed up in her head that get her upset and make her want to drink. And when she's not drinking, they make her want to stay in her room and sleep. That's how come her to go to bed after Christmas and not get up."

"Momma was tired."

"That's right. They call it depression. And down at Whitfield they got this special kind of machine that will suck up all the sad thoughts that can't get out by theirselves."

He put the hose up to his head to demonstrate and made a sucking noise with his mouth. Johnny's eyes widened. "That way, she'll have room for some brand-new ones. You and me'll have to be extra nice so all her new thoughts will be happy ones. Understand?" his daddy asked, the hose still up to his head.

"Yes sir," Johnny answered dubiously.

When Floyd dropped the hose to the floor, one of Johnny's rubber balls came rolling out.

"Hmm," Floyd said. "I guess it wasn't the motor after all."

Chapter Seventeen

HIDDEN IN CLEAR VIEW

A s Floyd drove over the Hopalachie County line, he said as fast as he could, "Half in and half out!" and for a brief moment the car and its three occupants were caught in between counties, belonging entirely to neither. For an instant Floyd Graham had beaten geography.

Hazel didn't pay him any mind. What did it matter where they were going? Let him take the highway all the way up to Memphis if he wanted to. Or all the way down to hell, for what she cared. It was the same to her now. She only stared out her window, not at anything directly, mostly just away from her husband. It wasn't the silence of somebody who had nothing to say.

"I know a little Mississippi town where the county line runs right down the middle of Main Street," Floyd chirped. "They got a sheriff for each side of the road. Different laws and everything."

Johnny shifted a little on the seat. He still wasn't accustomed to having the entire back to himself. When the family used to go driving together, Davie would sit behind their father and Johnny directly behind their mother. Johnny scooted a few inches to the left and then to the right, trying to find the exact middle point between his parents.

"What I want to know is, what happens if somebody shoots a person from across the street?" Nobody offered a solution to Floyd's dilemma.

The breeze from Hazel's window carried the sweet smell of gardenias into the backseat. Even though Johnny had visited his mother in the hospital several times, she had never worn any of her familiar scents. She only smelled of things that stung his nose.

Johnny inhaled deeply, to make certain, and then he smiled. Sure enough, his mother smelled right again. That had to be a good sign. Her skin, too, was exactly as it was supposed to be, white as milk and sprinkled with the cinnamon freckles she hated so. The ugly bruises on her arms from the straps had disappeared, and when she got into the car, she still sat straight as a plumb line. His mother never could tolerate slouching.

It was his mother's eyes that had disturbed him. They had dimmed from the crystal blue of a spring sky to the washed-out gray of winter. He could see no farther into her than into a pond on an overcast day. For the first time he did not know what she wanted of him.

Floyd slowed the car. "We're passing over the Big Black. Look out for gators!"

Beneath them, the current was deep and the water dark like iron. The river gave off a coolness that, even on a summer-hot day in late May, gave Hazel a shiver. Hugging herself, she rocked to and fro ever so slightly in her seat. If she would only scoot over some, the boy thought, his father would surely put his arm around her.

"Hazel, honey, ain't you got nothing to say to us?"

Hazel wouldn't turn her attention from a pasture of strange-looking cattle, trying to remember what they were called. They had grotesque humps up high on their backs and seemed to be watching her with baleful looks, stirring a memory of a warning her mother had offered long ago.

"Everything's going to be just fine now, Hazel. Even got a new maid coming tomorrow to help out," Floyd assured her. "Real go-gitter. Come right up to me and asked for the job. She'll be a real comfort to you. Wait and see. Everything's gonna get back to normal."

Floyd beamed reassuringly at his wife, who kept a tight hold on herself, staring out the window. It was anybody's bet what normal was for her anymore. For all Floyd and Johnny knew, maybe this was exactly the way a body was supposed to act after weeks and weeks in the ivy-covered hospital getting fixed.

His daddy's arm remained outstretched along the back of the seat. What was his mother waiting for? If she would only sidle over a foot, everything could get back to the way it had been.

Floyd switched on the radio. Somebody who had the voice of a jittery colored man was singing.

"Y'all listening to this?" He turned the music up loud. "That ol' boy's from Tupelo. Would you believe he's white, to boot?"

Floyd tilted his toward his wife and smiled hopefully. "Hazel, honey, just think. You might of scooped him up some ice cream when he was little." Floyd began to sing along:

You ain't nothin' but a hound dog
Cryin' all the time.

Hazel couldn't care less about the song. She was trying to remember something important. What was it? It had to do with the bluffs. No, beyond the bluffs. Gradually, as the road became familiar, it came back to her. Just on the other side of this narrow band of hills was that sudden descent into an endless flat floodplain. It was out there that she had put mile after mile on her Lincoln, looking for God knows what. Or was it God she was looking for?

She remembered the day Floyd had taken her up into these bluffs for the first time. From where, with the wave of his hand, like the devil tempting Jesus, he had shown her the frightening secret of what lay on the other side of these soft, eroding hills. That sharp decline into the largest collection of flatness on earth.

It was strange what stayed put in her head and what went missing. Of course she knew she had been the mother of two children, and now she was the mother of one. Johnny had stayed. Davie had gone. Yet she felt nothing about his leaving. There was only a dead spot, like ground that had been scorched by lightning. It was as if, in her feelings, he was still falling.

Yet she remembered, as if it were yesterday, that late afternoon she had stood by her husband on top of the bluff, how her head had spun at the wonder of it all and how she had trembled at the thought of so much unbounded space. Then, she had put her arm around Floyd for balance, and he made her feel anchored. How she had loved him so. She still had that memory. Now a memory was all it was.

After crossing the bridge into Delphi, Floyd decided to go right through the middle of town instead of turning off on one of the residential lanes and bypassing the Saturday crowds. He even turned at the courthouse, going out of his way to round the busy square.

For the first time during the trip Hazel gave Floyd a look, and it was by no means a nice one. But she didn't say a word. She put on her sunglasses and pulled down the visor. Her back was as straight as a fence post.

Like any Saturday in Delphi, the downtown was awash with people. They were talking in friendly huddles on the sidewalks and calling to each other from across the street. People stopped what they were doing to watch the Lincoln make its way through town. White and colored, everybody waved and nodded as Floyd drove past. Hazel ignored them, staring straight ahead through her butterfly sunglasses, holding her chin up high as if she had a big insect balanced on her nose and was disinclined to disturb it. That way she didn't have to see people shaking their heads and blessing her heart as she passed.

The Lincoln was a rolling advertisement of Hazel's last debacle, with the prominent dent in the hood where she had tried to run down the Baby Jesus. It would have seemed natural for Floyd, the owner of Delphi Motors, to have had the dent removed long before now, but that's not how Floyd dealt with his family's embarrassments. He once told Johnny that in a town as little and high-hat as Delphi, everybody knew everything about everybody else, whether it was true or not. He said a man looks plumb sorry covering up what folks already know. "Now take the killdee," he explained. "She lays her eggs in the gravel, right under your nose. But you'd never see them 'cause they blend in so good. Yep, honesty is the best policy," his father had concluded. "Sometimes dragging the truth out in the open, every jot and tittle, is the best way to hide things."

So Johnny's daddy had decided to display his wife for all Delphi to see the very day she got out of the mental hospital. He was hiding her out in public view like a bird egg.

☙

Despite Hazel's obvious feelings on the matter, Floyd slowed down in front of Gooseberry's Department Store. The Gooseberry twins were standing out front in their usual Saturday spot, calling people by name—first and last—as they walked by. They knew everyone. If you wanted to get word out countywide, people knew to tell it to the Gooseberrys.

Sid and Lou were hard to tell apart. Each was the size of a small barn. They smoked fat cigars and hadn't a full hank of hair between them. Matching tape measures were draped around their necks and hung down their stomachs resembling limp yellow suspenders that had given up the battle.

The brothers lived by themselves two houses down from the Grahams and belonged to that group of Delphinian families who passed down history as well as money. Floyd had once told Hazel the Gooseberry brothers were descended from Jews. "In fact their great-granddaddy was the South's only Jew Civil War hero."

"How come them to go to the Episcopal church if they're Jews?" Hazel had asked.

"What I heard was that the family had to turn Episcopal when Jesus picked up such strong support amongst the Klan."

Angling the car in front of the brothers' store, Floyd yelled too loudly, "Hey, Sid! How's business, Lou?"

Johnny noticed the tomato-sized splotches rise up on the back of his mother's neck. There was something she needed of him now, yet he couldn't figure out what.

Sid worked his cigar to the corner of his mouth and called out, "Why, it's ol' Floyd Graham." He loped over, placed his hands on the car roof, and leaned down into Floyd's face, his cigar still burning. "How in the world you been, Floyd?"

Lou came around to the other side. Hazel pushed the button for her window. Before the boy thought about doing the same, Lou had already placed his pudgy fingers over the ledge and thrust his jowly cigar-smoking face through the opening. "Why, is that Miss Hazel you got in here?"

"Welcome home, darlin'!" Sid shouted, as if Hazel had lost both her mind and her hearing.

"You're a sight for sore eyes," Lou yelled at the back of Hazel's head, which was rapidly disappearing in a cloud of smoke.

Floyd nodded in Hazel's direction. "Don't she look good, Sid?"

"I was about to say it. She sho' do look good."

"Bless her heart," the brothers said in unison.

Hazel's shoulders notched upward. Johnny noticed that the blotches had joined up, and now his mother's neck was a solid swath of red.

"We'll have you over to the house real soon," Floyd said, and then backed the car into the street, heading up Gallatin. The brothers waved them away.

Hazel finally spoke. "They all know, don't they, Floyd? The whole damn town knows."

Floyd smiled the same smile Johnny had seen his father use when an angry farmer had brought back his Mercury coupe. "Sweetnin'," he purred, "you know everybody would of found out soon enough. Now it's all in the open. Ain't that the way?" He smiled again sweetly and tilted his head to the side, not bothering to explain to her about the bird egg.

When Hazel didn't answer, Floyd answered for her, "Well, it is, honey. You got to trust me on this."

Then Hazel uttered one syllable. "Ha." It was hardly discernible from a cough.

BOOK TWO

LOST CHILDREN

Chapter Eighteen

THE KEEPER

Overall, Floyd was pleased with how things were turning out. As he told Johnny, one of the pills Hazel took would make her sick if she drank, and the other would keep her from getting all knotted up inside. Floyd said the medicine was already a great comfort to him, but to be safe, he showed Johnny how to use the phone—"In case your mother does something funny."

Johnny didn't know what he meant. His mother hadn't been fun in ages.

"You know how whiskey smells, don't you?"

Johnny nodded. He instinctively knew all the smells that attended his mother, and what mood each signified.

"Well, then, when you think you smell it on her or if she gets to walking crooked or starts to talking funny, you call me right then." He led Johnny into the stairhall, to the little cubbyhole built into the wall. That's where the telephone sat, squatting there in the hollow like a giant black toad. Floyd put a chair against the wall so Johnny could reach it.

"Just pick up this part shaped like a door handle and put this end up to your ear and this one to your mouth. When the lady says, 'Number, please,' you say real loud and clear, 'Four-oh-three.' I'll get here before you know it."

Later that morning, after Floyd had left for work and Johnny sat at the kitchen table eating his Cheerios, there came such a loud knock at the back door that it made him nearly jump out of his pajamas. He spied a set of dark, frightful eyes under a monstrous straw hat, peering hard at him through the screen.

"Anybody home in there?" came a shout.

He knew this woman! He had seen her skulking around the neighborhood for weeks, looking like she was up to no good. He'd tried to tell his father but he wouldn't listen. And now here she was dressed in a white uniform. *She* was the new maid?

"My name Vida Snow!" the woman boomed in a voice too big for her scrawny body. "I told to be here this morning. Y'all aiming to let me in or no, little boy?"

Johnny decided not to. They didn't need a maid, especially not this one. Not when he could take care of his mother. He decided to hide under the table and hold his ears until she went away.

"I ain't walking all the way back to Tarbottom. Little boy, I seen you. Now let me in!" She beat on the door with the handle of her dirty umbrella.

She stepped back from the door and in a voice raised loud enough for the neighbors to hear, she bellowed, "I supposed to clean house for a po' sickly white woman!"

Johnny heard his mother's feet hit the floor with a *blam!* "Good night in the morning!" she cried out, banging the door behind her and clumping down the stairs. "Who's out there calling me names and it ain't even noon yet?"

This was the most animated his mother had been in months. Maybe they could throw the woman off the porch together!

By the time Johnny crawled out from under the table, Hazel was at the door, clutching her pink chenille robe at the throat. She asked sharply, "What are you carrying on about?"

Looking up into Hazel's face, the visitor threw her a startled look of recognition. The look vanished as suddenly as it had appeared.

"Now, you must be Miss Hazel Graham. My name is Vida. Vida

Snow. I'm sure happy to be working for you."

Johnny noticed that the woman was at least pretending to be nice to his mother. Hazel only stared at her blankly.

"Maybe you ain't expecting me. Mr. Floyd hired me, and I get two dollars a day. He told me so."

Hazel sighed and opened the screen door. "Yeah, I been told, too. Come on in, I reckon."

The woman walked straight over to the sink, leaned against the counter, and crossed her arms like she was setting claim to that very spot. As Johnny hoisted himself back into his kitchen chair, Vida studied him closely. "How many children you got, Miss Hazel?"

Hazel didn't answer immediately. She poured herself a cup of coffee and eased herself into a kitchen chair. "Just the one," she finally said. "But I imagine Mr. Floyd already told you that, too," she added coldly. "What else did he tell you?"

Vida reached into the pocket of her maid's uniform and pulled out two bottles of pills. "Said I supposed to give you a blue one and a yaller one every morning. No more, no less."

"Anything else?"

Vida looked down and smiled self-consciously. "And he said to watch you close 'cause you be real bad to spit them out."

"He hire you to be my maid or my keeper?"

Vida shrugged. "I reckon it's time now." She took a clean glass from the drainboard, filled it with tap water, and then uncapped the pills.

Moving no closer than an arm's length from where Hazel sat, Vida bent over and cautiously slid the water and the two pills across the table, as if she were setting out a plate of food for a dog of questionable temperament. She stepped back to watch.

Hazel reached for the pills. "Don't worry. I ain't going to jump you. No matter what you been told by Mr. Floyd Graham." She swallowed the pills and then held her mouth open for Vida to see. "There. Ain't I a good girl?"

"Yessum," Vida said. She hung her hat on the rack behind the door and began bouncing on the balls of her feet, her eyes darting around the kitchen, appearing for the first time a little less than confident. "Where you want me to start, Miss Hazel? Washing, ironing, scrubbing?"

"How would I know? Floyd hired you. He can tell you where to start. I'm sure he gave you his number." Lifting herself up from the table, Hazel added, "Only stay out of my bedroom, if you don't mind." At that she turned and trudged out of the kitchen.

Vida didn't seem to take offense. Johnny watched as she went about taking inventory of the kitchen, squinting and shaking her head. She clucked her tongue at the sink. She bent over and whistled at the knobs on the stove. She scuffed her shoe against the linoleum, nodding curiously to herself. Only when she walked into the pantry did she lose her squint, for a long moment staring wide-eyed at all the cans and jars and boxes of food.

Her attention lit on Johnny again. The maid's eyes were now hard and alert. It was obvious that this was a woman of very few words and very many opinions. "What you call your name?"

He dropped his eyes to the linoleum. She had no right coming in here and asking his name and making his mother sad.

"Cat got your tongue? Don't matter none. I done been told. Johnny, ain't it?" She squinted at him and shook her head, rendering a silent opinion he did not feel was at all favorable.

"I'm Vida."

Still looking down, he said, "I know who you are. You the one been hiding in the bushes. I seen you there. Spying on the sheriff's house."

"Hmm," she said disagreeably. "And I know who you are. You the one riding in the back of that big old car while your momma slings gravel and tries to run folks off the road."

Johnny glanced up at her. "How you know?"

They glared at each other for a moment, neither one giving, and then Vida leaned against the sink once more, crossing her arms. "What's wrong with your momma?" she asked.

He crossed his arms as she was doing. "Tired," was all he said.

"Tired," Vida echoed and then shook her head. "Nosuh! It ain't tired."

She poured herself a cup of coffee and sat down at the table with Johnny, crossing her legs at the ankles, all of her energy seemingly spent. "Nosuh!" she said again, mostly to herself. "I know tired. And that ain't tired."

Chapter Nineteen

SWITCHING PLACES

H azel lay in her bed waiting for the clattering of dishes, the fall of footsteps on the stair, the two hard knuckle-knocks on the door, and finally the resolute face of that horrible little woman who doled out oblivion, two pills at a time.

Each morning the maid followed on Floyd's heels after he dispensed his morning kiss as efficiently as Vida did her medicine. With a pitying look, he assured her, "You get some rest and let me take care of everything for a while. Time is the best healer, you know."

She thought a moment about time. Since Vida had begun overseeing Hazel's medication, time ran like a clock somebody had thrown down a well. She could hear it ticking, loud and unceasing, and knew seconds and minutes and hours and days must be piling up somewhere, yet she couldn't remember what it had to do with her. Wasn't Johnny supposed to be starting to school soon? Or had he already begun? It wouldn't surprise her if he walked in with a high school diploma in his hand.

No, she could only deal with time in small doses. Each day she opened her eyes to see the world in a kind of stark, harsh glare. It was in the morning that she knew she had a husband who barely tolerated her, and one child that was alive and wanting and the other dead and gone.

Vida took care of that. Clutched in that tight, dark fist she brought the next kind of time, a fluid, river kind of time. At first she tried to resist, knowing it would take her away from her remaining child. Inevitably the medicine caught her in its current and gently drew her below the surface, and soon she was aware only of a beautiful refracted light and could hear nothing except the gentle hum of the water rushing in her ears.

Then there was the time of surfacing, when she would open her eyes and see her son, the remaining one, the determined one, waiting by her bedside staring at her, his worried eyes trying to catch her like a net, beckoning her upward. She didn't want to go. She wanted to stay warm and caressed by the river. Yet his stare was relentless, and finally the river gave her up.

Lastly there was the night, when sleep would not come. During these hours it was as if she stood at the mouth of a secret cavern, and memories, indistinguishable one from the other, thick as bats at feeding time, swarmed her in a great black cloud. In those late-night hours the screaming cries of voices she could hear but not understand forced her out of bed, and she roamed the darkened house like a ghost, randomly picking up objects—a shoe, a toy, a photograph—studying them, trying to coax from them their secrets until, exhausted, she returned to bed. It was during this time she most wanted to drink, just to make the voices stop. Once she had sneaked a glass of Floyd's bourbon to bed with her, desperate enough to test the pill that was supposed to make her violently ill if she mixed it with alcohol. It did, and after an emergency visit to the hospital, Floyd had mentioned going back to Whitfield—indefinitely.

From the bottom of the stairs she heard a rattling of the breakfast dishes. Here she comes, Hazel thought, right on schedule. Sounding her two warning knocks, Vida entered the room and without speaking set the breakfast tray down in front of Hazel.

"Good morning, Miss Hazel," she said without feeling. "Take your pills, and I'll sit here and keep you company while you eat your breakfast."

Hazel glared at Vida. She knew the real story. The only reason

Vida stayed was to make sure Hazel didn't stick a finger down her throat after swallowing the medicine.

"Suppose you came in here one morning and I told you I wasn't going to take your medicine. Supposing I locked the door on you. Then what?"

Vida waggled her hand in her face. "Come on now, Miss Hazel. I got ironing to do."

"I asked you a question."

"First thing, it ain't *my* medicine. It's yours. And two, if you was to act ugly, I suppose I have to call Mr. Floyd at his work." She reached into her apron pocket again and produced a skeleton key. "Or maybe use this thing he give me in case you was to try something funny like that."

"Y'all think you know me pretty good, don't you?"

"Nome. I ain't met nobody like you a-tall." She looked at Hazel warily. "Now, I might have *seed* somebody like you at a distance, but I ain't never met them up close."

"What do you mean by that?" Hazel hated it when people acted as if they had secrets on her.

"I ain't meaning nothing, Miss Hazel. Now take this medicine and swaller it down."

Hazel took the pills with orange juice. There was never any doubt that she was going to do as she was told. Only she didn't care for Vida bossing her like she did, acting as if she knew everything there was to know about Hazel, yet she didn't want to push her too far either. Something about this colored woman scared Hazel. The determined set of her face signaled that Vida was a woman who would do whatever it took to get her way.

After eating a few bites of the scrambled eggs and toast, Hazel lay back on her pillows and waited for the warm current to rise up around her, gradually lifting her and then drawing her out into forgetful depths.

She cast an eye toward the maid, who sat in the chair across the room, staring stonily out of the window. With her anger and despair muted, Hazel found herself becoming fascinated by this woman. She was so young, maybe even younger than Hazel, but her bossiness made her seem so much older. How did a woman that young get to be so sure of herself? What did it take?

Hazel wondered if Vida had ever known loss. Maybe if things were different, they could have been friends. Secret friends—the kind you tell secret feelings to. Hazel could tell her many things. About voices that spoke to her at night. About death and fading love. About faith, hope, and charity...and the greatest of these is charity...tied up and dropped in the river...cast away like trash...how it feels.

As the edges of her mind began to blunt, Hazel tried to stay focused on the woman's face. Really a pretty face.

No, Hazel thought, closing her eyes. It was a face that could have been set in concrete. Or carved from oak. Or painted on a screen door somewhere. There was no heart behind that pretty screen. This woman probably didn't feel at all.

That evil little boy was at the dinette table when Vida returned downstairs. He sat with his crayons and paper, looking like he had swallowed the catbird. What had he done now? She went to check the cabinets. Sure enough, he had switched everything around again.

Vida crashed about the kitchen, pulling out pots and pans, fussing out loud to herself. Johnny silently sat there, drawing the big letter *D*.

"Now I know good and well I didn't put my pots here," she grumbled loud enough for him to hear. When she looked up at him he rolled his eyes.

This was the third time this week she had had to rearrange her kitchen. She couldn't turn her back ten minutes on that child without having him restore everything to the way his mother had it.

"Pots don't belong by the sink," she complained at him. "They belong by the cookstove where they is used."

"It's called an oven. Never heard nobody call it a cookstove. That's silly." He rolled his eyes again.

"What be silly is for some little boy to go 'round switching my kitchen on me. When he knows I going to switch it right back. That's sure nuff silly."

"Ain't your kitchen," Johnny mumbled.

Vida walked over to where Johnny sat and planted her fists on her hips. "I heared that. How you get so contrary? If you ask me, six years ain't enough time to work up that much orneriness. You as nasty-tempered as an old woman."

"Ain't your pots, neither. Them's my momma's pots."

"What's your problem, boy?" she asked. "How come you getting crossways with me?"

Rolling his eyes again at Vida, Johnny turned back to the table, where he drew a big letter *H*.

"You put me in mind of a boy I once knowed called Tangle Eye. Never would look straight at you. Always peeking out the corner of his eyeholes. Sneaking around and looking cockeyed at folkses. Know how they come to call that boy Tangle Eye?"

Johnny exhaled loudly like his daddy to show how exasperated he was getting. Bearing down hard on the lead, he put a cross on his little letter *t*.

Vida was silent, still waiting for his answer.

"No, I don't," he said, trying to sound not the least bit interested.

"Well, since you so nice to be asking, I tell you. One day that boy roll his eyes a time too many and they got all twixed up. Don't you know when he cried, his eyes were crossed so bad, his tears rolled right down his back."

Keeping his eyes down, Johnny pretended not to hear her. She'd get hers soon.

"Humph. Why don't you go outside? Ain't you got no little play friends?"

"Ain't no boys around here. Just girls, and I hate them." He looked up at Vida, as if to underscore his point.

"Well, then, play by yourself," she said. "Go fishing for a doodlebug."

"I can't. *He's* out there."

It took Vida only a second to figure out who "he" was. Today she had brought her father to work with her. Knowing how much he missed praying, she let him bring his Bible so he could sit and read and preach at the bottom of the Grahams' sprawling backyard. She had hoped the yard was large enough for him not to attract attention.

Vida dismissed Johnny's concern with a wave of her hand. "I ain't got time for your foolishness. He ain't studying you."

"He's sitting in *my* backyard. Sitting on *my* bench. On top of *my* grass."

"He been eating your porridge, too? Who you? Goldilocks? They room for you and him both in that big ol' yard."

"He talks to himself. And he looks at me funny."

"Well, maybe you funny to look at."

"He called me Nate."

Vida was silent for a moment. Lord, she thought to herself, what was her daddy thinking of? "You ever playlike?" she asked.

"Sometimes," Johnny said hesitantly, sensing a trap.

"Well, that man out there is my daddy. And some days he play-like, too."

"He's old."

"Old people can playlike. So when he call you Nate, now you know he's playing like."

"Does he playlike every day?"

"No. Some days he don't playlike at all. And then some days he talks to hisself. Same as I heared you talking to yourself behind my back." Then Vida shrugged her shoulders as if the whole matter of people talking to themselves was no big deal. "So you see, there ain't no need tellin' on him. He ain't going to bother you. He ain't crazy, if that what you're thinking."

Johnny wasn't so sure. He took off in a run, and Vida watched as he scurried out into the yard, ducking behind trees as he went, mimicking a movie Indian sneaking up on a cowboy, until he was within spying distance of her father.

Vida shook her head. "Hope his mouth ain't as big as his eyes," she said to herself before going back to arranging her kitchen.

Truth was, sometimes even Vida didn't know if her father was crazy or not. Their fall had been hardest on him. Losing his church and his position in the community, their nice home—that was bad enough. However, the thing that broke him was the Senator turning his back. That nearly killed Levi. The sheriff poisoned the Senator's mind against Levi, convincing the Senator that the Klan had burned down Levi's church because he was in league with the NAACP. Turned him out of their nice comfortable house, which the Senator owned, and forced Levi to make a crop and live in a tumbledown sharecropper's cabin. That's when his mind seemed to slip. On those long afternoons of hoeing, chopping, or picking cotton, Levi would sneak off into the woods, leaving Willie and Vida to do all the work. One day she decided to see where he was going off to.

She followed him down the rows and he never looked back once, keeping his face pointed toward the east until he reached the bayou. There he disappeared into the swampy growth. Vida kept after him. She traced his footsteps to the very edge of the blackish water. She ducked behind a cottonwood tree.

From her hiding place she could see her father standing motionless on the bank beside a giant bald cypress. For a moment all she heard was the plunking of turtles slipping into the water, until she noticed a rushing sound where the water ran fast and made deadly whirlpools.

She understood. This was the place her father called his praying ground, the secret place where as a young man he had prayed day after day, night after night, to see the shining face of God. Finally

God called out to him from a whirlpool of churning water. This was the very spot where Levi had received the calling to become a preacher of the Word.

The frogs, now accustomed to human presence, resumed their chorus. Then came the dry rattle of the kingfisher that sat perched on a dead cypress stump. Next it was her father she heard. At first he spoke so soft and low she couldn't make out the words. But she soon recognized the slow, singsong chant he used when he preached, right before launching into his sermon, when he would take a phrase and repeat it over and over in his deepest bass until he got the people's blood to stirring.

As Vida listened, his voice became fervent and full, larger than the swamp itself, groaning with emotion.

"Let this cup pass," he called out. "Lift up this yoke. Let this cup pass me by, oh Lord."

Over and over he called, louder and louder each time, until she was sure his voice resonated beyond this swampy place and thundered at the very door of heaven. He pleaded with God not to hide His face any longer, not to desert His good and faithful servant. He asked God to give him a mighty purpose and to please, please, show His face one more time: "Send me a righteous story to live out."

His words became angry, as if he were mad at God, offended that He would keep hidden from him, reducing Levi to a common fieldworker and plunging him into darkness. He cried out with a fury until a sudden upsurge of emotion strangled off his words and dropped him to his knees. For a while he sobbed bitterly, his shoulders heaving. Then he began sputtering, "I'm sorry, I'm sorry, I'm sorry."

Vida's father was now only a shadow against the late bayou dusk, a vanishing soul crying out to his white-faced God. As fireflies began their twinkling throughout the swamp, her father slipped like one of those turtles under the surface into another world, one she could not enter.

Chapter Twenty

THE MAIDS

OF TARBOTTOM

For the rest of the day, as every other day, Vida found herself locked in a battle of wills with the fractious little boy. She tried her best to coax him into watching TV. He would have none of it. The child was worse than a buzzing horsefly—you were always aware of his worrisome presence but never sure where he was going to light next. He just wore her out. The only peace she got was when he disappeared to play under the house, until she began fretting that he was starting fires beneath her feet.

The long day was coming to an end at last. She rinsed her coffee cup and then pulled back the curtain on the window above the sink. She reminded herself why she had asked for this job to begin with. From here she could see clearly into the yard next door. Sheriff Billy Dean Brister's yard. That was worth being a maid for a crazy white woman. No, she wasn't here for the company. It was for the view.

As she was heaping food on a plate to carry home with her, she told Johnny, "Now, your daddy called to say he got a meeting out in the Delta, but he'll be back soon."

Johnny wouldn't look at Vida. He stood with his back to her, staring out the back door.

"Now, listen here to me," she said louder. "I done took a plate to your momma and I'm leaving you and your daddy's supper on the stove. When y'all get hungry, jest warm it up. You understand?"

Turning around, Johnny sniffed the air noisily. "Smells burnt to me. Don't you know how to cook?"

"Plain contrary," she said to herself, putting on her funny-looking hat. She reached for her flour-sack purse and her arm froze. "I didn't leave my sack on this peg." She looked down at Johnny. "*Somebody* been going through my tote sack."

Johnny turned an accusing eye her way. "I was looking for my momma's stuff."

Vida gave him a surprised look. "You think I'm aiming to steal something from y'all? Boy, you calling me a thief?"

Johnny glared back. "You taking my momma's food, ain't you?" He dropped his eyes to the floor and said with a world-weary sigh, "You got to watch colored people in your house. They bad to steal things. That's what my daddy says."

"Contrary as the day is long," she said, shaking her head. Vida took Johnny by the shoulders and steered him out of the way of the back door. "Beatin'est mess of people I ever seed," she grumbled as she took the steps down into the yard.

When she got to the bench she touched her father on the shoulder, waking him from his nap. "Less go home, Daddy. I done had my fill of white folks today."

Vida and her father made their way out of the Grahams' neighborhood, and as they did, other maids also finishing for the day exited from their employers' fine homes, many also pan-toting leftovers. They formed a loose little procession of starched uniforms, some blue and some white, gradually making their way past the point where the expansive sprinkler-fed lawns gave over to a tangle of dusty trees and vines. They descended still farther, past where the pavement ended and the road became gravel, then took a steep downward slope and wrenched itself around to the backside of the hill, as if turning its back on Delphi proper on its descent to the quarters.

Vida heard a familiar squeal. "Whoo-ee! Girl, don't I know you from somewheres?"

Vida turned. The woman wasn't hard to recognize, even without a man's arms wrapped around her butt. Although she was wearing a maid's outfit, her bright red earbobs and matching lipstick made her look ready for juking.

Sweet Pea fell in uninvited beside Vida and her father. "I sees you took my advice. You went and got Miss Hazel for your white lady."

Vida said coolly, "This my daddy, *Reverend* Snow," hoping that might tamp down the woman's enthusiasm a bit.

The woman batted her eyes at Levi. "Proud to know you," she cooed.

Don't this woman have no off switch? Vida thought.

Levi touched his old felt hat and nodded politely at Sweet Pea. "It's good to know you likewise," he said, as if he meant it. Vida could have sworn she saw him blush.

"I took my own advice," Sweet Pea told Vida. "I working for Miss Cilly Prevost, on down from your white lady. I'm done with the mens." Sweet Pea smiled again at Levi and then pulled a sassy red scarf out of her bag and tied it around her neck. "These ol' uniforms just ain't flattering to a girl, is they?"

Levi grinned shyly and opened his mouth to speak, but when he saw Vida glaring at him, he put his eyes back on the road.

As the group continued on to the river bottom, the road lost its gravel and became nothing more than two deep ruts. Sweet Pea prattled endlessly about the domestic goings-on in the neighborhood in which they worked. Which families lived in which houses and how they were connected to each other. Who was good to the colored and who wasn't. She talked without stopping until the road exhausted itself at a large flattened-out place, around which sat a community of wooden shacks, known as Tarbottom.

Sweet Pea was saying something about how the sheriff's wife, Hertha, was Miss Pearl's niece and the Senator's daughter to boot.

Realizing that she was talking about the sheriff's kin, Vida took a sudden interest in the brash woman's babbling. Maybe it wouldn't hurt getting to know these women. If anything big or little happened in a white man's house, the maids were the first to know it. After all, that's why she'd come to Delphi in the first place, to pry open a white man's secrets.

"And they all got maids, too?" Vida asked. "Them Pearl and Hertha women?"

"Sho! What you think? They do for theyselves?"

Vida's mind was working a mile a minute. "No, I jest...who—"

"Speaking of the devil!" Sweet Pea said, pointing. "See that big red woman down yonder sitting on her porch? That Creola. Miss Pearl be her white lady." A large freckled woman, her frame completely hiding the chair that was propping her up, waved a meaty arm in their direction.

"Miss Pearl," Vida repeated, carefully considering the prospects. "The Senator's very own sister." Then she asked anxiously, "Where the sheriff's maid live at?"

"The sheriff?" Sweet Pea gave Vida a sideways. "Seems to me you always asking about the sheriff." Sweet Pea pointed farther down the lane. "See that painted house up on river stilts, looking down on everybody else?" Sweet Pea paused a minute while her red lips curled up in a look of obvious disgust. "That Missouri's house. We all call her Misery for short. She never let you forget who her white boss be."

"Missouri," Vida said slowly and deliberately, determined to remember it.

"Yeah, ol' Misery about as whitewashed as the house she stay in. She so color-struck she think she poots Franch perfume." Smiling contritely at Levi, she said, "Pardon my language, Reverend."

"Fact of the matter," she went on, "she was bragging about helping the Senator's family get ready for their cook's funeral."

"Lillie Dee?" Vida asked. "She done passed?"

"You know her? That sounds like her name. Misery say the Senator loved her like a mother. You know how crazy them white folks is about their colored mammies."

Vida's pang of grief for Lillie Dee turned quickly into excitement. Lillie Dee had died and there would be a funeral! Everyone would be there. It was as if the sassy woman had taken a stick and stirred up a wasp's nest in Vida's head.

In fact her thoughts were buzzing so, she hardly noticed when Sweet Pea stopped at a tarpaper shack with a vine-strangled yardgate. As she lifted the wire noose from the post, she cut her eyes up at Levi. "Well, this be where I stays. All by my lonesome."

Vida could have sworn she saw the woman wink at Levi.

"It was sure nice meeting you, Miss Sweet Pea," Levi said. This time it was Sweet Pea who seemed to be blushing.

It struck Vida that though her father was almost sixty, he was still a very good-looking man. His face was creased with age, but he was tall and lean, and his features were still sharp. When he looked at Sweet Pea his eyes seemed to twinkle. She had never thought of her father as a regular man with regular-man needs, nor had she considered the effect of taking Levi away from his self-enforced isolation. Life was a lot closer here. People would be watching. Things could easily get out of hand. She had to buy some time before she made her move.

As she continued down the lane with her father, Vida returned nods to neighbors who were sitting out on their porches, escaping from the heat of cookstoves and enjoying the cooling of the early evening. For the first time, she felt she belonged. There was purpose for her here. She noticed how pleasant it was down in Tarbottom. How every porch was a poor man's Hanging Garden of Babylon. Ferns and mother-in-law's tongues and impatiens and verbena rose up from old enamel washpans, while petunias and moss roses and wandering Jews, planted in rusted syrup buckets and coffee cans, spilled down from eaves and railings. The yards, kept clean and grassless by the regular sweep of dogwood brooms, were filled with chickens pecking and dogs trotting and boys and girls racing around in games of chase. For the first time in a long time, she noticed the music that lives in the laughter of children.

Chapter Twenty-One

PLOTS AND
CONSPIRACIES

The first thing Vida did upon getting in from her day at the Grahams' was to open the front and back doors of the shotgun house to get a breeze channeling through the two rooms. Then she pulled a couple of straight-back chairs up to the wooden table that sat on a ragged patch of linoleum. She called to Levi, "Supper's ready, Daddy. Come on and eat."

Levi stood over the table and prayed, "Lord, bless this food to the nourishment of our bodies and—"

In the middle of the blessing, Vida plopped herself down and forked up a bite of squash. This didn't go without her father's noticing.

Levi finished his prayer and seated himself. "It wouldn't hurt to give Him His due, Vida."

"Hurt Him a lot less to give us ours," she said with her mouth full. "He the one got everything. I reckon it's up to us to get our own." Vida had a plan, and needed neither God's nor her father's permission.

"We got food to eat."

"Ain't even our food," she said, thinking of Johnny's meanness today. "If you got to bless it, put Mr. Floyd Graham's name on it. It's his holdovers we eating."

A long silence followed while Levi stared at his plate. Vida knew she had shamed him again. She couldn't help it. Looking at him was like staring defeat right in the face. Sometimes she had to take a swat at it. Her father was lost without Jesus or the white man propping him up. She couldn't afford to think that way. Not now.

"All I'm saying is we on our own, Daddy. We got to be strong. Ain't nobody going to save us but us. You understand that? Time for wishing and praying is long gone. We got to start being smart with what we got. And careful. If we make a mistake, ain't no sweet by-and-by for us."

"You want me to leave, I'll go. You don't have to feed me. Anyways, I'd just as soon starve than hear you blaspheme the Lord."

"Where you going to go, Daddy? Tell me that. Down to the bayou to do some preaching to the frogs? We too far away for that now."

Levi stiffened. "What I mean is, I can find me a revival somewheres. Things ain't always going to be this way. Things going to be set right again."

"We been all over this," she said, knowing it would do no good to say it again. She did it anyway. "The sheriff done put the evil eye on you. Ain't no board of deacons in this county going to stand against him. You can leave the county if you want. But I ain't going. I still got business here."

Vida studied her father as he sat there, his eyes cut down at his plate. What would he do without her? It was too late for him to start all over.

"Now, Daddy," she said, trying to soften her tone, "you need to be with your family. I going to look out for you."

"I need to be doing something. I can't sit around on that bench all day. With that boy staring at me."

At that Vida tensed up in her chair. "Which boy?" she asked, her voice hard again. "That white boy say you call him Nate. What you think those fine white people going to do if they catch you talking crazy to one of their precious little lambs. Be back to the fields for both of us, picking scrap cotton. Or worser if it be the sheriff hearing you."

"I took the boy for Nate's all," Levi explained. "He came up on me sudden."

Vida angrily crumbled a wedge of cornbread over her peas, wondering if her father even remembered what Nate looked like, after years of pretending he didn't have a grandson. "That boy don't look nothing like Nate," she said flatly.

"Same coloring. Them thin lips—"

"Ain't nobody in they right mind going to mix Nate with that boy," she snapped. "Ain't nobody looks like Nate." Vida stopped herself, biting her lip. They both knew that wasn't true. If it were, Nate would be sitting at the table with them tonight.

In a calmer voice, she said, "I'll talk to Mr. Floyd. Maybe he can find you a little piece of work to keep you busy in the yard."

Levi squared his shoulders. "I ain't no yard boy," he said. "I'm still a preacher of the Word."

Vida's temper flared again. "And I ain't got no business being no maid. And Willie weren't supposed to be no two-bit bootlegger just to settle your sharecropping accounts with the Senator."

Damn! she thought. Why couldn't she ever stop short? Why did she always have to come out fighting? Seemed sometimes meanness was the only thing she had plenty of. She silently cursed herself again. Then she cursed her father for taking it from her, wondering when exactly it was that she had become the adult and he the child.

"It's been a fall for the both of us, I reckon," she said. "And neither of us can't pick ourselves up from no place but where we fell. We ain't got a bushel basket of choices."

"One day it'll be different, Vida," Levi said, now sounding as confident as ever. "When the Senator finds out the truth of it all, things will get put back the way they was. The bottom rail will be on the top."

"I know, Daddy," she said, scraping a few more peas into her plate. "You lay more faith on the Senator than Jesus. And the both of them ain't listening. Now, my own self," she continued, shaking her fork in front of her, marking her words in the air, "I find it best to keep my head down, my eye clear, and carry a ice pick in my tote sack. That way I kin get a quick handle on my faith when I needs too. When the sheriff find out I'm working next door, all hell going to break out. We got to be careful living amongst white people. And smart. Least till I can make my move."

"You study too much on revenge, Vida. All white people ain't bad."

"Humph. They raised to be bad. Leastways to the colored." She chortled to herself, thinking of the fierce look on Johnny's face that afternoon. "You know, I figger that white boy would kill me if I kept my back turned long enough. He's some nasty."

༄

Johnny eased open the door to the darkened room. A shaft of light from the hallway caught his mother's face, and her eye opened to the light. He tiptoed over to the edge of her bed and carefully removed the tray with her uneaten supper from beside her. Then he stood staring into her face until she managed both eyes open. At last she recognized him with a half-smile.

Johnny pulled himself up into the bed with her and burrowed into the space under her outstretched arm, putting his back against her ribs. Tucked up close to his mother, he dutifully reported to her the day's events, including the part about the strange old man on the bench and the jumble Vida was making of their kitchen.

With outrage he told her of all the time Vida wasted. About how she would walk out to the front porch and stand there staring off into the distance at the sheriff's house, as if she were waiting for him. And how sometimes, after the sheriff got in or out of his cruiser, she would head back to the kitchen, walking very slowly, like all that looking had worn her out, and stand over the sink saying and doing nothing. Wasting his daddy's money.

"And Momma, one day she disappeared. She was out standing on the porch looking at the sheriff's house, and then she was gone."

When his mother didn't ask where to, he offered his guess. "I bet she been over sneaking around the sheriff's house. She's sneaky mean, Momma."

Johnny went on to list Vida's offenses and then waited for something to happen, as if his recollections would make his mother whole. Or mad. Anything. But she didn't seem to care.

He had only one item left, one even he knew was minor. "She took some food home."

His mother gazed at him with clouded eyes. Then from out of that dimness, he thought he saw a faint, familiar glimmer.

She whispered to him, "Nothing else?"

Johnny's heart began to beat faster. "No ma'am. I even checked her bag."

"You know your daddy won't tolerate stealing, don't you?"

Johnny nodded again. They both knew that was one thing Floyd could not abide. He had fired other maids when he only suspected they had taken something from the house. One time he told the sheriff. Floyd hated it when he thought he was being taken advantage of by the colored.

"But it needs to be something bigger than food," she said. "Something valuable."

"Yes ma'am!" he said happily, interpreting this as a full-out declaration of war on the maid.

His mother's breathing became even again. When she closed her eyes, Johnny kissed her on the cheek and climbed down off the bed. Checking to make sure his mother's eyes were still shut, he carefully reached into her nightstand, picked up a little garnet brooch, slipped it into his pocket, and tiptoed out of the room.

Chapter Twenty-Two

LILLIE DEE'S FUNERAL

Down the bluffs and out in the Delta, a multitude of mourners dressed in their finest were on their way to pay their last respects to the most sainted church mother in the county. Lillie Dee Prophet had passed on the stroke of six, sitting alone in the Senator's kitchen having her supper. The Senator himself had heard the platter of cornbread shatter against the floor and found his cook, the woman who had raised him and his sister, Pearl, and after them his own daughters, slumped over the kitchen table.

The road to the church was dry and unshaded, and after half an hour, the morning sun was bearing down on Vida as she walked, setting like a weight on her shoulders. Every now and then a car or a wagon pulled up, the driver offering a ride, and each time she refused, wanting to be alone with her thoughts. This morning there was much to think about. She had been so impatient for daylight, she had rolled from pillar to post the whole night through. The biggest part of it had nothing to do with mourning Lillie Dee.

Another car approached from behind. Vida closed her eyes and lowered her chin, waiting for the cloud of dust to billow over her. With her head bowed, a breath of air locked tightly in her chest, she prayed that by the end of this day she would be one step closer to Rezel.

꙳

Most of the mourners in Levi's rebuilt church paid Vida no mind, pretending they didn't recognize this common colored woman wearing lye-scrubbed gingham. However, a few looked at her woefully, certainly remembering a girl from years ago who used to come to church dressed in white organdy, her plaits tied with satin bows. Avoiding their pitying looks, Vida sidled over to a side of the church where ladder-back chairs from half the porches in the county had been carted in for the overflow crowd and lined up against the wall. There, off to the side and unobserved, she could focus on her business.

First she scanned the church, trying to take in all the faces at once. Where was he? Surely Rezel would come home for his mother's funeral. Unable to pick him out on first glance, she started with those at the back and methodically surveyed the crowd, one face at a time. How much can a person change in six years?

She worked her way to the front of the church. There was still no Rezel. Refusing to give up hope, she tried to recollect the faces of his brothers. Maybe the one who left his wife in Memphis had come. Toby was his name. Vida recalled him being lighter colored than Rezel. Or maybe the oldest boy had come home; Pinetop, they called him, because he was tall and lean. Was he there? There were seven boys in all. One was bound to know Rezel's whereabouts.

Since the one letter years ago, there had not been another word from Rezel, nor from any of Lillie Dee's sons for that matter. Probably ashamed, Vida guessed. They all moved to and from cities with cold, iron-hard names that scraped the back of your throat to say them. Akron and Scranton and Chicago. In and out of jail so many times, they probably didn't have the heart to tell their mother nothing except the same ol' bad news. Yet surely they would come to her funeral.

But no, she saw not a one. To keep her tears at bay, she told herself maybe later, at the graveside.

The whispering around her hushed. Levi's successor had risen from his chair and was striding up to the pulpit. He was a soft-looking man with raised brows, lids that seemed to never blink, and rimless spectacles that magnified his eyes, all working together to grant him a frozen look of surprise. As he mopped his forehead with a handkerchief, he opened his mouth to speak. Before he could utter his first words, the back doors were flung open and heads whipped to the rear of the church.

In streamed a procession of white people marching down the aisle as if they owned the building. The sight of that many whites in a colored church was so off-putting, it took a moment for Vida to recognize who they were. When she did, her insides shivered. The large man with the shock of white hair and thundering footsteps leading the group was the Senator. On his arm was his sister, Pearl, who breathed through a lace handkerchief pressed against her powdered white nose. Behind the two of them was Delia, the Senator's pretty daughter, whose cobalt-blue eyes flitted recklessly from the face of one young man to another, tempting them. That was a woman bound to get some colored man lynched, Vida quickly decided.

Bringing up the rear was Hertha, the Senator's older daughter, as dark and scary as any midnight visitation. She seemed to be fuming mad, casting menacing looks back toward the open door. A cold dread settled on Vida's chest. She knew the procession had not ended. There was one member of the family unaccounted for. Sure enough, it was the sheriff who finally sauntered in.

The man didn't bother to remove his Stetson. His hands were crammed in his pockets like a child in a sulk. With what appeared to be much reluctance, he joined his wife where she had halted midway down the aisle, her stone-hard stare telling him she refused to take another step without him.

Farther down the aisle the Senator had stopped beside one of the pews. The people began shifting uncomfortably about, but he didn't glance to the left or right, keeping his red-rimmed, watery eyes straight ahead on the dove-gray coffin draped with gladiolas. As the entire pew stood up and emptied to make room for the white people, the preacher stumbled over his words. "Ain't this an honor, now? Such a great honor...an honor to us all...to Sister Prophet, that is..." He paused to wipe his brow and then continued. "The Senator and all his kin coming to pay they respects. I know we all happy to have them amongst us today as we praise the life of our dear departed sister." He paused again, allowing a murmur of agreement to course through the church.

While the preacher continued praising the white people, Vida studied them one by one. First, the Senator, looking like God without His beard, all-powerful yet now weeping like a baby for his old colored cook. Lillie Dee always said he would mourn her like a mother once she was gone. She said she only wished she didn't have to be dead to see it.

Next Vida eyed the three white women. Their skin as slick and sallow as a slab of fatback. Haughty and pampered. Dressed like queens in silks and satins and looping chains of gold and pearls. Vida ran her hand over her own dress and felt the rough scratch of the fabric.

The one Vida was most curious about was blocked from her view by a large church mother's white-scarved head. Building her nerve, Vida edged over in her chair and furtively crooked her neck to steal a look.

She saw him in clear daylight for the first time in years. His arms were crossed, and he glowered down at his boots. He had changed little since that day at the store, a little thinner maybe, more hard-bitten. But it was still there, in the almond shape of the eyes, in the uplifted corners of the mouth, in the fine-boned cheeks—the beginnings of Nate. Vida trembled inside. Something so innocent peering through a countenance so evil. How was it possible to fully hate the man, when Nate's goodness shone through like foxfire?

The sheriff, as if sensing her gaze upon him, looked up at Vida. The man still had eyes resembling burned-out cinders. At first his expression revealed no sign that he knew who she was. Then Vida saw the trace of a taunting smile.

When she could get close enough, she swore to herself, she would drive an ice pick through his black heart. And it didn't bother her one bit that she had made this promise in a church.

The preacher called out, "Let that be a testimony to us all! By carrying her corner for Jesus, Lillie Dee touched many important lives." Then, shaking his head sadly, he said, "It is a piteous thing that Lillie Dee's own children won't be with us here today. They done scattered to the four winds. Only God Hisself knows where they are, and only our prayers can reach them."

Vida bit her lip. The words cut across her heart like a razor.

As the mourners muttered about the shame of it, Vida heard a high thin voice pronounce a word that sounded like "Rezel" and then giggle. She frantically scoured the church trying to find somebody capable of being so irreverent at a funeral and finally settled on a high-toned man toward the back. It had to be him. She memorized his face just in case, yet in his green pongee shirt and sharkskin suit, he would be hard to lose. When he noticed Vida staring, he winked.

After the preacher was done with the service and Lillie Dee had been carried from the church, he asked everybody to show respect and let the Senator and his kin pass first. Vida stood anyway, trying to catch the flirty man's eye again, but he wasn't looking in her direction.

When the last white person was gone and the rest of the church rose up to leave, Vida struck out like a hound on his trail. Once outside she spied him under a pecan tree, alone, studying the crowd moiling about in the churchyard. Vida sidled over next to him, and he smiled, seeming pleased to have her company. Looking around to make sure no one was listening, Vida said carefully, "I heared you say something 'bout Rezel. You know Lillie Dee's boy?"

The man pulled an ivory toothpick from a special pocket in his satin vest and eyed Vida wickedly. "Sho. I know Rezel."

Vida's heart was racing. "How you know him?"

He grinned. "What's it to you, good-looking? He your boy-friend?" The stranger worked the toothpick between his long white teeth. "If he is, you might better find you another man to tide you over." He winked again. "How about checking me out?" He flicked the toothpick from one side of his mouth to the other.

Vida gasped. "What you mean I better look for anothern? What happened to Rezel?"

Surprised she didn't know, he told her that he and Rezel had done time together. "In Joliet," he said. "But don't look for him back here. He say he ain't never coming back to Mississippi."

The man must have noticed the stricken look on Vida's face. "That's all right, baby. How about letting me soothe your broken heart." He reached out to stroke Vida's face with the back of his well-tended hand. She slapped it away.

"He never said nothing about Vida Snow? Or my father, Levi? Or a little boy named Nate?"

The smile caved on the man's face. "Rezel was a daddy? Sure nuff?" He took a step back. "Rezel never said a word 'bout being no daddy. How many children y'all got?"

Vida moved a step closer. "Where he go off to?"

He returned the toothpick to his pocket. "Looka here. Me and him wasn't best buddies or nothing. Rezel didn't talk. He did his speaking in his cornpone blues songs, not to me."

"So what he sang 'bout?" Vida asked, moving closer still. The man's back was now against the tree.

"Damn, girl. Give me some room. If you got to know, he was always singing about a sweet deal waiting on him when he got out of the pen. A meal ticket, he called it."

"A meal ticket?"

"Yeah," he said, waving to someone across the yard. " 'Drivin' a big black car for a big white man.' That's how it went. Sang it over and over till I told him I'd sure nuff cut him if he didn't shut up." The man took another step back. "Now I got to go see somebody about a dog."

⌒

Later that evening, Vida put away her gingham dress and changed into a plain cotton shift. Her father slept soundly on the bed next to the stove. It was time to think about supper.

After lighting a fire in the stove, she got down on her knees and, using the handle of her old parasol, hooked the edge of a wooden potato crate she kept under her bed. She carried it to the eating table. There she ferreted through the contents—her mother's cotton gloves, empty thread spools. She quickly leafed through photographs and yellowed sheets of piano music, crayon scribbled pages in a child's hand. A white satin ribbon Rezel had given her, now dingy gray. As she searched she kept repeating the verse the man had told her.

Drivin' a big black car
For a big white man.

What was the music that went to that song? she wondered. What were the rest of the words? Maybe something that went with car or man. Hand. Can. Land. Promised Land.

She came upon what she had been looking for. After carefully removing Rezel's letter from the ink-smudged envelope, she smoothed the page out flat on the table. The only word she had had from since he took off to Chicago. Bits of the oilcloth showed through from all the folding and unfolding. Reading the letter she knew by heart, she tried to weave its contents with the information she had received today, hoping it would add up to something new.

The thought was like a cold wind whipping through Vida's chest. What was it Rezel done for the white man? Was the answer in the rest of that song? Car. Star. Far. So far.

Vida folded the letter and dropped it back in the box. There were no new answers, only more questions. She was no closer to Rezel.

Maybe one step farther away. Feeling the tears well up, she rose from the table and walked over to the stove. With a stick of kindling she furiously poked at the embers, raising an intense heat.

She drew her skirt above the thigh. The old scars had grown ashen and tough, but beneath them was still lodged the buckshot, ever working itself closer to the surface. Vida stepped up to the stove. As the burn bit into her leg, she clenched her jaw and swore a silent oath to God. She had stood by and let others take away all that she loved. Nate. The father she used to know. Next time God tested her, He wouldn't find her weak and pitiful. She swore that if only He would give her a second chance, if only He would lead her to Rezel, God would find her tough-minded and strong, fierce enough to strike anybody dead who tried to take what was hers.

Chapter Twenty-Three

DREAMING NATE

The day after Lillie Dee's funeral, the last thing Vida wanted was company. That pesky Sweet Pea had other ideas. That morning she met Vida at her cabin door and said she would walk Vida to work. Though Sweet Pea chattered mindlessly all the way, Vida didn't bother responding once. It nearly took until they got to Delphi proper for Sweet Pea to comment on Vida's sullenness.

"Miss Hazel done wearing on you? I told you, she a pure-dee mess. Don't blame you for being down in the mouth."

No way would Vida entrust this woman with the truth of her grief. She hadn't even told her father about going to Lillie Dee's funeral. Vida shook her head. "It ain't Miss Hazel. She sleeps in her room all day."

"How 'bout her little boy?"

Vida rolled her eyes. "Mean as the day is long, always trying to get my goat. But I guess the worst of it is figuring out how to work them fancy machines. Washing machines and cooking machines and the coffeepot and the beaters and mixers. I ain't never been 'round nothing such as that."

"Now, why don't I drop over today? I'll show you everything you need to know. Ain't that hard. You pick it up in the time it takes for us to have coffee."

"Coffee?"

"Sure, I'll be by around ten, that when Miss Cilly goes to her beauty parlor."

"I don't expect Miss Hazel be happy 'bout me having company and serving them her coffee."

"How she going to know? You say she sleep all day. We be real quiet"

Vida had a hard time believing this brassy woman could do anything quiet.

⸞

Loud or not, Sweet Pea was a good teacher and in less than an hour had Vida working most of the kitchen gadgets. Miss Hazel didn't say boo, and the boy was off to vacation Bible school.

"And if you ever get stumped, come get me. I can always get away, mostly. I visit my friends all the time while they white ladies is out. And Miss Cilly don't never stay at home."

Vida poured them both another cup of coffee.

"No, being a maid to Miss Cilly ain't too bad, once I got her trained in. Course some white ladies is worse than others. Work you to a frazzle. And none of them pay as good as what I used to get from their husbands. You got any cake to go with this coffee?"

Vida's mouth dropped. "With their husbands?"

"Now, don't look at me thataway. Anyhow, I'm a churchgoing woman now. I don't do that no more." Sweet Pea leaned in and whispered conspiratorially, "What's it like living next door to the law? You see him much?"

"The sheriff?" The question startled Vida. "Why you want to know about him?"

Sweet Pea laughed. "Oh, I thought I told you. Him and me go way back." Then she winked. Sweet Pea slid her empty cup away.

Vida was about to clear the dishes when Sweet Pea said, "I remember you asking me once if he talked in his sleep about some boy. I got to thinking. He did ask me the beatin'est thing the first time he brung me to that old shack."

Vida looked up. "What? What he ask you?"

"He was yelling out in his sleep. I shook him awake and I could tell he was coming out of some kind of bad dream. Ask me if I ever heard tell of a light-skinned colored boy in these parts. Ask me if I ever seen one so light he could pass for white. Wanted to know if such a thing was possible." She laughed, "Ain't that curiousome? Never knew what he meant, he was crazy drunk when he asked it. Probably a nightmare of some kind. Don't you reckon?"

Vida didn't answer. She picked up the dishes and went to the sink, turning her back on Sweet Pea to hide the stricken expression on her face. However, Sweet Pea gathered enough to know it was a good time to say her good-byes.

It would be like her father's God to be this heartless, Vida thought, staring blankly out the window.

When Vida closed her eyes, she could barely recall Nate's face. Even when she pulled his picture out of the crate underneath her bed, he seemed more like a dream she'd had one night long ago than a flesh-and-blood boy who had once tugged at her plaits, the fussy little child who couldn't get to sleep unless he was holding on tight to her father's gold chain.

"Hands, Momma. Hands," he would cry. She remembered his words but couldn't hear his voice.

How cruel, that after all her praying to see her son in her dreams, to touch his face, to catch the smell of his skin once more, it was the sheriff Nate came to. He appeared to the one person whose dreams she could never get close enough to overhear.

⁕

Yet that night, for the first time in years, Nate did come to Vida.

Vida is perched in her swing, the one that hung from the porch of her childhood home. Pushing off higher and higher, she kicks up her baby-doll shoes and ruffles her petticoats for the world to see, for Vida delights in the envious faces of the plantation girls as they walk by on their way to chop cotton, dressed in raggedy field clothes and nappy-headed.

Her father in his best preacher's suit, with the golden hands hanging from his chain, tells her, "You are truly blessed to be the daughter of the Reach Out Man." He smiles upon her proudly as she reaches for heaven with the tips of her shoes.

From somewhere comes the shrieks of a baby, and the smile vanishes from her father's face. "Is that baby yours?" he asks. She is too frightened to speak.

By now the plantation girls have come up into the yard, giggling wickedly. In the dream they play their ring games, holding hands in a circle and dancing and kicking. They chant those mean rhymes made up about Vida:

Vida was sewing a hole in her dress
From popping her tail so high,
White man thread her needle,
Right through the eye.

Vida looks up at her father, hoping he won't hear, wanting to deny their accusations. They begin to sing louder, almost shouting:

Vida got her a baby boy,
Bright as a 'lectric light.
That's why she be grinnin'
Cause all she totes is white!

The crying starts up again. And then she sees Nate. He is at her father's feet, grasping for the golden hands. The hands seem to be alive, reaching down toward Nate. They almost touch.

"Tell me the truth, girl," her father says angrily. "Is this baby yours?"

Vida's throat is so dry she can't speak. She desperately wants to put the smile back on her father's face. Finally she blurts out, "No,

Daddy. He ain't my baby."

The crying and chanting grows louder, yet the refrain has changed. The girls are singing and Vida reaches up to cover her ears.

When she awoke from the dream, it was Vida who was sobbing. "I'm sorry, Nate. I'm sorry," she heard herself moan. Through her tears, she saw the darkened form of her father standing in the doorway.

"Vida? You all right?" he asked. "You been calling out in your sleep."

Vida wiped the tears away. "No, ain't nothing wrong," she said. "Get on back to bed, Daddy. I be fine."

He returned to his room. Vida bit her lip. What was Nate trying to tell her? Was he asking her to fix the past? To put things right?

As sad as it made her feel, she would not wish this dreaming to stop. It was proof that Nate was still working in her life, doing his best to reach out to her, to show her the way.

When she fell asleep, she dreamed once more. But not of Nate. Rezel came to her. She saw him clear as day. He was strumming his old beat-up guitar, smiling sweetly at her. His music made her want to dance. He began to sing "Driving a big black car for a big white man," and for some reason it filled Vida with a joy so rare, she smiled in her sleep.

Chapter Twenty-Four

WORD FROM
UP NORTH

A hundred miles north of Delphi, the man's headlights washed across the road sign: WELCOME TO MISSISSIPPI, THE HOSPITALITY STATE. When he read it, he got the distinct feeling that it didn't mean him, so he slowed the old Caddy to five miles below the speed limit. He'd heard about the kind of hospitality Mississippi served up to colored folks visiting from the North. Last year the papers couldn't say enough about that boy from Chicago they found at the bottom of one of those unpronounceable rivers of theirs. Sent that god-awful-looking corpse back to his poor momma. They put him out on display. Thousands of people snaked by that casket to get a look at what Mississippi white people could do when they got it in their minds to welcome you properly.

And Jesus! The stories those Mississippi boys in Joliet told about home-sweet-home. No wonder they ended up in adjoining cells. Life spent bent over double in a cotton field, yassuhing and naw-suhing every white man that could knot a noose—such a life was bound to shortchange a fella when it came to making sound business decisions. Of course, his own crime was the result of an understandable miscalculation. Cutting a man for drawing five of a kind out of a deck he himself had stacked. He figured if the brother could magically come up with an extra ace, he shouldn't have any trouble producing a new ear. The law thought different.

Daylight shifted ever so slowly across the Mississippi landscape, carried on the back of a thick, ghostly mist. As the shapes of trees emerged from the mist, he peered through the vaporous air to see if there really were bodies hanging from every limb.

Nope, he thought, if it wasn't for Rezel, you sure wouldn't catch my ass in this backwoods hell of a hole. But a deal was a deal. Anyway, Mississippi was on the way to the Big Easy, a town tailor-made for an expert gamesman such as himself. In New Orleans, they never stopped dealing and the dice never stopped rolling. The best thing was, nobody knew his face or his con. Be taking candy from babies.

On top of anteing up a C-note, Rezel told him he could keep the car, and the only thing he asked was to drop off a message to some girl he used to be sweet on. Must still be after all these years. Acted like it was the most important letter he ever wrote. Didn't even have an address. Drew out a map to some hick town called Delphi and said to begin asking about her there. "Make sure you stay away from that sheriff," he told him. "Don't let him catch you."

The man had laughed. "Might as well tell me to not slam my dick in the door."

Rezel went on to say she always used to dress in white. It was her trademark. Shoes, socks, dresses, and even little white bows in her hair and on her shoes. Sure sounded crazy. Rezel was kind of crazy anyway. Everybody in the pen was sure Rezel was going to end up singing the blues for drinks and chump change. But the day he got out of prison, a big-shot white lawyer was waiting for him with a job. Personal driver! Let Rezel have his old Cadillacs, like hand-me-down suits.

Crazy. Crazy like a goddamned fox. He hadn't done bad for a boy whose momma was a plantation cook. Lillie Dee. Always crying about his momma, Lillie Dee. Southern boys and their mommas is something else.

Again he wondered what con Rezel had pulled to make that white man do for him like that. Must have promised the man something golden. Be nice to run that scam a few times in New Orleans.

It was almost dawn, and this sign said simply, HOPALACHIE COUNTY, no welcome to it. The name squirmed around in the man's head before it finally leaped to his tongue. "Hopalachie!" he hissed. "Good goddamn."

Now he remembered why it sounded so familiar. That was the name of the river they dragged that Chicago boy out of. And me driving in here with Illinois plates! He noticed that the air now hung heavy with the sour-sweet smell of swampland. Without thinking, he rolled up his window and nervously checked his rearview mirror.

If he turned around and took the long way to New Orleans through Arkansas, Rezel would never know a thing. Why should he risk his neck going through someplace named after a river like that? All he needed was some redneck sheriff asking him what a Yankee troublemaker was doing driving through his personal county.

Nearing the outskirts of Delphi, he told himself he would ask the first colored person he saw, and if they'd never heard of no Snow White, as far he was concerned he had done his duty. He'd drive straight out of Mississippi and never look back.

Avoiding the white neighborhoods, he took a gravel road that seemed to head down toward the river. "I bet that's where they keep their colored folk," he told himself. Sure enough, as he descended the hill, trudging up the road toward him came a large colored woman puffing like she was late for a mess of ham hocks.

"Hey, you! Big Momma!" he shouted out his window. "Come over here a second."

Creola planted her fists on her hips and scowled at the man, her red freckles aglow. "Who you talking to like that? I don't know you from jump, and if I did I'd sure nuff lie about it. You one of the ugliest sharp-faced mens I ever seen. Somebody could use that face of yours to split wood. And why you talk so funny? I *know* you ain't from around here. People 'round here got some manners when they speaking to a lady."

The man held up a hand, trying to stop the woman from making a scene. "Hold on, Momma! I didn't mean to get you riled. I'm just 'turning a favor for a friend used to be from down here, and I'm in bad need of a little Southern hospitality is all. Sorry if I got off on a bad foot."

"Who you know from around here?"

"The person I'm looking for is called Vida. Vida Snow. You heard the name?"

Creola eyed the man carefully. "I ain't got time to talk with the likes of you. I'm already late for work, and Miss Pearl going to have my hide."

"You ain't answered my question. You heard of her or no?"

"Maybe I is and maybe I ain't. How I know you ain't up to no good? Why you keep looking over your shoulder? The law after you?"

"Look, Momma. It's a simple question," he snapped. "Do you know somebody go by the name of Vida or not? Dresses like a fuckin' snowball. I got a message for her. It's important, and she going to want it."

Creola snapped her fingers. "I bet you a fat man you a friend of her brother, Willie. Or Hannah, one. You carrying a load of shine in that car?"

"Yeah, that's it, Momma. I'm her brother's best buddy. Now show me the way, will you?"

"Well," Creola said, eyeing the big plush seats in the car. "I sure could use me a ride. You carry me in your big fancy car, and I show you where she be at. She don't work but a couple houses down from my white lady."

The man reached over and flung open the passenger door.

When they got to the Grahams' neighborhood, Creola told the man where to turn so he could drive up behind the house. "Just climb up on that big porch and she probably be in the kitchen right this minute." With that, Creola took off in a lope to Miss Pearl's.

༄

Johnny was under the porch digging in the dirt when he heard the sound of footsteps above his head and then a knock on the door. "Anybody in there?" a strange voice called out.

The boy scrambled into the daylight, brushed himself off, and clambered up the steps. "Who you looking for?"

The man studied the boy for a moment. "You got a maid in there called Vida Snow?" he asked.

Johnny considered the man for a moment.

"I'm asking if she works here. You following what I'm trying to say? You got a tongue?"

Thinking the man may have come to take Vida away, Johnny decided to answer. "We got a mean ol' colored woman claims her name is Vida."

"Well, where is she? I got to speak to her."

"She's on the front porch. Waiting."

"Waiting? Waiting for what?"

"Waiting for the sheriff."

The man swallowed hard. "The sheriff," he repeated, hardly believing his bad luck, "of Hopa...Hipo...Hap...whatever the hell this county is. That what you saying?"

Johnny pointed. "He lives next door. She waits for him every morning."

"Merciful Jesus!" the man spat. "I done landed smack in the middle of the snake pit." Looking around frantically, he pulled an envelope from his jacket pocket and held it out to Johnny. "Take it," he ordered.

Johnny took a step back.

The man jabbed the boy in the chest with the envelope. "You make sure she gets it, you hear? I ain't got time to hang around and chat with no baby crackers."

Johnny reached for it with dirty fingers. Relieved of his burden, the man flew down the steps, taking two at a time, and headed straight for his car, idling at the bottom of the hill. He took off, throwing gravel behind him.

Johnny studied the sealed envelope. There was nothing written on the outside, except where somebody had typed the single letter *V.* He glanced back toward the kitchen and then took the envelope under the porch. He knew he was doing a thing so bad, he could never tell anyone. Not even his mother. He would have to lie the very best he could.

And he did. When Creola came over later in the day to find out from Vida what it was Willie had sent the man for, Johnny pleaded ignorance, and in the face of all the hard looks Vida aimed at him, he stuck to his story.

Chapter Twenty-Five

A GATHERING

OF MAIDS

It was early afternoon, and Hazel was fighting against the current. Johnny stood at her bedside, beckoning her upward. "Momma. They coming. Wake up."

That's right. Today was special. She remembered that much. Now, what was it? Something good was supposed to happen. Something she and Johnny had been waiting for. But what?

Trying to draw herself up on her elbows, Hazel only succeeded in getting knotted in the bedcovers. She gave up and fell back on the pillows. Johnny busied himself with untangling her.

"They coming today, Momma," he whispered excitedly. "We're going to catch them red-handed, ain't we?"

That was it! They finally had something good on Vida. Today, after weeks of taking double doses of that woman's medicine and meanness, Hazel Ishee Graham was going to fight back.

Over that summer of river rhythms, as the current took and then released her, from up in her bedroom Hazel had studied the cadences of her household. Floyd floated in and out, but he no longer lived in this house. His heart had drifted elsewhere. His smiles and nods merely marked his coming and going, and meant nothing else, like Vida's two warning knocks when delivering food and medicine.

The afternoons brought Johnny, dirty from digging under the porch and breathless with news of fresh outrages, mostly about Vida and her father. Things he wanted her to get out of bed to attend to.

Johnny complained that Levi was always sitting on his bench, preaching out of his Bible, talking to ghosts. Sometimes Hazel could hear the sound of his mower in an adjacent yard. It had a strange comforting drone, like an old woman humming church songs on some faraway porch. She couldn't get angry at that.

No. What little spite she could muster she saved for Vida, who over the summer had remained sullen, sparing no more words than necessary to get the job done. Sometimes Hazel resisted taking the pills just to hear the voice of another woman, but she always regretted it. Vida's words were as comforting as barbed wire. Hazel nurtured her resentment each passing day. That maid had become the living symbol of everything she had lost.

Once, after dinner, Hazel had thought she heard the sound of strange voices, muffled laughter, and the clatter of china. She put it down to the dreaming. That is, until Johnny told her about what Vida was up to—having her maid friends over for coffee, using the house as a break room for the neighborhood domestic help. The more Hazel heard about that, the more riled she got. Vida knew Hazel was helpless to stop her, and she was rubbing it in Hazel's face. Like dancing on her grave. Well, today they would be dancing to a different tune. Johnny had learned that after dinnertime, the whole raft of them were coming over to drink up her coffee.

"When they do," she had promised Johnny, "we'll go storming into the kitchen like Jesus into the temple and drive out that gang of thieves." With right on her side, Hazel was going to show that heartless girl who was the real boss in this house.

"Johnny, you go on downstairs and watch," she whispered. "When they all get here and Vida starts passing out my groceries, you come and get me."

⁓

Johnny innocently situated himself at the yellow dinette table, practicing his alphabet on the back of the electric bill. He could feel Vida looking over at him from where she stood at the sink, finishing up the dinner dishes.

"What you writing on?" she asked over her shoulder. "The light company ain't going to 'preshate you marking up they bill. You might be writing something that makes them people cut off the 'lectricity."

Johnny didn't bother to answer as he drew the big letter *V*.

"You going to have them ABCs writ on everything in this house before school even starts. Anyways, why you fretting so about it? You not 'spected to know nothing yet."

Ignoring her babbling, Johnny cut his eyes toward the porch. He hoped he had understood right about today being the day. He heard the clinking of china as Vida gathered the coffee cups and lined them up on the counter.

"Are them ol' women coming over here directly?"

"That's right. You got something to say about that?"

Johnny looked up at the kitchen clock in the shape of a large yellow chicken. "How many minutes are they going to stay in my kitchen?"

"Till they gets up and walks out the door, be my guess." Vida turned around toward Johnny. "What you staring at? You can't tell time."

"Can't tell it what?" Johnny asked.

"I'm saying you can't read no clock."

Johnny rolled his eyes. He knew that.

After disappearing into the pantry, Vida returned with a can of Luzianne. It had a picture of a smiling colored woman pouring a cup of coffee. Johnny wondered why his father couldn't find a nice maid like that.

Vida broke off the little metal key, fit the tab into the slot, and coiled it around the top of the can, cutting away the lid. A thick smoky smell escaped into the kitchen.

"That's a new can of coffee, ain't it?" Johnny asked, grinding the dot on the little letter *i*.

"Yessuh, I believe it is. Seeing I just opened it."

"I guess coffee costs my daddy a lot of money, don't it?" He looked up at her innocently. "I was only asking."

She was still squinting. "What's your problem now?"

He tried to hold her stare but finally exhaled, to show how exasperating she was, and then turned back to his work. He knew what his problem was—her and that squinty ol' face. She was going to get hers real soon.

◦◦◦

A few minutes later the screen swung open with a screech and there stood Creola filling up the doorway and flinging a shadow over the whole kitchen. She was wearing a starched white maid's uniform similar to Vida's, only a hundred times as large. Under one meaty arm she toted an enamel dishpan.

"Come on in!" Vida called out as she stood by the counter, waiting for the coffee to finish perking. "Plop yourself down and rest a minute."

Creola set the dishpan on the table and pulled out the chair next to Johnny. She squatted down partway and then, after waggling both hands behind her to locate the chair and center it, dropped into the seat with a groan. Johnny grimaced when he saw those poor chrome legs flare outward. These women would surely wreck his mother's kitchen. He sneaked a look down the hallway and smiled. Not too much longer.

Creola glanced over at Johnny's work and beamed. "Look at all them purty letters! What you doing there, Mister John? You writin' the guv'ner? Tell him Creola say 'How do.' " She winked at Vida. "And while you at it, ask him to let my ol' man out of jail for Saddity night. He can have him back first light Monday morning when I'm done with him." Slapping her huge thigh, Creola burst out laughing at herself.

Johnny held up his printing for her to see. "I'm practicing my ABCs. I'm going to school in September." He cut his eyes over at Vida, to see if she noticed how nice he could be to somebody who was nice to him first.

"I told you, ain't no September," Vida corrected. "They be a September. They be a October. Ain't never been no Septober."

"Well, ain't you a big boy!" Creola exclaimed brightly. She grabbed the corners of her apron and fanned her face. She made sure to include Johnny in the breeze, too. "Hardly bigger than a porch baby and can already cipher. You sure nuff going to be teacher's pet."

The screen door sounded again as Vida unplugged the percolator. "Just in time for coffee," she called out.

"Lawdamercy! It's so hot I'm bleeding to death!" exclaimed Sweet Pea. Beads of perspiration glistened on her smooth face. In her arms she carried a grocery sack from the Jitney Jungle. Sweet Pea let out a high laugh. "Y'all, I saw Misery coming up the lane from the sheriff's house, and I swear that woman don't sweat. She cool as a cuke." She placed a hand beside her mouth as if she were going to whisper but didn't. "I guess them high-toned niggers ain't got no sweat holes." Glancing out into the yard with a contrite look, she said, "I better mind myself. She tell her boss on me, he haul my butt off to jail."

"Won't be the first time he haul your butt somewheres," Vida said under her breath. When Sweet Pea shot her a look, Vida asked innocently, "You want coffee, Sweet Pea?"

She gave Vida a forgiving smile. "It might be better if you had something cold to drank. It be uphill from the store, and I run the whole way." Checking the chicken-shaped clock, she said, "I can't stay too long today. Miss Cilly be 'specting me back with her groceries." She set the bag on the counter.

Vida opened the refrigerator. "We got some sweet tea left from dinnertime. Got some orange juice."

"Ice tea hit the spot."

"Well, stand there in front of the fan, and I'll pour you some."

Johnny watched as Vida cracked open a tray of ice and fixed a glass for Sweet Pea. Now she was giving away his mother's tea, too. It was a good thing his momma was going to put a stop to it today. If Vida's club got any bigger, pretty soon they wouldn't have anything left in the house.

Sweet Pea drained half the glass in one gulp. Smacking her lips she exclaimed, "Y'all, it's hotter than a billy goat in a pepper patch!"

"Now, I reckon that be hot!" Creola giggled as she wedged the dishpan into the valley between her massive thighs.

Pushing back a strand of her shiny black hair, Sweet Pea said, "Yessuh! It be as hot as a one-legged ho' in—"

"Mind the boy, Sweet Pea," Vida interrupted. "Ain't nothing he don't remember."

"Oops," she said, "I clean forgot he was there."

Sweet Pea leaned over the fan that sat whirring on the counter. Johnny peeked out the corner of his eyes as she stretched open the top of her uniform, aiming the breeze down her bosom. Noticing him staring, Sweet Pea winked at Johnny. "How you doing, precious?"

Johnny snapped his eyes back down toward the table and pretended to be writing. Whenever Sweet Pea spoke to Johnny he blushed, finding it impossible to speak. He had never seen anybody such as her. Brassy and big-hipped. She always wore shiny red earbobs as big as moon pies and her dress hugged tight every curving and rising of her body. He preferred to watch her when she wasn't looking.

"Cat got your tongue, baby?" She fluttered her eyes at him.

"That boy be ciphering up a fog," Creola said. "Ain't got time for no womens fussing over him."

While Sweet Pea continued to flirt with Johnny, the door silently opened and closed, and before anyone knew it, a bony, light-skinned woman was standing among them, looking around the kitchen with her nose up. When her eyes lit on Sweet Pea, she sniffed once and then sat down at the table without speaking.

"How you, Missouri?" Vida asked, cutting her eyes at Sweet Pea, warning her to behave.

Missouri ironed out the lap of her crisp uniform with the flat of her hand. "I swear I ain't had a minute to sit till now. We been working night and day getting things ready out at the Columns." Then she fell silent, as if waiting for someone to ask her what exactly she had been doing at the Senator's, and while she waited she ran her hand over the top of her head to smooth out her fine white hair, though it was pulled back as tight as a snare drum.

After a long moment of quiet while the other maids traded amused looks, Missouri said, "Me and Miss Hertha been helping the Senator get ready for Miss Delia's birthday party."

"Miss Delia, that's the Senator's younger daughter, ain't it?" Vida asked, knowing good and well it was. "The flirty one."

"Yeah," Sweet Pea giggled. "She be the daughter that *don't* belong in a zoo. Missouri, your white lady so ugly, she has to sneak up on a mirror—"

"The *Senator*," Missouri interrupted, "the Senator is inviting ever important person in the state. I 'spec the guv'nor hisself be there."

Behind Missouri's back, Sweet Pea placed her hands on her hips and made a "lah-de-dah" face. Vida had to put her hand over her mouth to keep from laughing out loud.

"So Miss Delia done been resurrected, huh? Praise the Lord," Sweet Pea said with a laugh. "And everbody thinking she was murdered."

"She got back home last week," Creola offered. "Told y'all she took off to Memphis. And I heard she paid money to get a tattoo put on her patootie."

"Where Miss Delia tell her daddy she been gone to?" asked Sweet Pea. "After the sheriff done searched half the county for the Senator's poor lost lamb."

"Nowheres," Creola answered. "And he don't ask. Afraid she might tell him the truth. And that girl would, too. Don't give a hoot about what folks thinks. Been wild since she was a baby." Creola lowered her voice. "I heared the last one she took up with was a colored boy from Tchula."

A shared sense of unease hung over the crowd until Vida broke the tension. "What you want, Missouri, sweet tea or coffee?"

Missouri pressed her lips together into a thin taut line and smoothed her hair again. "You ain't got nothing else? Feel like a soft drink, myself."

Looking back into the refrigerator, Vida said, "I just mixed up some purple Kool-Aid for the boy. Reckon he won't mind sharing."

Johnny shot Vida a murderous look.

Seeing the reaction on Johnny's face, Missouri smiled a tight little grin and patted her head again. "Po' me a big glass of that Kool-Aid." Johnny held his peace. Her time was coming. There was only one maid left to go, the craziest one of all.

No sooner had he thought this than there came a long slow creak as the screen door pulled back once more. Everyone looked up. It was the Gooseberry brothers' maid, Maggie. Her hair was in its usual state—a squirrel's nest of black and white bristles. Maggie walked with great difficulty, by rocking side to side, as if her legs had rusted long ago and had lost their bend. Her cotton stockings had given up their grip and bunched loosely around her ankles.

"How you doing, Maggie?"

"Ain't it good to see you!"

"You a little down in the hindquarters today, Maggie?"

Seemingly deaf to the chorus of hellos and inquiries about her health, Maggie pulled out the last empty chair and eased herself into it.

Johnny shifted his focus to Maggie and studied her for a while. She was a gruesome sight to behold. Where her left eye should have been, there was only a shallow crater, permanently sealed shut with a ragged flap of skin. When she looked right at a person, which was rarely, she appeared to be offering a sustained wink. Mostly she kept her good eye looking down at her leathery hands in her lap.

"Maggie, you want a cup of coffee?" Vida called out.

Maggie continued kneading her hands. Vida brought the coffeepot over to Maggie and lightly touched her shoulder. Maggie jumped. Her one eye shot open as wide as a silver dollar. "That be the Lawd's truth! Sure is!" she said emphatically, yet to no one in particular.

Vida poured Maggie a cup and eased it in front of her. Eyeing Maggie closely, Johnny tried to figure her out. Whatever she said never seemed to match what was actually going on at the time, always a hoofbeat off from the rest of the herd.

"Johnny," Vida said, interrupting his thoughts, "you get up and gimme your seat. Go on outside and play."

Flouting the fate of Tangle Eye by rolling his eyes at Vida, Johnny dropped down from the chair. This was his cue to go tell his mother it was time.

As Creola began a story about Miss Pearl, Johnny left through the back door, made a dash around the house, and tiptoed in through the front. He was startled to find his mother already out of her room, wearing a robe, hunched on a step halfway up the stairs, an ear cocked toward the kitchen.

"Momma, they all here!" he whispered. "Let's go!"

"I'm trying to hear," she shushed him. "Now they low-rating Miss Pearl."

"But..."

Hazel shushed him again. "Maybe they'll do Hertha next." She was enjoying this more than radio.

Disappointed that their plans had obviously changed, Johnny took a place next to Hazel where he could keep an eye on both the maids and his mother.

Creola was sitting hunched over Miss Pearl's dishpan, shelling Miss Pearl's butter beans and badmouthing the woman she worked for. "Well, you all know how Christian my white lady believes she

is." Creola dropped a handful of hulls in a paper sack Vida had set
by her feet.

"What you say!" Sweet Pea said with a laugh. "Miss Pearl think
she so sweet, she stays out of the rain less she melts."

Out of the blue Maggie exclaimed, "Praise Jesus!" like she was
in church.

Smiling affectionately at her, Creola went ahead with her story.
"Last week Miss Pearl come traipsing in the house and took a perfectly good chair and busted it with a hammer. I asked her, 'What
you doing, Miss Pearl?' She say, 'If you has to know, Creola, I'm
busting up this here chair so Mr. Ramphree from the hardware store
can fix it.' That what she told me. As my word is my bond."

"That woman is crazy!"

"Sure nuff is!"

Missouri, who was always up for defending the white folks,
seemed doubtful. "Now, why she be busting up her own chair? That
don't make sense."

"I told you it was curiousome," Creola said. "Know what she say
when I ask her how come?"

"Tell it, sister!" Sweet Pea whooped. "You done started something now."

"Well, seems while Miss Pearl was downtown on her way to the
beauty parlor, she passes the hardware store. Some gentleman think
she was going inside so he hold open the door for her. Miss Pearl
too nice to tell the man he be wrong and she didn't have no business
in that store, that she was on her way to get her hair fluffed out. No
ma'am, she don't tell him that. So she say, 'Thankee very much,' and
walks on in the hardware store."

Vida and Sweet Pea both told Creola to "hush up," which Johnny
knew meant just the opposite to colored people.

"You ain't heard it yet!" Creola dropped another handful of hulls
into the sack. "When Mr. Ramphree sees Miss Pearl in his store, he
ask her if he kin help her find something. She don't want to be ugly

and tell the man she come traipsing into his store by mistake, so she lies and say she got a broke chair and was looking for some nails and glue."

"Bless her own dear self," Maggie intoned sweetly, rocking her head back and forth, probably lost in a story all her own. Missouri frowned at her.

"Well, that Mr. Ramphree thinks she so sweet, he say he'll be glad to come by and fix up her chair."

Vida slapped her leg. "No ma'am, she didn't!"

"Yes ma'am she did," Creola said with a laugh. "Instead of saying 'No thankee,' like somebody with the sense God gave a billy goat, she go straight home and busts up a chair so the poor man would find something to fix when he got there." Throwing her head back, Creola raised both arms to the ceiling and shouted, "Law, Law! I *told* you that woman was a pure-dee mess."

Maggie looked up with her good eye and saw Vida and Sweet Pea bent over with laughter. Judging the story to be over, she nodded her head vigorously. "Uh-huh. That's right. Sure is."

Johnny thought he heard something behind him and was amazed to see his mother with her hand over her mouth. Had she really laughed?

Missouri shushed everybody. Her ear was cocked toward the stairhall. "I thought I heared something stirring." Both Johnny and his mother froze.

Vida, who was wiping her eyes from laughing so hard, reassured them. "All you probably heard was Miss Hazel's radio. She ain't coming out of her room before suppertime. We got the kitchen to our own selves. I told y'all who was boss in this house."

Again Johnny looked at his mother. The muscle in her jaw was jumping. Otherwise she was still.

"Now?" he mouthed. But she shook her head no.

Sweet Pea fished a couple of ice cubes from her glass and twisted them tightly in her handkerchief. "You right about that Miss Pearl.

She tries to act so nice it be scary." She daubed her throat with her ice pack. "Every time that Miss Pearl comes visiting my white lady, she bound to sneak back to the kitchen and hand me some trashy love story she done read."

"Uh-huh," Creola said. "She got herself into a racy storybook club. When one of them books comes in the mail she runs and hides it so Mr. Hayes don't see. She gives them to you just to get them out the house. And who you going to tell?"

"What you saying! She say she gives me them books 'cause I went to the eighth grade and don't hardly never say 'ain't.' And she say she *approves* how I straightening myself out by giving up the mens and getting respectable work." Sweet Pea shook her head. "I read them ever one and they all the same. About some weak-kneed white woman waiting for a big strong man to come along and pull her butt out of trouble. Miss Pearl say, 'Sweet Pea. It's so nice to know some of *our* colored can turn themselves around and aspire to life's loftier pursuits.' "

"You sounding like her now!" exclaimed Creola.

"What I want to say is, 'Why, thank you kindly, Miss Pearl, but if what you calling the lofty pursuits is counting on a man to rescue your pasty white ass, you can keep your books. I'll carry myself down to One Wing Hannah's and punch in some Bessie Smith records on the Seeburg. That's one lady who know what a man is good for. If Bessie's man ain't home by suppertime, she be moved on to the next pair of britches by breakfast."

"Uh-huh!" Creola agreed. "When the men go hunting, the womens can go fishing." She hooted at herself.

Vida laughed at Creola. "What you know about that? You been with the same man for thirty years."

Sweet Pea whistled. "Never met a man worth thirty years. Whoo-ee!"

Missouri patted the bun on the back of her head and sniffed at Sweet Pea's common talk. "If you so down on men, how come you always seem to be knee-deep in a fresh supply?"

"Don't get me wrong. I enjoys a man's company. But if his company turns bad, then out the door he goes. You can't do that if you counting on love to pay the rent. I pays the way for my own dear self." Shaking her head, Sweet Pea crunched a piece of ice. "Nothing worse than having to abide bad company."

"Praise the Lawd," Maggie said in a low whisper. She appeared to be nodding off.

Vida tried to steer the conversation back to the Senator and his family. "What was y'all saying about Miss Delia a while back? About her being crazy and running off to Memphis?"

"*All* them women in that family is crazy," Sweet Pea said. "Starting with Miss Pearl and ending with Miss Delia. Ever time that girl go missing, which is about once a month, it's katy-bar-the-door and hide your purties, 'cause the sheriff ain't long behind."

"What you mean, hide my purties?"

Creola nodded at Vida. "That's right. You ain't been here long enough. You don't know about the little show the Senator puts on ever time his girl gets a wild hair to take off and mess around." Creola, having seen all this many times before, told Vida that the Senator would right away get in a terrible state, convinced some ungrateful colored man had done his daughter harm. Next he would ride his son-in-law the sheriff until he did something official.

"He sending the fox after the hen," Sweet Pea said under her breath.

"The fact of business is," Creola continued with a chuckle, "everybody in Delphi know that Miss Delia going to come home by her own self. Probably after sneaking off up to Memphis and alley-cattin' with some man. They say she like the white trash the best." She lowered her voice and said guardedly. "Colored boys, too."

Then, like a wet dog, Creola shook her head furiously to throw off the sweat from her mop of red hair. Everybody ducked. "How be ever, you can't tell the Senator that," she said, pushing back the limp strands of her hair with both hands. "No, Lord! Both them girls—Hertha and that Delia—is the apples in his eyes. Can't do no evil. So he tell the sheriff, 'Boy, you better get your ass in high gear and do something about my little princess *now.*' " Creola whooped and stamped her foot. "And you should see that man move that skinny butt of his. Lord!"

Vida wasn't laughing. "I still ain't seeing what that got to do with hiding my purties."

"That's the part I'm up to now." Creola took a loud slurp of coffee. "To *keep* his job, the sheriff got to prove to the Senator he *doing* his job, so he put on these house-to-house searches. Except they ever one start and end in Tarbottom. He go down there and poke through a few of our houses. Stalling the Senator till Miss Delia drags her own dear self home."

"So the sheriff going to walk right in my house one day?" Vida asked.

"What you mean? Probably already has," Sweet Pea said. "He mostly go when nobody's home. And he's bad to pick up things that don't be his. Trifling things. Can't be worth nothing to him. But, to some poor colored person it is."

Creola frowned. "Last year he stole the locket my little niece give me for my birthday."

"Why he do that?" Vida asked.

Creola shrugged her shoulders and picked up a swatter lying on the table and waved it at her face. "Why white people do anything they do? 'Cause they can, I reckon."

Again Johnny looked up at his mother. What was she waiting for?

A heavy silence fell over the group, until Missouri spoke up with a sputter. "You all ain't nothing but a bunch of gossiping ol' hens. Sheriff Brister ain't no man to be disrespecting. The sheriff chosen by a wise God who knows when the people need a firm hand."

"Don't blame God for that man," Creola shot back. "He married

Miss Hertha, is how come he the high sheriff. The Senator's money what keep him running for office. And Miss Hertha's uglies keep him running after anysomebody with a tail to switch." Creola shook her head. "Say when he was a young'un, he went after colored girls. I hear he done moved on from that. Thanks the Lord for small favors." She winked at Sweet Pea, who looked away too quickly, none too anxious for Missouri to know about her times in the woods with the sheriff.

The comment also hit Vida hard, and she made an effort not to show it. She turned her attention to Missouri, trying to be nice. "I bet you part of that family, ain't you, Missouri? I seen how they always making admirations over you."

Missouri glanced at Vida suspiciously. "They do good by me. If you pay respect, you gets respect."

"Ain't that the truth," Vida said. "I bet you know everthing that goes on in that house."

"I reckon. What you rooting around for?"

"Nothing mostly," Vida said, trying to affect only mild interest. "Only something I been meaning to ask you."

"Like what?"

"Like what become of that ol' uncle used to be his deputy?"

"Humph!" Missouri sniffed. "That ol' fool? Sheriff run him off years ago."

"Did?" Vida refilled Missouri's glass. "Now ain't that something? How come he went and done that to kin? Sounds cold."

"Sheriff got good reasons, I'm sure. Anyway, ain't none of your business. Best kept in the family," Missouri said, letting everyone know that included her.

Glancing up at the chicken clock, Creola said, "Look at the time in that bird's gizzard." She caught hold of the table and hoisted her massive bulk vertical. "I reckon I best be getting back to Miss Pearl. She wake up from her beauty nap and find me gone missing, she be some mad. She liable to turn out the hounds."

The rest of the group followed suit and rose from their chairs.

Sweet Pea lifted her grocery bag from the counter and then stamped her foot. "Mercy! I plum forgot Miss Cilly be looking for her dish soap and I been gone all this time. She going to raise sand at me."

Vida disappeared into the pantry and returned with a new bottle of Lux. "Here, take this," she said, handing out Hazel's soap. "We got us plenty."

Johnny shot a glance at his mother. *Surely* that would set her off. They were stealing right from under her nose. But she sat there. If he didn't know any better, he would say she seemed pleased that they'd said all those mean things about white people.

The boy watched as the little club headed for the door. After almost an hour of gossiping and grunting and waggling their heads at each other, and the one with the scary eye mumbling and humming to herself, they exited the kitchen one by one.

His mother had let them go. Scot-free. She had them dead to rights, and now they had escaped. He looked at her and watched disappointedly as she carefully drew herself up and turned back toward her room. He became frightened. Why was she letting Vida win?

Chapter Twenty-Six

MISSING THINGS

No matter how many times she had been here, she was never prepared for the gloom the house exuded. Inside, it was darker than the Grahams', and cooler, almost tomblike. The furniture was ponderous and grave. Latched shutters behind silk damask drapes, their golden rope tiebacks loosened, both kept out the afternoon sunlight and kept in that morning's run of the air conditioner. The ceilings were higher, probably fourteen feet, and although the rooms were densely furnished, the house eerily echoed the slightest sound. It seemed to repeat even the galloping of Vida's heart.

The floor in the hallway was constructed of long, wide planks of heart pine, waxed to a deep honey glow. Over the century the soft wood had been dimpled countless times by the sharp heels of white people now long gone.

The creaking beneath her feet sounded out like thunder as she cautiously made her way into the library. She came to a stop before the fireplace. On the marble mantel shelf, the gold clock's tick-ticking was loud enough to wake the dead. For a moment she stood stock-still on the ancient French wool rug of muted colors and stared up at the oil painting of a long-dead ancestor that hung above the clock.

Vida slowly looked around the room, taking in its contents. She wondered if her own ancestors could have dusted and shined these very heirlooms. A great-great-grandfather could have planed and laid down the very floorboards beneath her and maybe felled the trees from the extinct Delta forests she had heard about, before cotton took over the world.

Vida's interest turned toward more recent times. She had stolen inside the house to watch and to listen, to touch and to gather up smells. She came to glean from the house any trace of a living, breathing inhabitant. Yet in the midst of the splendor, she could detect no sign of the sheriff. She closed her eyes and tried to imagine him in the house. Where did he sit? Where did he eat? Surely not at the grand mahogany table, in a chair with a hand-embroidered seat. Where did he sleep? In the giant four-poster bed upstairs with the canopy as big as the night sky?

No, this was not where he lived. Though she kept up with his comings and goings, watching him swagger to his patrol car in the morning and disappear into the house in the evening, she couldn't imagine him existing once he passed through those doors with the polished brass handles and the beveled glass that distorted like prisms. There was nothing of him here. This was old, and elegant and civilized. Where did a low-rate man such as him disappear to in a house like this? Where did they hem up the sheriff so he wouldn't upset the ways of fine, civilized white people?

One careful step at a time, Vida softly padded up the stairs. She wanted to see the bedroom again. Maybe there was something she had missed before.

Vida knew her way around the house very well by now. When Hertha took the girls out to the Columns to see her daddy, sometimes she would take Missouri along, leaving the house empty and unlocked. If she could get Johnny to take a nap or sneak away while he was busy under the house, Vida was free to roam through the rooms, touching their contents, hoping in some way to brush up against an understanding of Nate's daddy and perhaps bring her one step closer to his downfall, all the while remaining alert for sounds of an approaching car. Stealing her son away was the price the man paid to be sheriff. If it was the last thing she did, she would take that away from him.

Yet so far in all her visits, she had not come upon the sheriff here. No journals or records or old letters. No notes scribbled in a masculine hand. Not even the stink of stale cigarette smoke lingered. The only scents were those of Hertha and her blood relations.

In the bedroom she opened the giant doors of the mahogany armoire, where his clothes were kept. Taking her time, she went through the inside drawers and fingered each item, lifting it up to her face, smelling the fabric of undergarments and socks and handkerchiefs. Vida had never forgotten the sharp, piercing odor of the sheriff when he had fallen upon her. But it was not here. Everything was so freshly laundered as to be absent his presence. Missouri was more of a fact in this house than he.

She closed the last drawer and turned to look at where he slept, a massive four-poster bed with a flowered canopy. Did he ever dream of his son there? she wondered. Lord, she thought, did he even know his own son's name?

She knelt and looked under the bed. There was room enough for her to hide, and then to rise up in the dead of night. He would wake with an ice pick in his heart.

Vida crossed the room and climbed the bed steps. Carefully she sat herself down on the elaborately embroidered coverlet and ran her hand over the duck-down pillows. Did he ever feel any emotion for his son besides hate? she wondered. If not, she would settle for that. For if he still hated Nate, if in his heart he still raged at the boy, then that was evidence that Nate had once lived. Knowing even that would be a great comfort.

She descended from the bed and smoothed away any evidence that she'd been there. Her visit today was almost done. There was only one more place she wanted to look.

Downstairs, Vida stood for a moment in the hall, listening and watching. The house had darkened. It was getting late, and the sheriff would be arriving soon. Yet she heard no engine sounds or tires against gravel, only the clock in the library marking the seconds. She made her way stealthily to a little room off the parlor. She wanted to check the drawer again. In all the house, that one drawer in an old rolltop desk was the only thing kept locked, while silver, gold, and crystal lay out in the open for the taking. Whatever was in that drawer must be important indeed. She was determined to find the key.

She tried the drawer as she always did, and it resisted as usual. Then it lurched open. A fold of paper had wedged itself between the drawer and the frame and had kept the lock from catching. Someone must have been in too much of a hurry to notice.

She removed the paper, and there in the bottom of the drawer was a trove of treasure. Astonished, Vida reached down and stirred the contents about. On closer look, she saw breast pins with colored glass, bracelets going green, broken pocket knives, a tarnished Sunday school attendance pin from her father's old church. Junk. She picked up a dime-store locket and realized what she had found. These were the trifles Creola had complained about, the ones the sheriff had pocketed on his raids down into Tarbottom.

Holding the locket in her hand, she debated whether to steal it back for Creola. Deciding against the risk, she dropped the locket back in the drawer and pushed it shut. As she did, she shook her head in wonderment. This had to be the queerest place in the world! A house where a man can walk in through the door and then completely vanish, without leaving a trace. Where treasures are laid out for the taking and trash is kept under lock and key.

As she turned to leave, she noticed she was still holding the paper that had jammed the lock. She flipped it over and saw that she was holding an envelope. It smelled strongly of perfume. On the front somebody had written simply "Billy Dean." She opened it and found a single sheet of fancy purple stationery with pretty handwriting. It was from Miss Delia.

Maybe her daddy was right. Maybe indeed God had his good days. The letter was exactly what she had been praying for.

Vida shoved the envelope into her pocket and fled.

The very moment he saw Vida leaving through the sheriff's side door, Johnny thought, "Now we got something good on her." From his bedroom window he continued to watch as she scurried back across the yard.

For reasons he could not understand, his mother seemed to have softened her views on Vida. Each time the maids came by, taking over the house, she sat on the stairs and listened yet never sprang their trap. He was beginning to fear that Vida was taking over his mother as well, that his mother was going to be on Vida's side.

But *this* she couldn't ignore.

He found his mother sitting up in bed with the curtains pulled and the radio on, half hidden in the shadows. Tingling with excitement, Johnny jumped up beside her and breathlessly told her all he had seen.

When he was done, she said very softy, "I swan. Tell me again." After he had finished his second rendition, she asked, "Did you see her tote anything out?"

"No ma'am. Her hands was poked down in her pockets."

"I swan," she said again. "Ain't that something."

Johnny thought he saw the ghost of a smile flicker across her face. He had done well. He thought she winked at him when she said, "Let's have us a secret. OK?"

Turning toward the window, Hazel indeed felt her spirits begin to lift. Johnny's news confirmed what she already suspected. Lately she had lost a silk scarf and a hairbrush and a garnet pin. She had put this down to the pills and her volt-damaged memory. That is, until Floyd started complaining that he couldn't find his new gold-plated tie clip or his favorite hammer. The pieces were falling into place.

For the longest while Hazel was silent, gazing off into the distance like a gambler considering how to play a very good hand.

The next morning Hazel heard Vida stomping up the stairs, rattling the breakfast tray. Normally this was the part of the day Hazel hated the most. Vida coming in sullen, as gracious as a prison guard, plopping the tray down on the bed and saying only, "Medicine time, Miss Hazel." But this morning Hazel was certain there would be more words passing between them than those.

Vida rapped twice with a free knuckle, then pushed open the door with her foot. She took one step into the room and spied the empty bed. That stopped her cold. She almost fell out when she spotted Hazel in the armchair over by the closet door, wooden-backed and defiant.

Hazel had dressed herself in her favorite driving clothes, a navy-blue poplin with a box-pleated skirt and a little round hat bobby-pinned to her head. She had even managed some makeup.

"What you staring at?" Hazel asked, unable to hide a satisfied smirk.

"Nothing, I don't reckon," Vida stammered, not trusting what she saw. "Maybe 'cause I ain't never seen you in nothing 'cept bedclothes." She set the tray on the foot of the bed and considered Hazel again. Finally she asked, "What you-all made up for, Miss Hazel? You going out today?"

Sizing Vida up, Hazel said, "Thought I might. If that's all right by you."

"What I got to do with anything?" Vida reached for the glass of orange juice on the tray. "I'm your maid."

"More like my overseer," Hazel muttered.

"Yessum. Well, here your medicine." Vida stuck out her hand. In her palm were the two round pills, one blue and one yellow. In her other hand was the glass of juice.

Hazel set her jaw. It was now or never. "I don't reckon I'll be taking no pills today." Her voice was a bit shaky.

"I reckon you will, Miss Hazel."

"Not if I don't want to."

"Miss Hazel, 'want to' got nothing to do with it. Mister Floyd say you got to. You don't take your pills, I don't get my bonus."

Hazel's mouth dropped. "He pays you a bonus?"

"Yessum. Two bits a pill," Vida said matter-of-factly, as if this were common practice in households across Mississippi.

Her hand was almost in Hazel's face. "Here you go. Swaller them on down."

Hazel took a breath to steel herself. She knew she didn't have energy to waste. "Vida," she said, deciding to get to the point. "Things have been going missing around the house."

Squinting hard at Hazel, Vida asked in a measured voice, "And what that got to do with me?"

"Well..." Hazel hesitated. This was going to be harder than she had imagined. "Well, who else could have took them? I mean, after all..." Then she blurted, "Vida, please don't make me take no more pills!"

Vida, still squinting, thought it out and said, "You trying to blackmail me, Miss Hazel? You calling me a thief?"

"You don't understand. I don't care about the things you took. You see, nobody has to know," Hazel explained in a rush of words. "I don't want to take them pills no more. They make me tired. I can't think. I can't feel nothing. Vida, I don't care what you took. Keep it all. Take some more, I won't tell. I promise. Please. It'll be our secret."

"Miss Hazel, since the day I got here the onliest thing I took from this house is nasty looks."

"But things are missing," Hazel said, desperate now. "Floyd's going to be upset when I tell him it's been you. Don't make me have to tell him."

"You go on ahead and tell it on me if you want. Come on down to Tarbottom and search my house. Everybody else is. You ain't going to find nothing 'cause I ain't took nothing." Vida waggled her open palm at Hazel. Her voice was firm. "Now, you swaller these pills, Miss Hazel, before you get me and you the both in a fix."

The little gumption Hazel had been able to muster for the confrontation was ebbing fast. She panicked. Her one opportunity was slipping away. "But Johnny said he saw you sneaking around in the sheriff's house."

"You think I ain't got the sense of a June bug? If I going to take up thieving the neighborhood, you reckon I'm going to commence with the high sheriff's house? If you think that, then let's me and you call Mr. Floyd and see who he believes." Then she waited, patting her foot to the passing seconds.

Hazel sank back in her chair, defeated. What Vida said was true. Floyd would certainly side with his maid over his wife. Vida's explanation would be best because it was the simplest, the easiest to live with. Poor ol' Hazel was acting crazy again. It was the shortest distance between two points. Hazel dropped her head.

"Want me to help you in bed, Miss Hazel? Or you want to sit up for a while? Same difference to me." Again Vida held out her hand. "Long as you done took your medicine."

Hazel remained slumped in the chair. Couldn't even get a colored maid to be on her side. She had handled it all wrong from the start. She shouldn't have tried to blackmail Vida. Now she had made her mad. She would never listen. And there was so much she needed to tell somebody, even if it was a colored somebody.

She needed to tell about dreams and drowning, and about how it feels to be beat up, bound up, and thrown away, like that poor colored boy in the river. She needed to tell how he still haunted her.

She needed to tell about losing a child she never really knew to begin with, and about how it feels to see the remaining one fretting his childhood away, constantly staring at her as if she were already a dead body on the bottom of the river, waiting to be dragged up, his worried eyes scanning the surface above her, calling out for her; and about how she wanted to reach up through the currents for him, but was pulled back by the weight of knowing nothing she could do would make a damn bit of difference. She needed another woman to tell it to. That and more.

How she believed her husband had other reasons for wanting to keep her down. How Gardenia Paradise was last year's fragrance, and now when he leaned over to kiss her good-night, he smelled of something French and sophisticated. She wanted to tell how her own reflection had vanished completely from her husband's eyes and been replaced by another's.

She lifted her head to see Vida still standing there, unmoved, her hand outstretched. Hazel was a fool to think that just because she and Vida hated the same people, they themselves could be friends and share secrets. So instead of telling Vida all these things, Hazel took the pills as she was told and let herself be put to bed like she was a child.

Closing her eyes, she drifted back to that day she had stumbled across her father's jug in the woods, and how its wondrous contents had lifted her spirits higher than the chinquapins along the creek below her, higher than the hills that had hemmed her in. She had only been a silly, full-of-feelings girl. She should have listened to her parents and kept her eyes shielded against hope. Now she understood. It was important for her kind to steer clear of hope. Not because they weren't capable of it. But because they were unable to sustain it.

Chapter Twenty-Seven

IT'S ONLY

MAKE-BELIEVE

It was Wednesday, and regular as clockwork Delia had arrived right before twelve, ready for her weekly test drive. Floyd, like all the other business owners in Delphi, took each Wednesday as a half day, closing shop at noon. Come rain or shine, she would be there just before he sent Hollis, his shop mechanic, home and locked the doors. That way they could drive off together and no one would notice how long they were gone.

"Well, look who's here!" Floyd said, acting surprised. "Think I might could interest you in trading up today?" He grinned and cocked his head.

"Depends, Floyd," Delia purred.

"On what?"

"On how well you service after the sale."

Floyd blushed. She always made him blush. No matter how hard he tried to play along, attempting to match her insinuation for insinuation, she upped the ante until he had to retreat in embarrassment.

So instead of thinking of something clever to say, he just admired her for a moment. Today she had on a misty sea-green dress made of some delicate fabric as wispy as smoke, causing her to shimmer before him like a mirage. He looked up into her eyes. Even with all her joking, something was different about her today. It was something he didn't know she was capable of. Delia was obviously sad. Though Floyd wasn't one to encourage negative feelings, he asked her about it.

Laughing unconvincingly, she said, "Nothing's wrong with me that a test drive with you won't cure, Floyd."

Still her mood bothered him, somehow making what they were up to more real. "We got to be more careful," he said. "I think we better find another way to meet. You been test-driving that Mercury Montclair for three months now. If word gets back to the Senator—"

"Daddy?" She rolled the bluest pair of eyes Floyd had ever seen, even bluer than Hazel's that day at the Tupelo Rexall. "It's coming up on ginning time," she said. "He'll be too busy to care about anything or anybody except getting his cotton picked."

Floyd knew that wasn't true. The Senator doted on both his daughters, Delia as well as the ugly one. "The Beauty and the Duty," as the sheriff himself had once let slip about his wife and her sister. The Senator would first ruin and then kill any man who harmed either one.

He got up from his desk and walked across to where she stood. His office had windows on three sides and jutted like a peninsula into the showroom, and he came as close to her as he dared, close enough to catch the smell of her perfume and see the flecks of gold in her eyes. How could someone as high-class as Delia really want to be with him? he thought. Somebody who had come out at the Delta Debutante Ball. A woman who wore cashmere like a second skin.

"You sure there's nothing wrong?" he asked again. "You ain't tired of me, are you?"

"Tell me again, Floyd."

"Tell you what, Delia?"

"Stop teasing. You know." She slid her finger slowly up and down his tie, tracing the vertical lines in the pattern. "The reasons you like me." She looked up at him as if the fate of the world rested on his opinion.

His face fired up again, and he quickly scanned the showroom to make sure no one was getting an eyeful. He cleared his throat. "I like you because you're the most beautiful woman I ever seen. I like you because you know what you want and go after it." Floyd smiled bashfully. "Me included."

"Serious, Floyd."

"OK, serious. I like you because you understand the way the world works. And you keep me positive. That's important to a man such as myself. I like you because you make me believe I I can do anything. Make me believe I'm a winner. You—"

"Do I really, Floyd? Do I make you feel like a winner?" she teased. "Well, I guess I wasn't head cheerleader at Ole Miss for nothing. Score, Floyd, score!"

Her laugh was hard-edged now, derisive. "Now *you* be serious," he said firmly. "You're good for me, Delia. That's all there is to it." Floyd moved closer than he should.

No longer laughing, she said wistfully, "I merely distract, I'm afraid. I help you forget all you've lost."

Maybe, thought Floyd. It was true that Delia kept him positive and sure, the way he was before family, death, and craziness ganged up together and conspired to bring him down. Being with her was like spending an afternoon with Norman Vincent Peale. Well, almost.

When Delia looked back up at him, he saw the tears in her eyes. She said, "But I use you, too, Floyd. It's as if we cover each other's losses."

He waited for her to say more, only to see her smile at him sadly.

☙

Later that afternoon he found out what she meant by her comment. They were two counties away and across the river in Arkansas, at their little honky-tonk hideaway on the levee. Instead of her usual beer, Delia was drinking bourbon, and lots of it. She began making jokes about the live entertainment, some local tractor driver with an impossible name, tuning his guitar not five feet from where they sat. Delia tried to think of all the funny words that rhymed with Twitty, some of them not very nice, and laughed out loud in the boy's face.

The boy looked right at Delia and said he was going to sing something he had just written about illusionary love. When that plowboy began growling out his song, Floyd could tell from the tragic expression on Delia's face she wasn't going to make it through the whole tune.

And he was right. When the boy got to

My only prayer will be,
Someday you'll care for me,
But it's o-o-o-o-o-nly make believe,

Delia burst out into loud ugly sobs. Everyone was staring.

Panicking, Floyd rushed her out of the honky-tonk and back to the car, where she cried uncontrollably into Floyd's shoulder. Eventually, sitting there in that hard dirt yard, the poor white boy still grinding out his music from inside the shack and Floyd nervously scanning the darkening grounds, she confessed her secret.

"Oh, Floyd," she cried. "I'm pregnant."

"But we never. . .How could. . .?" Floyd hadn't done much more than hold her close and stroke her hair. She had not even allowed him to kiss her on the mouth.

She pulled back and looked up at him through her tears as if he were an imbecile. "Not *you*, Floyd."

"Oh," he said, at first relieved, then hurt. "Oh."

"Yes, exactly!" she cried. "Oh."

"You been seeing somebody besides—"

"That's right," she said. "And I'm in love with him, Floyd."

As it slowly sank in that he had lost Delia, or rather never had her to lose in the first place, he was overcome by that old crippling sensation. The same one he'd had when Davie died, a trapdoor feeling like he was doing a free fall through space, all his insides floating up and bunching high in his chest. Gripping the wheel tightly as if to keep from being pulled through the floor by an ancient gravity, he stammered, "Who...who..." even though he was certain he didn't want to know.

She wouldn't answer anyway. She did go on to tell him other things he would rather not have heard. She said she was frightened. Her lover had been outraged when she had asked him to marry her. He had made threats. With tears glistening in those cobalt-blue eyes of hers, she looked up at Floyd and said, "It hurts all the more knowing the man you cherish would bring up the topic of killing you."

Despite his sorrow, Floyd could see her point. "Maybe we should tell the sheriff, Delia," he suggested.

That had stopped her tears. "No. No. No," she said, as if that were the stupidest idea in the world. Then all at once her face unclouded and she became thoughtful. Looking at Floyd earnestly, she said, "Floyd, if anything does happen to me, even though in my heart I don't believe he would hurt me, you tell Billy Dean. But only afterwards. OK?"

Floyd thought it a strange request. "After?"

"Promise me," she insisted. "Not before. Only after."

༚

The incident with Delia had sent Floyd for a loop, and his lapse in emotional control caused him to do one of the silliest things he had ever done, something worthy of Hazel. On that last test drive Delia had left a bottle of her perfume in the car pocket, and one day Floyd rode around in the red-and-white Mercury for hours, all the way to the river and back, the windows up and the Chanel open, crying his eyes out.

That's when Floyd hit bottom. It forced him to get a grip on himself. Using his best logic, he began to reason himself out of his grief. He told himself it was to be expected. Everybody knew Delia was a bit on the wild side, with two ex-husbands up North. Take it as a lesson, he told himself.

After only a few days Floyd had mostly put the whole thing behind him. It was a sterling testimony to the Science of Controlled Thinking. If anybody asked Floyd what his greatest secret to success was, as he often imagined them doing one day, he would have to say it was his ability to take feelings that would sink a less mentally trained person and discharge them like so much ballast.

He only regretted that he couldn't tell Hazel how he had handled the thing with Delia. If he could get that one thing through Hazel's head: When you can control your thoughts, you control your emotions. No need for hospitals and pills and such. But no, some people refused to put out the mental courage it took.

Chapter Twenty-Eight

MANY MANSIONS

From where he sat, in the shade of an oak in his own backyard, Johnny studied the crazy old man over at Miss Pearl's, raking the ground beneath her stand of pines. Though he had been watching for quite a while in the midafternoon heat, Johnny couldn't figure out what he was up to. After the man filled his barrow, he would bow his head over the load of straw. Then he appeared to talk at it and make gestures over it. When the man was done with his little ritual, he would wheel the barrow over to the flower bed and spread the straw among the gladiolas and azaleas and then talk at it some more.

Johnny decided to get up close and hear for himself what the man was telling the pine straw. It might be something his mother needed to know about.

"The harvest is great, but the laborers are few," the man said, in a voice unlike any Johnny had ever heard before. It reminded him of thunder rumbling and rivers rushing and trees bending in the wind. Yet it wasn't loud on the outside. It only felt loud on the inside.

The man wheeled his harvest over to the flower bed, with Johnny tagging along behind. It occurred to him that the man was wearing overalls, a hat, and a long-sleeve flannel shirt in the afternoon heat. The shirt was dark with sweat. Johnny thought he should be wearing khaki shorts and a thin nylon shirt like him if he was going to stay outside. "Ain't you burning up?" he yelled out to him.

Levi started at the voice coming from behind him. When he turned and saw the boy, all he said was "No," and then went back to his straw.

Even though the man still sat out on the bench once in a while, Johnny had mostly avoided him. He was Vida's father, after all. But now he decided to get a closer look. As he ventured nearer, he saw that his face was lined with deep wrinkles that reminded Johnny of the folds in his mother's black velvet dress. When the man completely uncoiled himself to give his back a stretch, only then did Johnny notice how tall he was.

Johnny threw his head back to see into the man's face. When the man looked back, Johnny decided those had to be the largest, roundest, deepest eyes in all the world. They were oceans of chocolate, and big enough to see him all at once. Most people's eyes took in little parts of him at a time, his dirty hands or his uncombed hair or his untied shoes. This man's eyes swallowed him whole.

"How come you wearing them long sleeves?" he asked.

The man quickly looked around, as if to see if anybody was watching. "I ain't studying you," he said very low. "Get on from here 'fore you get us both in trouble."

Though the man wasn't being very nice to him, for some reason Johnny wasn't afraid. He wanted to be looked at again with those big eyes of his. So he asked once more, "Ain't you hot, dressed that way? Did Vida make you wear them clothes?" It would be just like her to do something that mean.

The man gave Johnny a bemused look. "Vida? You think Vida puts my clothes on me?"

"I don't know," he said, secretly pleased he had got the man to look at him again.

"Well, she don't. And if you has to know, young man, I dress this way because it makes you sweat more."

"Why you wanna sweat more?"

Levi took off his hat, revealing hair so white and fleecy, it reminded the boy of a lamb he had petted once. Johnny would have petted the man's head if he had offered.

With a bandanna from his back pocket, Levi wiped the inside brim of the hat, without bothering to answer the boy. So Johnny asked again. "So why you want to sweat more, huh?"

"You ask a lot of questions," Levi said. He replaced his hat and then looked down at Johnny.

"Yeah, but why?"

"It be like this here. Sweat makes the air cool. Sometimes you got to get hotter before you can get cooler. Sometimes things got to get worser before they get better. Can you understand that?"

Johnny thought it was something his daddy might say. Maybe the man wasn't crazy after all. To make sure he asked, "You know what my name is?"

The man looked up and again surveyed the yards around him, as if to see who had put this child up to testing him this way. Finally he said, "I reckon they call you Johnny."

"What's yours?"

"Levi Snow."

"Why was you saying them Sunday school words to that wheelbarrow?"

Levi shook his head at the boy's question and then leaned over the load of straw to resume his work.

"You playing like you a preacher today?"

Levi quickly drew himself up again. "I *am* a preacher."

Johnny doubted it. If he were telling the truth, where was the man's preaching uniform, the snow-white suit with the cross-of-diamonds stickpin? "You ever bury anybody?"

"Course. I done told you I'm a preacher. Now you best get on away from here and let me work."

"Davie got himself buried."

"Yeah, I heard about that," Levi said, his eyes swallowing Johnny whole again. "If you believe in Jesus, you going to see him again."

"We been waiting on him," Johnny said.

Levi nodded. "In my father's house there are many mansions."

Yep, Johnny thought, that sure enough sounded like something a preacher would say.

Then Levi picked up an armload of straw and scattered it in the bed of red and white gladiolas while speaking in his special voice. "I send you like sheep among wolves."

As Johnny contemplated how pine straw was like sheep and wondered where the wolves were, the scent of face powder drifted his way. Miss Pearl was strolling through the yard showing her niece, Miss Hertha, her prize roses. Always happy to see her, Johnny called out, "Hey, Miss Pearl."

Johnny couldn't understand what his mother had against her. She had blue cotton- candy hair and carried herself the way the fairy godmother did in his Golden Goose Classics and all the time acted as sweet as she smelled.

She looked over and, upon seeing Johnny, waved her handkerchief and began approaching, Miss Hertha by her side.

Johnny tried not to look directly at Miss Hertha's face. At least he and his mother were agreed on her. Her buckteeth gave Miss Hertha a mulelike appearance, an impression reinforced by a long sloping nose and protruding brow. His mother said that even though she herself had been born ugly and poor, she had managed to do something about both. However, Miss Hertha, born ugly and *rich*, didn't have the least excuse to go around looking like a field animal. His mother had made up a little joke about the woman.

"You know why they named her Hertha?" she would ask.

"Why?" was Johnny's part to say.

"Cause it *hertha* look at her," and then she would giggle.

"What are you-all doing out here?" Miss Pearl asked.

"Just talking to Mr. Snow," Johnny said, trying to be proper around Miss Pearl.

Miss Pearl smiled, yet Hertha was quick to reply. "No, no, child!" she said, shaking her head at Johnny. "Levi here is not a Mister. Levi is a nigruh."

"Leave the boy alone, Hertha. He's only practicing his manners."

Hertha wouldn't be stopped. She motioned in Levi's general direction. "He's plain Levi. Understand, child?" she asked. "Only white people get to be Misters. And one day Levi will call you Mister, but never the other way around. Isn't that right, Aunt Pearl?"

Pearl said nothing. She simply touched her lace handkerchief to her cameo choker. Johnny watched as she used her handkerchief to dab at the moistness that had gathered in dewy drops above her rose-tinted lips. Next her hand went to her neck and then her lips again. For a crippled hand, it sure got around. Then she turned to study her gladiolas, ignoring her niece.

As for Johnny, he hadn't discerned any meanness in Miss Hertha's voice. Instead, it was like someone firmly telling him not to talk with his mouth full or to keep his elbows off the table. When he looked back at Levi, he saw that the old man stood there looking much smaller, his shoulders slumped. He was turning his hat around and around in his hands and his huge eyes studied the grass at his feet. His face did not contradict anything Miss Hertha had said. If Levi didn't mind, Johnny figured that must be the way things were. Anyway, Miss Pearl would say so if it were wrong.

"Well, let Levi get back to his work, now, child," Miss Pearl said. She looked over at the man and touched his arm. "Levi, when you finish up with the beds, the verbena by the front gate needs shaping."

"Yessum," he said, studying the ground. With his head still bowed, he addressed the woman he had known since childhood. "Miss Pearl, ma'am. If you don't mind me asking, next time you see your brother, would you tell the Senator, Levi Snow sends his regards?"

Miss Pearl smiled affectionately at Levi. "Now, Levi, when you want some lemonade, knock at the back door and Creola will fix you some, do you hear?"

"Yessum, I sure will do that," Levi answered, and then bent himself down again to the wheelbarrow.

As Miss Pearl pointed out her gladiolas to her niece, and Johnny stood there wondering if he had missed Miss Pearl's answer to Levi's question, the big reddish maid Creola came bounding out of the house and down the hill to where they were all standing. As usual, she was out of breath when she arrived.

"Miss Pearl!" she puffed, holding a hand to her heaving chest. "It's the Senator on the phone. It's about Miss Delia."

"What now!" Miss Pearl said, clearly exasperated.

Miss Hertha exclaimed, "I just knew my sister would do something to scandalize Daddy right before her party. What's she done?"

"She gone missing," Creola said, puffing.

"Oh, is that all?" Miss Pearl dismissed Creola's message with a wave of her handkerchief. "Tell my brother there's a difference between an emergency and a predicament."

Creola looked at Miss Pearl quizzically and then said, "All I know is the Senator say it's for real this time. He says Miss Delia went out hossback riding and that hoss done come back empty."

"Oh, my," Miss Pearl exclaimed, her eyes shifting to her poor broken hand. "Her horse. That is different."

Hertha wasn't convinced. "She's up to something. I know it. Always trying to get attention."

"Poor Senator," Levi said as he watched the women rush back up the hill. "It going to sure nuff kill him if something happens to Miss Delia."

"Miss Delia?" Johnny asked, at first not remembering. Then it hit. "She's the pretty one," he blurted proudly.

Miss Hertha, who was already halfway to the house, whipped around and gave Johnny a look that made him take a step behind Levi for safety.

"Um-hmm. Boy, you better hide," Levi chuckled, "least till you learn who you supposed to practice your manners on and who you ain't."

⚮

Vida was in the parlor dusting the furniture when Johnny got back to the house. It was a task she saved for this time of the day, just before her programs began. Sure enough, when she finished wiping off the television, she clicked it on and settled back into a Stratolounger. Even when the maids came over for coffee, they had to leave before the start of her first show, the one where a poor white woman told about how hard her life was and they made her queen for the day. Vida always got a real kick out of that.

Johnny stood furtively in the hall, waiting for the set to warm up before he crept past the parlor doorway and slipped upstairs. This was one of the few times during the day he could spend with his mother without fear of Vida calling out for him, trying to meddle in their business.

When he came into her room, the lights were off and the radio was on. She hardly ever went down to watch TV, and when she did, she seemed to tire quickly of all those happy families doing their best to make her laugh.

Today, the radio was playing a song without words. It was the kind of music he and his mother used to make up rhymes to as they drove fast in the Lincoln. Only now Hazel lay there quietly with her eyes closed. Without making a sound, Johnny pulled the dressing table chair to her bedside and seated himself. He stared through the filtered afternoon light at his mother.

Her hair was flattened against the sides of her head and pitifully pooched out on top from lying on it all day. Later that evening he would ask her if he could brush it for her. He looked at the arm that lay crooked on her stomach. Her skin was the same pasty white color as the china poodle that sat next to her on her nightstand, the one his father had given her for a surprise present, for no reason at all. Her fingernails were ragged and chipped, the last vestiges of polish from her failed escape about to flake away. He noticed how the bedspread rose and fell at regular intervals and knew that to be a good sign, having watched his father lean over Davie, yelling at him to breathe.

She needed to get up soon. Time was coming unloose. Countless days and hours and minutes were passing undesignated and unaccounted for, flowing into one another like little streams coursing into an unnamed river. Although Time lived in the clock, his mother was the only one who could tell Time, who could tell it what to do. Time to rise and shine. Breakfast. Dinner. Supper. Time for a story. Time for bed.

Without her, all the ticks on the clock bled together, and he couldn't be sure the day had been done right, that some things hadn't been forgotten and left out. He sighed. So many things to be remembered. Nobody talked about Davie anymore. He needed to be remembered so he could come back home.

His mother took in an extra-deep breath and then, forcing it out, opened her eyes. Neither of them spoke, each watching the other. His mother's face was expressionless, and he tried to make his likewise.

Once, while out driving, his mother had pulled the car to a stop on a country road without warning. She had reached over, touched him on the shoulder, and pointed, all in a way that told him to be as still as he could. Looking along the line of her finger he saw the lone doe. For several minutes he and his mother gazed upon the deer, and the deer gazed back. The world stopped breathing. It was as if the slightest movement of the tiniest muscle would break the spell and frighten the deer back into the woods. So now, Johnny watched his mother quietly, asking nothing from her except that she keep her eyes on him, to notice that he was there.

A single tear trickled down her face. "Johnny, I wanted to be a good momma," she whispered. "I really wanted to."

A few moments passed, and her face went heavy with the weight of some realization. Johnny watched as she closed her lids and said sadly to herself, "Damn."

∽

After tiptoeing downstairs and sneaking past Vida, who was at that moment fussing at a contestant on a quiz show, he went out through the back door, catching the screen so it didn't slam, and descended the porch steps.

The elevated porch was supported by brick pillars, and between the pillars on three sides were giant screens of crisscrossed green lattice, framing a cool patch of earth underneath. Parting the Confederate jasmine that climbed the latticework, Johnny removed a small inset wide enough for a worker who might need to get at the pipes under the house and crawled through, replacing the little latticed door snugly behind him.

Squatting down there in the dirt, waiting for his eyes to adjust to the dark, Johnny remembered what the old colored preacher had told him earlier in the afternoon about funerals and believing in Jesus and seeing Davie again. It certainly sounded like what Brother Dear had said.

Maybe Levi Snow was crazy. After all, he *had* been talking to pine straw. Johnny was beginning to think that the world was chockfull of crazy grown people on the loose, seeing Jesus and preaching to pine straw and sneaking in and out of other people's houses. To think that his mother was the one that got picked on.

Johnny took the little china poodle out of his pocket and cradled it in his palm and kissed it on the nose. "Who do you love the best?" he asked the dog. "Whose side are you on?"

Setting it gently on the ground, Johnny took a silver spoon from his pocket and began digging among the dozens of little mounds arranged in neat rows in the dirt. After he had dug his hole, he placed the dog in a bread wrapper and then laid it carefully in the grave.

"Now, stop that crying. Close your eyes and go to sleep. Jesus is gonna come by soon and get you up. And then you can come home again. I ain't gonna forget."

He scooped dirt over the dog with the stolen tablespoon. There were so many graves now. Johnny was having trouble remembering what was buried where. He crawled along the ground touching each grave with his finger, and as he did, he said the name of the person who had forfeited some possession to his graveyard.

Over the hammer he said, "Daddy," and over the garnet pin he said, "Momma," over the toy tractor, "Davie," and "Vida" over the envelope he'd got from the man with the straight-edged face.

He went on this way until he had recalled them all. Little lost things that others would miss and consider gone forever, and only he knew how to stop their grieving. It was up to him to remember where everything was buried. This was, after all, his graveyard, and here, he was the one who measured out death, one tablespoon at a time.

"Johnny!" came Vida's voice. "I know you up under there. Get on out right now! Got to get you cleaned up before your daddy gets here."

The boy took another moment to finish his remembering. Then he told them all, "Good-night. Sleep tight. Don't let the bedbugs bite."

Chapter Twenty-Nine

TRUE STORIES

The next afternoon found Vida hurrying upstairs to make sure Hazel was set for the next hour or so. She hated being disturbed when her friends were visiting. In the bedroom the lights were off and the radio was on low. So as not to wake her, Vida gently closed the door behind her and quietly descended the stairs.

Hazel flipped opened her eyes and turned off the radio. She rose up out of bed, groggy, put on her robe, and dragged herself to the door. Carefully easing it open, she peeked out and, seeing that the coast was clear, took her listening post on the stair. By that time Johnny had tiptoed up to join her.

For Hazel, in this summer of drugs and depression, the time she spent listening to those maids carry on in her kitchen, loud talking and low-rating everybody they knew, was the only thing that kept her going. She wouldn't miss a session for the world. Something about the way those colored women could tell it on people. It was one of the few things that did her heart good anymore.

When Vida returned to the kitchen, Creola was already telling the maids about how she had overheard her boss, Hayes Alcorn, Miss Pearl's husband and Delia's uncle, carrying on about a men's club he was forming.

"That man getting crazier-actin' every day," Creola said. "Ever since that hoss came back by hisself, he keeps telling Miss Pearl,

'This nigger problem done got outa hand.' "

Vida pulled out a chair for herself. "How come he already know a colored man done it? How come he know anybody done it? Ain't even found her body yet."

Creola shook her head. "She dead, all right. They found her pretty silk scarf dangling on a branch reaching out over that whirly pool near to Bryson's Bayou. She probably floated all way down the Mississippi by now."

"Well, she mighta fell off in that whirlpool by accident," Vida suggested. "It's slick on that bank." She knew the spot well. It was near her father's praying ground.

"Girl didn't slip," Missouri said, her eyes glaring at Vida. The sheriff's maid was acting as if it were her own sister who got drowned instead of her white lady's.

Enjoying how riled Missouri was getting, Vida became flippant. "Maybe she flung herself in there on purpose. Don't always take a colored man to make a white woman do something crazy. They's a dead cat on the line, if you ask me."

The group was quiet for a moment, waiting for Vida to hang some meat on her suspicions, but she said nothing more. For now she wanted to keep the contents of the purple-and-white letter a secret. Especially with Missouri present.

"Mr. Hayes say it's got to be a colored man done it," Creola said. "Mr. Hayes say the colored done got above theyselves. He say we getting some dangerous ideas from the outside."

"What kind of ideas we been getting?" Vida asked.

"Oh, about voting and integrating and sleeping with the white folks. He told Miss Pearl his little club going to take care of the colored problem once and for all. White supremer he calls hisself now."

"Praise Jesus," Maggie sang out. "He rule supreme."

"He sure do, Maggie. 'Cept we ain't talking about Jesus right now." Creola was growing angry. "We talking about a little no-assed varmit calling his own puny self supreme. Mr. Hayes is foaming at the mouth about some colored preacher named King over in Alabama. Said he done outfoxed the bus company and the whole town of Montgomery. He say Mississippi going to be next."

"Colored man do that?" Vida asked. "How?"

"He got all the colored folks together and told them to stay off them buses till they could ride up front like first-class citizens."

"Sure!" Sweet Pea squealed. "I read about it in one of them colored papers from Chicago somebody was passing round at One Wing Hannah's. But it wasn't no man who got it started. It was a colored woman done it."

"Goodness gracious!" Creola said. "If Mr. Hayes knew that, he sure nuff have a duck fit."

"Her name Rosa somebody. Parks, I think." Sweet Pea continued. "She riding back home from work on the bus and wouldn't let go her seat to a white man. Say she was too tired to move."

"That what she say? Too tired to move?" Creola started laughing as if that was the funniest thing she had ever heard. She began singing the words like a gospel song. "Too tired. Too tired to move. Law! Law! Too tired to move." She laughed harder, setting her mighty breasts to wobbling.

Sweet Pea and Vida broke up, too. Maggie mouthed the words, but didn't seem to recognize the tune.

"Um-hmm!" Creola said, wiping her eyes. "I know how Rosie feels. Bone weary. Ain't that something? So that's what started it all. Rosie not getting up off her feet."

"Rosa," Sweet Pea corrected. "Hauled her off to jail for it."

"Thank you, Lord!" Maggie sang out, sounding as if she thought the more colored folks in jail the better.

"Rosie a maid?" Vida asked.

"Rosa, I believe her name was," Sweet Pea said. "No. Weren't no maid. I believe it said she sewed clothes."

"Law, Law," Creola chuckled to herself. "That's what we sure nuff need around here. Somebody too tired to move for the white man.

Maybe Rosie come here, you reckon? We throw together a club like Miss Pearl and her white lady friends. League, they call theyselves. I 'spect we can be a league just as good as they can."

Sweet Pea slapped her hands together. "Yes ma'am. We can be Rosa's League of Uppity Colored Maids!"

"We ain't got no buses," Missouri said flatly.

"That ain't the point," Vida snapped. She wasn't in any mood to hear Missouri take up for the white man today. "Somebody need to teach the white folks in this town a lesson or two. Can't keep messing with us the way they do."

"Who been messing with you?" Missouri challenged.

Vida bit her tongue.

Creola answered for her. "That boss of yours, for one. Sheriff been tearing up every colored house in Hopalachie County looking for who drownded Miss Delia. How many white doors you 'spec he busted down?"

"The sheriff doing his job," Missouri said. "What he was elected to do."

Creola stomped her foot, rattling the dishes and sloshing the coffee out of the cups. "*I* sure didn't elect him. *I* can't even vote in this county."

Vida had never seen Creola this upset before. Her face freckles were glowing as bright as lit cigarettes on the inhale.

"What you want to vote for?" Missouri spat. "What you care which white man get elected?"

Vida couldn't help but smile, seeing Missouri tempt her fate with Creola this way.

The large woman shifted her bulk and then leaned in toward Missouri, getting right in her face. "I tell you how come me to care. My baby niece only just turned fourteen and I seen the way that man is looking at her. I can tell he ready to go back to his old habits. If I gets the vote, your sneaky-eyed, bony-assed, fork-dicked boss sure be out of a job."

Missouri's face swelled up like a biscuit in a hot oven. "Voting is the white man's business," she said, clenching her teeth. "Ain't no colored preacher or no uppity girl from Alabama named Rosie or Rosa neither one going to make it otherwise. All they do is leave a mess everybody else has to live in." While they all shot her furious looks, Missouri continued to lecture them righteously, "We need to keep our minds on the Lord, not on the vote. The Good Book says, 'Pay honor to God.' "

"And everything else to the white man," Vida snapped.

Missouri smiled her tight little grin at Vida. "We could all take a lesson from Vida's daddy," Missouri said. "Sheriff say he used to be a biggety preacher out in the county till he got hisself mixed up in this voting mess. Course y'all see how he do more yard work than preaching nowadays." Looking quite satisfied, Missouri puckered her lips and took a noisy sip of coffee.

There followed a charged silence. Vida knew they were looking for her to say something in his defense, but she kept quiet. What could she say? "You wrong about that; Daddy was a white man's nigger like you, Missouri"? Explain how he had curried favor with white folks, thinking he would have him an angel when he needed it?

Then Vida smiled. She knew how to get even with Missouri. Thinking again of the letter she'd found at the sheriff's house, she said, "I bet I know who Miss Delia was carrying on with."

Before Vida could tell her theory on the matter, Sweet Pea piped up. "You mean it's true? Here I was thinking it was crazy talk. "

Vida was confused. Had Sweet Pea heard about Delia and the sheriff? "You know?" she asked.

"About Mr. Floyd and Miss Delia? Sure! I heard some old drunk down at Hannah's talking about how they seed the two of them out at Friar's Point. Being mighty close, they was."

Up on the stair, Hazel's shoulders slumped. Johnny looked up at her. "Momma," Johnny whispered, "are they talking about Daddy?"

Hazel didn't answer. She didn't even breathe. Slowly she rose up from the stair, went back into her room, and closed the door behind her, shutting Johnny out.

Johnny looked back down the stairs. These women had hurt his mother. It was all Vida's fault. If his mother wasn't going to get rid of her, he would have to. And he knew how to make it happen. Just as soon as the sheriff got home.

Chapter Thirty

THE CITIZENS' COUNCIL

B ack at the dealership, Floyd stubbed out his unsmoked cigarette and slowly got up from his desk, clicked off the light, and pulled the blinds so Hollis couldn't see him. Standing there alone in his darkened office, Floyd took a handkerchief from his back pocket, wiped his eyes, then blew his nose. He needed to be alone for a few minutes to pull himself together.

Settling behind his desk again, he took a deep breath and closed his eyes. He had to get his attitude right. Get back on top of things. After all, attitude determines altitude. Floyd blew his nose again and dropped his head down on the desk. He tapped his forehead against the laminated surface. "I'm a winner. I'm a winner. I'm a winner."

He had just got over losing Delia, and now it looked as if he would have to start all over again. Two days ago, after he had got his attitude back on track, Brother Dear had called, saying Delia had been drowned. It almost killed him this time, imagining her lithe body floating face down, her blond hair a silky net for leaves and twigs and river trash.

Only Wednesday, she had been standing right here in his office, smiling at him, tossing back her hair in that free and easy way of hers, eyes bluer than they had a right to be. For a moment he thought he could detect a whiff of her perfume and hear her silvery laughter.

No matter how hard he tried to push Delia into the past where she belonged, she refused to budge. He tried muttering his favorite motivational sayings, but his guilty mind would have none of it and countered by churning out dire prospects for his future. It occurred to him that he was probably one of the last people to have seen Delia alive. That would make him a suspect.

And wasn't he a witness of sorts? Delia had told him directly that her boyfriend had threatened her life, surely crucial information the sheriff would want to know. He had promised her he would tell if anything happened. Yet how could Floyd explain to the sheriff where he got that little piece of news without revealing his own lusting heart?

Oh, my God! he thought, as he began mixing and matching facts in his head. There was that phone call from Hayes Alcorn, about a meeting at the barbershop. He'd said it was important and had to do with the future of Hopalachie County, and he needed Floyd's help. The sheriff and some others town leaders were going to be there. Maybe it wasn't a meeting at all. They were setting him up for an arrest! That was it. It was a trap. They were going to surprise him so there wouldn't be a scene.

It might not be such a bad idea to leave a little early, drive around town and collect himself. Maybe arrive at the barbershop before Hayes started up the meeting. That way he could get a sense of the crowd. Not that he had anything to be worried about.

⁓

Pulling down the visor of his truck, Floyd reread his saying for the day: IT'S NO GOOD BEING A MENTAL GIANT IF YOU REMAIN AN EMOTIONAL PYGMY. As he drove up and down Gallatin, committing the saying to memory, trading nods with folks as they emptied the stores and headed on home for supper, Floyd's spirits gradually began to lift.

He gave himself a little pep talk. Attitude was everything, and he needed to keep his on track. Couldn't let this Delia thing get him down again. He had overcome worse. Take yesterday's saying,

"Whether you think you can or you think you can't, you're going to be right." It was all a matter of not getting detoured into negativity.

By the time he got to the barbershop and stepped in through the door, tripping the little bell, there was already a crowd gathered. Hayes Alcorn, Brother Dear, and half a dozen others looked up and nodded at Floyd, and said their heys and howdys. The old shoeshine boy grinned his usual grin. Nobody looked at Floyd with the least bit of suspicion, not even the sheriff, who sat slouched in his chair acting bored.

The others quickly returned to the amusement at hand, making fun of the new Yankee in town who was at that moment up in the chair getting his hair cut by Slats. As usual, Marvin was taking a ribbing about his accent.

Hayes Alcorn was the one talking now. "Say 'school' again, Marvin."

Marvin said it, making it sound like two words. Everybody howled.

"Y'all hear that?" Hayes said. 'Skew all.' Don't that beat all."

Marvin joined in the laughter. He even looked like a foreigner, with his swarthy complexion and severely pocked face, probably from some northern affliction. Marvin had married a local girl and got the job managing the Nehi bottling plant in Greenwood. But he was a real sport, never taking himself too seriously.

Floyd took the chair next to Hayes and felt so relieved he decided to join in. "What's that thing on top of your house, Marvin?" Floyd asked.

"Roof," Marvin said good-naturedly. There was another round of laughter.

"Sounds like a dog barking, don't it?" Floyd said with a chuckle. "Ruff. Ruff."

Marvin cocked his head so Slats could get the stiff little hairs on the side of his neck. "Now that you mention it," Marvin said, "a Negro family who lived in our town pronounced it that way. I think they were from down South."

An ugly silence gripped the barbershop. It was Hayes who finally spoke up. "A *neee*-gro?" he said derisively. "What's that?"

Marvin's face reddened. "Negro. The colored. You know."

"How many *neee*-groes lived in that town of yours in New York?" Hayes asked, dead serious.

"Illinois."

"Same thing."

Slats whisked the back of Marvin's neck. It was almost quiet enough to hear his falling hair hit the floor.

"There were two families, I believe," Marvin answered carefully. They all shook their heads in amazement.

"Well, you ain't no expert then, are you?" Hayes said. "What we got down here is *nigruhs*."

Then Hayes glanced over to the shoeshine stand. "That right, Ben?"

The balding colored man who had been sitting there quietly smiled bashfully and said, "That's right, Mr. Hayes."

"See," Hayes said. "We expert at nigralogy."

Trying again, Marvin said carefully, "Nig-gruhs. Is that how you say it?"

Hayes slapped his leg and guffawed. "We gone make a Mississippi boy outa you yet, Marvin. You know, you can't just marry into it."

There was an immediate burst of relieved laughter from the crowd. Slats carefully loosened the barber's sheet from around Marvin's neck and then whipped the cloth in the air with a loud crack. Snippets of coarse black hair rained on the floor.

Marvin paid Slats for the haircut and bid the group good-bye, chuckling to himself and repeating, "Nig-gruh. Nig-gruh," as he walked out the door.

At that moment Shep Howard, the insurance agent, walked in with Gaylon King, the publisher of the *Hopalachie Courier*. They took chairs along the wall with the others.

Hayes Alcorn rose to his feet, which everybody always joked was a quick trip for Hayes, considering how short he was. "I think that's everybody. Slats, would you mind pulling the blinds? It's time we started up."

Hayes stepped up into the barber's chair and looked down with great satisfaction upon the gathering of county leaders. Not a hair over five-foot-four, he was a man who enjoyed being looked up to. Even though he was Princeton-educated, he took every opportunity to prove to people he was still one of them, only more so. That including speaking as if he'd never got out of high school.

While Slats pulled the blinds, Ben hurriedly packed away his tins of polish, trying his best not to make a sound. He carefully folded his blue apron, laid it on the shoeshine chair, and then moved like a phantom across the shop floor, opening the door in a manner that kept the bell from ringing. Though the day was fair, Ben stuffed his fists in his pockets and hunched up his shoulders as if he were stepping out into a bitter wind. Slats locked the door behind the old man.

Hayes cleared his throat. "Before we get started, I want to thank y'all for the prayers and all the kindness you've shown to my wife, Pearl, the Senator, and me. And I'm sure I can speak for Billy Dean and Miss Hertha, too. You-all made the unbearable a bit more bearable."

A quiet murmur rose up from the group of men as they crossed and uncrossed their arms and shifted in their chairs. Again Floyd imagined all the eyes were now on him and that Hayes was about to dramatically point a finger and accuse him of illicit test drives with his niece.

To Floyd's relief, Hayes turned his attention to Billy Dean. "And I think we should continue to keep the sheriff in our prayers as he pursues the monster responsible."

The sheriff, who was sitting cross-legged, slouched down in his chair, did no more than nod in Hayes's direction, seemingly more interested in flicking the lid of his cigarette lighter.

After Hayes let a little memorial silence pass, he announced, "Well, that brings us around to why I asked y'all to come today." He reached down and gave the lever on the chair a little pump, sending him up a couple of inches, and then continued. "All this integration mess coming out of Washington, D.C., is giving the nigruhs ideas that they can get away with other things. Take what's going on over in Alabama right this minute. One solitary nigruh woman refused to take her rightful place in the back of the bus. And now not a single nigruh in Montgomery has ridden a city bus for nearly a year. How she do that? Not by herself, you can be sure. They being organized against us, gentlemen. And it's not just Alabama. Y'all know as good as me this talk about equality is nothing but a Jewish-Communist conspiracy. A way to mongrelize America by letting the nigruhs have their way with our women." Hayes let the obvious sink in.

Was Hayes implying that Delia had been molested by a colored man? A surge of feeling for Delia welled up in Floyd. He gripped the arm of the metal chair and tried to think of something positive to stem the sadness. Well, at least they were looking for a colored man, he told himself. That got him off the hook. Then he hated himself for thinking it.

Hayes continued, "Seems every other county in Mississippi has already formed them a Citizens' Council to resist it at a local level. Now, Delphi, being the progressive town we are, needs to get on the bandwagon before we get left behind. I think it's up to us as forward-thinking county leaders to get the ball rolling."

Denton Prevost, who had planting interests in the Delta along-side the Columns, asked, "How's the Senator going to feel about this council thing? I can say for a fact, he don't abide the Klan in this county."

Hayes nodded. "You right about that. Why, many a time I myself have heard the Senator say, 'Hayes, the only thing worse than the Klan in their white sheets is the Supreme Court in their black ones. Neither one,' he'd say, 'got no business telling me what to do with my niggers.' "

There was a round of appreciative laughter for the Senator's sentiments and Hayes's fine impersonation—laughter from everybody except the sheriff. Floyd was keeping a close eye on him, and right now Billy Dean seemed bored to tears. As Floyd watched, the sheriff lit a cigarette and inhaled, blowing a jet of smoke up at Hayes in his barber's chair throne. It might have been judged an aggressive gesture if Billy Dean's expression revealed anything other than pure indifference.

Hayes cranked himself above the cloud and continued. "I know for a fact, if the Senator wasn't grieving, he'd be here with us this evening, lending his support. You see," he said, "the Citizens' Council is not the Klan. We're not a bunch of yahoos out to lynch nigruhs. We are a legitimate association of civic leaders who will work with the Sovereign State of Mississippi to protect its constitutional right to be led by white people." He paused to survey the group face by face, and then concluded, "We'll have the full support of the state and its governing bodies, as well as the complete backing of my brother-in-law, the Senator. We're talking respectable."

"Like the Rotary?" Floyd asked hopefully. He sure didn't want to be involved in anything mean-spirited.

"Yes," Hayes heartily agreed. "Exactly. Upright, patriotic men operating by the full light of day in the community's best interest. Why, just between the eleven of us here plus the Senator, we can evict, cancel credit, cut off commodities, or fire anybody who wants to make trouble. No need for lynching anymore. This is a new day for Mississippi." Hayes paused while a murmur of agreement rippled among the men.

"Why, over in Indianola, they got it locked up so tight that if a nigruh even starts *thinking* about voting he has to leave the county to earn penny one. And it's all on the upright. No violence. Ain't that right, Sheriff?"

Not bothering to look up, Billy Dean stubbed his cigarette on the sole of his boot and yawned. "Yep," he said. "That's the way to do it, awright. Lawful."

Floyd noticed Brother Dear nodding vigorously, throwing his vote firmly on the side of nonviolence. He didn't know what it was about some of these people in Hopalachie County. Back in the hills there was a lynching now and then, but these Delta people were damn near nigger-crazy. Talking about how the colored wanted to take over the schools and the churches and the bedrooms. To hear them tell it, every white woman in the county was in danger of waking up one morning and finding herself impregnated with a colored baby.

On the other side of the coin, it certainly was an honor to have been asked to be a founding member of this thing. The way Hayes explained it, maybe this Citizens' Council wouldn't be so bad. What harm could it do? It sure wouldn't hurt business any.

"Well, if we all in agreement," Hayes said, "I think we should start by electing officers and then plan a recruiting drive to get the rest of the county involved."

Floyd even took vice president.

჻

Floyd stuck close to the sheriff after the meeting broke up, pretending to be going in the same direction. As Billy Dean reached for the door of his cruiser, Floyd stopped in his tracks and snapped his fingers. "Sheriff!" he called out. "Something come to me this here second. Something that must of slipped my mind before." Floyd hurried over to where the sheriff stood waiting for his revelation.

Floyd began talking in a rush. "Delia was at the dealership one day last week looking to trade in, and she said she sure loved that Mercury Montclair we had on the side lot, but then she said she didn't know if the fella she was seeing would like it, and I told her why not surprise him and see if he don't, and she said he hated surprises and that he had threatened to kill her over the last one she give him."

Floyd waited for the thousand follow-up questions he had practiced the answers to. The sheriff looked at him unblinking. "Well,
how come I didn't bring it up before," Floyd said, proceeding with
the interrogation he had imagined, "was I didn't think she was serious about it. You know how you can get so mad at somebody you
love, you liable to say things you don't really mean in a million years?
I was thinking it was that kind of thing. How come me not to mention it before now."

Floyd knew he was talking too much for an innocent man, and
his face began to burn hot. He just couldn't seem to get his mouth
stopped. "You know what I mean," he rambled on. "I thought it was
one of those things, like we all do. Like, 'I'm gonna *kill* you, Hazel.'
You know what I'm saying, don't you, Billy Dean?"

Floyd was finally able to get himself to shut up. The sheriff studied him coolly. After a long moment he reached to open his door
and turned back to Floyd. Without a hint of emotion, Billy Dean
said, "I'm sure you're right about that. Done the exact same thing
myself on occasion."

The sheriff drove off, leaving Floyd on the sidewalk a free man.

Pulling up to the house, Floyd had convinced himself for the thou-
sandth time that everything was going to be fine. Like his book
said: "To rise above your petty problems, tackle even bigger problems. Successful men are known by the size of the problems they
choose to focus on."

Today his fellow citizens had entrusted him with grave respon-
sibilities. By anyone's standards, Floyd was a successful man. An
important man. A man of the community. A man who could be
trusted with larger problems and purposes. Yes, at last he had a firm
grasp on things.

The house was dark when he stepped in the door. Vida had left
hours ago, and Hazel would be asleep in her room. It was the solid,
reassuring quiet of things under control. Yes, he told himself again,

things were going to be fine. "Johnny!" he called out in the dark. "You here?"

Johnny came bolting down the stairs at the sound of his father's voice. "Big Monkey!" he called out. The boy ran over to his father and bounced happily up and down at his feet.

"Hey, Little Monkey," Floyd said.

Floyd lifted Johnny up, not thinking. He only felt love for the boy, wanting to share with him the exhilaration of the moment. He swung the boy downward and then raised him fast on the upswing, as if he were about to toss him into the air. Yet this wasn't Davie, who had trusted Floyd's grip.

Even before Johnny's scream, Floyd felt it. He himself was pierced by a panic so absolute it shut down his senses. Losing his balance, he staggered forward, holding on to his son for dear life. After reeling there in the dark for what seemed an eternity, he was able to set Johnny down, carefully, both feet on the floor. Still trembling, Floyd knelt down before the boy and looked into his face, only to see his own terror repeated in his son's eyes. Floyd reached out and drew Johnny to him again. This time he began to sob, clutching his boy to his chest.

Chapter Thirty-One

A BURNED-OUT SHACK
IN THE HEART OF THE WOODS

The cruiser was well hidden behind a curtain of kudzu-strangled pines. As he sat waiting, Billy Dean flicked open and closed the lid of the nickel-plated lighter. He didn't know why he'd bothered taking it. Just couldn't seem to help himself when he saw stuff lying around. He had quite a collection now, mostly dime-store flash. The kind of thing niggers hold dear. The kind of stuff his mother had cherished.

He snapped the lighter shut on the thought.

A couple of maids walked by yammering. He cricked his neck out the window to get a look, and then resumed flicking the lighter.

Normally Billy Dean wouldn't mind driving down into Tarbottom in broad daylight to arrest somebody. Today, however, he didn't want to be seen, didn't want to risk it getting back to the Senator. He had to be careful. When it came to Levi and his family, the Senator made it clear they were off-limits. He hadn't trusted Billy Dean from the very beginning on that count. He remembered how suspicious the Senator had been when Billy Dean told him somebody had burned down Levi's church for starting up all that voting business.

The Senator had been infuriated. "Levi's church, hell!" the Senator shouted. "That was *my* goddamned church!"

How was Billy Dean to know the Senator had built it himself, to keep his field hands contented? "I reckon the Klan burnt it down," Billy Dean had said, thinking as fast as he could.

"What Klan?" the old man asked, eyeing Billy Dean doubtfully. "I don't tolerate no Klan in my county messing with my labor. Daddy and me ran them out back in the twenties."

"Musta been from somewheres else. Lusi'ana Klan, maybe."

"What about that little boy?" he asked. "Who shot Levi's grand-baby? That don't sound like no Klan to me."

"Boy's daddy done it," Billy Dean answered. "Found another mule kicking in his stall. Got crazy jealous and shot wild. He prob-ably up to Memphis by now."

"All this happen in one night?"

"Big night," Billy Dean said lightly.

"Yeah, big load of shit, if you ask me." The Senator had been blunt. "Here's the quick of it, Billy Dean. From here on out, you let Levi and them alone. If anything happens to him or his, I'm going to hold you personally responsible. Got it? I done run the Klan out and it'll take a lot less to drop-kick your sorry ass over the county line. The nigruhs in Hopalachie County are *my* business. Levi Snow is *my* nigruh."

He blew a thick cloud of cigar smoke at Billy Dean. "I'll take your word this once about that voting business, but I swear, if I ever hear anything different, if anything ever happens to Levi, if you lay one hand on him or his girl or his boy..." The Senator stubbed out his cigar in his silver ashtray. The gesture wasn't lost on the sheriff.

"Yes sir. I hear it. They your niggers. Not mine."

"Good. And now that we having this nice father–son chat," the Senator had continued, "let me tell you one more thing I got on my mind." The Senator had tilted forward in his chair and slammed his elbow on the desk, pointing his trigger finger straight at Billy Dean. "I know your kind, Billy Dean. Common as pig tracks. If I ever find out that you been fooling around on Hertha, I won't bother kicking you out of the county. I'll personally bury you ass-up, right under my back step, just so I can tromp on it every morning on my way out the door."

Thank God for the Senator's stubborn pride. If he and Levi ever had a heart-to-heart, Sheriff Billy Dean Brister would be history. The experience had made an impression on Billy Dean. Since that one close call, he had sworn off colored women. Except for Sweet Pea, of course. One nigger baby looking like him running around the county was plenty.

Sometimes he wondered who got the best end of this deal. For two terms he had done the Senator's bidding as his plantation sheriff—patrolling the train station to make sure no tenants skipped town owing the Senator money, keeping the local yahoos away from the colored prisoners until the traveling electric chair could get to town, closing down the jukes during times of short labor, shooting up any stills not personally sanctioned by his majesty, not to mention trying to keep his ugly-as-sin daughter happy.

Now, to add to it, every day the Senator was hounding his ass to "find the nigger that killed my little girl!" He was going to have to come up with something pretty damned soon to satisfy the Senator on that count.

Billy Dean tossed the lighter and snatched it in midair. On the other side of that same nickel, he had become accustomed to the jangle of the handcuffs and the tug of a pistol on his hip, deputies who had to do for him. For the first time in his life, Billy Dean knew how it felt to have something to lose, and it wasn't that bad of a feeling. This was as far as his kind ever came. He sure wasn't going to let somebody's colored maid come between him and that.

Through the tangle of trees and vines, Billy Dean saw Vida. That gold-toothed whore was with her. He pocketed the lighter. After letting them walk a little farther down the road and out of earshot, he cranked the engine. Then he slowly pulled out from the trees and rolled after them, coasting at a snail's pace with his foot on the brake.

They never even glanced around.

Pulling up alongside, he leaned across the seat and glowered at Vida through the opposite window. "You! Girl! Get in the back."

When Vida didn't respond at once, the sheriff slammed the car into park, sprang out, and marched around to the other side. He jerked open the back door and shoved Vida inside, striking her head against the roof edge in the process. "I ain't got all day," he said, banging the door shut.

As Vida sat hunched in the backseat, holding her head, he looked at Sweet Pea, whose face was stupid and blank. "Keep on ahead, minding your business, you hear?"

The sheriff got back in the car without another word. He just drove. A light rain began to fall. Every once in a while he checked Vida's expression in the rearview. Cold as a stone. The same way she looked every morning and every evening when she stood outside the Grahams' house, staring him down. No sir, he thought to himself, no colored girl was going to kill his gold-shitting goose.

༄

They were miles out of town and speeding down a road that coiled through the bluffs as it ran north. The sun had already dropped below the tree line and the fields were mostly shadow.

Eventually the sheriff turned off the blacktop and onto a gravel road cut on a deep downward slope that would inevitably strike out into the open Delta. Before reaching the bottom of the descent, the sheriff turned again, this time onto an ungraded and much narrower road cut between high earthen banks. The farther they traveled, the narrower the road became and the more disused it looked, until it was nothing but a double footpath with goldenrod and jimsonweed growing up between.

When there was no path left at all, the sheriff pulled to a stop. Sitting off in the growth of weeds and brushwood sat a half-burned shack, much of it covered with vines. It leaned crazily to one side, as if the green twisting tentacles were ever so slowly lowering the house into the underbrush.

The sheriff lit a cigarette and then sat motionless, looking off in the direction of the house. Vida stayed dead still in the backseat. She was damp with fear. Her hand was down in her bag, her fingers firmly gripping the wooden handle of the ice pick.

From the glove compartment the sheriff produced a half-pint of whiskey and then got out of the car. He opened her door. "Out." It was the first word spoken since they'd begun their journey.

Still she didn't move. Looking down at his boots, considering her options, she tightened her grip on the pick. When she saw him reach for her arm, she jerked her hand out of the sack, empty. She struggled to exit the car on her own, revolted by the thought of his touch. On her feet, Vida's legs buckled and she nearly fell, finding her balance just before the sheriff shoved her, sending her stumbling into the wild tangle of a yard.

Briars bit her legs, but she kept moving toward the house, clutching her sack. She stopped when she got to the fire-scorched porch. There were no steps.

"Keep on ahead," came the dry growl from behind her. He pushed her again and she caught herself against the plank edging.

She hoisted herself onto the porch and walked toward the door. Each step made a loud hollow sound that seemed to reverberate through the woods. The sheriff followed close behind.

Once inside the shack, Vida saw that the far wall was mostly burned out, nothing left except charred boards. The vines had stitched over the breaks, keeping the house dark and cool, the smells thick and musty. All the windows were busted out, and dirt daubers busied themselves around the stone fireplace, filling in the gaps where the chinking had fallen out. It was past twilight and the house was alive with shadows, half-real shapes that seemed to loom about in the room, vanishing when looked at straight on.

Vida's eyes adjusted to the dark. She noticed broken chairs and pieces of a table strewn across the floor; against the wall was an empty pie safe, its screened door hanging askew like a broken arm. The place gave off a sense of death and despair.

Vida judged the distance across the floor to the window. If she didn't get shot first, she figured she'd make it in three steps and then take off into the woods. Or, if she could get a grip on her pick...but again she felt his hand at her back. He shoved Vida so hard, she went stumbling through a doorway into the back room. On the floor in the corner lay a ruined cotton mattress, its striped ticking darkened to a dingy brown. Strewn about were dozens of empty whiskey bottles, a chair with the cane seat busted out, tatters of old clothing. It was exactly as Sweet Pea had described it.

A flicker of hope rose up in Vida's chest. Maybe Sweet Pea would find Willie and tell him what had happened! Willie had a gun. Could Sweet Pea remember where this shack was? Then just as suddenly, the hope vanished. She remembered that Willie had gone to Louisiana on a run for Hannah. Vida was alone in the world with this man.

The overpowering smell in the room was not of old smoke, but of rot and mildew. The stench, laced with her own terror, gripped Vida's belly. More afraid of the mattress than of the gun, she turned to face the sheriff. She did not dare look into his eyes, yet she could feel them running over her body like cold hands.

The sheriff opened the whiskey and flung the cap across the room. "Go on, girl. This what you been wantin', ain't it? To get a close-up view? Well, here I am. Take a look."

Vida began to shake. Still she kept her eyes riveted to the floor.

Then he roared, "I said *look*, goddamn you!"

She tried, but was able to raise her eyes only to the level of his badge before dropping her head again. All she heard was the pounding in her ears and the ugly grunts as he drank from the bottle. When he spoke at last, his voice was like the cold edge of a blade to her throat. "What kind of games you playing with me, girl?"

Still she remained mute. She closed her eyes and saw Nate's face.

"What's the idea, you working right next door to me?"

"Needs the money," she was able to mumble.

"The Senator know how you done run off his place?"

"Yessuh," she said. "He know it. We all paid up with the Senator."

"And what you doing with that whore?"

"Who that?"

"You know the hell who. The one you was walking with."

"She ain't a whore no more." Vida bit her lip, not meaning to contradict him.

He laughed. "Sure thing? She been revirginated, I reckon."

"Yessuh. She Miss Cilly's maid now."

There was another pause while the sheriff raised the bottle and took a long pull. She lifted her eyes for only a moment and saw him wiping his mouth with the back of his hand. He had seen her look. Again he laughed. "You still wearing white, I see."

"Yessuh," she mumbled.

"Same as the first time I seen you. I bet you remember that night good, don't you, girl?"

"Yessuh," she said, thinking again of the ice pick the sack held.

He took a step closer to her. "What was his name?"

"Whose name?" She knew, but she couldn't believe he had really meant it.

In a hoarse whisper he said, "The boy's name."

"The boy you. . ." Vida said, stopping short of what she had intended.

"*Your* boy," he said. "His name. What was it?" He moved closer again.

Her head still bowed, she could see the pointy toes of his boots. She began again,

"The boy. . .the boy you kilt."

Once said, now she had to find the courage to study his face. His reaction meant the world. Would his expression at least tell her he remembered that night? That in one blast of a shotgun he had destroyed the lives of her son, her father, and herself? Did it matter to him at all? She lifted her eyes. The room went perfectly quiet. In that moment, nothing else existed except for the man's face and the message it held.

She saw his thin, pinched lips, his jaw that jutted out sharply, the dip in the chin like a thumbprint. Yet nothing in his face moved, except a muscle under his ear that hardened and released and hardened again. Then she dared to glance quickly into his eyes. There was nothing. Nothing apart from cold and darkness. She shut her eyes to him.

"Wha'd you call him?" he asked, terrifyingly patient with her. "How old would he be?"

"Nate," she said, thinking how peculiar to be telling a father the name of his own son. What would he do with it? What *could* he do with a name?

"Nate Snow," he said almost to himself.

"Nine years old," she said. "He would have been nine."

She waited for more, but he only stood there holding his bottle at the level of his star, still nothing telling on his face. She glanced quickly at his eyes again. They were as dead as burnt-out coals.

No longer able to bear not knowing for another second, Vida blurted, "How come you asking me that? Why you want to know?"

He smiled, as if amused at her boldness. "No reason particular," he said coyly.

"What you going to do with me?" she asked, though she was now certain he meant to hurt her bad. "Why you carry me out here? What you want?"

The sheriff drained the bottle and tossed it out the window. She heard it land with a clink somewhere out in the brambles. Sensing that his eyes were no longer on her, she looked up and watched him as he slowly surveyed the room, as if he were able to see what she couldn't. Vida half expected something to melt out of the shadows.

That's when she knew it. What this place was. If thinking about someone made it so, she knew this man better than any man in her life. Fearing him. Studying him. Turning him over and over in her mind, till she believed she could prophesy his movements. This was where Billy Dean Brister belonged. This was where he watched his mother burn to death. This was where the biggest part of him was buried, what he kept coming back to find.

It was as if Billy Dean had snared her thoughts and didn't like them one bit. He struck like a rattler. Sudden and swift, in the blink of time between two thoughts, he had her by the throat.

Vida fumbled at her bag. Before she could touch her pick, he flung her bag across the room and lifted her by the neck to her toes. "Think you smart, don't you? Spying on me. Sneaking in my house."

The sheriff's face was in hers. His breathing was hard, and she could smell the sourness of whiskey. His eyes had caught fire. "You know what I'm going to do to you now, don't you?" His spittle flew into her face. "Answer me," he said.

He had cut off her breath. "Nosuh," she gasped.

"Nosuh, Sheriff! Nosuh!" he raged. "That it? That's all you niggers know how to say?"

Vida couldn't have said anything else if she'd had to. The sheriff's face was now a glowing ember at the center of a darkening sky.

He pulled the gun from his holster and carefully placed the bore against Vida's temple. He eased back the hammer, and like thunder she heard it lock into place. "Let this burned-down shack be the last thing you see. My daddy set fire to it, his own place, before he'd let the bank take it. And that's how far I'll go to keep what's mine. Shooting you ain't going to mean jackshit to me."

The red ember that was his face burned out.

∽

When Vida came to, she was lying with her face flat against the stinking mattress. She had no idea how much time had passed. She only knew she was still alive. The second thing she knew was that she hadn't been raped, not yet.

The house was dark and cool now. A breeze stirred in the room. She reached to touch the searing pain in her throat. When she turned herself over, the sheriff was standing several feet away. He seemed to be studying her through the dark.

"Girl," he said, his voice low and even. "I'll say it once. Stay out of my house. Away from my wife. Away from my girls. Do you understand that?"

"Yessuh," Vida whispered hoarsely.

"And next time your daddy tries to get a message to the Senator, through Pearl or anybody else, he'll be one dead nigger. Tell him."

"Yessuh."

"Now, you be a good girl and let sleeping dogs lie." The whites of his eyes shone in the dark. "Remember, I'm watching you. Like you watching me."

He reached down and picked up her sack. After he removed the ice pick, he tossed the sack on the mattress. "I'm glad we have reached this understanding," he said, eerily formal. "Now, let's you and me get on back to the car."

As the sheriff headed toward Delphi, Vida rubbed her throat, thinking hard about the man driving. She had more questions now than ever. Why hadn't he killed her? He could have, easy. Nobody would have been the wiser. Killing now must be so easy for him. The letter she had taken from his house proved that.

Yet he had let her live. Why? she asked again. To carry a warning to her father? Why hadn't he killed them all long ago? She could think of no reasonable answer. Any more than she could figure out how a little colored boy could draw so much hate from a grown man.

⁓

Vida had no idea what time it was when the sheriff pulled over at the spot where he had picked her up a lifetime ago. He simply told her to get out. In the dark of a starless night, she stumbled down the hill and through the mud to Tarbottom.

When she neared her house, she could see Willie's car parked in front and his silhouette on the porch.

"Vida!" he shouted, jumping to his feet and scrambling down the steps to meet her in the yard. As he approached she noticed the pistol he was toting.

"Vida, you all right?" He strained to see her face in the dark.

"I'm fine, Willie. Please, put up that gun."

He shoved it in his belt. "I been driving 'round the country for hours looking for you. Sweet Pea was waiting at Hannah's when I got back from Louisiana. She was crying so hard I couldn't hardly make it out. Then she told me about the sheriff. I tried my best to find you, but. . ." He paused, narrowing his eyes. "What he do to you, Vida?"

She looked up at the darkened cabin. "Where's Daddy at?"

"Inside, sleeping. I ain't told him nothing. Said you was out visiting."

Vida was relieved. "Don't wake him up. Come on. Let's go around the back to the kitchen."

Once inside, Willie got the lamp lit, then turned to Vida. Seeing her holding her neck, he grabbed Vida's wrist. She resisted, but Willie was stronger.

Her skin was already bruising. Willie spat, "That son of a bitch! I'll kill him." His hand automatically touched the gun. Gripping Willie by the arm, she drew him down into a chair, then sat down next to him. "Willie, I'm all right," she said in her calmest voice. "Let it alone. It don't hurt." She managed a smile.

Willie stared angrily at her throat, his jaw clenched. Vida could tell he was ashamed, probably because he hadn't been there to stop it. "Willie, listen," she said. "I know how to get the Senator to turn on the sheriff. Just like he did on Daddy. I found a letter from Miss Delia. Him and her—"

"That's real good," he said evenly.

Vida reached over and shook him by the shoulder, trying to

break him out of his mood. "Willie, now we can get him. We got to play it right, but we got to do it soon."

He looked into her eyes and, as if hearing for the first time what she was saying, smiled tenderly. "Yes, Sister. I want that, too."

He got up, went to where his special coat hung on the back of the door, and retrieved a milk of magnesia bottle from a hidden pocket. Setting it on the table beside Vida, he said playfully, "How about a drink? Might do you good."

"What you meaning by this?" Vida asked, having to smile.

"Open it and take a swaller."

"You crazy? Don't need no laxative. I ain't backed up."

"Go ahead on and open it. It ain't what you think."

She unscrewed the top and lifted it to her nose. "This is hooch!"

Willie laughed. He was his smooth, charming self again. "It was my idea. I make deliveries to white women all over the county. They rather get it from a colored man who ain't going to tell it on them, like a white bootlegger might do. Smart, huh?" He laughed again. "I pretend I'm from the drugstore dropping off medicine to constipated white ladies."

"You crazy," Vida said, unable to keep from laughing with him. She gave his hand a pretend slap. Vida screwed the top back on and handed the bottle to her brother. "But leave me out of your schemes." She reached up and touched her neck.

Willie's face went serious again. "Sister," he said gravely, "I thought you might could use you a drink."

"No," she said, "it don't hurt that bad."

"No. Not that." Willie was speaking very carefully now. "I got some news, too, Vida."

"What's happened?" she looked toward the front room. "Is it Daddy? He done something, ain't he?"

"No, it ain't Daddy." Willie reached for her hand. "Now listen to me. While I was in New Orleans picking up a shipment, I stopped off to shoot a little craps."

"Willie, I told you no good going to come out of that kind of living. What trouble you fell in now?"

"Just listen, Vida. There was this boy in the game, and when I told him where I was from, he said he had been through here once. Back in June, he said it was. Vida, he said he came to Delphi looking for you."

"For me? Why. . ." Then it dawned on Vida. "Creola said there was some man come looking for me at the Grahams'. I told you about him."

"Vida, he swear he brung a letter for you. From Rezel."

"Rezel! Lillie Dee's boy?" She gripped his hand tight enough to stop the flow of blood. "Oh, my Lord almighty in heaven! You got the letter, Willie? Give it to me!"

"I ain't got it, Sister. He said he left it with the Graham boy."

Then her eyes flared. "That damned white boy! He got my letter!"

⁓

It was everything Willie could do to keep Vida from taking off that minute to grab Johnny out of his bed and shake him senseless. She reluctantly agreed to wait until morning.

She didn't sleep the whole night through, and by first light she had figured out where the letter had to be. She didn't bother with breakfast or even with waking her father. Instead, she threw on her wrinkled uniform and raced up the hill toward the Grahams'. She was the only one on the road.

Halfway there, the sun had already disappeared behind a weak gray sky. A misting rain had started to fall. She had forgotten both her parasol and her hat, and the fine mist gathered on her skin into droplets that trickled down her face. She didn't notice to mop it away.

When she arrived at the Grahams', she didn't bother going inside and headed straight for Johnny's digging ground under the porch. After she'd crawled through the little door, she stopped.

At first she couldn't see a thing. She waited there, on her hands and knees in the dirt, for her eyes to adjust, and when they did, she saw a piece of white paper that seemed to be growing out of the ground. Her heart began to race. Was that it? She crawled in that direction. There was another one. And then another. Rows and rows of scrap paper—used envelopes, grocery lists, bills, paper plate— each piece run through with a popsicle stick and stuck in a dirt mound like a sign. Dozens of them.

She plucked one out of the ground. In crayon was written the word "Daddy." Scooping up the dirt with her hand, she found one of Mr. Floyd's tie clips. Other signs read "Momma" and "Davie." Frantically, she began tearing the sticks out of the ground, one after the other, reading the names, until finally Vida found the one she'd been looking for. A marker with her name drawn in black crayon. She dug down into the ground with her fingers, pulling out fistfuls of dirt until at last she saw, lying in a bread-wrapper coffin, an envelope with a neatly typed *V* on its face.

Vida's first reaction was disappointment. "This can't be from Rezel," she told herself. "This writ with a typing machine."

With her hands shaking like leaves, she carefully tore off the end, blew into the envelope, and fished out a single page of white stationery.

Sitting there under the house in dim morning light strained through lattice, she moved her lips to the words.

Dear V,

I'm sorry I haven't tried to reach you before this. There are too many reasons, none of which make any difference now. Besides, I know how the white folks down there like to read the colored's mail. I was especially afraid to send something with your name on it. After Momma passed, there was no one I could trust to send a letter to.

For years, I told myself it would be best if you knew nothing. I'm still not sure I made the right decision, but when my friend said that he was going down that way, I took the chance of him finding you or your family.

First off, the boy is fine. If you haven't heard, soon after I left Memphis I was sent to prison for a couple of years. It was impossible for me to keep him. There was a man who was real good to me through it all and he said he would take him. He and his wife are raising him as one of their own. They love him and he has nothing to want for.

V. they are white people and the boy is passing for white. The white life is the only life he knows.

I can't tell you where he is. It may break your heart to hear this, but you must realize that he doesn't remember Mississippi or his short time there.

Please try to see that it is best this way. Mississippi is not a place for a colored man or boy. Pray for him and wish him the best. Let him have his chance now.

I won't be back either. I hope you and your family are well and weathered the storm all right. I'm sorry I let you down.

Sincerely,

R.

She stared at the paper for a long time, unblinking. Then she hardened her face and said out loud, "Nosuh. Rezel didn't writ this letter. This was writ by somebody with book learning. Reads like a teacher done it."

She shook her head at the letter, denying what it said. "Ain't none of it the truth. How could it be?" She had to disprove it before it killed her.

She forced herself to remember back to the last time she'd heard from Rezel, weeks after Nate's funeral. She went over every detail of that night.

༄

She remembered standing in the parlor of their old house, looking out of the window. It was nearly dusk and time to begin her nightly trek to Lillie Dee's cabin. It had rained most of the day, and the low-hanging clouds threatened more, but there would be no stopping her. Even the persistent pain from the gunshot wounds couldn't keep her from taking to the road.

"You going to get wet," Willie warned. "Ask Daddy to carry you."

Vida glanced over at their father, who sat in his chair in a darkened corner, fingering the links of his gold chain, the one Nate used to cling so tightly to. She looked out the window again.

"It might be lightening up some," she said, studying the paler shade of gray on the horizon. "I be all right." Then she whispered, "Willie, I got a good feeling about tonight."

Willie smiled, not saying she always had a good feeling, when she left.

As she walked past his chair, Levi took no notice of Vida. Anyway, it wouldn't do any good to ask him to drive her the five miles to Lillie Dee's. He refused to leave the house anymore, afraid he would be absent when the Senator finally sent for him. Any hour now, any minute, word might arrive and Levi would be called into conference with the Senator, his oldest friend, the man he used to be boys with. All Levi needed was one conference and the world would be set right again.

Vida knew the truth. Levi had been out to the Columns so many times in the past two months, the Senator had sent word through Lillie Dee that if he wanted to speak to Levi, he would send for him, and to stop coming around and bothering the help.

The day after the fire, when nothing remained of his church but a pile of ashes smoldering behind a kerosened cross, rumors began to spread about how Levi must have been working with the NAACP, trying to get the vote. His deacons were quick to turn him out, forever marking him as a troublemaker bound to draw the white man's fire wherever he showed up to preach.

Vida reached for her parasol hanging by the door and was taken by the memory of the day it had arrived, and how she and her father had danced around the sun-drenched yard in a shade brought from Memphis. She turned back toward him and almost called out that she loved him, wanting only to draw the same from him.

When she saw him sitting there in his make-believe world, the words caught in her throat. Things would never be the same between them. She knew that now. Had known it since that day in the graveyard.

❧

By the time Vida neared Lillie Dee's place, she was limping, but it didn't slow her down. She had learned to put her weight on the parasol like a walking stick.

Lillie Dee's cabin sat in the darkness, back off in the field her boys had worked before they left her one at a time and headed up North. There were no lights on in the house, but Vida knew Lillie Dee was there nevertheless. She always ate her supper in the Senator's kitchen, and later he had one of the tractor drivers take her home, where she would sit outside rocking on her porch until it was time for sleep.

Vida approached the shack and heard the sound of the rocker creaking like a rain frog in the night. She made out Lillie Dee's silhouette on the porch. When the rocking stopped, she knew that Lillie Dee had spotted her.

Vida sucked in her breath, braving herself against the old woman's first words. Would it be the usual discouraging greeting: "Baby, I ain't heard one lonely word." Or would tonight be different?

Lillie Dee called out brightly, "I bet you a fat man that be Vida Snow coming down my path!"

Vida's heart leaped to her throat. For the first night in weeks and weeks, Lillie Dee was glad to see her.

"Say it, Miss Lillie Dee!" Vida shouted, running the rest of the way, splashing puddles as she went. "Say you got word. You did! I can tell."

Through the dark Vida could see Lillie Dee lift her hand. It held an envelope. Vida dropped her parasol on the porch and grabbed at the letter, letting out a shriek.

"Light the lantern there behind you and read it out loud. I

couldn't hardly tell one word from t'other. Except I'm sure it be from my boy. I knows the writing for Rezel's name."

Vida's hands shook so she nearly dropped the globe. It took three matches before she got the lamp lit. As the kerosene sputtered, she fumbled with the envelope. She was so excited she couldn't get it open. So she held it to her chest and shut her eyes tight. Vida was sick with fright.

It had been the only choice, she told herself yet again. Her father had sworn to her it was for the best. He'd said it had been God's will, the man passing out face down in the cotton after firing off his shotgun. Never seeing what he had hit. It had been God working on the old uncle's heart that had made him run up to where Vida lay bleeding and Nate screaming, telling her to get her baby out of the county that very night.

"Better yet," the man had said, "get him out of the state of Mississippi."

Even as Vida frantically searched her child's body for wounds in the dark of the field, she could hear the panic in the uncle's own voice. "Bury an empty grave box," he said. "I'll vouch the boy's dead." He glanced over to where his nephew lay. "I know Billy Dean. It's the only way he ain't going to hunt the boy down. He's got it in his head if the Senator finds out that's his boy. . .Well, once Billy Dean gets ahold of something, he's bad as a snapping turtle. Won't let go till lightning strikes him in the ass."

The old man tried to get Vida to her feet, but she was too weak to stand. He hefted her into his arms. Trembling and bloody, she tried to read the man's face in the moonlight.

"But girl, if you do it," he had said, smelling of sour mash and shaking as bad as she, "you can't never tell it. Be the end of me and you both." He looked down at the child that clung to his pant leg. "End of your baby, too."

That night as he tended her wounds, her father told Vida that God was giving her a second chance. Before the man had shown up with his gun, she had refused to send her baby away. Now he said they didn't have a choice. They had to act fast. Perhaps they could ask Rezel's help after all, her father said, since he was so determined to go up North. It would be a simple thing to sneak Nate to safety on the train. It would fool the man.

"I'll even pay Rezel's way," her father had said.

"Without me?" she cried. "No!"

"It's the only way we can save the child," her father had said. "Rezel's oldest brother got a family in Memphis. That's not far. He can drop Nate off with them. They take good care of him. He be safe there. We won't have no explaining to do."

"No!" she cried. "I can't let go of my baby."

"Just for a while," her father had pleaded. "We can go get him soon as you get healed up and I conference with the Senator. I promise."

⌒⌣⌒

Vida clutched the envelope to her chest and whispered, "Oh, God, please show me the way to Nate."

She opened the letter and then held the paper to the light. First thing she did was drop her eyes to the bottom of the page. Sure enough, there was Rezel's name. He had finally written. The night he caught the Memphis train with Nate, Rezel had promised he would write as soon as they got to his brother Toby's. That was so long ago.

Taking a deep breath, Vida began to decipher the wild scribble. As the words piled up, she shook her head in disbelief. Then she read the letter again.

Lillie Dee leaned forward in her rocker. "What's it say, baby?" She waved her hand in front of her face, swooshing the night insects drawn by the light.

"Rezel say he got to Memphis."

"Praise the Lamb!" Lillie Dee clapped her hands together. "They made it 'live out of Mississippi."

"But, Miss Lillie Dee," Vida said with panic rising in her voice, "they ain't there no more." Vida turned the envelope over and checked the postmark. It was true.

"They ain't? Where is they?"

"They couldn't find Toby. They in Chicargo."

"Chicargo," Lillie Dee said to herself. "Cold-sounding word."

Vida went through the letter yet again.

"Chicargo," Lillie Dee repeated. "Where that be at, exactly?"

Like a stone falling through water, Vida slid down against the wall to the porch floor. Her leg burned as if aflame. To quiet the pain, she tried to recall the map that hung in the front of her classroom. The one with greens and blues and yellows she ignored year after year, when it was not important to know where any place in the world was, except home.

She shook her head hopelessly. "I don't know where it be at. Maybe on the other end of the river. Maybe clear on the other side of the Promised Land."

⁂

Vida wasn't aware of how long she sat there under the porch, amid Johnny's graves. She didn't even notice when Floyd walked out the kitchen door and descended the steps to his truck parked between the house and the dry-docked Lincoln.

At some point, she told herself she should be grateful. "Least he's still alive," she said without conviction. "That's something."

Yet she also knew that he was alive to some white woman. A white woman he was now calling Momma. He didn't know Vida at all.

"And if he ever do see me," she thought, "who he going to see? A nigger, is who." She breathed in and forced out the breath, her shoulders caving in on the exhale, as if all at once feeling the cumulative strain of eight years of waiting without word.

"I'm dead to my boy," she said bitterly, staring at the letter. "Worse than dead. He one of *them* now. Nate, you ain't never going to want me for your momma."

Later, inside the Grahams' kitchen, Vida sat trancelike, staring at the letter spread out on the table before her. She only moved to touch her throat. This morning she had even forgotten about Hazel's pills.

The kitchen had grown steadily darker with the weather, and she hadn't bothered to turn on the lights. As the thunder began to rumble outside, her only response was to clasp her hands and lay them on top of the letter. The unlit kitchen rapidly filled with shadows.

She looked up. There was the boy, wearing his pajamas and sleep still in his eyes. He stood there, a grave look on his face, considering her carefully. Knotting his brows, he asked, "What's the matter? Why's your dress so dirty?"

She gave him a searing look. In a bloodless tone she said, "I been up under the house. You want to guess what I found?"

Johnny's eyes cut down to the letter and then back up at Vida. He took off in a frantic dash for the bathroom. Before he could get the door closed, Vida was on him. She pushed back hard, knocking Johnny to the floor.

She yanked him up by the waist and hauled him under her arm as if he were a sack of cornmeal, his legs flailing in the air. She plopped him standing up in the tub. Then she grabbed him by the wrist.

"*Ow!* You're hurting me!" he shouted.

"Stand still or I'll shake you like a 'simmon tree." He tried to pull away from her, and she yanked him viciously.

"Momma! Momma!" he yelled.

Vida turned on the faucet and a loud rush of water splattered into the tub, drowning out his screams.

"Go ahead and holler your head off," Vida shouted. "She ain't going to hear you. She ain't going to do nothing to save her little white boy. You and me both knows that. Now who you going to tell it to?" She scalded him with her eyes. "You going to tell it to the sheriff agin?"

She gripped his wrist tighter and reached for the bar of soap. "You know what they do to bad little boys with dirty, lying mouths, don't you?"

"Leave me alone. Nigger!" he shouted.

That did it. Vida flung the bar of soap against the tile wall. It hit with a *thwack* and then splashed into the tub. "Damn it, Nate!" she screamed, "shut your goddamned mouth!"

"I ain't Nate!" Johnny screamed back. "I'm Johnny Earl Graham. Big letter *J!* Little letters *o! h! n! n! y!* That's who I am. Don't you people call me Nate no more!"

It was as if somebody had slapped Vida across the face. Her mouth still agape, she stared at Johnny long and hard. His breathing was furious, his bottom lip quivered, and his little fists were clenched. In a voice strangled with a murderous rage, he seethed, "And you better leave my momma alone or I'm gonna kill you."

For certain, Vida thought, this boy would kill her if he had half a chance.

She let go of his wrist, and as if that had been the last thing holding her up, she slumped to the floor. She sat there in a heap with her eyes closed and her hands limp in her lap.

Johnny remained tensed, ready for whatever this crazy woman might do next.

Vida looked up at him. Here was a son who loved his mother so much he was prepared to kill for her. For the first time she realized why she hated Hazel so.

Vida shook her head wearily. "Johnny Earl Graham," she said, barely loud enough to be heard over the sound of the running water. "You got a wagonload of fight in you."

Now with tears streaming down her face, she carefully reached up toward the boy. He raised his fists at her as his own tears fell.

"And child," she said as she gently wiped a single teardrop from his cheek, "in this bad ol' world, I 'spec you going to need ever last ounce of it."

Chapter Thirty-Two

MORNING PICNIC

Vida's steps were leaden as she slogged down the muddy road to Tarbottom. She couldn't work today, that was all there was to it. Anyway, Miss Hazel didn't need her. She had a son to tend to her, to love her, to worry over her. As for Vida, her thoughts were of her own bed, in her own room, her own dreamless sleep.

When she got to her cabin, her father was sitting out on the porch. She felt his eyes on her as she climbed the steps. She knew he was waiting for some explanation but she said nothing. She passed through the open door and didn't stop until she fell hard upon her bed, collapsing under the weight of losing Nate for the second time. It had crushed the very breath out of her.

Levi followed her into her room. "Vida, you sick?"

How could she answer him? How could she put into words her sickness. Years of plotting and scheming. Childish plans that had put them in Delphi, within striking distance of the man who wanted her whole family dead. Thinking she could weave a web around an entire town and snatch up every word spoken about her son. Only to be undone by a six-year-old. She had been so foolish.

"Daddy," she said, her eyes closed. "I ain't never going to see Nate again. I know it now." She wasn't sure why she'd told him. Maybe she just needed to say it out loud to someone. To make it real. To let go of the folly. She looked up at Levi.

He was watching her with blank eyes. Did he even understand? She had lived so long with her silly connivance, never telling him what she was feeling or thinking or hoping. Her plans had been all she'd needed. Even her dream of killing the sheriff now seemed ridiculous. What did any of it matter now? She was alone again. How could he ever understand her loss?

A faint smile appeared on Levi's face. He looked down on her dirt-streaked uniform and her muddy tennis shoes. "Snowflake Baby," he said finally. "You still my Snowflake Baby, ain't you?"

She could feel the emotion rising in her throat. "Yes, Daddy," she said, her eyes filling with tears. "I reckon I am."

Her father sat down on the edge of the bed and held open his arms to her. Reaching up around his neck, Vida laid her head against his shoulder.

"That's real good," he said softly. "I been so sad about losing her."

❧

Hazel waited for Vida's approach, but it never came. When Floyd had dropped in earlier to dispense his morning kiss, at first she could hardly look at him. She had long stopped asking if he loved her. He couldn't say it without that "anyway" sound to it. She wondered how much patience he had left with her. How much time did she have before he moved her out, and moved in the one with French perfume?

The maids had given Hazel's fears a name. Delia. The same woman who had come into her house and laughed at her. Humiliated her. Made fun of her furniture and her food, all the time scouting Hazel's home for her third husband. Not for one minute did Hazel believe she was really dead. Mainly because her own jealousy was so alive.

When she did manage a look at him, even with his salesman's grin and head-tilt, he appeared nervous.

"What's wrong?" she had asked.

"Nothing," he said too quickly, glancing at this watch. "I really got to go." He made a beeline for the door.

"Floyd," she called after him, "let's get away from here. Take a trip together. Maybe drive down to the coast? Maybe stay at that Edgewater Beach Hotel."

With his hand on the door handle, he turned over his shoulder and for a moment she thought he was going to cry. Or confess, maybe. Her heart stopped.

Then he seemed to recover. "It's ginning time. Everybody's flush. I'm going to be plenty busy, what with the new models arriving soon and all the trade-ins. Now's not a good time."

It had to be Delia. Maybe she was hiding out somewhere, waiting for Floyd to run away and join her. Why else would he be acting so jittery?

"What about Johnny?" she almost blurted after he had shut the door, wanting to remind him there was more to consider in this world than just himself and Frenchie. Yet she said nothing, knowing that in a few moments the river would be there to fetch her and for a few hours wash away any regrets.

However, it was Johnny, not Vida, who came to her room. Hazel thought he looked as guilty as Floyd.

"What's going on here?" she asked the boy. "Where's Vida?"

Johnny looked down at his feet. "She's gone home."

"Why?"

He only shrugged.

A cold shiver ran through her. If Floyd had fired Vida, did that mean he had new plans for her, too? Had he decided to send her to Whitfield again? That sounded about right, she figured. "New models and trade-ins," he had said. Hazel guessed that was as nice a way as any to be told. That way Floyd could be all alone with his new model while his trade-in was getting rewired.

"We don't need her no more," Johnny said, breaking into her thoughts.

"Huh?'

"Momma, I can take care of you. We don't need Vida coming in our kitchen. I can feed you."

"Johnny, what are you talking about?"

"I made you a picnic. It's ready."

"A picnic? You mean outside?"

He nodded excitedly. "A breakfast picnic. Orange juice and toast and Cheerios and grape jelly and chocolate cake. Vida never did that, did she?" He reached for her hand and tugged. "Come on. It's on the ground. We got to go before the dogs get it."

"But..."

"Please," he begged. "I got it all ready. Come see."

Hazel didn't have the energy to argue. Anyway, with Vida gone and no antidrinking pill this morning, she was having her own picnic ideas.

Johnny found her pink quilted housedress in the closet and selected a scarf for her hair. Hazel slowed briefly before the makeup mirror yet talked herself out of looking. She did make a stop at Floyd's collection of Jim Beam decanters in the kitchen. Finally, with Johnny leading the way, Hazel walked out of the house with her yellow tumbler and into the dreary morning light.

Deep in the yard under an oak, on his *Wagon Train* bedspread, Johnny had laid out plates and napkins and knives and forks and most of the food from the house. He had even set out a large bouquet of fresh-cut roses in a Mason jar of water—roses that looked suspiciously similar to the ones from Miss Pearl's garden. Somehow he had managed two kitchen chairs down the porch steps.

"Johnny, it's so nice," she said, touched by his efforts.

"Better than Vida. I told you so."

Carefully, Hazel sat herself down in a chair. She balanced her bourbon on her lap, trying to remember how long that doctor at Whitfield had said the Antabuse stayed in her system. Was it fourteen hours? Or fourteen days?

As she contemplated her drink, sitting before the spread laden with the odd assortment of foods, Hazel was haunted by a vague memory, as if she were acting out some scene from long ago. Where had it been?

She raised the glass to her nose and took a whiff of the liquor. Yes, that smell was part of it. But there was more. What was missing?

Johnny climbed into the dinette chair beside her. "It's wet today. So we got chairs to sit down on."

"I see," she said, still trying to remember.

"On a real picnic," he explained, "you supposed to sit on the ground."

"That's right," Hazel said.

"Like we did by the bridge. Remember? We had moon pies and grape Nehis. The big fish they pulled from the river? And remember how Davie took off for the bridge and I caught him? Do you remember, Momma?"

"Davie," was all Hazel said, and she began to cry, only a little bit at first.

"What's the matter, Momma?" Johnny asked, panicking. "What did I do wrong?"

"Nothing, honey. Nothing." The more she tried to reassure him, the harder she cried. "It's...not...you," she sobbed.

Johnny didn't believe her. He started to dance frantically around the bedspread, picking up servings of food and bringing them to her. And when she shook her head, trying to tell him it wasn't the food, she would break out into a new round of sobbing, which only sent him in search of the dish that would make her stop.

Not able to bear his repeated efforts to make her happy, she hid her face in her hands and wailed, and she would probably have continued for hours if it had not been for the voice of an uninvited guest.

"What a lovely idea," the intruder chirped, her crippled hand waving her lace handkerchief over the feast. "A morning picnic. Now, whose idea was this?"

Shocked tearless, Hazel peeked up over her fingers into the perfectly composed face of Miss Pearl Alcorn.

"I suspected something special was up when I saw Johnny in my rose garden."

Johnny looked up guiltily at Miss Pearl.

She said nothing else about the roses. Instead she turned to his mother. "Hello, Hazel."

Hazel didn't speak at once. All the ugly things she had rehearsed over the summer to level at Miss Pearl had vanished from her head. Still holding her hands up to her tear-stained face, a soggy "Hello" was the best she could do.

Miss Pearl smiled sweetly and then looked up at the sky. "Who said picnics are best saved for sunny days? I think we have more need of them during the gray, gloomy times, myself."

She looked down at Johnny. "Child, would you hand your mother and me a paper napkin from your elegant setting there? The ragweed is dreadful this time of year."

Pleased to learn how to be of help, Johnny quickly did as he was told.

With her good hand, Miss Pearl took the napkin and touched it to her perfectly powdered face, giving Hazel a chance to blow her nose and dry her eyes.

"It's been a fretful season, hasn't it, Hazel? So many offensive things in the air. Pollens and such. Smells of cotton poison wafting up from the Delta."

Hazel nodded, not sure what the woman was talking about.

"I want to apologize for not visiting this summer. To tell you the truth, I was a little intimidated by that unpleasant little maid of yours. Levi's girl. How did a sweet man like Levi manage to raise a...oh, never mind. I'm sure it's a shoddy excuse on my part." Miss Pearl looked down on Hazel and smiled sadly. "I know it's all been a trial for you."

Hazel studied the woman curiously. Something offensive in the air? That dreadful little maid? Was Miss Pearl attempting to sum up

Hazel's entire hellish summer?

"Anyway, even though I haven't called, doesn't mean you haven't been on my mind." With what Hazel discerned as a definite look of pity, Miss Pearl asked, "Hazel, dear, how are you?"

Hazel dropped her eyes to the glass in her lap. How in the world was she supposed to answer that question? My husband has been cheating on me with your dead niece? I'm one sip away from the nuthouse? I'm the sorriest excuse for a mother since Ma Barker?

She wished Miss Pearl would leave so she could down the contents of the tumbler and several more like it. But Miss Pearl's regal presence kept Hazel from moving at all. She tried to remember what the maids had said about Miss Pearl. She seemed so laughable then. However,, today she was as scary as ever. Hazel smiled weakly and made a feeble attempt at smoothing her hair.

"And how's that hardworking husband of yours? A regular Horatio Alger, isn't he? I haven't seen him around much."

Hazel opened her mouth to answer but found herself having to choke down a sob. She put the napkin up to her mouth and dropped her head.

"I see," was all Miss Pearl said. And for a moment they were all very quiet. Miss Pearl handed her napkin back to Johnny and said, "Child, would you be a dear and get me a glass of ice water? And maybe some fresh napkins."

"We got tea," Johnny offered, eager to do anything for Miss Pearl.

She smiled and nodded. Johnny took off at a dead run for the house.

Miss Pearl looked into the distance again and waved the handkerchief in an arc over the neighborhood. "You know, my ancestors used to own all this land. Most of the county, as a matter of fact. In the days when this part of the world was considered frontier. The backwoods."

Miss Pearl seemed to be speaking more to the landscape than to Hazel. "We go way back. Men in our family put their names to the deeds and handed them down to their sons. It's always been that way. We bred some great men, they say. Big part of this state's history. And you know what I'm struck with, Hazel?"

Hazel was getting irritated. She was not in the mood for another history lesson that ended up exposing her own poor-as-dirt roots. "No," she said at last, "what strikes you?"

"That most of the men I have known personally, especially the ones they call great, are dull to the point of genius. Don't you find it so?"

"Huh?"

"No imagination. They really don't seem to know what they want." Miss Pearl solemnly touched the handkerchief to her bosom. "Not deep down."

She turned to Hazel, "You see, I have a theory. I think men are able to see one thing at a time. Usually the last thing that happens to be dangling in front of them at any given moment. The more shine and glitter the better. As you might imagine, this gives them the tendency to lurch. This way and that. To and fro." She waved her handkerchief in time to her words. Her whole body was undulating absurdly, as if she were acting out her theory to some audience larger than just Hazel. The maids were right. This was the silliest woman she had ever met. All she needed now was a maypole.

Miss Pearl continued her little dance. "Always unbalanced," she said, leaning farther to one side to demonstrate. "They break the surface like pond minnows striking at shadows." Miss Pearl giggled at the thought. "And the little ripples they make convince them they are oh so very dangerous and bold. Ultimately it merely makes them predictable."

Hazel had no idea what Miss Pearl was trying to say, much less why she felt so strongly about it, acting it out the way she was. Hazel was beginning to feel a little embarrassed for the woman.

Unabashed, Miss Pearl went on with her theory. "Women, on the other hand, aren't as prone to lurching. You know why?"

Hazel shook her head.

"Because we *do* know what we want, and we hold on for the duration. We know what will fill us up. We are more attuned to life's vital essences."

Without warning, Miss Pearl thrust her crippled hand into Hazel's face. "*We* grab and hold on to what is important." Hazel snapped her head back, frightened by the twisted fingers.

"Hazel, *we* don't let ourselves become distracted by the fancy of the moment. *We* are the steady ones. Never, ever," she said fiercely, shaking her hand in Hazel's face, "lean on a man for balance. You know why?"

Staring at the hand, Hazel took a wild guess. "Because they lurch a lot?"

"Exactly!" Miss Pearl exclaimed, throwing her hand over her head.

Not knowing what to say now, but pleased to have got the right answer, Hazel shook her head knowingly, as if she had grasped this crucial difference between the sexes. It did sound familiar. Hazel wondered what Miss Pearl would say if she knew how much she sounded like Sweet Pea.

Miss Pearl fell back into the chair next to Hazel and took a few moments to catch her breath. Then, in a much more somber tone, she said, "Hazel, let me tell you the story of someone who will never be in the history books. Or have a statue in the capitol rotunda at Jackson."

She drew her handkerchief to her heart, as if swearing to the truth of the story, and began. "Many years ago, my great-grand-mother on my mother's side was abandoned by her husband. For an octoroon in New Orleans, no less. He left her with forty acres of undrained swampland, six children, and a blind mule. Yet the woman knew what she had to do. Somehow she was able to raise her a plot of corn, and with that produced her first batch of whiskey. Once a month she loaded up that whiskey on the back of that blind mule and led it and six children twenty miles to an old beech tree that grew on the Natchez Trace. She camped out under that tree until she had sold every last drop. To travelers, drifters, and high-waymen. To whoever had a dollar. Later she built her a little house on that very spot and hired two girls to work the back room, if you know what I mean. She may have even pitched in herself."

The woman's pale blue eyes misted over.

"No," Miss Pearl said sadly, "you won't see her picture in the history books. I once saw a tintype of her when I was a little girl. It was hidden away at the bottom of a steamer trunk. I still remember. It was taken when she was eighty-two years old, and she was still a beautiful woman, if you can imagine that. She sat erect, her head unbowed, unapologetic. When my father saw me looking at that photograph, he took it from me and tore it to pieces. I was told I would risk scandalizing the family if I spoke of her in polite company. Hazel, that woman raised a governor and a secretary of war. Today nobody even knows her name."

Hazel nodded. She liked the story very much yet had no idea why Miss Pearl was telling it to her. "She must have been a fine woman," Hazel offered.

Miss Pearl smiled. "I thought you would like her, Hazel." As if she had read Hazel's thoughts she went on to say, "Now, I know they say the women in my family are silly, maybe even crazy. Well, perhaps we are. But you see, we come by it honestly. We don't make it a habit of leaning on men. Now Hertha, bless her heart, wanted Billy Dean, God knows why, yet through hell and high water, she got him and she's kept him. And I know good and well, once he's outlived his usefulness, she is not above pitching him out in the street. And poor Delia..."

"Delia," Hazel repeated, wincing. For a moment Hazel had forgotten. But now she had to ask. "Is she really...I mean..."

"Dead? I doubt it. Even if she is, I don't mourn her. I'm quite certain she died going after her heart's desire. And in Delia's case, that would probably be an insatiable taste for variety. She was true to it up until the very end."

Hazel wondered about Floyd having been in love with a dead woman. Would he mourn Delia? Would he come back to Hazel now? Was the point of Miss Pearl's story that she shouldn't even care?

"And you, Hazel..." Miss Pearl said.

Hazel looked up into Miss Pearl's penetrating gaze. "Me?"

"The first day I saw you, at the little gathering at your house, when you answered the door...do you remember that day?"

Hazel grimaced.

"Well, the minute I laid eyes on you, I said to myself, this woman has something special. She has a deep, unquenchable thirst."

Hazel looked down at her glass, embarrassed.

"A thirst for *life*, Hazel," Miss Pearl clarified. "I saw it in your eyes, the way you dressed. Oh, my! That elegant blue dress you wore. And the manner in which you wore it. The way you stood there. Regal. I was so impressed, Hazel. I never in my life saw anything like it." Miss Pearl smiled fondly. "Except maybe once."

The world had gone dead quiet around Hazel. All she wanted to hear was Miss Pearl's voice. Nobody had strung together that many nice words about Hazel in years. Since she and Floyd first dated. It was as if somebody knew her. She was so rapt, she wasn't even aware that Johnny had arrived with Miss Pearl's tea.

"Now, correct me if I'm wrong, Hazel, but the way you were dressed that day, the way you held yourself. You weren't born to that, were you?"

Hazel shook her head.

"No, I thought not. That's what makes me so sure that at some time, you must have wanted that more than life itself. Didn't you?"

Hazel nodded. It was true, she had.

"You grabbed ahold of something deep inside yourself. Some private hope or dream. And you started pulling. Regardless of what other people said."

"You're right," Hazel said, amazed. "They all laughed at me 'cause I wanted to look nice."

"Why, Hazel, what I saw that day was not about pretense or pre-sentation. Or even a fine wardrobe. It was something else."

"What was it?" Hazel asked breathlessly.

"It was a heartfelt yearning for something more. And I wager, if you are rigorously honest, it didn't have to do with any man, did it?"

How did she know this? Hazel wondered. Her hoping had begun long before Floyd Graham ever showed up.

"That thing you grabbed hold of. You know what I believe it was?"

"What?" Hazel whispered, ready to be convinced of anything that came out of the woman's mouth.

"Dignity," Miss Pearl said. "That's what I saw that day." Miss Pearl extended her arm out before her, her handkerchief fluttering in the breeze. "A woman reaching out with all her might for her share of dignity."

"Dignity," Hazel said reverently, thinking she never heard such a beautiful word in her entire life.

"Diggity," Johnny whispered, deciding that the word must be like abracadabra, and that somehow things would never be the same. The little breeze that ruffled the handkerchief in Miss Pearl's still-outstretched hand seemed to confirm it.

They both watched Miss Pearl as she receded into the distance. For a very long time Hazel sat without moving, with Johnny just as motionless in her lap. Hazel needed time to think. Not only about the future, but about the past. It was like that decoder ring they'd offered on the radio when she was a girl. Miss Pearl had given her something that turned the whole alphabet on its head. *A* was really *D,* and *E* turned out to be *Z.* Hazel started paging through memories, decoding them, reordering all the letters. So many lies she had believed.

It was dignity! Not silliness. Not stupidity. Not worthless and ugly and helpless and hopeless and crazy and bad, bad, bad. Dignity. That was it all the time.

Chapter Thirty-Three

FIREFLIES

Wearing a slightly dazed expression, Hazel got up from her chair and returned to the house, softly repeating to herself the new word Miss Pearl had given her. She emptied her tumbler into the decanter and went to her room. She spent the rest of the day there, alternately sobbing, calling out Floyd's name, and then becoming quiet once more, staring out the window. Johnny found her sitting before her makeup mirror, looking blankly into the glass. Miss Pearl's visit had altered his mother in a way he didn't understand.

The good thing was that Johnny had a whole day without Vida, and he certainly needed it. There was a lot to do. The rest of the morning he spent in his graveyard, digging up the mounds. His father was going to be furious, not only for his taking things from the house, but for stealing from Vida as well. When Vida came back, she was sure to tell on him.

Later he sat at the table practicing his name for school, which he understood would be starting Any Time Now, whatever that meant. "Almost Time for school," people would say. "Are you getting excited?"

Sitting there in the empty kitchen, he studied Time—right where it lived—in the wall clock shaped like a chicken. There Time stretched its arms and pointed to the numbers that told everybody where to go and what to do and when to stop doing it. Always circling. Widening its reach only to bring its arms together again, squeezing out the space between, and slowly opening its embrace once more.

Johnny had yet to figure out the secret language of Time, but when he did, he believed Time would tell him important things. Like when it was going to heal his mother and send Davie back home. He copied down the numbers from its face. "Time is the great healer," his father was always saying. Time, he thought, must be as powerful as Jesus.

His father arrived home later that afternoon looking tired and worried. He headed straight for the TV. As Johnny sat on the couch, Floyd aimed the rabbit ears toward Jackson and then leaned back in his lounger, letting the gray and white men who pointed fingers and shook hands and signed papers on the evening news cast light and shadows across his father's face and send him directly to sleep.

He thought about crawling into his father's lap, waking him. There were questions he needed answers to yet did not know how to ask—the questions of Time and the secrets it held. He had put these questions to his father before, and his father had only become frustrated, not understanding what he was asking. "Time is the currency of life," was the best Johnny could get.

There was someone else who might know about Time and Death and Jesus. The sounds from his mower had drifted over from the Gooseberrys' yard earlier.

It was already first dark when Johnny stepped outside, and the shadows had finished their lengthening and let go completely, flooding the entire yard in deep, cooling shade. Mourning doves welcomed the evening by cooing softly from somewhere nearby. As if in rebuttal, a brown thrasher protested with a harsh cry from a cherry laurel.

Amid the sounds of the evening creatures, Johnny heard a lone voice deep in the yard. It was exactly the person he was looking for, sitting down the hill on the cast-iron bench.

Johnny slowly approached the man until he was right up behind him. Vida's father wasn't exactly talking to himself. It seemed he was talking to someone who wasn't answering back.

"Hey," Johnny said.

Levi spun around on the bench, surprised. For a moment he searched the boy's face with those dark, bottomless eyes, and Johnny could almost feel the earth come up to meet his feet. Levi said, "How long you been standing there spying on me?"

Johnny only shrugged, still watching the man's eyes.

"What is it you want?"

The boy was still silent, not sure of that answer either.

"You go inside now," Levi said. "It's getting dark and time for supper. They going to come looking for you and put the blame on me."

Johnny took one step back and stopped, still staring up at the man. "Ain't nobody home," he lied.

A few more moments passed while Levi considered this. Finally he said, "Well, you best come over here so I can see what you is up to. No good, be my guess."

Doing as he was told, Johnny walked right up to the man.

The man asked simply, "You lose something?"

Johnny considered the question for a moment. It was a good question. The right question. And Johnny knew the answer. Death was not a hide-and-seek game you played with Jesus. You can pray. You can be good. You can try hard not to forget. You can do everything right, but some things will stay lost forever.

He decided to ask anyway. "Is Davie coming back?"

Levi's gaze softened. "Your little brother?"

Johnny nodded.

Levi shook his head gravely. "No. I don't think he's coming back."

Johnny considered this for a moment. "I don't think so neither. I used to believe it when I was little. But I don't believe it no more."

"I can tell that," Levi said. This time they both sighed.

Then, looking up at Levi, Johnny asked, "Why you always sitting in my backyard?"

Levi eyed the boy tentatively. "You got a problem with it?"

"No. I just wondered who you been talking to back here."

Levi considered the question. "Ever man need him a place to talk to God."

Johnny nodded to himself. "God," he echoed softly, and climbed up on the bench next to Levi.

Minutes passed as they both looked down the hill into the darkening distance. Little breezes began to play high up in the trees. Levi had his arms stretched out over the back of the bench and he gave off smells of earth and sweat, and to Johnny they were substantial and comforting. He leaned into Levi and felt the dampness of his shirt. Levi shifted, as if trying to push the boy away with his movements. Johnny held fast. Levi looked around and then carefully lowered an arm around the boy.

"You seen him?" Johnny asked.

Levi quickly looked about. "Seen who?"

"God. You seen God?"

"Oh. Yes, I have."

"How'd he look?"

"Well, it's hard to say. The first time He showed hisself to me he was in a mighty whirlpool of churning water. 'Course I knowed it was Him, all right."

He asked Levi, "You seen God around here lately?"

"No. Not for a while. He got His own timetable, I reckon. But you can be sure He always seeing us. His eyes don't miss a thing. Not the littlest sparrow."

"He looking at us right now?" Johnny asked, wondering if God's eyes were as big as Levi's.

"No doubt in my mind. Ain't that a comfort?"

The boy shrugged. "I want to see His face."

Levi laughed. "Me, too, I reckon."

For a moment they scanned the yard together, as if trying to pick out the face that was said to be turned their way, invisible and unblinking. A firefly flickered in the twilight.

"Lightning bug winking at us," Levi said.

"Uh-huh. I seen it. He's gone now."

"He's out there," Levi said. "Why you say it's gone?"

"'Cause I can't see it no more. He's gone dark."

The firefly blinked again. "There he is, over there!" Johnny whispered, not wanting the firefly to know they were onto him, figuring they might be as skittish as fish. He pointed in the direction of the porch.

"Now he's gone dark again, ain't he?" Levi asked, sounding as though the disappearance was a worrisome thing.

"We got to be quiet and wait till he blinks," Johnny explained, not wanting Levi to give up too soon.

Levi laughed as if he had known it all the time. "That's the way it is with God, don't you reckon? He always around somewheres, if you can see His face or not. He's out there watching through the dark. Sometimes that's got to be enough, I suppose. Knowing He sees us even if we can't see Him back."

Johnny didn't know what to say to that. He thought they had been talking about fireflies.

Levi surveyed the yard again. "You know, I'm starting to think it's more God's nature to move unseen through the darkness like them bugs out there. He ain't going to stay put in no church or on no riverbank or even in no Bible. You see, I know. I done found Him and lost Him again in all them places."

"Me and Davie used to catch lightning bugs in a mayonnaise jar," Johnny said, thinking it much easier to talk about fireflies. "Daddy poked holes in the top with an ice pick. They died anyway."

Levi nodded. "Can't keep God in no jar neither, I reckon."

Levi continued talking about God for a while, in a voice that seemed at home with the croaking and whirring and cooing and the rustling of leaves, all the night music that was rising up around them. Like those sounds, his words didn't insist upon answers or require understanding. Johnny found himself wishing his mother could hear Levi talk. He asked him, "You know my momma?"

"No, I can't say I do. Vida tells me some."

"She don't feel good no more. Stays in bed all the time."

"That's what I heared." Levi removed his hat and set it on the bench. "You know, I reckon what we been talking about is the same with people. They can sure nuff go dark, too, can't they?"

Johnny nodded, not really knowing, but he was willing to believe.

"Myself, I got so used to seeing the faces shining their love at me, I thought it would stay that way forever. My wife. Vida. Nate. My flock. They was so much love in them days. All them faces shining just for me." Levi brushed his nose. "But pride goeth before the fall. The Lord giveth and the Lord taketh. And God done took it all from me. Put out them shining lights."

Then Levi squeezed Johnny's arm gently. "I reckon that's got to be the hardest thing about loving, ain't it, child? Calling out in the dark. Pleading with love to show its face again." He laughed sadly. "Maybe we all living from one blink of love to the next."

The firefly winked over by the elephant ears. It seemed to be working a wide net around the yard. Levi lifted his finger in the direction of the bug, about to say something. Instead he formed a fist and brought it down hard on his leg. "Old fool!" he said with so much intensity Johnny jumped. "The dark *was* his sign! Right in front of my face!"

Levi's gaze was firmly fixed on a spot somewhere beyond. Afraid, Johnny peered out into the deep dusk, wondering if somebody had come up on them. He saw no one. There was only the firefly.

Levi kept talking in a slightly raised voice, leaning into the gathering dark. "All this time I thought it was *you* abandoned *me*! Punishing me with your darkness!" Levi shook his head with strong feeling. "Old fool! I been cursing the night. Thinking it was hiding you away from me."

Levi sprang to his feet. He held his arms extended and shouted, "I see it now. My own church, going up in flames. It was a burning bush. A sign. All things working together for the glory of God!"

Surely his voice was loud enough for his father to hear. Then Johnny noticed that the insects and frogs and evening birds had gone into riot, rising up like a night choir as if to cloak his words. The wind picked up and the trees shuddered and swayed.

"I see it, Lord. With the eyes of a child. I see it clear. It wasn't a sign to stop, but to step out."

He fell back onto the bench, as if now under a heavy load. "I know what must be done. I hear your voice calling to me, 'Step with me into the darkness. Step with me *into* the darkness.' "

As if in reverence for Levi's now heavy heart, the wind died to a whisper and the creatures around them hushed to a deep, soft murmur, almost a lament. Levi dropped his head to his chest, which was heaving mightily. Just before he covered his face, Johnny thought he saw tears glistening in the man's eyes.

No longer afraid, he reached out to touch Levi's other hand, which lay open by his side. Now it was Levi who was hurting. So many people were hurting, he couldn't keep track of them all.

Johnny stroked Levi's hand, trying to soothe away his sorrow about the darkness. He thought of Davie in the dark. About his mother lying in the dark, fading a little every day. Everything seemed to be going to darkness.

Almost imperceptibly, his body began to tremble. His breathing became shallow because it hurt his chest to bring the air deeper. He moved his eyes around the yard. Now there was a second firefly, circling and flashing. It was impossible to tell which firefly was his. He had lost it.

The little breaths hurt, and the tightening continued upward to his throat. He squeezed Levi's hand, trying to hold it back.

"What is it, child?"

Johnny looked up. Levi wasn't crying at all! His eyes were burning bright, his face shining. Before Johnny himself knew what the words were going to be, he blurted, "My momma's gonna die forever, ain't she?"

Levi gripped Johnny's shoulder and pulled him close. He held on to the boy tightly and let him sob open-mouthed into his shirt. His tears flowed fast and free, as if all the fear and dread in the world were thawing to sorrow, and not until the tears had slowed did Levi move. He took Johnny by the shoulders and looked him solidly in the face.

"Listen to me, child, and remember what I'm saying." His voice was clear and strong now. It was the same voice that had once prayed over pine straw, the kind of voice that made Johnny quiver on the inside and caused his flesh to tingle. "Even though you can't see Him, and even though you can't feel Him, He's loving you, right now, through the darkness. He's loving your momma, too."

Searching Levi's eyes, Johnny wanted to believe.

"I know it for a fact. Everthing going to be all right. He promised it to me."

Levi paused, smiling down on the boy. "I been wrong. As wrong as a man can be. The darkness ain't been hiding God at all. He revealed the truth to me, and I'm going to tell it to you."

His eyes were pools of light, he whispered the secret to Johnny. "Child, the darkness *is* God. And you and me and your momma and Vida—we all been moving through His very heart." Levi motioned out into the night. "See? He ain't forgot about us."

Johnny looked to where he pointed. The yard was now studded with fireflies, their twinklings multiplied through the prism of his tears. It was as if all the stars in heaven had settled in around them.

Chapter Thirty-Four

THE MAMMY

Vida had never before spent the entire day in bed. But yesterday she had. A good thing, too, because her father had kept her up most of the night. He had come home late, scaring her half to death with wild talk of visions and lightning bugs blinking in the night, going on about God giving him a new story to live. It was worse than she had ever seen him down at the bayou.

"God done set me out a path to walk," he had said, "a path through the wilderness. It was Him who set my church afire. A burning bush to get my attention. The Lord was trying to speak to me, same as He spoke to Moses. But I didn't hear Him then. God wasn't taking, He was giving. I know now. It was a sign. A sign that God has a greater story in mind for me."

Vida wasn't sure she could handle any more stories. It was through a story that her father first told her to let go of her son. It was his stories that kept him wandering in the past, blind to the present. Now she feared his stories had set him adrift downstream in his mind for good.

Though she tried her best to draw it out of him again this morning, what it was that God was telling him to do, all he would say was that he was called to preach, and preach he would. And how at that very moment God was preparing him a church like none other—

one that could never be set afire. One of iron and stone. "From there I will deliver a sermon that will touch the hearts of our people, Vida. God said, 'Don't fear the darkness.' He said to be ready to step into the darkness with Him."

She tried to dismiss his talk as nothing to worry about, the wishful thinking of a man on the short end of his life. So far she had not yet convinced herself. All she knew was that she would need to watch him closer than ever.

⁓

The first thing Vida noticed as she climbed the hill up to the Grahams' house was the boy sitting hunched on the back porch steps, his shoulders drawn close, shadows veiling his face. Then the boy's father stepped outside, his eyes on her approach. Oh, Lord, she thought, something about this don't look right already. Levi probably scared the boy so bad last night that Mr. Floyd was going to have her daddy run out of Delphi on a rail.

The closer she got, the more her mind kept churning out dire possibilities. The boy surely had told Mr. Floyd about her being so rough on him yesterday. That was it! She was about to get fired. Or maybe even arrested for laying hands on a white boy. No telling what the boy had piled on top of that story, bad as he hated her. Vida glanced over at the sheriff's house, to make sure he wasn't at that moment storming across the lawn with his pistol drawn.

As she came up to the porch, Vida avoided looking at the boy's face.

"Morning, Vida," Floyd called, his tone businesslike. "The boy said you were feeling poorly. Left early." He took a sip of coffee and then peered at her over the rim of the cup. "Let's see, what did he say was the matter?"

Vida opened her mouth to answer, but before she could utter a sound Johnny said, "She had a headache."

"That's right," Floyd said, remembering. "Well, I'm glad you made it back today." Still watching Vida, he asked, "You gave Hazel her pills yesterday before you left, didn't you?"

Again before she had a chance to answer, Johnny said confidently, "Yes sir. I saw her do it."

Satisfied, Floyd set his cup on the railing and headed across the porch. As he took the steps, he reached down and tousled Johnny's hair. "Bye, Little Monkey."

"Bye, Big Monkey," Johnny said, surprisingly cheerful.

First thing Vida thought was, that little devil can lie like a convict. But why?

Floyd turned back to Vida. "By the way, where'd you find my cufflinks and tie clip and all the other stuff that's been gone missing? I've looked high and low for them things."

She glanced down at Johnny again, who was looking back at her with pie-pan eyes. That was it! The rascal was striking a bargain with her.

"Just 'round, Mr. Floyd," she said casually. "You know how things likes to wedge up in and betwixt."

"I'm sure glad." He laughed awkwardly. "I was ready to think you been taking them. If I didn't know any better." Johnny beamed at Vida.

◦⌒◦

After Floyd left, Vida went into the kitchen with Johnny following close behind. When she got to her spot at the sink, she turned to watch him as he climbed into his regular chair. They looked at each other uneasily for a few moments.

"You know," Vida said finally, "I'm sure sorry about yelling at you. And for treating you so rough. I want you to know I don't hold no madness against you."

He studied her for a moment. "I'm sorry I called you a nigger." Then he dropped his eyes and said softly, "And for hiding your letter."

"Well," she said with a long exhale, "I guess we both right now done a big thing, ain't we? Ought to proud of ourselfs."

"Yes ma'am."

"Ma'am?" Vida laughed to herself. "Well, I be."

Vida had turned back toward the sink to begin the coffee when Johnny asked straight out, "Who is Nate?"

She was caught off guard. "What?"

"The one y'all always calling me. I was just wondering. Levi said Nate don't smile at him no more. Is Nate dead, too?"

"Daddy said that?"

"Levi said Nate don't smile at him and his light went out and that makes him sad, and I figured he might be dead same as everybody else."

"No," she said thoughtfully, touched that her father would say he missed Nate. "Nate ain't dead."

"I know a lot of dead people," Johnny said, sighing heavily. "Papa Graham is dead. Davie is dead. Old Miss Floy down the street is dead. You know, Vida," he said gravely, "the dead stay gone forever and ever."

"Nate ain't dead," Vida said again, firmly.

The boy was now looking at her with wanting eyes. Her father had tried to get her to feel sorry for the boy last night. Said that boy's mind was too much on death. Well, this white boy was looking to the wrong person. Her own loss was too fresh. Anyway, Vida Snow was not one of those old-time mammies the white folks were so fond of—treated like slaves when they were alive and mourned like family when they died. No ma'am, she told herself, I ain't no Lillie Dee.

She turned back to the sink again. There was work to get done. No telling what state that white woman was going to be in this morning, after being without her medicine for a day.

Sensing something at her back, Vida turned and saw the boy still staring. "You want something?

"Un-uh," he said.

"Then why you drilling holes in me?" she asked. Whatever he was up to, she told herself, it wasn't going to work. Not the way it had on her father. Finagling. That's what he was doing. Trying to boll weevil his way into her feelings. He wanted something from her that wasn't his to have.

"If all you got to do is stare at me, you might as well give me a hand with breakfast. Get me four eggs out of the icebox. And the orange juice. Then count out three pieces of bread for toast."

Johnny hopped down and did exactly as he was told.

He'd be off to school in a couple of days, she thought, out of the house and out of *her* kitchen. She cracked an egg into the skillet, shaking her head and thinking, that white momma of his been so busy feeling sorry for herself, she probably don't even know school is about to commence. Mr. Floyd is sure too busy to worry about such things.

Looking down at the boy whose gaze was locked onto the toaster, she asked, "You ready for school?"

His eyes shot up at her. "What do I have to do to get ready?" The bread blasted out of the toaster, making them both jump.

Just as she thought. Nobody had even talked to him about it.

"Not much," she said, buttering a piece of toast, sounding as casual as she could. "I imagine you need you a lettering pencil and a doodling pad."

"I ain't got none. What they gonna do to me?"

"Don't fret. I'm sure your daddy going to find you some. Plenty of time before school commences."

"But what they gonna make me do with a pencil and a doodling pad?" His eyes were beginning to jump about again.

"Nothing you can't already do," Vida said. "I expect they going to show you things to copy down. Like them ABCs you been practicing all summer. And your name. I seen you writing that down on everything in the house."

The boy hung on every word. "What else they gonna make me do?"

"I expect they going to show you things and tell you to count them up on your fingers. You can do that. And probably copy ciphers out of a book. Know you got that licked." Why did she bring this up? They had been doing so good. "Now, settle down," she said in her most even voice. "You going to get the fidgets. I expect the teacher will be real sweet and think you mighty smart."

It didn't work. He let loose with a torrent of questions. "Can I come home if I don't like it? What do I do if somebody pushes me down? What if I get sick? What if my momma needs me and I ain't here?"

Vida became more annoyed by the second. I can't be this boy's mother, she told herself. Anyway, he has a perfectly good one. Well, maybe not. Still that ain't no reason for him to go around acting an orphan. Vida had lost her own boy, but it had been out there in the big, wide world. How, she wondered, could a boy get lost in his own house?

Yet there he was. With his own momma in a bedroom not ten feet from his. And him as lost as a babe in the woods. What kind of mother would let that happen? A white one, she answered herself. With nothing better to do than feel sorry for herself, that's what. Vida took a spatula and flung the eggs at the plate.

The tears surprised Vida. She quickly wiped her eyes with the back of her hand and thought angrily, why couldn't nobody see it except her? 'Cause everybody around here had their damned heads up their butts, that's how come! Mr. Floyd seeing whatever he wants to see. And not seeing what needs to be seen, right under his own nose. And that woman upstairs? She done lost one boy to death and afraid to touch the other, lest she kills him, too. Don't need no doctor to tell Vida that.

The whole thing landed squarely in Vida's lap. Just like a white woman to cause this much trouble and get off scot-free. Laying up in bed. Acting helpless and piteous, trying to win queen for the day. But not so helpless she couldn't blackmail her maid into letting her go out and get drunk. Vida might buy the whiskey herself if Hazel would put in a little time being a mother. It made Vida's blood boil. That white woman was aiming to turn Vida into a mammy, sure as rain.

Well, she thought, dropping the plate on the tray, that Hazel woman had another thing coming if she thought she was going to win this easy. Staring hard up at the ceiling as if she could see right into Hazel's room, Vida said under her breath, "Lord, give me the strength to help this child without killing his momma first."

BOOK THREE

RELUCTANT
HEROES

Chapter Thirty-Five

HELP ARRIVES

One day off those pills and Hazel felt like a new woman. She was in no mood for that foul-tempered maid with her hard looks. The idea of treating a white woman in such a way. It was. . .it was. . .undignified, that's what it was! Why, Miss Pearl would never stand for such a thing. Neither would the new Hazel.

This morning, Hazel Ishee Graham was itching for a fight.

Down below she heard the sound of Vida clattering the china louder than usual and taking the stair steps in heavy tromps. Without the two courtesy knocks, the bedroom door flung open and in fumed Vida, jostling the breakfast dishes. She practically dropped the tray on the bedside table, sloshing the coffee, then stood over Hazel's bed with her fists planted on her hips. She narrowed her eyes at Hazel.

Hazel narrowed hers back. *"What?"* she said. "I ain't done nothing to you." This morning Hazel believed she could take this woman if she had to, wrestle her to the ground if there was need.

"No ma'am!" Vida said expansively. "You ain't done *nothing.*" Bending over the breakfast tray, Vida mumbled under her breath, "That be the nub of it, awright. Ain't done one damned thing." Vida turned toward Hazel with the most unreal smile plastered to her face. Handing Hazel her coffee, Vida oozed venom. "I expect you want cream in that, don't you, *Miss Hazel?*"

"What was it you said?" Hazel asked, doubting her own ears.

"I 'spect you want cream with that coffee," Vida cooed ever so sweetly. "I membered the little cow jug this time."

"No. Before the cream part. About the nub of it. What did you say to me?"

"Oh, that," Vida said, with the coat-hanger smile still on her face. "I was just meaning this house sure has gone to hell in a bucket. If you don't mind me saying it, *Miss Hazel*."

Hazel eyed Vida warily. At the moment she was holding out the little cream pitcher in the shape of a heifer with a painted-on grin, much like Vida's. Hazel took the cream and poured a cloud of it into her cup. "Well," she said, stirring her coffee, "I wouldn't count on seeing me up anytime soon, if *that's* what you getting at."

"You seem feisty enough this morning."

"What? You think I been putting on? You think I enjoy being kept up here like a two-headed uncle?"

"Who been keeping you up here?"

"Who?" Hazel looked incredulously at Vida. "You the biggest one. And Floyd. And them doctors. And them pills. And—"

Vida cut in on her list. "Like I say, you seem mighty fit this morning. Fit enough to get outside and walk. Take that boy with you, maybe."

"Not after you give me them pills, I won't. In less than an hour I'm going to be fogbound, and you know it." She looked at Vida out of the corner of her eye. "Reckon you got them pills right there in your pocket, itching to put me out so you and your friends can go back to having the house to y'allselves." She smiled tightly and then took a sip of coffee. Vida didn't bite.

"Of course," Hazel continued, almost wistfully, "they told me one day I'd get used to feeling like I've got a sack of seed on my back and cotton lint between my ears. They said I'll come 'round to it."

Hazel looked up, sad-eyed, but Vida didn't appear very sympathetic, standing there like a wooden Indian. There was no getting to that woman.

Hazel fussed with the napkin on her chest. "Anyway, I don't know why you need to fret about it. You still get your little bounty for every pill you can cram down my throat." She looked up and grinned, "Ain't that right?"

A moment of frozen silence passed as the two women stared at each other, both smiling mightily and neither meaning an inch of it.

Vida threw her hands in the air. "Calf rope!" she cried out. "I give up. It ain't worth putting up with your mess no more. What's your price, white woman?"

Hazel lurched backward, sloshing coffee on her bed jacket. "What the hell are you babbling about? My price for what?"

"To make you do right! What it is you want out of me?"

"What I'm wanting is a little dignity!" Hazel answered.

"Dignity? Dignity! What you talking about dignity?"

"I didn't think you'd understand. What would somebody like you know about dignity?"

"Enough to know you ain't done nothing to rate none of it," Vida said.

"Well, then, if you can't give me none, then what I want is for you to leave me alone."

"Lord, that be what I want too. I'd love to leave you alone. That be my fondest dream. 'Cept it ain't just you and me. They's that boy downstairs. What we going to do about him?"

"*We?* Ain't no *we* to it. He's *my* boy. Do you hear?"

"I hear it, but I don't see it."

"Listen to me," Hazel said, her teeth clenched. "What I *don't* need is you coming in here and making me feel guilty about what a bad momma I am. The whole county knows it already. Why, I been sermonized in the Baptist church and writ up in the *Hopalachie Courier*. Ain't you read it yet?"

"Lord, girl! You got enough pity in you to float a boat upriver."

Hazel gave Vida a look of pure viciousness. "I don't think you ought to be talking to a white person that way. I hear it ain't healthy."

Vida's eyes blazed. "All I'm asking is what's it going to take to get you up!"

"That's between you and Floyd, ain't it? He the one paying you to keep me down."

"Well, it ain't nowheres near enough," Vida shot back. "I got a boy downstairs worrying me like a bone. Asking me questions his momma ought to be answering." Hazel opened her mouth to protest, but Vida kept it up. "All summer he been lettering his name on everthing in the house. Like he leaving a trail for somebody to follow. Like he lost. Why he doing that?"

"I—"

"Well, I don't know neither. And that ain't all. Did you know he got him a graveyard up under the porch? Spends all day in his hidey hole burying Lord know whatall. Making funerals and saying prayers over graves. It ain't natural. What's all that supposed to mean?"

"I don't know. Why you asking me?"

"Well, you his momma, ain't you? Who else I got to ask? That bedpost?"

Hazel tried to answer, but again she wasn't quick enough.

"And he frets worse than an old woman. Talks like a undertaker. I swear! I ain't seen the boy in him yet." Vida gave Hazel a scalding look. "That child is in a plumb mess, and I ain't the one who's going to clean it up. You his momma."

"I know it!" Hazel shot back and then glowered out the window.

"Well, don't that mean *nothing* to you?"

When Hazel wouldn't look at her, Vida said, "Miss Hazel, a momma is the one that tells a child where he belongs. Every child need to know that. He got to know where home is. That's the biggest thing what a mother does."

For a moment, Hazel thought the woman sounded half human. "I done told you," Hazel said. "It's them pills you got in your pocket. They keeping me down. That's all's wrong with me."

Vida reached into her apron pocket and pulled out Hazel's daily dose of medicine. Rolling the pills around in her palm, she studied them seriously. Finally she said, "These here pills is supposed to keep you from dranking, ain't they?"

The way Hazel's face colored up told Vida she was right.

"Now, I ain't dumb. I know about you getting all looped up and galvanating across the countryside in your car. I *seen* it!" Vida said, remembering when she first encountered Hazel out in the Delta, dodging her whiskey bottles. "Running folks off the road, slinging your gravel in our faces. Trying to act like you somebody."

That right there was enough set to Hazel off. "That ain't it!" she shouted. "That ain't it at all. And why should I tell you about it?" Without waiting for Vida to answer, Hazel let loose on the maid. It was her turn now. "I drive because then I'm free. All my whole life it's felt like I got a fence around me, bull high and hog tight. No way out. Being moved from one pasture to the next. But when I'm in my car it's *me* who's deciding which road to take. Or *not* to take. Or even if I want to take any road at all. Sometimes I just head off through a field. I can go as fast as I want to. I can laugh, I can cry. I can stick my fool head out the window like a gold-plated idiot and hoot to high heaven. I can cuss God and my momma and my daddy and Floyd and Jesus, too. Then step on the pedal and make them all disappear in a cloud of dust. If you close by I can make you disappear, too. And yeah, I can get as drunk as I damn well please."

Vida stood there openmouthed, gazing at a red-faced woman. It was as if she had come uncorked.

"So maybe you right," Hazel said after finally taking a breath. "Maybe you hit it on the head. When I drive, I do feel like I'm somebody. Not *somebody's* somebody. Not somebody's pitiful wife. Not somebody's sorry excuse for a mother. Just plain somebody. Me. Hazelene Brenda Ishee. A woman in a car with a full tank of ethyl, reaching for a little dignity. Is that selfish?"

Vida almost answered, but Hazel beat her to the punch. "OK. It is selfish, I'll give you that one. Still, if I can have that two or three days a week, maybe four, the rest of the time is tolerable. Who's it hurting, I'm asking? You don't know what I been put through." Hazel clenched her teeth. "And you know as good as me, Floyd's been cheating with another woman. And then he pays you to get those pills down my throat. How would *you* feel? Well, I'll tell you exactly how *I* feel." She looked at Vida fiercely and then crossed her arms over her chest, her whole body shaking. "I'm sick and tired of feeling beat down. Can you understand that? I'm sick and tired of plowing other people's fields. When am I going to get some acreage of my own? My own little piece of dignity?"

As Hazel lay there, breathing heavily after her outburst, Vida looked back and forth between the white woman and the pills in her hand. Then she asked carefully, "This here dope you taking. It supposed to make you forget about all that?"

Hazel sighed. "That's the big end of it, I reckon."

Looking back at the pills, Vida said, "I reckon forgetting can be a blessing."

Hazel shut her eyes and sank back into her pillows. There was no way she could ever win with this woman.

After a long pause, Vida continued. "I heard tell of this colored woman called herself Rosie."

"Yeah, seems I heard tell of her, too," Hazel said, her eyes still shut, not saying she had heard about Rosie the same time Vida did, from downstairs in her own kitchen. Hazel seemed to remember her husband's affair had also been on the program that day.

"Well, anyways," Vida continued, "Rosie's stirring up a lot of trouble for the white folks. They say she forgot who she was. Forgot her place." Vida shook her head. "I figger it was the other way 'round. I figger she remembered who she was. Remembered she was as good as anybody else. That's what folks didn't like."

One of Hazel's eyes flipped open. "What's a colored girl got to do with me?"

"Well, I 'spect if Rosie was taking these here pills, she might of give up her seat and dragged herself on to the back of the bus. Same as ever other day. Forgot all about how tired she was."

The other eyelid went up. "I ain't asking to ride in no bus. It's the Lincoln I want."

"Don't matter," Vida said, still looking into her palm, "All I'm getting to is this. I ain't no doctor, but I say you done forgot too much already. I 'spect it's time you start remembering, like that Rosie Parks done."

"Remembering what?"

"Remembering you a momma, for one," Vida said. "I don't know about all that other craziness. About the dranking and the driving and the yelling out the window and such. Don't sound like no dignity to me." Vida shrugged. "Maybe that go along with the remembering."

Hazel thought about that for a moment. "You know," she said softly, "I never was a very good momma, no way."

"I don't doubt that for a minute," Vida said, as if she figured they were both telling the truth now. "But that boy don't know it. Good, bad, you the one he want. That there is a blessing. More than you know, Miss Hazel. What could be better in this whole world than having a little boy who don't want nobody 'cept you for his momma?" Vida smiled sadly. "A little boy who would kill to keep you safe."

"That ain't all," Hazel said, touching a freckle on the back of her hand. "I lost my Davie. You don't know what it's like to lose a child."

"Well," Vida said, "I reckon—"

"Vida," Hazel whispered, tears filling her eyes. "I could see it coming. I knew. I might could have stopped it, and I didn't. There's no making up for that."

Vida dropped her eyes. "No ma'am, there ain't no making up for that," she said, rolling the pills around in her hand. After a few moments she looked back at Hazel and said, "And Lord knows, they sure ain't no forgetting it." There was a tremble in her voice.

Vida dropped the medicine into her pocket. "Now, you listen," she said, tough once more. "I ain't going to be no mammy. How be ever, if it means getting that boy out from under my feet, maybe I can figger something out."

"Why should you?" Hazel asked.

Vida shrugged and exhaled heavily. "Beats me." When she spied what could have been a misty look of gratitude welling up in Hazel's eyes, she said sharply, "Just remember one thing. I ain't doing it for you."

"Then why?" Hazel asked again.

"Maybe there ain't no reason," Vida said, poking both fists into her apron pockets. She looked past Hazel and out the window, as if searching. "And then again, maybe if I did have a little boy walking 'round lost, I'd sure want somebody to get him back to his momma." Nodding to herself, still staring out into the distance, she said, "Maybe it's as simple as that there."

Hazel wasn't fooled. "No, it ain't that simple, is it, Vida?"

"'Ma'am?"

Hazel smiled in recognition. "You been a momma, ain't you?"

Vida caught her breath and stared incredulously at Hazel. "What you meaning?"

For a long time the two women looked at each other, searching the other's face, wondering who this person had become before their very eyes.

At last Hazel patted the side of her bed. "Sit down here next to me, Vida," she said. "Tell me about your boy. I want to know."

⁂

On Johnny's first day of school, Vida broke an egg into the skillet and then hollered at the top of her lungs, "Scrambled or fried?"

"Scrambled!" came the answer from upstairs.

Stabbing at the yolks with the spatula, she yelled again, "Well, get on down here. Breakfast almost ready."

A moment later Johnny came tearing down the stairs. "Vida! Vida! Momma ain't in her room! Where's my momma at?" He was on the verge of tears by the time he burst into the kitchen. Then he stopped dead in his tracks.

Hazel was already at the breakfast table, sitting plumb-line straight in her red sateen dress. Her hair was brushed and her makeup was on neat. The scent of Gardenia Paradise mixed gloriously with the smell of frying bacon. "Momma!" he gasped.

"I been wanting me some sugar from a real live schoolboy this morning. You know any?"

Johnny reached his arms around her neck. She kissed him and then rubbed the lipstick off his cheek with her thumb. "Momma," he said, "you look beautiful."

"Why, thank you!" she said, as if she really believed it. "And don't you look nice and growed up! Your hair all smoothed down. I swan! You even dressed yourself!" She reached over and finished tucking in a shirttail. "When did you learn how to do that?"

"Vida showed me."

"Well, she did real good, didn't she?" Hazel smiled at the maid, who continued setting the table.

"Now, sit down and eat," Vida said. "You going to be late your first day."

Johnny couldn't stop staring at his mother. "You ain't tired no more?"

"I feel just fine. Ready to dance a jig."

Vida set the biscuits on the table and then leaned against the sink, her arms crossed. "All right now," she said, her tone business-like. "What all this young man need to know about his first day at school, Miss Hazel?"

Hazel looked up at Vida blankly.

"You know. Remember what you was telling me?" She gave Hazel a piercing look. "Like when he need to go peepee. The part you was saying about holding up his hand."

There was a flicker of recognition in Hazel's face. "Oh, yeah! If you have to go to the bathroom, raise your hand."

"That's right!" Vida said, reaching behind her for the coffeepot. As she filled Hazel's cup, she prompted again, "And how about not sassing the teacher?"

"Yep. Don't break your manners," Hazel said. "Be real sweet and say 'Yes ma'am' and 'No ma'am.' "

"Anything else?" Vida asked. "Like, maybe, don't cut up in your seat and don't leave the schoolyard and be sure to get on the bus right after school lets out?"

Hazel nodded. "Yep, all them things is important, too, Johnny."

Taking her spot against the sink again, Vida asked, "You want to give him the stuff *you* bought him?"

"Oh, yeah!" Hazel reached under the table and pulled out a little plastic satchel with a picture of a cowboy painted on the front. "This is for you."

"It's the Cisco Kid!" Johnny yelled. "It's so pretty!"

"It really is!" Hazel said, looking up at Vida.

"Ain't y'all going to look inside?"

"Good idea!" Hazel said excitedly. "Let's open it up and see what's in it."

Inside they found a blue plastic ruler, a box of crayons, a pencil nearly as big around as Johnny's wrist, and a lined tablet with the ABCs on the cover—big and little letters—and a banana moon pie. "My," Hazel said thoughtfully, her eyes on the moon pie. "They think of everything, don't they?"

Vida shook her head at Hazel.

Johnny climbed up into his mother's lap and held her close, not caring in the least that he was smearing her makeup and mussing her hair and that he would spend the day smelling of Gardenia Paradise.

"We're going to be fine now, baby," Hazel whispered to him. She kissed her son again on his cheek. "I'm your mother and I don't know a lot of things, but I know exactly where you belong, honey.

You never have to worry about that. We ain't going to be lost no more."

Vida slapped her hands together. "Time for the bus! We need to get moving."

"My boy ain't gonna take no bus his first day!" Hazel proclaimed. "Nosiree! I'm gonna drive him." She turned sheepishly to Vida. "You know where Floyd hid them?"

Vida hesitated for a moment. Still reluctant, she opened the ice-box and reached into the freezer. She handed Hazel the keys to the Lincoln.

As she held them there in her hand, Hazel gazed at the keys with a look resembling real affection. She grinned big and clenched her fist tightly, warming the cold metal. "Vida," she announced, "don't expect me home no time soon. I'll be out driving some." She winked at her maid. This time it was Vida who needed prompting. "You know what we talked about. What you promised?"

"Oh yeah," Vida grumbled. "So much for that dignity." She walked across the kitchen and reached into her tote bag. Pulling out a cobalt-blue bottle, she muttered, "If you ask me, which you ain't, you just swapping the devil for the witch."

Not really understanding her little saying, Hazel only grinned at Vida, and then, as if the maid might have a change of heart, Hazel snatched the bottle from her outstretched hand. Clutching the moonshine in one hand and the ignition key warmed and ready in the other, Hazel made a dash for the Lincoln with Johnny scrambling close behind.

Chapter Thirty-Six

HAZEL GETS A FRIEND

Hazel Graham swung the Lincoln up to her house and pulled to an easy stop, the front passenger-side door lined up flush with the sidewalk steps. It was a crisp fall afternoon, the air golden with sunlight and thick with the smell of burning leaves. She honked the horn twice, bringing Johnny tearing out the front door and down the walk, with Vida following a moment later, her bag swinging from her shoulder.

Clambering up into the front next to his mother, Johnny breathed deep and hollered, "We got a new car!"

"Ain't it nice?"

Hazel waited for him to close his door and then eased the car up a few feet for Vida. The back door now in position, Hazel leaned down to receive her peck on the cheek. "How was school today? You do good?"

"I got to tell another story," he said.

"In front of the whole class?"

"Yes ma'am. And the teacher told them to clap."

"I swan."

Vida opened the door and ducked inside. She gave the backseat a couple of bounces, checking out the springs in her regular spot.

"How you like my new car, Vida? It's a '57!"

Vida rolled her eyes. "Same as the old one, ain't it?" Like Johnny, she took a sniff. "Except it don't got that medicine smell. And it ain't got no caved-in hood."

"Make it squeal, Momma!"

"Hold on to your taters!" Hazel yelled, and then, leaving the smell of rubber in her wake and neighbors scurrying to their windows, the trio headed off to Tarbottom, with Vida in the back gripping the door handle.

Hazel was turning down the hill toward the river while simultaneously touching up her lipstick when Johnny shot up in his seat. "Stop, Momma!" he screamed. "You gonna hit him! Stop!"

Hazel stomped on the brake pedal, throwing gravel and fishtailing the car within inches of the ditch. Vida went hard up against the front seat. The car skidded to a stop and Johnny hopped out, scampering back up the road through the dust. Watching him from the rearview, Hazel saw him pick up a very lucky box turtle she had straddled with her tires. Johnny took the turtle back to the side of the road, turned him around, and patted him on the shell. When he got back in the car, Hazel asked him, "Why'd you point him thataway?"

"So he could get on home before he hurts hisself."

Vida gathered herself up in the backseat, growling. "Just going to turn hisself around again." She pulled the apron out of her sack and mopped the nervous sweat from her brow. "He going to cross that road no matter what you do. You see if he don't." Vida cut her eyes at Hazel in the mirror. "You see, Johnny, some of God's creatures you can't tell *nothing* to. Hardheaded as that turtle's hull. They ain't going to change their ways even if it kills them and a load of other folks."

Nodding thoughtfully, Hazel said, "Johnny, Vida's right. You go put that turtle on the other side of the road. If you want to help a thing, you got to help it in the direction it's headed." Hazel beamed, delighted with herself. Floyd wasn't the only one who could come up with snappy little sayings, and she told Vida so. Vida rolled her eyes.

ᴄ~ᴏ

In Tarbottom, Hazel pulled the car close alongside Vida's front porch. Johnny and Vida got out. Hazel made herself comfortable where she was. Sucking on a peppermint, her legs dangling out the car door, she was feeling especially good. She always did on her driving days.

"I had me some kind of fun today!" she announced. "Even better than when I come up on that town run by nothing but colored people. Remember me telling that? Started by the slaves of Jefferson Davis hisself!"

"Seem to," Vida replied from where she sat up on the porch. Her eyes were on Johnny, who was playing pretend with a family of cornshuck dolls she'd made for him.

"Today I saw me some real live Gypsies!"

"Gypsies?" hollered Johnny, jumping to his feet.

Hazel worked the peppermint to the opposite cheek and then continued. "Yep. I was coming down off some old ridge road and there they were, camped out by a branch. A whole herd of Gypsies."

"A *band* of Gypsies, Momma."

"Mighta been," Hazel said grudgingly. This was *her* story, after all. She gathered up her excitement and continued, "They had these wagons with roofs. You should have seen them. Painted red and blue and green and yellow. Pictures of flowers and animals and such. And there were snow-white horses grazing on the hill. Their bridles had little gold bells."

"Yes ma'am, sounds like you sure nuff had a big day. Shouldn't you be getting on home now?" Vida glanced nervously up and down the road.

"There were real live Gypsies?" Johnny asked.

"Sure! A mess of them. I mean, a band of them. With gold hoops in their ears and the men wore bright-colored head rags. They had real dark skin and these mysterious black eyes. They was something! And real friendly folk."

"You talked to them, Momma?"

"I did. I said, 'Nice day to be outdoors, ain't it?' Invited me to sit around their fire. Gimme a drink of something out of a bottle that had a real worm in the bottom. Brought it up all the way from Mexico. They told me they was on their way to Meridian, where the queen of all the Gypsies is buried. Going there for some kind of a Gypsy powwow."

Fishing another peppermint from her bag, Hazel sighed contentedly. "The things you learn in this ol' world. I swan. One day I'm going to come across that colored girl from the circus and find out where she got them pretty clothes."

"Yes'm," Vida said, mostly to herself.

Hazel loved these chats with Vida. They were a perfect ending to her driving days. These days started with Vida showing up early in the morning with a little blue bottle in her flour-sack tote bag. After they got Floyd off to work and Johnny off to school, Hazel would pack a couple of sandwiches or some cold fried chicken and head out by herself, staying gone till late afternoon. When she was done, she would pick up Johnny and Vida at the house and then head back to Tarbottom. Hazel was getting good at angling the Lincoln within a hair's breadth of the front steps. That way Vida and Hazel could hear each other talk without Hazel having to get out of the car. Floyd had told her it went hard against tradition for a white man or woman to put both feet on a colored person's porch. A man might could put one foot up maybe, as long as the other stayed on the ground. Hazel didn't mind pushing a few conventions, but she wasn't taking any chances on getting sent away for being crazy again. Besides, this way was just fine. Vida seemed to be able to hear Hazel perfectly as she related from her car all the strange and wonderful things she had seen during her drive. At least, Vida had never asked Hazel to repeat anything.

Hazel looked on contentedly as her son pretended the dolls were Gypsies and made them do a little Gypsy dance. At first Hazel had been leery about Johnny playing with dolls instead of his cowboy toys. No doubt that boy had his own way about him. After living under the house in the dirt for most of the summer, he now insisted on dressing in his Sunday clothes for school. Refused to put on a pair of jeans. He looked like a little businessman, with his white starched shirt and dark blue pants, toting his Cisco satchel. Even his teacher said he was special, all right.

Hazel smiled proudly as Johnny sang a peppy Gypsy dance tune. She figured she would take her own advice about helping a thing in the direction it was headed. Vida said a mother is the person who shows a child where home is, but Hazel figured there was more to it than that. A child's not going to stay at home forever. Like her, Johnny was reaching out for something. It took Miss Pearl to recognize and name what Hazel herself had been reaching for all these years, and now Hazel wanted to do the same for her son. She figured that though a mother might not be able to change the direction her child was heading, at least she could make sure he got there with a fistful of hope. If acting out stories with cornshuck dolls was what it took to make Johnny happy, then more power to him.

Maybe I'm not such a bad mother after all, she dared think.

With her friend close by on the porch and her boy lost in play, the sun setting on a world with plenty left to explore, for the first time in a long time Hazel was actually at peace. It was as if her own far-flung hopes were coming home to light.

Chapter Thirty-Seven

ANSWERED PRAYERS

Levi reached on top of the chifforobe and brought down the brown paper sack. Very carefully he drew out his felt hat with the oval crown, the brim that was still stiff as new. After removing the newspaper stuffing from the hollow of the crown, he held the hat out before him and lightly touched the small satin bow on the shiny band. This was the hat he had worn only to deacon meetings and to conferences with the Senator, on occasions when he needed to use his sway. The hat hadn't seen the light of day for years. He hadn't needed it. There wasn't anybody who would listen to him.

Today they would listen.

Next Levi pulled out his gray preaching suit that hung flat against the back wall of the wardrobe. He remembered those early dawns after he had lost his church. Vida would lay this suit neatly across the bed with a fresh starched shirt and dark tie. She would tiptoe soundlessly around the bedroom, trying not to disturb him as he prayed on his knees to the Lord to give him another chance. He would dress and spend the day traveling the county, begging every cotton-field church he came across to let him say a few words. All Levi had ever wanted was to preach.

Today his prayers were being answered, exactly forty years from the morning he stood on the banks of the Hopalachie River and first saw the face of God looking up at him from that whirlpool of churning water. Forty years. The same amount of time Moses spent in the wilderness before leading his people to the edge of the Promised Land.

He held the suit up before him. The moths had got to it, but it would do for today. He smiled sadly, thinking there might be bigger holes in it by sundown.

Levi put on the fresh white shirt he had paid a woman to boil and starch so Vida wouldn't know. Standing before the cracked mirror that hung on the chifforobe door, he knotted his silk tie with the hand-painted butterflies he got hand-me-down from the Senator; then put on the vest and coat. The cracks in the mirror broke Levi's face into four distinct pieces. Levi smiled at that, too. "Thank you, Lord," he prayed simply, "for today is the day you make me whole again. I step into the darkness with you."

The only thing left to do was to loop his gold chain across his vest, the watch having been sold years ago to put gas in the old Buick. He rummaged through the fruitcake tin and the bottoms of all the drawers, in the pockets of his clothes. The chain was nowhere to be found. Vida would probably know where it was. She often pulled it out when she got lonesome for Nate. He gave up the search and took it as a sign from God against his vanity. Levi carefully positioned the hat on his head.

He looked up into the sky when he stepped out the door. He had never seen such a sight! Curiously shaped clouds in a multitude of unearthly colors, moiling and swirling, like heaven was still mulling over what kind of a day to turn out. When he understood, tears came to his eyes. It was the whirling, ever-changing face of God, looking down upon him, showering him with blessings, showing him the way out of the wilderness.

⟡

Billy Dean Brister sat in his office with his new air conditioner going full bore. It was coolish for November, but he liked to watch the lazy curl of smoke rising innocently from his cigarette, until the shaft of cold air from the vent blasted it. The unsuspecting smoke would rupture and be whisked away across the room in a thin cloud. It helped him think.

Delia had really put his ass in a crack this time. What had she been thinking of? Now the Senator was telling him if he didn't find either her body or the nigger who killed her that Billy Dean would have to resign. Pompous old fool. All the time going on about how they were *his niggers* and nobody knew *his niggers* except him. But just wait. The minute somebody or something went missing, he was the first one yelling, "Which one of them sorry ingrates did this to me?" Don't even have a body to examine and he knows for sure that Delia was drowned by some grudge-holding darkie specially out to get him. Served one term at the lousy state house a hundred years ago, and that supposed to make him some kind of know everything god?

Billy Dean blew another jet of smoke into the stiff current of air. The question was, what the hell was he going to do to buy some time? Wasn't as easy as turning over a few shacks in colored town. If the Senator found out about him and Delia, he would do more than ask him to resign. The Senator would have him take Delia's place at the bottom of the river.

He should have known Delia would bring him nothing but trouble. Trouble was her middle name. Always living on the wild side. Doing things to shock everybody. Like marrying those nose-talking Yankees. The woman even had the nerve to bring them down here and rub it in everybody's face. And those love letters of hers. Leaving them under his windshield wipers. On the seat of his desk chair, right in his office. Any reckless place she could think of. That purple-and-white paper was her personal calling card. He'd told her a million times to leave off with them purple letters.

"Don't say purple, Billy Dean," she'd purred at him. "That's too common. Like you. It's lavender and cream. With a touch of *Chanel*. Like me."

Once, when Hertha threw a dinner party, Delia had sneaked off upstairs and put a steamy one right under his pillow. Right there in her sister's own bed! She reveled in the possibility of getting caught. When she got pregnant, the game got serious. She taped one of those purple-and-white envelopes to his front door. It said that unless he left Hertha, whom she despised in a way only a sister could, and ran away with her, she would make sure her daddy knew everything. She would ruin him. If Hertha had come home thirty seconds earlier, he would have been ruined anyway. Plus castrated and shot. As it was, he was barely able to get the desk drawer shut and locked before she walked in. Billy Dean had been furious. That's when he'd threatened to kill Delia. That had been a big mistake.

Just then his deputy flung open the office door, barging in on his thoughts. "Dammit, Lampkin," he snarled. "Ain't I told you to knock first? I didn't hang no screen door there for a reason."

"Sorry, Sheriff," the baby-faced Lampkin said, not seeming to take the sheriff's mood too personally, "I thought you'd want to know it first. They's trouble over at the courthouse. Nellie Grindle is pitching a fit."

"What's wrong this time? She trying to take all the Senator's dead friends off the voting rolls again? She knows he ain't gonna stand for that."

"Nope. You better come on. They's a nigruh over there says he wants to vote."

⟡

Billy Dean had been waiting for something like this to happen. Only a few months ago, down in Lincoln County, some nigger called himself Lamar Smith had tried it and got shot dead right there on the courthouse lawn in broad daylight. Some say the county sheriff had done it himself, but of course nobody would testify to it. If Billy Dean was called on to do the same thing, he'd be more than willing.

He got to the circuit clerk's office to see the colored man still there, his hat in hand smiling respectfully at a pinched-faced woman with pointy glasses who by now had gone purple in the face.

"Sheriff!" she cried out in an annoying squeak of a voice, "it's about time you got here. This nigruh's trying to register for the vote. And when I told him to leave the premises, he flat-out refused."

It took a moment for the sheriff to recognize the man dressed in the suit as baggy as a rodeo clown's. "Well, lookee who it is!" he said. "I always said you was a troublemaker, boy. You been biding your time, ain't you?"

Levi smiled shyly at the sheriff. "You sure were right about me, Sheriff. I been biding my time, like you say. I been weighing the matter and now I wants the vote."

The sheriff studied Levi's face and then frowned. This is all I need, Billy Dean thought. The Senator watching me like a hawk, and now his old pet nigger has gone crazy. Strolling right in here in front of God and everybody. No telling what he was liable to say. Billy Dean walked over to Levi and shoved him hard, slamming Levi into the doorjamb. "Get outa here!" he shouted.

When Levi opened his mouth to speak, the sheriff shouted louder, "Now, goddammit! Not another word out of your sassy mouth."

Nellie dropped her chin. "Aren't you going to arrest him for disturbing the peace or something?"

"Nellie, don't you know Levi? Well then, let me introduce you two. This here is one of the *Senator's* niggers. You know we got special rules just for them," Billy Dean sneered. He looked back at Levi, who remained by the door with a pleasant grin on his face. "I don't see you moving, boy."

"That's right, suh," Levi said politely and bowed his head. His manner was almost courtly. "I was telling Miss Nellie, I come to take that voting test."

That set Billy Dean back for a moment. "Are you deaf? Did you hear what I told you to do?"

"Yessuh," Levi said. "But like you explained to the Senator, I'm a born troublemaker. Don't know no other way to be. Guess you going to have to do what Miss Nellie say and toss me in the jailhouse." Nellie clutched her old woman's breast and gasped, "Of all the...I've never in my..."

The sheriff studied Levi warily. "You want me to arrest you? That it? You trying to rain the Senator down on my ass?"

"I want to vote, sir," Levi said again, respectfully. "And I reckon if I can't vote, I might as well go on to where they puts all the colored that try."

Billy Dean grinned. "The years ain't been good to you, has they, old man? I believe you crazier than a coot." All the more reason to get him out of here fast, before he starts to raving, thought the sheriff. Something sure wasn't right here. Smelled fishy. If he arrested him, people might take the old man serious. The Senator would get involved for sure. The sheriff had another idea.

He grabbed Levi by the arm and yanked him out the door and down the corridor. By the time they got outside to the courthouse gallery, word had spread and a small crowd of whites had already gathered on the lawn. Among them Billy Dean thought he saw the glint of a gun. All the black faces had wisely pulled back to the safety of the other side of the street.

All anybody saw, black or white, was the overworked sheriff of Hopalachie County clutching an old colored man dressed in a ridiculous suit, with a foolish grin on his face. People started shaking their heads at the pitiful sight even before the sheriff pushed him down the steps.

As he lay there sprawled out on the sidewalk, his hat crushed beneath his backside, Levi nodded respectfully to Billy Dean, who stood with his hands on his hips at the top of the steps. "Sheriff, sir, I still want the vote. Now all these good people is my witness. So if you ain't going to let me take that voting test, you best take me on to jail."

A few gasps went up from the crowd, and they began mutter to one another, yet every eye stayed on their sheriff, waiting.

With only a wink from the sheriff, Levi Snow would instantly become just another colored killed by "unknown assailants." All Billy Dean had to do was turn his back and walk back into the courthouse. Would the Senator still put the blame on him?

Billy Dean shook his head and grinned. "Crazy as a coot," he laughed loudly. "Nothing a good sobering up couldn't help."

Reassured, the crowd laughed with the sheriff and then began to scatter.

As he walked away, Billy Dean said to himself, "Now let him tell his story and see who listens. That's almost as good as dead."

Not everybody was laughing. Later that afternoon, Floyd got a frantic call at the agency from Hayes Alcorn. He was convening an emergency board meeting of the Citizens' Council. He said to be over at the bank in fifteen minutes.

Again, Floyd was convinced that it was about him and Delia. The sheriff was still looking for the murderer, and Floyd, a nervous wreck for more than three months now, had decided that somebody was bound to inform on him sooner or later. He would probably be called in for questioning and interrogated about all the time he stole from his poor, nervous wife to be with the Senator's twice-divorced daughter. All the sordid details of their pathetic little affair would be on the front page of the *Jackson Daily News*. The word "illicit" haunted him in his dreams. Floyd left Hollis in charge and as he crossed the street to the Merchant and Planters repeated to himself, "I feel healthy! I feel happy! I feel terrific!"

It was after banking hours, but Hayes was standing at the entrance, holding the door open for the members as they arrived and pointing them one by one to the conference room across the marble lobby. "Glad you could make it," he told Floyd, looking truly appreciative. "These are troubling times."

Floyd breathed easier. From the grateful look on Hayes's face,

Floyd could tell he was still considered to be on the right side of troubling times. Much relieved, he went on in to join the other members.

Floyd was met by a weary look from the sheriff, who sat pulled back from the mahogany conference table, his legs crossed, the Stetson pushed back on his head, flicking that old nickel-plated lighter. Billy Dean looked as if he had been run through the wringer all right, and it showed—months of chasing leads and tracking down suspects, running the hounds till they dropped, tromping through woods and thickets and digging up fields, dragging miles of creeks and swamps and rivers by the light of day and by torch at night, and so far only coming up with a couple dead bodies and neither of them white. Everybody knew his job was on the line. Floyd forced a smile at Billy Dean and then took a chair, angling it so his guilt-ridden face was out of the sheriff's line of sight.

Hayes walked to the head of the table and cleared his throat. He always ran the meetings standing up, all five-foot-four of him. "Like I told everybody already, we got a crisis on our hands. A well-known nigruh agitator walked right in the circuit clerk's office as big as broad daylight, and demanded to be registered to vote. Nearly scared poor ol' Nellie Grindle to death. Twenty years, and she ain't never had no nigruh to suggest such a thing."

"Who was it?" asked Gaylon King, the newspaper publisher. "Levi Snow," Hayes said as if the name itself would raise alarm. He plopped down dramatically in his personal chair with legs six inches higher than all the rest. "You can see we got a problem."

The county attorney, Hartley Faircloth, looked at Hayes incredulously. "You mean that old colored man who tends yards? What he do, threaten Miss Nellie with his rake?"

Everybody laughed.

His face pinking up, Hayes shot out of his chair and leaned over the table. "The man is a known agitator. Ain't that right, Sheriff?"

The sheriff didn't bother looking up from his lighter. "Was once," he mumbled.

Hayes waited for the sheriff to tell the rest of the story, but it was obvious that Billy Dean was all talked out on the subject. Narrowing his eyes at the sheriff, Hayes said pointedly, "Nellie told me you didn't even arrest him. That right?"

"I took care of it," the sheriff said.

Hayes shook his head and pulled back to address the whole group. "The way I understand it, he use to be one of them NAACP preachers trying to stir up the colored. Y'all might remember that nigruh church getting burnt down out in the county a few years back."

Nobody seemed to. Yet Hayes said, as if they did, "Well, that was his!"

Hayes planted his little balled-up fists on the table and leaned in toward Billy Dean again. "Ain't that right, Sheriff?"

"'Fore I was elected," Billy Dean said, clicking the lid of the lighter shut.

Johnelle Ramphree, from the hardware store, piped up. "That old man's harmless, Hayes. Maybe a little addled, is all. I don't think we got nothing here to worry about. Not from a poor ol' afflicted colored man. He's nothing like the one that tried to vote down in Brookhaven."

Hayes was not one to be dismissed so lightly. "That's only a front. He's been biding his time. He told the sheriff as much. Right in front of Nellie. Given this mess in Montgomery with that King preacher and the Supreme Court going pinko, and nigruhs asking to vote right here in Mississippi, he knows the climate is right. No telling how many he can get stirred up if we don't do something immediately. Gentlemen, it's up to us. Hopalachie County is in the grips of a Jewish-Communist conspiracy. We might have another Martin Luther King right in our midst."

Floyd shifted uncomfortably in his chair. It was Floyd who had first talked his neighbors into using Levi in their yards, and he had the man's daughter working right under his own roof. He decided he better weigh in on this thing before it turned on him. "Now, I agree with Johnelle," he said. "I been around Levi, and he seems a pleasant enough colored—" He stopped and corrected himself, "I mean nigruh." He better talk in Hayes's language if he was going to head this thing off, something he'd learned from that book about influencing people.

"Floyd!" Hayes said. "You ought to be more concerned than anybody. I've seen him out there talking with your boy. Johnelle said he was criminally insane."

"I believe I said 'addled,' " Johnelle corrected.

"No matter. Did you ever see how big that nigruh is? Six and a half feet if he's an inch." Hayes was reaching up over his head as far as he could, but Floyd figured he still came a few inches short. "And those hands could choke a cow," Hayes added.

The nickel-plated lighter shut with such a crack, everybody's head snapped toward Billy Dean. It was clear that something had caught his interest. Straightening up from his slouch, Billy Dean said, "He might well be dangerous, at that." He stuck the lighter in the pocket of his khakis and pulled up to the table as if he had decided to join the meeting after all.

Thrilled to finally be getting support from the sheriff, Hayes went after Floyd. The little man looped his arms out in front of him dramatically. "Why, I've seen him tote a two-hundred-pound tree trunk the length of my yard. Ain't you the least bit worried, Floyd? At least for your boy's sake? For your wife's?"

Of course, Levi had also been seen by the whole neighborhood talking to Hayes's wife, Pearl. That wasn't being mentioned. But Floyd decided not to be antagonistic. Try to see the other person's point of view. "Maybe we should hear Hayes out," Floyd said, settling into a reasonable position. "Why don't you tell us what it is you're suggesting, Hayes?" Floyd was impressed with the the sound of that. Almost statesmanlike.

"Thank you," Hayes said, acknowledging Floyd's contribution. "It's not as if I'm advocating violence. I told y'all from the beginning that's not what the Citizens' Council stands for. Like our charter says, we stand for a peaceful yet firm response to any attack on our way of life. I suggest we make an example of this nigruh by guaranteeing he never works again in this county. We boycott him. And what's more, he doesn't get credit from any Delphi merchant nor service from any professional."

Gaylon King wasn't convinced. "Seems like a little overkill for a poor ol' broke-down colored man, don't you think, Hayes? I agree with Johnelle. This don't compare at all to that agitator in Brookhaven. By the way," the publisher added with a sly grin, "this wouldn't have anything to do with the rumors about you announcing for governor, would it? How about a quote for the paper?"

There were a few sniggers. Gaylon went on, "I can run it as my lead story: Hayes Alcorn Single-Handedly Starves Out Old Colored Man."

That drew an bigger laugh. Hayes ignored it and continued outlining his all-out campaign to save the county from the conspiracy at hand. "And I suggest we extend this boycott to all members of his family." Hayes looked down at Floyd. "That means you need to get rid of his girl, of course."

Floyd sat up in his chair. "I don't see why that's necessary, Hayes," he protested.

"Well, exactly what do you see as *necessary*, Floyd? What does our vice president suggest?"

"Well," Floyd said, taking a breath and diagramming the situation in his head. He could already see the sparks flying if he had to tell Hazel he was going to fire Vida. She was sure to throw a duck fit. Things around his house had changed dramatically over the past month. Hazel was all fired up and full of grit, dressing nice and out driving the Lincoln like the old days. Maybe even drinking, but not enough to tell it. She seemed happy. Though he would prefer to believe his positive mental attitude had rubbed off on her, he was more convinced Vida was somehow behind it.

"Well?" Hayes said impatiently.

Floyd cut his eyes to the ceiling and exhaled deeply, letting Hayes know he was still in a mulling mode. Maybe it would be better if Vida were gone, he thought, taking the other side of the issue. He had probably trusted her too much. Truth was, Floyd had no idea what was going on in his home. This thing with Delia had sapped all his extra energy. Floyd got the feeling that as a result of his lack of attention on the home front, he was now surrounded by a conspiracy between his maid and his wife. Could be his own son was in on it. Still he didn't want to rock the boat. Floyd had the vague feeling that Hazel knew about Delia, and he wasn't anxious to find out how much. Let sleeping dogs lie.

The room was still waiting for Floyd's best thinking on the subject. He cleared his throat. "Well, maybe we can give Levi a good talking-to and tell him to get back to his yard work," he said hopefully. "I bet that's all it would take."

Hayes's response was immediate. "No! No! No! That's not the way it works at all," he cried, sounding like his chances for governor were slipping away before his eyes. His reaction was so violent, Floyd began to worry about the extension on his business loan.

Then Hayes started strutting around the room like a banty rooster. "We're the Citizens' Council! We're supposed to strike fear in the hearts of agitators. We don't give them a good *talking-to*. Now, y'all got to get behind me on this. And Floyd, you of all people. The vice president for Christ's sake." He glanced quickly at the other end of the table. "Sorry, Brother Dear."

Brother Dear, sheathed in his white linen suit, had been listening intently to the debate and used the opportunity of Hayes's blasphemy to insert himself on the Lord's behalf. He smiled at Hayes forgivingly and then leaned forward to address the group. "I've been listening carefully to what's been said here today. Now, I know that each of you comes here with the well-being of your community foremost in your thoughts and prayers. So I think it's safe to put aside any doubts you might be having about the motivations of others at this table."

Hayes nodded aggressively.

Brother Dear's beatific smile and melodious voice had already given a new gravity to the proceedings. The men around the table now wore the sober expressions of civic responsibility. "I believe what Hayes says bears listening to," he continued. "Since the Supreme Court handed down that Brown decision a couple of years ago, our community institutions have been under constant attack from Washington. Our local government. Our schools. Our businesses. Next in logical sequence, like the falling of dominoes, will be the church. And finally it's the family that will topple."

He let that sit a minute before he went on. "Our local traditions make up a complex weave." Brother Dear made a dramatic sweep of his hand over the sleeve of his white suit to demonstrate. He was well known for using visual aids in his sermons. "That weave, our community fabric if you will, is a living, breathing testimony to our shared Christian faith." To emphasize that point, Brother Dear reached up and lightly touched his cross-of-diamonds stickpin.

Then he shook his finger at the group. "And this is not about prejudice and discrimination. Why, look at us here. We have Baptists and Methodists and Presbyterians and Episcopalians all sitting around the same table together."

Everyone grinned sheepishly, acknowledging the private reservations they had had about such a thing in the beginning. Everyone grinned, that is, except for Billy Dean, who, when Floyd glanced over at him, seemed to be deep in thought. From where he sat, Floyd could see the sheriff's hands under the table, and instead of the lighter, he was fiddling with a gold chain of some kind, fingering the links one at a time. Floyd noticed a charm shaped like praying hands dangling from the chain.

"Nor is this simply about a yardman and a maid," Brother Dear was saying. "It represents a kind of gnawing at those fibers that hold together our community. We need to take righteous action before more threads are broken and the fabric loosens. Before we disintegrate—desegregate if you will—into social chaos. You all know what that means."

Floyd rolled his eyes. Yeah, he figured he knew what it meant. All those colored men had been biding their time for three hundred years, working the fields, getting out from under slavery, getting themselves lynched, burned, and drowned, and finally going all the way to the Supreme Court—all that, just to get them a white woman. If that was true, Floyd thought, they ought to get some kind of blue ribbon for pure determination.

No, he couldn't figure out the logic of some of these people. Yet what he could figure out by the silence around the table was that Brother Dear's sermon had pretty well clinched the deal for Levi and Vida. All that was missing was the amen and hallelujahs.

⁓

Floyd hardly looked at Hazel all through supper, and when he did, his expression was tinged with guilt. It wasn't as if she hadn't seen it coming for a long time now. Hazel prepared herself for the worst, the other-woman confession. Delia might be dead and gone, but so was Floyd's affection for Hazel. She was certain that he had already replaced Delia with another.

She watched apprehensively as he took the last bite of his minute steak and carefully folded and unfolded his napkin several times. He glanced at Johnny. "Go up to your room and play. OK, Little Monkey?"

"All my doll people are at Vi—" Johnny caught himself before he broke his and his mother's secret. "Yes sir," he said, and took off upstairs like a guilty man set free.

"Hazel," Floyd said gravely, unfolding the napkin again and somberly laying it over his plate as if he were covering the face of a dead friend. "I got something I need to tell you."

She closed her eyes and bit her lip. Here it comes, she told herself.

"Bad as I hate to..." Floyd said.

"Oh, God," Hazel moaned, slumping down in her chair.

"Bad as I hate to...we going to have to let Vida go."

It took a moment for it to register. "Vida?"

"It's for her own good, Hazel."

Hazel knew she should be thankful he wasn't asking for a divorce, but it wasn't gratitude or even relief she was feeling now. Not even fear. Something else was taking hold.

"You're going to fire Vida? That's what you're trying to say?" There was a boiling down deep in her gut. The floor seemed to quake under her chair. In her mind she saw a tattered lace handkerchief tied to a flagpole and whipping valiantly in a gale-sized wind.

Shifting into his most logical voice, he said, "Now, she's only a maid, Hazel. I can find you another one just as good by suppertime tomorrow."

When she saw him begin to rise up from the table, it was like another person took over inside. Her fist came banging down on the tabletop hard enough to rattle the silverware in the drawers.

Floyd fell back into his chair, covering his head. Hazel heard herself speaking to her husband in a voice that was flat and final. "Ain't no way you getting rid of Vida." Her face burned hot, and she was not sure where the voice had come from, only that it had been too long in the coming.

It took a few moments for Floyd to regain his composure. His voice was still a little shaky. "Now, don't upset yourself. You been doing so good and all. You're letting your emotions get the best of you. Calm down and listen."

She crossed her arms over her chest and shook her head vehemently, trying to block out his words. He reached for her hand, still clenched at her side. "Hazel, we got to be a team on this now."

"Team?" She erupted in a burst of angry laughter. She snatched her hand from his. "My whole life long I ain't never had a real friend before. Somebody in this world who would be on my side no matter what. Somebody I can tell everything to. Who listens without interrupting. Who don't list out everything I should have done different. Who don't want me to be nothing except what I already am. No way you're gonna make me give Vida up, Floyd Graham. No way in hell. Vida stays! She's the one on my team."

The words had tumbled out in such a rush that Hazel wasn't altogether sure what she had said. When she looked up at Floyd he seemed to have been struck dumb. He cleared his throat a couple of times and struggled to give her one of his trademark grins, yet the rest of his face wasn't able to get behind it.

"Hazel, you're talking about a colored woman," he said. "She can't be your friend."

"Don't go telling me what Vida is or ain't. You got no right."

"Now, I got to insist, Hazel," Floyd said, his tone less confident than his words. "It might come down to staying in business or not. And I know you want what's best for the family. Please, Hazel."

As went on begging, Hazel almost felt sorry for Floyd, until he said, "It might seem like a problem now, but we got to look at it as an opportunity."

This time Hazel banged both fists on the table. "Stop spouting those things at me!" she screamed.

Floyd covered his head again. "What things?" he called out from his crouched position.

"Those sayings of yours. About how what is—really ain't. And what ain't—really is. About if you call something by a different name, all your troubles will disappear. Floyd, all you doing is tying my brain up in knots."

"All I'm saying," he ventured, "is if you take what looks to be your very worst problem and think about it positively, what you might have before you is something you can use. I already told you all this. Remember? Lemons and lemonade?"

Floyd found his salesman's grin again. "Now all I ask is if you would take ten seconds and think about what I just said. See if you can make the problem work for you. Make some lemonade, so to speak."

Hazel eyed him dubiously yet did as he requested. She gave it seven seconds, then she said, "OK, let me see if I got it. If I take the most awfullest thing, and look at it different, try to hang some hope on it, so to speak, then I might can figure a way to make it turn out good?"

"Exactly, honey. That's all I'm saying." Floyd was real excited now, as if there might be hope for her after all. "It's the Science of Controlled Thinking."

"I see," Hazel said. "Like if I thought you cheated on me with another woman, for instance. There might be a way to make that work *for* me instead of *against* me?"

Floyd opened and closed his mouth several times as if he were straining for air. He stammered, "Wha...wha...what are you asking again, honey? Would you repeat that question for me?" His voice was all bluff.

She smiled innocently and said, "I'm asking, is that the way it works, Floyd? Am I a controlled thinker now?" There was a long moment of silence while Hazel's big blue eyes looked expectantly at Floyd, waiting for his answer.

Floyd blurted out, "Hazel, I ain't cheating on you! I swear it!"

Maybe he wasn't...not now, this very second. Maybe there was no new woman in his life. Even if Floyd was technically right, he was still cheating with his words. He was sacrificing his dignity for a lie. He didn't have the courage to tell her the truth.

"What's the matter, Floyd? You look sick at the stomach."

"What's got into you?" he shouted. "Stop it, whatever it is, you hear?"

She knew she had won something and lost something at the same time. "Maybe I don't understand your little saying after all, Floyd.

Maybe I'm not sophisticated enough."

She pushed herself away from the table and rose to her feet. When she stood, she noticed how strong and solid her legs felt beneath her. Hazel said more sarcastically than she meant to, "But please don't fire Vida. Would you do that one thing for your poor, ignorant wife?"

Chapter Thirty-Eight

SET UP FOR A FALL

Vida had the fidgets so bad she had already chipped two of Hazel's dishes, and it wasn't even noon.

Levi had stunned her the evening before with the news about his day at the courthouse. His eyes had shone bright, the way they had the night he came home raving about the lightning bugs and his church that couldn't be burned. That had been over a month ago. She thought he had got it out of his system.

"I wish you could have seen it, Vida," he told her. "You would have been proud. It's what God been leading me to do. I'm walking with the Lord again. Stepping out in faith."

Vida had been so stunned she collapsed on the bed in disbelief, hiding her face in her hands.

"You should have seen how they looked at me, Vida," he said. "Like I was dangerous or something. Like I was a man to be dealt with. It was like Moses calling on the Pharaoh."

Vida looked up at him and shouted, "Don't you never say nothing about no Moses again! You hear? We ain't people in no book. You can't go plopping us down in some make-believe story 'cause it suits you. We is real!" She jumped to her feet, furious, and held her arms out to her father. "See? Flesh and blood. We got feelings. We can hurt. We can die. You got no right."

Levi seemed bewildered by his daughter's reaction. "Vida, you don't know what you're saying. It was God's will. I had to do it."

"No you didn't!" Vida said, furious. "You didn't have no right get-ting up one day and out of the clear blue deciding you was going to be Moses. 'Cause tomorrow when you wake up, you got to go back to being Levi the nigger yardboy. You'll still be living in Mississippi. The white man still be on top. And then what you do? You think God going to get you out of this mess? Well, he ain't. Case you ain't noticed, he ain't parted no seas for us lately."

Levi had been undeterred. "It is the path, Vida. I got to go where the Lord leads me. Don't you see it? It was God sent the sheriff to burn my church down. Made him spread the lie about me working for the vote. But the sheriff's lie was God's truth. God wants me to stand up for my people. Like that King preacher in Alabama. Like that Rosie Parks girl you told me about. She stood her ground and got dragged off to jail for it. The Lord done set out a story for her, and she ain't backing down from it. I ain't neither."

"Don't lay it on Rosie," Vida said sharply. "That ain't our story neither. No more than Moses is." Yet when she saw his look of incomprehension, she gave up. All she could do was shake her head sadly, bite her tongue, and walk away.

They had hardly spoken the rest of the evening. Levi sat out on the porch praying, and Vida stayed inside, terrified the sheriff might show up any minute to firebomb their house. After an hour passed with the cabin still standing, Vida had almost convinced herself that her father had imagined the whole thing. Then Creola came crash-ing up the steps. After nodding uncertainly to Levi, she rushed to Vida's side. She breathlessly confirmed Levi's story, saying that it was all Hayes Alcorn had talked about during supper.

The next morning at breakfast, things were strained between her and her father. Clearing away the dishes, Vida suggested the only workable idea she had been able to come up with. "Maybe we ought to go on up to Memphis," she said. "Borry some money from Willie and leave Delphi. I ain't got no reason to be here no more. Crazy, just waiting around to get killed."

"No. I ain't running," Levi said firmly. "I got to wait right here. This is where my church will be. The Lord promised it to me." His face softened, and he smiled patiently at Vida, as if she were a little girl who didn't understand her Sunday school lesson. "Don't be afraid, Snowflake Baby. He ain't deserted us. He been watching and directing our feet all the time."

He reached over and cupped her face in his giant hand. She knew then that there was no way she could talk him out of this. Her father had finally set his world right again. He had found a story he could weave himself into. He was a self-proclaimed prophet of God, a leader of his people, the kind they wrote up in newspapers and put on TV. It didn't matter that not a soul was following him. He was the Reach Out Man once more.

Now Vida was looking out the Grahams' back door for the umpteenth time that morning, hoping to get a glimpse of her father working in the neighborhood, when Hazel came up behind her and said, "What's got you on edge?" Vida nearly jumped out of her skin.

"You expecting company?" Hazel asked. "Your friends coming over later?"

Vida yanked the screen door shut. "Ain't nothin' the matter with me. Didn't sleep much, is all." She walked over to the oven to check on the corn bread.

"Well, if it's about what your daddy did, I don't want you to worry one bit," Hazel said, sounding proud as could be. "I done fixed it."

Vida slammed the oven door shut. "Fixed it?" She spun around to face the white woman. Hazel had a satisfied grin on her face. That's all I need, Vida thought, a woman the whole town knows to be a crazy drunk coming down hard on my side. She'll get us all killed. "What you mean, you fixed it?"

"Floyd's little boys' club told him he had to fire you," Hazel said. "But I put my foot down. 'No way in hell,' I said. I said, 'Nobody's gonna fire my Vida.' " Hazel's eyes seemed to mist up. "Oh, I wish you could have heard me, Vida. I really stood up for you."

Hazel looked as if she expected a "Praise the lord" and a "Thank you, Jesus" to come bubbling out of Vida's mouth. Instead, Vida's face went to stone, and she angrily wrenched herself around to the sink. She began scrubbing a pan so hard, it looked like she was trying to take off the enamel.

Hazel didn't move. She kept standing there in the middle of the kitchen, waiting for her due.

Rinsing off the pan, Vida said curtly, "Why don't you go on and do your driving now? Your hooch is in my sack behind the door."

Hazel was unfazed. "How about I carry you on home later? We can chat for a spell at your house." Hazel stood there, as dense as molasses, waiting for her answer.

Vida began scrubbing the same pan again, cursing to herself. White women! God, she hated white women! She slung the pan into the sink with a splash and whipped herself around toward Hazel. "Tell me something, Miss Hazel," she snapped. "What you want from me, exactly?"

"What do you mean?" Hazel asked, caught short.

"Why you bother saving my job for me? It can't be the hooch. You can get that for your own self now."

"But Vida—"

"And I been meaning to ask, why you all the time coming down to Tarbottom and letting peoples see you sitting in my yard talking to a colored woman?"

Hazel opened her mouth to speak and then closed it again. Vida could tell she had hurt the woman, which only made her want to strike again. "Why you want to talk with me at all? Why don't you talk to Mr. Floyd? Or some white womens?"

"You don't enjoy our little chats, Vida?" asked Hazel, sounding small.

"You the onliest one chatting. I the one jerking my fool head up and down like a chicken in a yard full of corn. It ain't natural." Vida dropped her eyes to the floor. "Anyways, my peoples is starting to talk. And I reckon so is yours."

"Well, let them talk. What they gonna say, anyway?"

"I can't speak for the white folks, but my peoples is asking if you trying to be colored. And some want to know if I trying to be white."

"That's the silliest thing I ever heard!" Hazel said. "I talk to you because you understand me. I can tell you things I can't tell nobody else."

Vida shot Hazel a look sharp as a pick. "Why is that, Miss Hazel?"

"Because—"

"'Cause why?" fired Vida. "'Cause I won't tell nobody?"

Hazel gripped the back of a kitchen chair, like her legs were going wobbly.

"How do you know I don't tell nobody?" Vida pressed. "How you know I don't tell my friends everything you say? And all about you dranking and driving?"

Hazel looked as if she could cry. "I don't care what you tell your friends."

"No, I reckon you don't. All my friends is colored. Don't matter what colored folks think."

"Vida, you're putting words in my mouth. I care about what you think."

"Then tell me," Vida demanded, "what do I think? What I thinking right now? Tell me what it is I fret over every day? Tell me what keeps me up at night worrying. Tell me what you know about *my* suffering. What it is *I* done lost."

Hazel's eyes were tearing up. "I thought we was friends."

"I clean your house," Vida said sullenly. "That makes me your maid, not your friend. That's the difference between colored folks and white. You get to pick me as a friend and I ain't got no say about it."

Vida turned back to her dishwater so she wouldn't see the hurt on Hazel's face any longer. But her insides felt as if they were crumbling, caving in like a house afire, one floor at time.

༄

The sheriff was tilted back against the wall in his chair, boots up on the desk, waiting for his deputy to return with the evidence—evidence the grand old man would insist on before he would let Billy Dean act. It just might work, he told himself again. At least it would buy a little breathing room. Give him some time to figure his way out of this fix Delia had put him in.

If he worked it right, he could put a stall into things for a couple of months. Get the good citizens off his back. Give the newspapers somebody else to crucify besides him. And most of all, keep the Senator from replacing Billy Dean with Lampkin Butts as sheriff. The old man had threatened it often enough. Said he didn't even need an election to do it. Billy Dean was his personal sheriff. Like all them *personal* niggers he looked out for. Billy Dean reached into the drawer and pulled out Delia's note to read it one more time.

I'm holding you to your promise, Billy Dean. Leave her or I'll tell Daddy. It's me or nothing, sugar. And you know you could never stand nothing.

He studied the handwriting. All those pretty swoops and curves and curlicues masked the cold hand of steel that had written it. He brought the letter up to his face and sniffed it. "Oh, Delia. You sweet, conniving thing," he whispered. "Why didn't I do it your way from the start? It wouldn't have had to come to this."

It wasn't the first time he'd wished he'd just gone ahead and given her what she wanted. Done it before the threats began. Gone ahead and told Hertha the truth. Hell, it would have been worth it to see the look on that godawful face of hers. Anyway, it wasn't as if he was ever going to get his hands on the Senator's money. He used to be under the impression that when the old man died, the plantation and the gins and the bank shares would pass on to him. He would be fixed for life. Could do things his own way. Then Hertha told him there was no way he was getting his hands on it. She said *she* might keep him on as sheriff, but the Columns was a separate thing. A family thing. *He*r family, not his. And the family lawyers would make sure of it.

To hell with her family. And their land and their money and their personal niggers nobody could lay a hand on. You touch one, you touch them all. That was the problem with the Senator and them. They couldn't tell where one thing ended and another began. They were all wrapped up in one ball, and it was *theirs*. Billy Dean couldn't imagine such a thing. With him, the fewer strings the better. He'd cut them all loose if he could.

To hell with them all, he thought again. The only one of the whole bunch he ever gave a good goddamn about was Delia. And now...

In the middle of his thought, the door was flung open and in rushed his deputy, panting like an overworked mule. The sheriff quickly shifted himself about and got his boots on the floor. He shoved the letter into the drawer and slammed it.

"I told you about knocking, Lampkin."

The deputy struggled to catch his breath. "Looka here what I found at the murder site," he said, puffing. He handed Billy Dean the watch chain. "You was right. Funny how we missed it all them other times."

"How about that? I had a feeling."

It has to work, the sheriff told himself again. What was the worst that could happen? The old preacher might spend a few weeks in jail until this thing was settled. He sure seemed willing enough. Of course the best solution would be for him to get lynched before things unknotted themselves. That wouldn't be Billy Dean's fault. Not if he played his cards right with the Senator. The sheriff pocketed the chain. For the first time in months, he walked out of the redbrick jailhouse with a spring in his step. He got in his cruiser and headed straight out to the Columns.

༄

That night Vida sat up alone, waiting in the pitch-blackness of her shanty for her father to return, trying not to think the worst. The truth was, she didn't know what to think anymore. The last twenty-four hours was proof that her father was liable to do anything. Already several of the other maids had come by to tell Vida the pieces they knew of the last day's events. Even Missouri. She said that everybody laughed at Levi when he tried to register. That Vida had nothing to worry herself about except having a fool for a father. Vida had been so happy to hear that, she had wanted to kiss the spiteful woman. Next it was Sweet Pea, who said she had overheard a call between her white lady and Nellie Grinder. Nellie was all upset because the sheriff had refused to arrest Levi. Said he laughed it off.

So for a few moments, Vida felt some welcome relief. Then Creola came chugging up Vida's steps, sweat drops as big as bullets glistening among her freckles. Vida could tell Creola had something to say and was fighting hard against it. Finally she blurted, "Mr. Hayes is telephoning all over the state about Levi. Calling him an agitator. A civil righter. An NAACP nigger. Going on about how dangerous he is. Say something got to be done. And the sooner the better."

Creola reached out for Vida's hand. The woman was trembling. "Vida, I sure would feel a lot better if you come and stay with me and Rufus tonight."

"I can't go, Creola. Things going to work theyselves out. I be all right."

Creola bit her lip and then said what she had come to say all along. "Vida, when a colored person starts up with that voting business, his whole family liable to get hit. Night riders drive by shooting off they guns. Even fling dynamite sticks through your window." Creola's whole body shook. "Vida, I'm afeared for you."

Vida reached out and took the big woman in her arms and

thanked her. But Vida still wouldn't go, determined to wait up for her father. "I owe him to be here. It's 'cause of me we come to Delphi in the first place. I ought to got him away from here a long time ago."

Reluctantly, Creola left the cabin. Vida closed the door behind her and dropped the crossbar. She would wait for her father in the darkness. As she sat in a corner of the room, Vida heard coonhounds down by the river, their barks high-pitched and sharp, like they were on the scent of game.

"Please, God," she whispered. "I ain't spoke to you in too long a time. I been holding a lot of madness against you. And you got to admit, you ain't been the easiest thing to love. Still, I promise, if you let my daddy live through this, I see what I can do about softening up some on you and him both."

Vida heard the hounds again. Their barking was different. Harsher now and lower, like their heads were slung back. The dogs had something treed. And then came another sound.

Vida's heart nearly stopped. It wasn't dogs this time, but the low whine of a car engine. Easing cautiously across the floor, as if a careless creak would give her away, she peeked out her window. Sure enough she saw the approach of a pair of headlights, painting the row of shacks in a gleam of white.

There was nowhere to run. All the houses around her were darkened now. Word had spread fast about the trouble the Snows were in, and nobody wanted to be lit up when trouble came calling.

Vida went back to her chair and waited, listening as the sound of the engine came closer, and closer and closer still, until she imagined she could hear the tires whispering against the dirt track. She said a last prayer for Nate and another for her father.

The shack exploded in light. The car's headlights were aimed right through her window. In that instant, Vida was hurled back in time, to the awful night the sheriff had come for Nate, when her room had lit up, distorted images thrown against the walls, the horrible glare in her eyes.

The engine cut off but the headlights stayed on. Her heart pounded like a wild animal trying to bang its way out of its cage. Still she did not move. She sat there listening, waiting for it to happen: An explosion. Gunshots. A voice summoning her out into the night.

So far there was only silence behind the lights. Finally the lights themselves cut out. Still she waited.

Able to stand it no longer, Vida rose up on wobbly legs and peeked through the board shutters. She couldn't believe her eyes! There was the Lincoln sitting in her front yard. "Miss Hazel," Vida whispered. Then louder, "Miss Hazel!" Her voice raw with fear. "Is that you out there, Miss Hazel?"

"I got to talk to you, Vida."

Vida was never gladder to see anybody in her entire life. Nobody would dare hurt Vida with a white woman in her yard. "Sure thing, Miss Hazel," she called out the window. "I'll cut on the porch light. You can talk as long as you want this evening. I even got coffee."

Vida quickly lifted the crossbar, and by the time she had opened the door, Hazel had both feet on the porch. "Miss Hazel...?"

"Let's go inside, Vida," Hazel said, pleading. "Can we, please?"

"I reckon we can," Vida answered, but she was thinking, what has this white woman gone and done now that would make her ask to go inside a colored person's house? Once inside, Vida turned on the light and offered Hazel a chair. She's looped up and can't go home, Vida guessed. "You want that coffee, Miss Hazel? Won't take but a minute or two."

Hazel shook her head. "Vida, sit down beside me, will you?"

Vida eyed Hazel warily for a moment, and then retrieved a chair from the kitchen for herself. Seated across from Hazel, Vida could see there was something very wrong. A look of physical pain had settled on Hazel's face. "What is it?" Vida asked, her voice flat. "Tell it."

Speaking carefully, Hazel said, "I got some real bad news, Vida."

Vida searched Hazel's face. Who was this going to be bad news for? she wondered. Vida braced herself, now fearing the worst.

"Vida, it's about your daddy. He's been arrested," Hazel said. "Vida, I'm so sorry."

Vida closed her eyes and gave out a deep breath, relieved. She had imagined much worse. "Then Daddy ain't dead," Vida finally said.

"No, Vida, no!" Hazel exclaimed. "He ain't dead at all."

"All right now, Miss Hazel," Vida said. "Tell me everthing what happened. Don't jump over nothing."

"I don't know it all, but I'll tell you what I heard. Floyd got a phone call a few minutes ago, and I picked up the upstairs extension and listened in. Thinking it might be. . ." Hazel dropped her eyes for a second and then continued, "That part's not important. It was Miss Pearl's husband, Hayes, on the line. He told Floyd that the problem was taken care of." Hazel stopped for a moment, making the connection. "Oh, Vida, if Floyd had anything to do with this..."

"Go on, Miss Hazel. What Mr. Hayes say?"

"Hayes said he guessed they wouldn't have to worry about Levi doing any more agitating for the vote."

"So let me get it straight what you saying, Miss Hazel. Daddy ain't been hurt. He's alive and they got him in county jail."

Hazel nodded.

"I see," Vida said, and thought for a moment. "Surely they can see he ain't no agitator. Only feeble-thinking. They ain't going to hold him for that silliness at the courthouse. They bound to see."

Hazel was confused. "What silliness at the courthouse?"

"For trying to get his vote!" Vida said impatiently. The woman couldn't keep her own story straight! "You the one said it. The reason he got hisself in jail. Agitating for the vote. Them's your words."

Hazel shook her head sorrowfully. "No, Vida, no. That ain't why he's in jail. Your daddy got arrested for killing Miss Delia."

Vida's eyes widened. She cupped her hand over her mouth and let out a muffled cry, then began shaking her head stubbornly. "No.

No. No," she said. "That don't make no sense. They talking about somebody else. Probably not my daddy at all. Probably you heard wrong. They got Daddy in jail for voting. He was just confused in his head, he didn't mean nothing by it. They let him go in no time."

"No, Vida. I heard what Hayes said." Hazel took another deep breath. "Vida, there's more. I hate to tell you, but you need to know it."

Vida could feel herself going numb.

Hazel reached out and gently shook her shoulder. "Vida? Are you still listening?"

"Go on," Vida answered dully.

Hazel took a deep breath. "Vida, Hayes told Floyd that they might could overlook a crazy colored trying to vote, but not a crazy colored murdering a white woman. That the Senator and his family ought to be spared the spectacle of a public trial. That Levi was going to be..." Hazel reached for Vida's hand. "That they were going to bust your father out of the jail and..." Hazel began to cry. "Oh, Vida, it's...Hayes said they were going to lynch your father."

At first Vida didn't catch what Hazel had said because she was so shocked to find her hand in the white woman's. Yet those words, "lynch your father," kept beating against her brain like birds throwing themselves against a windowpane, until she at last had to let them in.

Vida lifted her face to Hazel, who with her other hand reached out to gently stroke Vida's cheek. Vida jerked her head away. Her hand still in Hazel's grip, Vida rose on wobbly legs, then dropped to her knees. She tried to wrench her hand from Hazel's, but Hazel refused to loosen her hold.

With no place to go, Vida laid her head on Hazel's lap and at last began to cry. Loss filled the room—fathers and mothers and husbands and sons, dead and forfeited and snatched away. Vida looked up to see the other woman's tears. She rubbed her cheek against Hazel's hand. In their private grieving, each tried to comfort the other.

Chapter Thirty-Nine

THE FREEDOM RIDERS

School was letting out early because of the storms popping up all across the Delta, not to mention a tornado sighting over toward Little Egypt. As children inched their way in orderly lines from the school building, lightning lit up the dark sky while thunder shook the ground and rattled the windows. The children broke ranks and ran screaming for the buses. As they pulled out of the school lot, the sky opened up and the rain fell in sheets. By the time Johnny's bus had turned down his lane, roofs had become waterfalls and the streets gushing rivers.

Johnny made a run for it up the sidewalk and through the front door. He was halfway down the stairhall, wiping the water from his eyes, before he noticed that the house was unlit. The rain, noisily beating down on the world outside, contrasted eerily with the dead silence inside the house. He worried that his mother and Vida might be somewhere out in this storm. He scurried back toward the kitchen, calling out "Momma! Vida!" No reply came back to meet him.

He tore through the kitchen door, then stopped in his tracks, taken aback by the sight of the maids sitting silently in the shadows. They looked up at him with weak smiles that quickly faded.

Vida got up without speaking and walked into the laundry room. She returned with a towel and began to dry Johnny's head. "You'll catch your death," she said, but she sounded as if she were thinking of somebody else.

"Where's Momma?"

"Out driving."

"What y'all doing in the dark?" he asked, peeking out from beneath the towel.

"Lights is out," Sweet Pea answered.

"And we can't go home 'cause the river suppose to flood," Creola said. "Again."

The way everybody slowly nodded their heads up and down, Johnny could tell they were really sad. Since Levi's arrest, they had been low. Even Maggie's "Praise Jesus" sounded wobbly to him.

"Fourth time this year," Sweet Pea said glumly. "Get a little rain and the bottom floods out ever time." She was slumped over in her chair, her arms propped against her legs. The cleft between her breasts was more prominent than ever. Vida jerked Johnny's eyes away as she continued to towel his hair.

"Nobody going to build no levee for colored folks, that's for sure," complained Creola. Her wet red hair was hanging stringy from her head, making her already huge round face appear more balloonlike than usual.

"Yeah," Sweet Pea grumbled, "Miss Hertha put Misery's house up on stilts. I bet she down there grinning like an albino possum, sitting high and dry up in her tree."

A clap of thunder shook the house, but only Johnny jumped.

The sound of stamping feet came from the back porch, like somebody trying to shock the mud off their shoes. A moment later Hazel entered, smiling at everybody, and when she opened her mouth to speak, the dreary scene in her kitchen silenced her. She walked over to Vida, who was standing at her place by the sink, looking forlorn. "Oh, Vida, I'm so sorry. I heard them tell it on the radio."

"Tell what?" Johnny asked.

"Now, I'm sure it's for the best. Your daddy will be better off in

Jackson. The sheriff was right to ask for it."

"He ain't there yet, Miss Hazel. You don't know the sheriff. Lot can happen between here and Jackson," Vida said, close to tears. "And, Miss Hazel, the sheriff won't let me see my daddy. Only way I gets to see him is if I stand in front of the jailhouse and stare up at him in his window. He always there, looking down through his bars like a zoo animal. Mob of white men always gathered 'round. Calling him names. Some laughing. Some cussing. I saw one old man standing on the steps, cackling like the devil and swinging a...a noose." Vida stumbled on the word.

Hazel put her arm around Vida. The other maids glanced at each other, their eyes big.

"He didn't do it, Miss Hazel. They framing him."

"I'm sure they are, Vida," Hazel comforted her. "It's a shame on everybody claiming to be a white person."

"But I know for a fact he didn't. I got Miss Delia's letter. I knows who did it."

"Who?" Hazel asked. "If you know, you got to tell it to the sheriff and get your father set loose."

There was a disbelieving silence. Vida and the maids shook their heads at Hazel and laughed sadly.

"What?" Hazel asked, hurt. "Why y'all making fun of me?"

"We ain't, Miss Hazel. Just what you said. You done marked off the difference between being white and being colored as clear as if you drawed a line in the dirt."

"Amen," Sweet Pea said.

Flustered, Hazel said, "I don't know what you-all are talking about."

"Let me count it out to you plain," Vida said. "First off, we colored. We ain't got no sheriff. And second off, I seen the evidence. I know who kilt Miss Delia. But it comes back around again to me being colored. How's a colored woman going to speak out and get believed? Well, she ain't."

There was a chorus of "That's right" from the maids.

Vida picked up steam. She started counting on her fingers for emphasis, which reminded Hazel uneasily of Floyd. "And third off, since I'm *still* colored, how can I speak out the first word if that word is against the sheriff *hisself.*"

"That's the truth," Creola hollered and Sweet Pea chimed in with an "Amen."

"And fourth off," Vida said, "if I do say that first word, it will sure as hell be my last one. You know why?"

"'Cause you colored?" Hazel ventured.

That brought a response of grievous howling from the maids.

"That's right, Miss Hazel. That's why we was laughing at you."

"You saying Billy Dean Brister did it?" Hazel sounded doubtful.

"Makes me so damned mad," Vida grumbled to herself. She surveyed the room. "We a piteous sight. Things keep coming down on top of us like that storm outside, and all we can do is sit around in the dark with our tails tucked."

Hazel pulled up a chair, let Johnny climb into her lap, and sat with the maids in silence, listening to the rain drumming on the tin roof over the porch.

After the rain had finally slacked off to a sprinkle, Hazel spoke up. "You know what helps me when I don't think I can take it no more? A little drive. Never fails to get me cheered up."

Vida looked at her as if she had cracked, yet Hazel insisted, "Let's all go for a ride. Come on, now! Everybody in the car."

Johnny jumped down from her lap, excited to go with his mother, but the maids only stared at her. Hazel went around the room grabbing their arms and pulling them up off their chairs, one by one. By the time she had herded them onto the porch, the rain had completely stopped and the wind had died. It was deathly still. The skies had lightened to an eerie Coke-bottle green. There was an unholy calm all around, like tragedy suspended in midair. Tornado weather.

Hazel wasn't deterred. On the way down to the car she told them all about a man she'd met the week before on one of her drives who

said that when he was a boy he was picked up by the Great Tupelo
Tornado of '38 and carried clear into another county, at a mile a
minute, and set down unharmed into the Buttahatchie River. "He
told me you got to cooperate and not fight it. Since I heard that, I've
felt real peaceful about the weather."

Hazel situated herself behind the wheel, and Vida slid in next
to her. Sweet Pea took the front-seat window. Creola and Maggie
loaded into the back, wedging Johnny between them.

"Lord have mercy!" Creola called out. "We going to sure nuff
bust out the sprangs in Miss Hazel's new car!"

"Don't you worry about nothing, Creola," Hazel reassured her.
"Everything's paid for." She opened up her purse, retrieved a little
blue bottle, and handed it to Vida.

"This is your hooch," Vida said, taken aback.

"It don't do nothing for me no more," Hazel explained. "Take it.
Y'all sit back and relax. Enjoy the ride." Hazel mashed the gas pedal
and the big Lincoln roared to life, taking off like a rocket for where
the sun was about to break through the clouds.

They drove along winding roads, through masses of trees and
vines growing so dense that the inside of the Lincoln grew dark and
cool, until they burst out again into the dazzling light of open fields.
Confident and in charge, Hazel worked the wheel as if she were
a Talladega pro. No terrain could discourage her. She took back
roads—gravel, dirt, sand, washboard, rutted, overgrown, and completely washed out. She navigated abandoned logging trails and mere
pig paths. When it looked too muddy to continue and everybody
swore she would have to back herself out, Hazel swerved off onto a
shift road appearing out of nowhere and skirted the bog completely.

Even Vida was impressed.

Now and then Hazel pulled the car over, and heading off on foot
she would reach behind a log or into the hollow of a tree or under a
gnarly root and return with another blue bottle and hand it to Vida,
telling her to pass it around. Hazel didn't touch a drop.

The passengers surrendered to Hazel's driving as they might lose themselves in the lament of a soul-scarred blues veteran or in the words and cadence of a revivalist burning with the holy spirit or in the rhythm of an old woman piecing up a quilt with nimble fingers skittering along the patches. It was obvious that Hazel was inspired. Creola turned to Johnny and said with reverence in her voice, "You momma can drive like Peter can preach."

That sounded about right to everybody.

As the sun began to set they came upon a pasture blanketed with a smoky mist. "Look," Creola said pointing to the field. "The rabbits is cooking they supper!"

"Ain't it purty," Sweet Pea said wistfully. "Looks like a cloud bedding down for the night."

With the cool November wind blowing gently in her face, Hazel inhaled deeply. "Don't this make you feel free as a bird? Nobody in the world to bring you down."

Turning to Hazel, Vida said in a sad voice, her words a little slurred, "That's just it, Miss Hazel. We ain't free. Don't believe we ever going to get free."

Hazel nodded as if she had heard all of this before. However, she was careful not to say anything lest she encourage this kind of talk. No telling where it could lead.

Vida continued anyway. "One day we going to take our freedom. Going to stop waiting for somebody to give it to us in the sweet by-and-by." Vida took a quick little nip. "Anyway, I figger freedom really ain't yours unless you take it. Nothing free if you owing somebody for it. Nobody give it to Rosie. No ma'am. She reached out and snatched from the white man."

The maids erupted into a chorus of "Uh-huh" and "That's right." Nobody could mention Rosa Parks without soliciting some kind of heartfelt response from maids.

"Now, Vida," Hazel cautioned, "that's civil righter's talk. You got to mind where you say things such as that. We all free in this car, but when we get out, we got our places. You have to be careful. People might take you for an agitator."

Feeling no pain, Sweet Pea stuck her head out the window and yelled "Agitator! Agitator!" She snatched the bottle from Vida and took a swig. Wiping her mouth, she said, "I'm sick of y'all white folks blaming everything on agitators." She passed the bottle back to Maggie.

Maggie held to it tightly, looking a little confused as to why somebody had handed her a bottle of laxative. "Take it to the Lord in prayer!" she sang out.

Reaching across Johnny, Creola eased the bottle from Maggie's grip. "I'm sick of it, too," Creola added. "And I don't even know what a agitator is. Puts in mind of something that go crawling 'round in the swamps."

Hazel said she wasn't real sure herself what one was, but whatever it was, she was sure it was up to no good, and they should make sure they didn't mess with any. It might get them shot or hung or drowned. "And I seen it done," she said, thinking of the boy in the river.

"We all got to die sometime," Vida said, sounding resigned to it. "What's the difference how? Only matters why."

"Might as well be something you believe in," Sweet Pea said.

"That's right," Vida said. "My daddy sitting in jail thinking he going to die for the vote. Instead everybody wants to get at him for drowning a damned white woman. And he didn't even do it." Vida pounded her fist on the padded dash. "White man done took everything he got. Only thing left was his story. And I'll be damned if they didn't go and snatch that, too."

"Poor Reverend Snow." Sweet Pea began to cry. "Now, he was a righteous man. He was surely looking on the face of God. And such a good-looking man, too."

"Y'all stop that kind of talk," Hazel said firmly. "Levi ain't dead. And Vida, you wrong. I do care how you die."

Vida thought about that for a moment and turned to Hazel. "But do you care how I live?"

"I don't understand what you saying," Hazel said, not at all enjoying the turn in the conversation. They had been having such a nice time.

"I know you don't want me to die, but that ain't enough," Vida said, and then took a quick pull on the bottle before continuing. "Being my friend and all like you claim, you got to want me to live my life free and equal."

"You talking to the wrong person. I ain't free neither. Only one mistake away from being sent back to the state hospital for the insane myself. They got a bed with my name on it."

"Well, maybe you got some figuring to do, too, Miss Hazel. As for me, I'm getting to be more my daddy every day."

"Tell it now," Creola called out.

"You know I got a little boy out there I ain't never going to see. He ain't never going to know me as his momma. I has to live with that, I reckon. I can't raise him up to do right nor wrong. Can't help him with his homework. I missed teaching him everything a momma needs to teach a child. But my daddy say they is one thing I can leave him."

No one spoke. For everyone except Hazel, this was the first anyone had heard of a boy wandering the land without his mother.

"Daddy say I can leave Nate *my* story. And my story is how I live my life. I can live it afraid or I can live it strong. I don't understand it all my ownself. But Daddy say if we live our story, we get to pass it on. If I try to live strong and free, somehow that make Nate more strong and free, wherever he be at."

Nodding to herself, she said, "That's what I done decided to leave my son. A free life."

Hazel was nodding, too. "What you want me to do, Vida?"

Without hesitating, Vida answered, "Walk with me to the courthouse and say 'This here is a first-class citizen who wants to vote.' "

"Amen!" Sweet Pea seconded, before Maggie could open her mouth.

But Vida wasn't through. "Let's you and me go to Mickey's Diner and tell the waitress you want a table for the two of us."

"Uh-hunh!" Creola called out from the back. "I wants to go in there with y'all. Where it's air-cooled and they set your food down on a table in a china plate and not shove a greasy bag at you through a window in the alley. Ask for us all a table, Miss Hazel. Say it's for the Rosie Parks League of First-Class Citizens."

"And," Vida said, "when we pass somebody you know on the street, I want you to say, real proud like, 'This is my friend *Miss* Vida Snow.' "

Everybody in the car was quiet now, imagining such a thing. Finally, Sweet Pea announced, "I gots to pish bad as a racehorse."

They decided it was a good time to drop by One Wing Hannah's and see her brand-new indoor toilet. They'd heard she had put a sign above the tank that read FLUSH GOD DAMMIT!

As they sat around the table at the juke with a new bottle, Johnny in his mother's lap, the women told their secrets. For the first time, Vida told about how she came to have a boy named Nate. And Hazel told about how she came to lose a boy named Davie. Creola cried about knowing every lullaby there was yet never having a child of her own to sing them to. Trembling like a virgin, Sweet Pea told about her first and only true love. Hannah came over scratching her wig to see what all the crying was about and plopped herself down and told right out about how she had once loved a woman like a man, and damned if she had found anything since to beat it. Maggie sang a hymn so fractured nobody could recognize it to sing along. Still, everybody knew it was from her heart.

❧

It was going on ten o'clock by the time Hazel had dropped off the maids and returned to the house. She hoped she might be able to sneak Johnny up to his room before Floyd discovered them home, but he was waiting for them in the kitchen and fit to be tied. Word had already got back to him that his wife had been seen as far as fifty miles away riding around with a carload of colored maids. Somebody from the filling station called and said most of the bunch looked pie-eyed drunk. And with tornadoes touching down all over the county!

First thing, he threatened to take Hazel's car away. She drew herself up and said fiercely, "You do and I'll leave you for sure."

"Where would you go?" Floyd scoffed. "How would you live?"

Without missing a beat, Hazel shot back, "I'd move in with Vida. I'd help her clean houses. I'd wait tables at One Wing Hannah's. See what that does to your year-end closeout."

That stopped Floyd, but only for a moment. "Do you want me to send you back to Whitfield? You know I could have you committed again. There ain't a judge in four counties that ain't already heard about you riding those niggers around and having a high ol' time." Floyd looked down at Johnny as if noticing him there beside his mother for the first time. "And with innocent children!"

"Don't say 'nigger' no more," Hazel said. "It ain't dignified, and we don't care for it."

"Don't tell me what dignified is, not after what you been up to. And who the hell is 'we'?" Floyd asked. "You're a white woman, for God's sake. You got it all. Any other woman'd be proud to be the wife of a Lincoln dealer. Any other woman would take advantage of that situation and make a place for herself in the community. Get in the Trois Arts League. Join the Baptist Ladies Auxiliary. Raise money for the Lottie Moon Offering so the missionaries can save the niggers in deepest Africa."

Hazel opened her mouth to object.

"Excuse me," Floyd said bitterly. "*Colored* people. But not you. You want to throw it all away. And take me down with you. Well, no deal, Lucille! I won't let you do it."

"Send me away then, Floyd," Hazel yelled back. "Tell them to snip the wires in my brain this time, why don't you? Matter a fact, why don't you cut out a magazine picture of the kind of woman who would make you happy, tack it on my forehead, and tell them doctors to have at it. Don't accept delivery till I meet your factory specifications."

Turning on her heel, Hazel stormed away, and Floyd, stunned, listened to her stomps recede up the stairs. Her bedroom door slammed shut.

Johnny and Floyd now stood alone in the kitchen. As Johnny watched his father, waiting for him to say something, he noticed a color in his face he had never seen before, a kind of cherry red heading toward grape. His eyes were anxiously searching the kitchen, as if he was looking for something to turn off or on. Up or down. Anything he could make do what he wanted it to. Finally his gaze settled on Johnny, who stood there wearing his Sunday pants on a Friday. "Why can't you dress like a real boy?" Floyd snapped. "For God's sake, buy you some blue jeans."

"But—" Johnny said.

Floyd didn't hear him. He was busy storming out the back door.

Chapter Forty

THE ROSA PARKS LEAGUE

Hazel angle-parked in front of the two-story redbrick building that sat across the square from the courthouse. Not wanting to draw any unnecessary attention, Vida occupied her customary spot in the backseat. Today they were making a visit to the Hopalachie County Jail.

Vida got out of the car hesitantly, dreading the encounter with the sheriff. When she looked up, she froze. Through the bars of a second-story window she saw her father, his face bruised and his lip cut. One eye was swollen shut. His body swayed from side to side, the way he used to do in the heat of his sermons. He seemed to be gazing down upon her with one eye, his expression vacant but his mouth moving to form words she could not make out. Vida felt Hazel's hand touch her shoulder.

"You all right?" she heard Hazel ask.

Vida nodded, still looking up at her father.

"Still want to do this?"

Vida nodded again, yet Hazel could feel a tremble under her hand. "Well, then, let's go on ahead, OK?"

Hazel carefully led Vida toward the jail and guided her through the ever-present knot of glowering white men occupying the steps.

One grizzled, whiskey-soaked man leaned in too close and muttered into Vida's ear, "Your daddy ain't going to live long enough to get to Jackson, girl." She saw he was holding up a necktie with hand-painted butterflies like a trophy. "Nearly got him last night," he cackled.

Vida picked up her pace.

It had been Vida's idea for Hazel to go along with her to see Levi. That morning after breakfast, Vida had explained, "Daddy been there for three days, and the sheriff ain't let me in. And even if I do get in, probably won't let me out again. I need me a white woman there."

"Vida, maybe you're exaggerating," Hazel said. "After all, he's the law now. Maybe he's changed since before." Hazel had always been partial to the sheriff and had never forgotten how he'd pulled her out of many a tight spot, not once laughing at her or scolding her or making her feel stupid.

"Miss Hazel, I'm telling you. You seen the letter."

"I did and she didn't say Billy Dean was going to kill her."

"He got to be the one who killed Miss Delia." Vida was annoyed at having to explain this again. "She was blackmailing him, Miss Hazel."

Hazel looked doubtful.

"Well, what would you call telling him to leave Miss Hertha and run away with her and be the daddy to her baby, and if he didn't she would tell the Senator on him? Now, the sheriff I remembers ain't going to stand for that. No ma'am, he ain't changed." Though they'd been alone in the kitchen, Vida had lowered her voice. "He told me personal he would kill before losing what he got. He be the kind that takes matters in his own hand. Believe me, I knows."

"Well, Vida," Hazel said sadly, "you know I got my own opinions about this Delia."

"Yes'm. I know."

"And if you ask me, she can't be trusted to be dead. I don't believe a word she wrote."

Though she still wasn't convinced, Hazel had agreed to go. Maybe she could show Vida how Billy Dean Brister was nobody to be afraid of.

When they walked through the door of the jailhouse, Hazel in the lead and Vida close behind hugging a bag with a change of clothes for her father, they entered a large open area with several wooden desks scattered about. A couple of deputies were standing in the center of the room talking. Behind them were barred gun racks filled with fierce-looking weapons. Over in the corner was a closed door with a frosted glass pane that read SHERIFF in big black letters.

The only desk occupied at the moment was the shabby one closest to the entrance. Sitting there was a plain young blonde who eyed the two women curiously.

"Yes ma'am?" she said to Hazel, talking over the crackling of a dispatch radio that took up most of the desk.

"I'm Hazel Graham and I—"

Just then the corner office door swing open and Billy Dean Brister stuck his head out, his mouth already fixed to yell something at the blonde. When he saw the two women, he smiled instead and sauntered up to greet them. "Miss Hazel," he said,, looking happy to see her. "How can I help you today?"

Vida glowered at Hazel. The woman was blushing like a schoolgirl.

"Well, Sheriff, we—me and Vida—are here to visit with Levi Snow. If you don't mind."

The request seemed to amuse Billy Dean. He glanced back at the blonde, who was also smiling. "Any reason I should mind, Rose?" he asked the blonde.

Rose shrugged at the sheriff's question. Billy Dean looked back at Hazel. "No, I don't mind. It ain't as if he's under arrest or anything."

"What!" Vida and Hazel gasped at the same time.

"I ain't charged him with nothing. Not yet, anyway. He's in what we call protective custody. I hear there might be those who want to do him bodily harm."

Billy Dean shook his head at the thought of such a thing, and then sat down on the edge of Rose's desk. "I don't even keep the door locked. No call to, really. That old man don't want to be nowhere in the world 'cept in that cell. Don't that beat all?"

"See, Vida?" Hazel said. "Things aren't as bad as you think. He ain't even arrested. Ain't we been stupid!" Hazel then gushed to Billy Dean, "I sure am glad you looking out for him."

Vida tried her best to scald Hazel with her look. Didn't she realize she was flirting with the man who'd probably torn up her father's face?

"Well, Miss Hazel, since we swapping compliments," the sheriff said, "I think it's real generous for you to take an interest in a man everybody else is out to hang." At the mention of hanging, he smiled big at Vida, acknowledging her presence for the first time. She looked down, horrified. To Hazel he said, "But I guess you've heard all the talk."

"It's terrible, ain't it?" Hazel exclaimed. "That's why I was so pleased to hear them say you were going to get him to Jackson. That's real gracious of you to go to so much trouble."

Vida clenched her teeth. The woman was talking as if she were on a date with the man!

"We trying our best. But it ain't done yet. Our illustrious head of the city council, Hayes Alcorn, don't agree with me on it. Wants to keep him close by. Might be out of my hands. Either way, there's only so much I can do."

He smirked at Vida, taunting her. "I'm afraid a couple of dissatisfied citizens already snuck into your father's cell and roughed him up a bit while no one was looking. Got clean away. But like I say, I'm doing my best with what I got." He shrugged and smiled at Hazel. "That's enough shop talk. We do what we can, don't we, Miss Hazel?"

When Vida saw Hazel blushing again, her eyes all starry, she blurted, "How bad my daddy hurt? Let me see him!"

Even Vida seemed surprised at her own abruptness. She dropped her eyes again and mumbled, "Please, sir."

"Right to the point, ain't she?" he said to Hazel. "I see your generosity also extends to his family. That's mighty brave of you."

Hazel smiled stupidly and started to say, "We do what we can," as he had. Then she came to her senses and asked, "What do you mean, Sheriff? Brave?"

Billy Dean grinned. "Oh, nothing really. Except maybe to keep that girl on as your maid and all. The daughter of the nigger suspected by most people of murdering a white woman. I'd call that brave. Or something."

Hazel was red again, but it wasn't from puppy love. She looked down at Vida, uncertain, and again at the sheriff. In a trembling voice she said, "Now, I don't much like you calling Vida a nigger, Sheriff Brister. That ain't good manners."

"Well, Miss Hazel, you could be right about my manners," Billy Dean said loud enough for the deputies in the back to overhear. "But if you are, I suspect in your case it would be a lucky guess. Where I come from, it ain't mannered for a white woman to drive around juking it up with a carload of *coloreds*."

Hazel stood there with her mouth agape. She heard snickering coming from somewhere in the office, but she was too ashamed to look.

"Well, if that's all," the sheriff said, rising from his perch, "I'll get my deputy to take you and your *friend* here upstairs to see our guest. Enjoy your visit."

The sheriff turned, and as he headed back toward his office shouted, "Lampkin! See if you can't help the girls here. And check the paper sack. Make sure Miss Hazel ain't planning on serving no illegal beverages while she's up there."

There was outright laughing this time.

⁓

"Daddy!" Vida cried when they opened his cell door.

He looked worse up close. His white shirt was stained with blood and the left sleeve of his suit had been ripped away. "They done hurt you so bad, Daddy!"

As damaged as his face was, Levi beamed when he saw his daughter. Vida rushed into his arms.

Over Vida's shoulder he smiled at Hazel and nodded, but she didn't notice. Numb with shame, Hazel walked into the cell and edged over into the corner, between the bars and the cot. She stood there silent, her eyes on the cement floor.

Levi returned his attention to Vida. "I'm fine, daughter. I took that first step and the next move is His. Like the Good Book says, it ain't meant for man to direct his own footsteps. Rosa Parks took her step into the dark, and look what all God's doing with her. Them buses still ain't running—"

"Oh, Daddy. Can't you leave that alone? It ain't getting you nowhere 'cept in trouble. Look at you. Have you seen your face?"

The truth was, even with a closed eye and cut lip, Levi's face appeared to glow. "It ain't trouble. They finally listening to me, Vida. That's because the Lord give me a story to live. The people always need a story to look to. When the people don't have no vision, the Lord say they shall perish."

"Daddy, you got to stop it! Don't you know what story they telling about you? It ain't the one about you standing up to the white man asking for the vote. They saying you went crazy and killed a white girl." Grasping him by the arms, she cried, "Daddy, they saying you drowned Miss Delia."

He looked down at Vida. There was a glint of remembering in his face. "Miss Delia. I knew her since the day she was born. The Senator named her after his momma. Pretty little baby. Willful, too."

"They say they can prove it. They found your watch chain down by that whirlpool, Daddy."

"My chain?" Levi touched his vest. "I ain't got my chain, Vida.

Couldn't find it nowhere. Remember how Nate used to love that chain? How he wouldn't nod off till he could take aholt of it in that little hand of his? He'd grip it till daylight, wouldn't he?"

Vida shook her father and shouted. "Daddy! Don't go off on me now. Listen! What you think it mean, the sheriff puts you in here with the door unlocked? Don't you understand? Anybody can get at you again. They mobbed up out on the steps right now. I'm scared for you."

Yet Levi's face was serene. He whispered to his daughter, "I told you, Vida, don't be scared of the darkness."

"Daddy, the sheriff say you ain't under arrest. Let's go home. Maybe Willie can find a way to get you out of Delphi."

"Vida, God done set everything in motion. I got to stay and keep my promises. He's sure keeping His." He beamed at his daughter. "Look here!" He walked over to touch the back wall of his cell. "See. A church of rock." And then he reached for the barred window through which she'd spied him speaking earlier. "A pulpit of iron."

Vida slumped to the cot, her eyes staring with disbelief at her father. "Oh, my lord, Miss Hazel. What we going to do?"

There was no answer. Vida looked over to see Hazel still standing there in the corner, wooden. "Miss Hazel, don't you go mindless on me, too. Somebody need to get ahold of this thing. It's liable to throw us all off in the creek."

Hazel looked down at Vida. "Let's go home, Vida. Please?"

⟡

In Hazel's kitchen, Vida fixed a pot of coffee and the two sat down at the table, neither speaking. They were well into their second cup when Vida broke the silence. "If my daddy bound and determined to die," she announced, "at least I want them telling the right story at his grave. I got to let people know."

"How you going to do that?" Hazel said sullenly, still smarting from her rough treatment at the jailhouse. "You said yourself nobody was going to listen to a colored woman."

"Well," Vida said carefully, "maybe you could help."

"Me?" Hazel checked to see if she was joking. When she saw Vida was serious, Hazel dropped her eyes to her cup. "I guess you could tell today how much weight I carry around here."

"So you giving up? Just 'cause you got treated like a nigger one day of your life, you going to quit?"

"You don't need me," Hazel said. "I'll only get in the way. Can't you see? I'm the town joke."

Vida reached for Hazel's hand. "Miss Hazel, what I *sees* is a woman who told the baddest man in this here county not to call her friend a nigger. Ain't nobody else I know going to do that. What I *sees* is a woman who got so much dignity that she willing to share some with a friend."

Hazel began to mist up, but before she could get too far Vida pulled her hand back. "And the fact of business is, I need your help."

"To do what?" Hazel asked. "To get yourself killed?"

Vida gave Hazel a determined look. "It's what I *got* to do."

"It's what you got to do, huh?"

They were both quiet for a while, avoiding each other's eyes. A few moments later, as she studied her coffee cup, Hazel smiled to herself. "Vida," she said, "you going to be like that turtle, ain't you?"

Vida looked at her blankly. "What turtle?"

Grinning slyly, Hazel said, "I know somebody who's going to cross that road somehow or the other, even if it means getting run over."

That made Vida laugh. "How's your little saying go again, Miss Hazel?"

With a stern look, Hazel said in her best Floyd voice, "Like I always say, Vida, you can only help a thing in the direction it's headed."

Vida laughed again. "I believe you right. That's as good as anything Mr. Floyd ever come up with."

⌒⌢⌒

All the maids were game for the idea except for Missouri, of course, whom they knew better than to ask. Her allegiances were no secret. But the next day, when they met in Hazel's kitchen, they were stumped over how to go about getting the real story out.

"Can't work with the preachers, like Rosa done," Sweet Pea said, rubbing her chin. "Preachers around here carry it back to the sheriff like a dog toting a bone."

"Can't take out an ad in the *Jackson Daily News*," Hazel said. "That's for sure."

"Maybe we copy what the white folks do," Creola suggested. "The ones that trying to get elected. Take the word door-to-door and talks to the peoples."

"Take a year," Vida said, her tone harsh. "Daddy ain't got a year."

"It's something," Creola said. Then she grumbled to herself, "Ain't heard nothing better coming from nobody else."

"Now, if we had the vote—" Sweet Pea began.

"We ain't," Vida said, cutting her off.

Sweet Pea looked over at Creola and lifted her brows. Creola gave her a welcome-to-the-club look. Maggie shifted her weight and opened her mouth to speak, looked around the group, and closed it again.

After a spell of silence, Creola asked offhandedly, "What do it take to get the vote? When I was in school, somebody razor-bladed that part out of my gov'ment book."

"Three things," Vida growled, lifting her fingers for the count. "One, you got to pass they reading and writing test. Two, you got to pay they poll tax. Three, you got to be white. Any more questions?" she asked scornfully.

All four women were now staring at Vida with hard, sharp looks. Finally she dropped her head and shook it. "I'm sorry for it," she said. "I'm as bad-tempered as a hornet. Guess it's getting to me. It was my idea, and now it's me who don't see no hope in it."

Creola waved it off. "I thought you was bound and determined to carry the load yourself."

"We just wants to help," Sweet Pea said. "This thing be everybody's problem."

"Well, maybe so," Vida conceded. "But I can't think of no idea ain't going to end up getting us all killed. I don't want that on my head."

Creola spoke up. "I had an ol' uncle used to say the way to get supper is to aim at one rabbit at a time. And the way to go hungry is to aim at all of them at once."

"I like it," Hazel said. "What's it mean?"

"Well, I always suspicioned the reason the sheriff never have no trouble with the colored is he keeps us split apart. Picks us off easy that way. Now supposing we gets together like they did in Montgomery. Crowd the courthouse with rabbits. Get a bunch of colored people to take that test and show him we can vote him out of office next time if we set our minds to it. Let him know we all is watching him. Sheriff won't know where to aim first, less he hits some white man's favorite nigger in broad daylight. What he going do then?" Creola hooted at the thought. "He be staggering 'round like a blind dog in a meat house."

"You think it would really work?" Hazel asked.

"Well, all I know, it sure be Mr. Hayes's worst nightmare come true. Coloreds lining up to vote. Must be something to it if they working so hard to keep us from doing it."

"You right there!" Sweet Pea cried out. "If the white man is so afraid of us getting the vote, then I imagine we closer to it than we know. Anyways, it'd sure make the sheriff think hard about hurting Reverend Snow. Just can't go pushing our people 'round no more."

Creola slammed her mighty foot on the floor, making everybody jump. "Sure it'll work! I bet you a fat man that it do. Specially if we get some upstanding colored folks to show up with us."

For a while the group was silent, each testing the weight of the idea. Vida began mulling it over aloud. "It'd sure nuff need to be a mob of us. Even then, it ain't going to be safe."

"He'd probably go for the ringleaders after dark," Creola said.

"And the timing's real bad," Sweet Pea added. "Picking season about over, and they don't have no use for coloreds till spring. What's a few dead ones now?"

Creola frowned. "Kill a mule, buy a new one. Kill a nigger, hire a new one. That sure what they say."

Vida began nodding to herself. "How be ever, might be a way to start getting the truth out about who killed Miss Delia for real." Vida nodded faster. She seemed to be pumping up her conviction from a deep well.

Creola had already caught fire, so excited she was shaking. "We oughta get everything writ down on some handbills like them politicians do, 'splaining about the vote and the test and the poll tax and about what kind of sheriff we got and how we can throw his sorry butt out next time if we all stick together. We tell them about Rosie and them buses and about being 'Too tired to move!' " Creola said it again, louder: "Too tired to move!"

"Tell it to Jesus!" Maggie sang out.

"Her name ain't Rosie," Sweet Pea said. "It's. . .never mind." She decided to let it go.

"We need us a mimeograph machine," Hazel suggested, sounding so smart she felt the need to explain herself. "I used to get the circulars done for the Tupelo Rexall. Now, who in Delphi got one we can borry?"

"Oh, won't Reverend Snow be proud!" Sweet Pea squealed. "I think he started something after all. He some kind of special man." She had stars in her eyes.

Vida scanned the joyous faces in the kitchen and then shook her head. "Y'all know this is crazy, don't y'all? Crazy as anything Daddy ever did. Chances are we going to end up dead." Yet her comments didn't dampen the growing enthusiasm in the room.

"I feel funny about it myself," Creola said. "I know it be dangerous. I know we liable to get blowed up. And I sure is scared. But it's a good kind of scared. Like my belly trying to tickle up against my backbone. So scared make me want to rise up and dance it out. What is that, you reckon?"

"I know exactly what it is," Hazel said, smiling big, again feeling the expert. "It's hope, Creola. Pure-dee, one hundred proof hope."

Chapter Forty-One

DELIA'S LAST REQUEST

The sheriff opened the door of his cruiser and stepped out onto the pavement. The migraine was about to split his skull clean open. He scanned the courthouse square. It was empty except for the old men sitting on the benches under the pecan trees, as stone-still as the Confederate soldier. Like old cats they were soaking up the weak November sun. He closed his eyes for a moment against the afternoon glare. Then he zipped his leather jacket, lit up a cigarette, and stepped across the street to the jailhouse.

As he walked up to her desk to collect his messages, Rose said, "Hayes Alcorn is in your office."

"Where's he been?" he asked, shuffling through the papers in the wire basket. "I ain't seen him but six times today already."

Rose pulled out an envelope from her drawer and purred, "Another letter came today, Billy Dean, you old dog." She winked and held the lavender envelope with swirls of cream up to her nose. "Smells nice, too. Expensive."

"Shut up, Rose, will you do that for me?" Billy Dean snatched the letter from her hand and quickly tucked it away in his jacket pocket. Then grinning at her as if he didn't mean it, he said, "Go buy me another pack of BC Powder, would you, honey? I'm almost out again, and my brain's committing suicide against my skull."

He walked into his office to find Hayes pacing back and forth.

His stride was barely long enough to take two tiles at a time.

"Hello, Hayes. Long time no see. What's it been, ten minutes?"

"It ain't funny, Billy Dean. I called Jackson. I told them we don't need any help tending to our problems. We can handle things nicely here."

"You shouldn't ought to have done that, Hayes. Now I might have to go over your head." The sheriff had to smile at that.

When Hayes planted his hands on his hips, Billy Dean thought he resembled a little loving cup, and couldn't help smiling again. "Billy Dean, you obviously see some humor in the situation, but you listen. I'm going to have your job for this. You hear me?"

"I been hearing you all week, Hayes. I just think it's best if we get him out of town."

Billy Dean dropped his cigarette to the floor and crushed it under the toe of his boot. "We ain't got the manpower to protect him night and day. No telling what could happen if he stayed here. I don't want to be the one's responsible."

"I told you, you won't be. If anything happens, it's the people of Mississippi who'll take credit. Hell, *I'll* take credit."

"That sounds good and all, but—"

"What's got into you, Billy Dean? You the last one I would expect holding back popular justice. And you not even charging the man yet. That's not sitting well with folks, I got to tell you."

"Well, sometimes this is not a popular job."

"Not a popular job! Don't give me that crap!" Hayes let out a derisive laugh. "If it meant keeping the job, you'd be out there throwing up the rope yourself. What's your angle?"

"Well, Hayes. We don't have a body. We don't have a witness to the killing. We don't know for sure she's even dead. And you know what I heard? That's the same place the old man used to go to and shout to Jesus! Could of lost his chain then. Too much circumstance and not enough meat. I ain't going to kill the Senator's boyhood playmate and have it come up that somebody else did the deed."

Hayes wasn't buying it. "Bullshit, Billy Dean! You are bullshitting me and I know it. I can smell it from here. You got something else going on the side."

"Yeah, right, Hayes. You found me out. I love getting calls from sawed-off little fuckers like you twenty times a day telling me my business so they can go out and get elected governor. It tickles me, seeing my name in the paper calling me soft on the colored. It does my heart good to tell Delia's daddy that he's just going to have to hold off on his revenge a little longer. You onto me, Hayes. It's a laugh a minute."

"Goddammit, Billy Dean, I'm telling you. If you send that nigruh to Jackson, I'm gonna—"

"I know, Hayes, you gonna have my job. Well, stand in line. Ever damned body wants my job this week." Billy Dean patted Hayes on the head and smiled. "And I got to tell you, Hayes, they's bigger boys in line ahead of you."

At that Hayes sputtered something incoherent and spun on his heel.

"Governor, my ass," Billy Dean growled as he kicked the door shut, rattling the glass. He stood dead still, waiting for the vibrations from the banging door to finish ricocheting against his skull. Now the pain was like a hot poker behind his eyes. He reached up and switched on the air conditioner that stuck out of a hole in the wall above his desk. It shuddered for a moment like an animal before it settled into a dull, deadening roar. Billy Dean tore open the envelope and read the letter.

"Shit," he said. He wadded it up and threw it against the wall. Shutting his eyes tight, he dropped back into his chair and held his head. His migraine was exploding thanks to the sudden burst of rage. After a few moments he sighed and said out loud, "You ain't leaving me much wiggle room, are you, girl?"

He thought *Hertha* had been conniving. What'd the Senator do, raise them both on rattlesnake milk? Delia had it thought through and through, down to putting the tail on the *z*. She knew when she staged her drowning, with the horse and scarf and the whole show, that her daddy would assume the worst like he always did, and then, just like he always did, put the screws to Billy Dean. She had it figured perfect. There would have to be a body and a killer, or he'd find a sheriff who could produce them. But the kicker was, Billy Dean couldn't take the killer to court. Not even a nigger. Couldn't even charge him. Because as soon as Billy Dean brought the poor slob to trial, Delia would jump out of the bushes yelling "Perjury! False arrest!" Her and her daddy would see to it he was picking cotton, chained ankle to ankle with the same niggers Billy Dean himself had sent off to prison.

She hadn't left him one single hole to crawl out of. Had him right by the short ones. Any false move on his part, and she shows up a wronged woman, pointing a finger. Delia was bound and determined not to have this baby without his name stamped on its forehead.

"I'm being generous," she had told him before she went missing. "I could force your hand now, Billy Dean. Instead I'm giving you some time to put your affairs in order. This way you can ask for a divorce like a man. I'd hate for people to think you were marrying me because I was holding a gun to your head."

Yeah, right, he thought.

That's when he'd threatened to kill her. Probably wasn't the wisest thing to do. Knowing Delia, it only made her want him more. He wondered sometimes if that was the only reason she wanted him, because she couldn't have him.

His only stroke of luck so far in this whole deal was when that crazy nigger came along, begging to go to jail. It was as if he had been sent by God. Didn't even have to arrest him. Loves it there. Acts like he *wants* Hayes Alcorn to take him out and lynch him.

Of course, that was the solution Billy Dean was counting on. Sooner or later Hayes or one of those yahoos on the steps would get tired of waiting and haul old Levi out of his cell and string him up.

People were getting impatient. Only last night, somebody driving through town had shot up into Levi's cell window. God knows Billy Dean would give folks every opportunity to take justice into their own hands, as long as it didn't look like he had a part in it. If he had to, he could get some of the Klan from over in Rankin County to do the job. But why should he take that risk? Billy Dean figured he had just about pushed Hayes to the breaking point. Senator or no Senator, Levi Snow would be history within the week. Threatening to send him to Jackson had lit a fire under Hayes.

The sheriff smiled. Talk about sweet justice! When Delia showed up alive and Levi dead, it would be Hayes's ass the Senator would be after. His own brother-in-law. Make Billy Dean Brister come off as the only voice of reason in the whole family!

The sheriff picked up the letter and smoothed it out on his desk. You cocky little bitch. Sending it right through the United States Mail. Directly to the Hopalachie County Sheriff's Office. With his thumbs he rubbed his throbbing temples. The screws they are a-tightening.

He read the letter again. The final screw in the lid.

Dear Billy Dean,

I hear an old friend of mine is lodging with you. Tell Levi I send my love. You know how I feel about that dear old man, don't you, Billy Dean?

Anyway, I'm sure you're anxious to know the latest. I just got back from the doctor. All is well. December 1 is your drop-dead date. Think of it: A new year. A new life and a new wife. Have you asked H. for the D. yet?

It's an easy decision, darling, even for you. Come to me or we'll come to you. See how simple?

Love and devotion,

Delia

She would do it, too, crying about how ashamed she was and how she'd had to run away because ol' Billy Dean had done her wrong. Woman loved to shock her daddy. And boy, did she hate her sister. Delia would get all three of them with that one shot. The woman could have fought the whole Civil War and never reloaded twice.

By God, that's what he liked about Delia. Jesus, she was a sight.

December 1. That gave him less than three weeks. Maybe in that time he could put some added pressure on the jukes and bootleggers and slot machine operators. Put a little heat under folks owing back taxes. Get some money stashed. Never again would Billy Dean Brister find himself beholden to one of the Senator's girls for his upkeep. Maybe he could do a few of those one-shot deals he had his eye on. Siphon off the tax receipts. Pocket a few pieces of his wife's jewelry. Clear out her bank account. Get into her safe deposit box.

He wondered if he could keep the Senator in line for a little longer, especially with him getting crazier every day, yelling to high heaven for a body.

"Lord!" Billy Dean had told him just last night "I ain't saying that she's dead, Senator, but Lord! Do you know what it would look like if she was to wash up after all this time?"

Didn't make any difference. "You keep dragging, boy. Throw a net over the Port of New Orleans if you have to."

Staring at the letter he grumbled, "Right, Delia. Simple as Simon shit." Billy Dean took a headache powder dry.

Chapter Forty-Two

A GAME OF CATCH

Floyd was in his office going over the books, preparing for his meeting with Hayes on his loan extension. Though he'd lost a few customers for not firing Vida, the year hadn't been all that bad. But he definitely needed to expand his inventory to compete with those dealers from Memphis and Jackson. It was only a matter of time before they would advertise him right out of business. Maybe he should pick up the whole Ford line, he thought. He had it on good word that next fall they were going to announce a sure fire winner. They were so confident, they were naming it after Henry Ford's poor dead boy, Edsel.

That sure wouldn't hurt. The Mercurys were turning out to be slow movers. He looked out his back window and saw the red Montclair parked on the side lot. It still hadn't sold. Just sitting there looking at him, serving up a daily reminder of Delia.

Floyd slammed the ledger shut and grabbed another from the stack. Get a hold, he told himself. No need to go all sentimental. Get your mind on business. Remember, success is a frame of mind.

"Nineteen fifty-four," he sighed, opening the ledger. Now, that was a good year. Everything under control. Back when he took his own advice. Floyd had always told himself to stay focused on his own business and don't get caught up in other people's craziness. "Play the game you're in, not the one you ain't," he liked to say. That was exactly it: lately he was not playing his game. There was all this Citizens' Council stuff. He was up to his neck in something that he didn't understand. Gave him a queasy feeling. The same feeling he got seeing Billy Dean with that chain the day before he was supposed to have found one identical. Now Hayes was lathering at the mouth about a hanging. If it wouldn't kill his business deader than a doornail, he'd drop out of that council business. No, this was not his calling at all. Need to stick to your fastball, that's what Floyd always said.

It wasn't only the council. It was his family, too. Hazel driving and drinking like the old days. It was a guaranteed time bomb ready to go off in his face. People were starting to talk again. Why couldn't she drink and sew? Or drink and can vegetables? Why did she have to be going ninety to do it? Then there was Johnny. Hell, they got him playing with dolls now! The boy didn't even have a pair of jeans to get dirty in. Insists on wearing his dress pants to school.

Yep. It was time Floyd stepped in and took that bull by the horns. Let the rest of the world go to hell in a handbag, but maybe he could at least get back at the head of his own family again, before it turned and drove him over. Floyd figured he was due for a success on at least one front. "Little successes breed big successes." On his way home, he stopped by the Western Auto.

⌒

Floyd walked into Johnny's room and found his son down on the floor. He had about ten homemade dolls with their backs against the wall and another ten facing those. Floyd's spirits lifted a little. "You playing war?"

"It's a square dance," Johnny answered.

Floyd shook his head. He didn't want to know any more.

Looking up at his dad and seeing the bag in his hand, Johnny jumped to his feet and ran to Floyd, grabbing hold of his leg. "What you bring me in the bag? You get me a present?"

Floyd pulled out his purchases. "Look at this!"

Johnny looked curiously at the fielder's glove and then back at his father. "It's a football mitten."

"Close. Want to play a little catch? It ain't the season, but maybe if you take to it, one day you can try out for Little League. You never know until you give it a shot. Everything takes practice. Like I always say, a goal without action ain't nothing more than a wish. Hey! I could even coach your team. How about that?"

Johnny had no idea what Floyd was talking about, yet the prospect of playing a game with his daddy delighted him.

"Let's go outside and toss a few," Floyd chirped. Johnny grabbed the glove and ran to the backyard.

Floyd lobbed the first few balls slow and easy, and Johnny tried catching them in his ungloved hand. He used the glove as a kind of lid to keep the ball from bouncing out again. Johnny thought he was doing pretty good until his father said, "Catch the ball in the glove, son. That's what it's for."

On that advice, Johnny took off the glove and held it out in front of him with both hands like a net, but the ball kept dropping between his arms.

"Put it on your left hand." His father held up his own. "This one. And then let the ball drop into the pocket. Where those stitches are."

That didn't seem to help much either. Johnny thought it worked a lot better his way. And he could tell that it wasn't going very well for his daddy by how he would sigh heavily and draw a little closer after each missed throw. Finally they were only inches apart, and his father was merely dropping the ball into Johnny's outstretched glove. They were close enough to talk without breaking out of a whisper.

"How you doing in school?" Floyd asked.

"I like it."

"That's good. That's real good. Your ABCs coming along OK?"

"That's for babies! I can make words. And I can add up apples. And I told the class a story about a turtle that crawled all the way Uptomemphis without getting runned over."

"Where to?"

"Uptomemphis."

"Now, that's fine. Just don't get the big head. Remember, you don't own success, you only rent it out one day at time."

"Yes sir," Johnny said, wondering if his daddy had just said something complimentary to him.

Floyd held the ball for a moment. Without looking at Johnny, he asked, "How's your momma doing, son?"

"Huh? I mean, sir?"

His father studied the ball in his hand as if he had found a message stitched in the horsehide. "I mean, you're with her all afternoon. At least I reckon you are. Like when you go on them little drives of hers."

Johnny froze, the glove still in place to catch the ball that didn't seem to be coming. Finally he looked up guiltily at his father.

"Don't worry. I ain't mad about that no more. It's just that I need some help. We got to watch her, you know, and it would be a great comfort if I knew I could count on you. Are you daddy's boy?"

Johnny nodded his head tentatively, waiting to learn what the job entailed.

"You remember what whiskey smells like, don't you?"

"Medicine," he said without thinking.

Floyd raised his brows. "That what she got you calling it?"

Johnny's face colored.

"What I want is if you would pay attention to how your momma acts. Anytime she starts talking funny or walking like she's got the blind staggers—you remember how she used to get—I want you to go up and hug her. If you ever catch that medicine smell again, call me. That way I can come home and help her. You understand?"

"Yes sir."

"You never can tell about your momma. We got to keep close watch, so she don't get herself in trouble again. She's walking close to the edge." Floyd tossed the ball from hand to hand for a minute, mulling something in his mind. Then he said, "I need you to tell me something else." Reaching into his pants pocket, he pulled out one of Hazel's blue bottles. "I found this in her hat box. It's got whiskey in it. Do you know where it come from?"

Johnny dropped his eyes. "I don't know."

"Son, this stuff is illegal in Mississippi. Now, we can't have her breaking the law and going to jail, can we? You going to help me?"

Johnny didn't look up. There was a scuff on his dress shoe that he became obsessed with.

"Well?" his father said. "Look at me when I'm talking to you."

Johnny did look at his father but remained mute, and the longer he went without speaking, the bigger the cords became in his father's neck. After a while, Floyd cleared his throat, then kicked at something invisible on the ground, embarrassed. Without a word he turned away and headed back toward the house, taking the ball with him. Halfway there, he turned back around. His face was wooden.

"I thought I told you to get you some jeans."

"But I—"

"No buts. Saturday I want you to go to Gooseberry's and tell Sid to fit you in a pair." Floyd tossed the ball in the air once and then snatched it hard. "Some sneakers, too."

"I don't want no jeans," Johnny said firmly, bringing his glove down to his side.

"You need you something to get dirty in."

"I don't want to get dirty."

"All boys like to get dirty," Floyd said flatly. "Don't argue. Just do what I say." Floyd headed back to the house, having to settle for a smaller success than he had planned.

Chapter Forty-Three

THE INFORMER

"Rose! Get me a Coke," Billy Dean yelled from his office. When she didn't answer, he stuck his head out the door. "You hear me?"

Rose was talking to a colored man dressed up in a preacher's suit.

"Rose," he shouted, dry-mouthed, "I'm waiting on my Coke!"

She cocked her head toward the man. "Been waiting to see you. Said it was important." She got up and headed for the soft-drink box.

As he worked his mouth to make the headache powder go down, Billy Dean studied the man. He stood there with his hat in his hand, eyes on the floor, waiting to be acknowledged. Billy Dean didn't have time for this. He had only a few days left to plan his getaway, and he was way behind in amassing his traveling money.

"What you want, preacher? I'm up to my ass in gators today."

The man looked up, unblinking, through steel-rimmed spectacles.

"Well, what is it?" Billy Dean took the Coke from Rose.

The man mumbled, "Can I have a word with you, Sheriff? It's oh-ficial."

Billy Dean almost spit out his Coke, laughing. "*Oh*-ficial, huh? What you know from official?" Billy Dean shook his head. "Hear that, Rose? It's *oh*-ficial."

"Yessuh," the man said. "It's about Miss Delia."

The smile dropped from Billy Dean's face, and he quickly looked away from Rose. "Yeah? Well, get on in here, I reckon."

Despite the air conditioner pumping a steady breeze into the sheriff's office, big drops of sweat were running down the preacher's face. Holding his hat in his lap, he shifted in his seat, waiting for the sheriff to tell him it was OK to start talking. But Billy Dean knew he couldn't act as if he were in any big hurry. These preachers were slippery as eels. You had to handle them just so, like a June bug on a string, or they would take off in the opposite direction of what you needed to know. He told the man he could have a cigarette if he wanted one.

"Now, I don't as a habit, Sheriff Brister, but since you so generous to be offering..."

The sheriff nudged the pack a couple of inches toward the preacher, indicating that it was OK for him to cover the rest of the distance himself.

The preacher rose up and leaned over the desk. Then he fumbled with the red-and-white package, finally wrestling one out. The man sat back down and placed the cigarette ridiculously in the exact center of his mouth, so that it stuck out like a peashooter. He sat there, paralyzed, his look as fixed as a mounted deer's. Billy Dean sneered at him. Too scared to ask for a light.

The sheriff pulled out the nickel-plated lighter from his khakis and sent it sliding across the desk. Trembling, the man held the lighter with both hands and flicked it three times before he struck fire. He squeezed his eyes shut as if he expected an explosion and blindly brought the flame to the cigarette. He pulled weakly and coughed once.

"Real diehard smoker, ain't you?" the sheriff said.

The man rose up out from his chair and, bowing over the desk again, held the lighter out to the sheriff. Billy Dean nodded toward the desktop, telling him with his eyes where to lay it.

"You the preacher over on the Senator's place, ain't you? Used to be Levi Snow's church?"

"Yessuh, that's right," the man admitted, and then added quickly, "Now, I never knew the man. Nosuh. Not personal like."

"That's right healthy of you, I reckon." Billy Dean lit a cigarette for himself. "You mentioned you got something for me."

"Yessuh." He carefully pulled a folded paper from his inside coat pocket. "I been hearing some things. We got folks trying to stir up trouble twix the races." He held the flyer out to the sheriff.

As the paper shivered in the man's outstretched hand, Billy Dean leaned forward and read the headline out loud: "We Must Vote Now." He snatched the paper. "Where'd you get this?"

"Somebody. . . one of my congregation give it to me," the preacher stammered. "She told me they been showing up all over her settlement."

"It says down here it's put out by the Rosa Parks League. What's that?"

"I don't know much of nothing about it," the preacher said. "Now, of course they got an uppity colored gal over in Alabama named like that. But ain't no Rosa Parks here. If she was, I'd sure tell." Pinching his cigarette between his thumb and index finger, the preacher squinched up his face and pulled, straining with all his might. He coughed again.

Billy Dean eyed him suspiciously. "You ain't got no idea at all?"

"Well, now," the man said, shuffling his shoes on the floor, "I can't name no names, but I can say for sure they are not from my congregation. I suspect they town coloreds."

"How many of them?"

"Only two showed up to Sister Raynelle Johnson's door. They both women."

The man timidly looked around and, finding no ashtray within reach, balanced his hat on his knee and flicked the cigarette ash into the palm of his hand.

"And they were colored, you say?"

"Yessuh. That's what I was told. Mostly." The man dropped his eyes to the floor.

"Mostly. What the hell does 'mostly' mean?"

"Well, now. I been told all this, remember. I ain't seen nothing my own self."

The sheriff took a slow breath, trying to keep from grabbing the man by the throat. It was as bad as pulling teeth. Why couldn't these preachers come out and say a thing without beating all around the stump? "Yeah. I know," the sheriff said wearily. "You ain't seen shit. Go on. Were they all colored or not?"

"I heard there was another one waiting in the car. Now they say that one coulda been white. Or maybe just light."

"What kind of car?"

"Big car. Big new car. Blue or green or gray or something like that."

"Out-of-state tag?" he asked.

"Said the tag light was burned out."

"On a new car?"

The preacher shrugged.

"Man driving?"

"Don't know that neither."

Billy Dean looked down at the flyer again. It told all about everybody's right to vote, about electing a sheriff to serve all the people, how and where to register, what a poll tax was, and when the next sheriff's primary was going to be held. Sheriff was the only office it mentioned. No, this wasn't the work of no town niggers, Billy Dean thought. Too slick. Hayes was probably right. It had to be some Jew-Communist outfit from up North messing around in his county. But why were they singling out the sheriff's office? Did they know he might be a tad vulnerable? Billy Dean said, "I don't see anything here about Miss Delia. That *is* what you said you came about, weren't it?"

The man swallowed hard. "That's right. Yessuh."

"Well?"

"Now you got to understand, I don't believe a word—"

"Damn it, preacher! Just say it. I ain't going to hold it against you."

"Well," the man said, talking to the tiles, "these two women was saying as how...Well, what they telling everybody is, you was the one killed Miss Delia." The man looked up and then quickly averted his eyes.

"And?" Billy Dean said, somehow knowing this wasn't the worst of it.

The smoke from the man's cigarette was curling into his eyes. Though he was starting to tear up, he didn't shift either his hand or his head. "And they say you killed her because she was...you got her in the family way."

At that the sheriff's head almost exploded. "Jesus H. Christ," he said through his clenched teeth.

Wisely, the man wasn't looking up to catch Billy Dean's expression. "Not that I tell on folkses as a custom," he said, "but you the sheriff ,and needs to know about these things or chaos is going to reign."

They sat in silence for a few moments, Billy Dean deep in thought, staring blankly toward the preacher, and the preacher studying his own shoes, the cigarette now burning dangerously close to his fingers. Still not looking up, the man said barely loud enough to be heard, "Well, suh. That's about the big of it, I reckon."

The sheriff's attention snapped back into the room. "Who else you told?"

The preacher looked up and for the first time blinked. "Who-all I told?"

"White people, I mean."

"I brung it straight to you, Sheriff."

"Well, keep it quiet for now. Till we can find who's been spreading them lies."

Billy Dean stood up, letting the preacher know his time had run out. He watched the man with contempt as he struggled with the doorknob, holding his hat and his cigarette in one hand, and the ashes in the palm of the other.

When he had finally managed the door and before he walked into the outer office, the sheriff called after him, "I need to know names. You hear?" Then Billy Dean pressed his thumbs to his temples again, the sound of his words were like the firing of cannons.

Chapter Forty-Four

ALL IS WELL

"Congratulations, boys." Floyd pushed the papers across the desk on an imaginary axis between the Gooseberry twins, not knowing which one would want to take charge of the signing. "Y'all got a real good deal out of me. That Mercury Montclair is quite a car. Put all the miles on her myself." Floyd sighed. "All easy miles." He wistfully looked out the window, bidding a silent farewell to the last evidence of Delia in his life. The perfume had dried up weeks ago.

Taking their cue from Floyd, the brothers each reached under identical tape measures draped around their necks and retrieved the silver Cross pens from their shirt pockets. First Lou scanned the agreement carefully, moving the pen along the paper as he read. Then he slid the paper across the desk to Sid, who automatically signed it.

So that's how it works, thought Floyd, finding the whole thing fascinating. Anybody else would have missed a detail that small. Floyd figured that was why he was so successful in business. He strove to understand the psychology behind things that most people took for granted. After all, that's all sales was, psychology and attitude. The study of human behavior.

"How's the family, Floyd?" Sid asked, stoking up a cigar and then handing the lighter to his brother.

"Fine. Real fine. Never better." Floyd said it as if he meant it. Because he did mean it for a change. It had been touch-and-go there for a while, but now everything was under control. Floyd had amazed even himself at how fast he was able to whip his family into shape. It proved to him that his instincts for the psychology of people were sharper than ever.

There was a thousand percent improvement in Hazel. Talk about a turnaround! After all the wisdom he had tried to impart to her over the years, and after all the hardheadedness she had paid him back with, who knew the thing she would latch onto was his suggestion for her to do church work? The idea was hardly out of his mouth and then lickety-split, she off and gets a job volunteering in the church office, putting her bookkeeping skills to good use. She was Brother Dear's right-hand girl. Even help put the weekly bulletin out. Besides that, she visited sick folks and delivered food to the needy evenings, becoming a regular pillar of the community. He hadn't smelled liquor on her in weeks. Something inside Floyd must have instinctively known what to say, even if it was in the heat of anger. Instinct. That's what it was. Pure-dee, unadulterated instinct.

"Yep. Real fine," Floyd said proudly. "And Johnny's becoming a baseball fanatic. Only the other day we were out tossing the ol' horsehide around. He's going to be a real sports nut, I can tell." He winked at Lou. "You know how boys are." Floyd had always wanted to say that.

"That's mighty fine," said Lou.

"He's a real boy, ain't he?" said his brother. They both lifted their large bulks from the chairs.

"Now, I'll have that car gassed up and sent right over to y'all's house. Be there before you get home for supper."

"You tell Miss Hazel Happy Thanksgiving," Lou said.

"And that boy of yours, too," added Sid. "Going to be reading about him in the sports pages."

"I'll sure tell the family y'all asked after them."

At that, the twins proceeded one after the other through the office door, like a pair of freighters through the Panama Canal. Floyd followed in their wake.

"Proud y'all came by," he called out as they headed down the sidewalk to their store, the smoke from their cigars curling above them into a single column. Floyd stood there for a moment, watching traffic, counting the cars and trucks he himself had put on the road. He thought about the many lives he had touched. No man is an island, that's for sure. With her charity work, he knew Hazel was finding out about that, too. A sensation of pride welled up in Floyd's chest and his eyes filled with tears. Things really were fine.

⌒

Hazel parked her Lincoln behind an old abandoned filling station on the edge of town. It was a half hour before first dark, and the temperature had begun to drop. She got out and opened the trunk, loaded with turkey hens for the needy. After locating the wires, she disconnected the light over the license plate and then got back in the car and waited.

A few minutes later, a battered pickup came grumbling down the two-lane, braked to a complete stop right in the center of the road, and then died. After starting it up again, the driver turned and came lurching onto the broken apron of concrete, torturing the gears. The truck was soon followed by a red-and-white Chevy. Both automobiles joined the Lincoln in the rear of the cinder-block building.

The doors opened, the cars emptied, and the women fell to work without speaking. Hazel removed a cardboard box from among the turkeys and took it to the hood of the Lincoln. There she and Creola began divvying up the circulars, hot off the Baptist church mimeograph machine.

Sweet Pea went to the trunk of Willie's car and lifted out a box of blank paper and a couple of gallons of mimeograph ink he had donated to the women for their next run. She transferred it all to Hazel's trunk, alongside the birds.

Vida was crouched over a county map spread on the fender of Creola's husband's truck. Holding a flashlight with her one good arm, Hannah stood over Vida's shoulder aiming at the map, though it wasn't dark enough to need it yet.

Maggie remained in the backseat of the Chevy, gazing out the window with her single eye, admiring the darkening blood-red sky, humming serenely to herself.

As they completed their tasks, the women gathered around Vida. The energy of the group was charged tonight. A current of constrained panic seem to hum about their heads.

"You hear from that NAACP yet?" Sweet Pea asked. "We need to get some help. It's getting scary. I'm starting to feel eyes all over me in the dark."

"You ought to be used to that, girl," Creola said with a giggle.

"I talked to them, all right," Vida said. "They going to be as helpful as tits on a boar hog. They say all they leaders is being blowed up and run out of the state. Told us we might better slow down and let them catch up. Say we done jumped the gun a couple of years. They ain't got no organization yet in Hopalachie County." Vida sounded disgusted. "'Sides, when they found out we didn't have no *man* running the show, that's when they almost hung up. Thought I was lying."

"What about Rosie?" Creola protested. "You tell them about her? She a woman."

Vida laughed darkly. "They say this ain't Alabama. Things is worser in Mississippi."

"Glad it ain't just my imagination," Creola said with a weak chuckle.

"They told me in Alabama the Law is bad to stand around and let you get kilt. But in Mississippi the Law be the ones trying to kill you. Don't matter if you is a woman."

The women exchanged nervous looks and anxious smiles. They knew what Vida was saying was true.

"So," Vida concluded, "if people going to hear the word about being a first-class citizen and getting the vote in Hopalachie County, it'll have to come from us womens, I reckon."

Sweet Pea shook her head. "I knows they need to hear it, and I hate to be no doubting Thomas, but we been talking up the vote for weeks. Not one soul say they going to go down to the courthouse with us. The sheriff got everybody scared to get off they porch."

"Ain't just the sheriff," Creola added bitterly. "It's them white niggers like Misery admiring over the white man. Makes my blood boil. And them chicken-eating preachers. Telling everybody to wait for the sweet by-and-by. 'Don't stand up in the boat,' they all say. They ain't noticed but they the only ones got a boat. The rest of us is in the swamp fighting with the gators."

"Y'all want to quit, y'all go ahead," Vida said glumly. "I can't blame you. I only come to it recent. Ain't been just a few weeks since I told daddy he was crazy for doing what he did."

At the mention of Levi Snow, the women got quiet for a spell. The only sound was Maggie's humming.

Sweet Pea broke the silence. "Awright. Show us where to go."

Relieved, Vida took the flashlight from Hannah and clicked it off, using the skinny end to point at the map. "Now, Hannah, you and Maggie take Willie's car and head on out to the Shinetown settlement tonight. Take the old Satterfield Road. Sheriff's people hardly ever patrols it."

"Let that sumbitch come ahead on," Hannah said angrily, lifting her clenched fist in the air. "Sheriff going to pay for doubling his take on me. I can't hardly afford to stay in business no more. Let him come ahead on and pick a fight with ol' Hannah! I'll beat his ass till his nose bleeds." Hannah was so agitated she was flapping her stump now. "Let him come on ahead, is what I says!"

Vida put her hand on Hannah's shoulder, trying to calm the woman down. "Don't get so worked up, Hannah. You got to be careful. Willie skin me alive if you scratch his new car."

"Don't you worry none," Hannah said. "I know how to handle that boy and his car both."

Vida grinned at Hannah. "Other way 'round, if you ask me. Willie got you wrapped around his little finger. Serves you right for trying to rob the cradle."

"Where is that boy?" asked Sweet Pea. "Why ain't that little brother of yours helping us?"

Hannah answered for Vida. "Willie say don't bother him till the shooting starts. Say that's the onliest way things going to change in this county."

"I hope he wrong," Vida said. "That's how come we got to try Rosie's way first." Then she went on with the business of the evening. "Creola, how's your driving coming along?"

"I got here, didn't I?" Creola answered a little defensively.

"Just barely!" Sweet Pea declared. "Thought I was going to have to stand in the middle of the road so Creola would have something to aim at."

"Hush! I didn't come close to no ditches this time out. I getting good as Miss Hazel." She smiled admiringly at Hazel, who beamed at the compliment. The women thought she was the best driver in the whole state of Mississippi, better than any moonshine runner they had heard of.

"Now, y'all remember to unhook your back lights so nobody can get your tag number," Hazel called out as they dispersed. "And cut off your headlights when you moving from house to house. Somebody might be watching."

Somebody was. As they left, no one noticed the car sitting across the road behind a screen of trees. It pulled out shortly after Hazel and took off in the same direction as the Lincoln.

Chapter Forty-Five

THE CHASE

The Lincoln rolled onto a tabletop landscape of straight lines and perfect right angles, a twilight world uninterrupted by hills or curves or contours. Endless rows of stalks, recently picked over and streaked with white scraps of cotton.

Hazel laughed softly to herself and said, "I remember the first time I saw this Delta. I was standing in them bluffs behind us, looking down on it all at once."

"Humph," Vida snorted. "I was probably out here with a hoe in my hand, looking up at you and cussin'."

"It took my breath away, scared me so," Hazel said, continuing with her memory. "Floyd and me looking over the flat floor of the world. Me gripping on to him for dear life." She chuckled softly to herself. "We was so excited. It was a brand-new world. Nothing but hope in front of us. Stretching as far as from here to China."

Vida looked over at Hazel. "I remembers the first time I seen you. Hope done fled the coop."

"I already give up by then." Hazel shrugged and smiled. "I couldn't get the hang of being somebody's wife and momma. Some folks just fall into it, I reckon. Me, well, I couldn't see it to save my life."

"And I can't see myself being one of the lovely Lennon Sisters," Vida said. "Everybody don't take to things the same way. Daddy says we each got our own story calling out to us."

Hazel laughed. "I guess the trick is to get everybody else to shut up long enough to hear it."

"Amen," Vida said.

"Of course, there's a lot of things I'd do different," Hazel confessed. "Take Floyd. I'd of stood up to him a lot quicker if I knew it'd make me love him more. Ain't that something? As soon as I found out I didn't need him, that's when I knew I wanted him. He's a good man. But he's only a man." Hazel laughed. "Lord knows, long as he has his little sayings, he can yank his world around any way he wants it. Now Johnny—he's in for some hard times, I can tell. You know how he is. He's..." Hazel looked over at Vida for the word and then said, "I don't know, special maybe. The world don't seem to fit him right. And he's trying so hard to make it fit. I only hope he don't have to give up too much. It's always the best parts they want to take away from you. I hope they don't take his story away."

Vida smiled. "Johnny too much like you. He'll have to find his own way, but he'll do it. I know that boy. When the time comes, he got a heap of fight in him. A heap of fight." She laughed, remembering. "One time he near about poked my eye out with his little fist. Now, that don't change. I know. It's the fight what gets you through. It'll be there when he needs it. It was you give him that."

Sniffling, Hazel said, "You're a good friend to me, Vida."

"Don't do that!" she fussed. "You know I can't stand it when you get all boo-hooey."

After Hazel took the next right off the pavement and onto a gravel road, she saw another car making the turn behind her. It was coming up fast. "Uh-oh. Vida, hold on." Hazel wasted no time. She flattened the gas pedal to the floor and the tires bit down hard on the gravel. The car seemed airborne.

Behind them, in a white Buick, two men urged the driver to speed up. Driving was Hollis, Floyd's shop mechanic.

"That's him, all right," said the man with the gun. "Just like Billy

Dean said. Look at that car go. Can you catch him?"

"Who you talking to?" Hollis scoffed. "I got a V-8 322 under my hood. Watch this baby strut her stuff."

Hazel was going sixty now, and even though she couldn't see the car through the cloud of dust gushing from her rear, she was sure it was back there somewhere.

"They's a wide place in the road up here," she told Vida. "When we get there, I'm going to mash the brakes hard. Mind your head."

"Jesus Lord, Miss Hazel!" cried Vida.

Hazel was as cool as a riverboat gambler. "Don't you worry, Vida. I'm going to take care of you. I can do this."

"I knows you can, Miss Hazel." Vida covered her face with one hand and braced herself against the dash with the other. "I got faith in you."

Hazel hit the brakes hard. The Lincoln skidded forward a few yards and the other car kept coming, then swerved trying to miss her. As Hazel continued in her skid, the rear swung around. The car spun once and then twice, each time veering farther to the left side of the road, until when it finally stopped, Hazel had the car sitting off on a sandy shoulder aimed in the opposite direction. The other car skidded off the road through a barbed-wire fence and came to a stop in an empty field.

Waving good-bye through the blanket of dust, Hazel took off and sped back toward the paved road. By the time she began to slow for the turn, she saw the other car coming up on her again. She turned hard and swung onto the blacktop, heading the Lincoln back toward town. As she powered the big car into the advancing twilight and the distance between her and her pursuers increased, Hazel began to breathe easier. They would be safely home in less than twenty minutes.

"I don't mind telling you now," Hazel said, "that was close."

Vida was holding her chest, unable to speak. When she turned back to look, there came a loud series of pops followed by a dreadful pounding noise. The car began to shimmy. It was if the Lincoln had a mind of its own. The rear of the car began fishtailing crazily, fighting Hazel. She gripped the wheel with both hands and struggled mightily against the wild sway.

"I think they shot out a tire," Hazel said, trying to remain calm. "Anyways, we sure got a flat."

"Can we make it to town?"

Hazel looked up into the rearview mirror. "Not ahead of them." The car was almost on her again.

Hollis yelled, "He's swerving all over the road. Flat tire. I'll be damned. You're one lucky shot."

"Luck, hell. It was my good shooting how come us to be catching him. 'Cause that ol' boy sure outdrove your ass."

Hollis sulled up. "Shut your mouth and get ready. Remember, he said just to scare them. I'll pull up even, and you fire off a couple of rounds. Aim over the roof."

The man readied himself at the window with his .38. "Damn. Be careful. He's all over the road now. He's liable to ram into us."

There was little daylight left. As the car pulled up next to the Lincoln, the man with the gun stared into Hazel's window. She glanced at him. For a second their eyes locked.

"It's a woman!" he shouted at Hollis. "A goddammed white woman. Did he say it was a white woman we was after?"

"What difference does it make? Shoot!"

He looked again. "Jesus, I think she's got a nigger right up in the front seat with her! Goddamn. Looks like a nigger man."

"Hurry up and shoot!" yelled Hollis. "Let's get out of here before she hits us."

"But it's a goddammed white woman!"

Hollis looked over to see what his friend was talking about. "Jesus Christ, don't shoot! That's my boss's wife. She knows me."

"Makes me sick to my stomach," the shooter said, not hearing. "White women out looking for niggers to fuck." He lifted the gun and fired twice, shattering Hazel's window. Hollis pressed the pedal to the floor, leaving the Lincoln behind. In his rearview mirror he saw the car veer sharply and fly off the road without slowing.

Hazel managed to jump a ditch, negotiate her way through a roadside stand of pines, over a cattle gap, and finally settle the car safely in a field of soft winter rye.

"Lord, Miss Hazel! Is you OK? Let's get out of here before they come back."

Hazel didn't answer. She sat erect, looking out over the steering wheel into the distance.

"Miss Hazel, you hearing me?"

"How'd I do, Vida?" Hazel said, her voice small, with a strange gurgle to it.

"Miss Hazel, you done real good. You showed them up."

Hazel turned and smiled at Vida, pleased, and then she slumped over the wheel, still smiling. She knew she had done well. Except for the shattered window and the stream of blood slowly seeping into the fabric, the car was miraculously unharmed. And, as promised, so was Vida.

Chapter Forty-Six

MAGGIE'S DIME

Floyd carefully set the phone back into its cradle. For a moment he stood stone-still in the darkened stairhall, not breathing. He reached out into the dark to no one, but wanting it to be Hazel. Wanting her to take his hand, stroke the scars on his fingers, and tell him she loved him. He staggered backward, needing the wall, and finding it, he slid himself slowly to the floor. He put his head in his hands and began to sob.

Unaware of how long he had been crying or when the persistent knocking had begun, Floyd managed to get to his feet and then reeled toward the door. Outside, glowing under the porch light, was Brother Dear. He smiled tenderly at Floyd, letting him know that he was not alone in his trials. The love that radiated from the preacher's face provoked a new round of tears. Right there in the stairhall, Brother Dear and Floyd knelt down together while the preacher prayed for Hazel as Floyd wept.

After his prayer, Brother Dear insisted on driving Floyd to the hospital. "Mrs. Dear is waiting in the car. She'll be here in case Johnny wakes up. My wife is real good with children at times like this. Knows every Mother Goose there is."

"Johnny would like that," Floyd sniffled, grateful to have the confidence of the preacher to lean on. "He sure loves a good story, him and Hazel..." Again Floyd was leveled by his need for Hazel, by the pure necessity of her, missing her worse than he knew was possible. He let the preacher guide him out to his car.

"Why did this happen, Brother Dear?" Floyd sobbed as the preacher drove.

"That's the way Satan operates. He sees a soul leaning toward Christ, and he wages full-out war. Hazel was wounded in the line of duty to Jesus. You can take comfort in that."

"I do, Brother Dear, I do." Floyd tried to smile in a courageous way. "The hospital said she was out ministering to the sick and needy when somebody..." Floyd couldn't finish.

Brother Dear reached over and put his hand on Floyd's shoulder. "Your wife is a real inspiration to the whole community, Floyd. Why, the way she's come around, her life is a sermon. A sermon I am not good enough a man to preach." He removed his hand from Floyd's shoulder to brush a tear from his own eye.

All of a sudden Floyd blurted, "Get me to her, please. She needs to know."

Brother Dear was calm. "What does she need to know, Floyd?"

"Everything."

"No," Brother Dear said carefully, "she doesn't. I don't know what it is you got to confess. Right now she only needs to hear you say one thing. And don't let me catch you telling her anything except that. Do you understand me? Man to man?"

Floyd nodded.

"And are you ready to tell her that one thing?"

"With all my heart," Floyd sobbed.

"That's good, Floyd. That's real good."

⁓

The cabin was growing heavy with stale air. Mattresses had been dragged across the floor and positioned over the windows. Though it was a chilly November night, the maids were drenched in sweat as they huddled together in Vida's darkened house, sitting around a sputtering oil lamp. They kept the light turned low, expecting white folks to race down into Tarbottom any moment, shooting off shotguns and tossing sticks of dynamite from car windows. This was going to be a nightly ritual, the maids had decided—taking turns staying together in each other's homes while Hannah and Willie sat up guarding the juke.

"Y'all know this is crazy," Sweet Pea fussed. "If they going to get us, we just making it easy for them peckerwoods. Us sitting here together like fish in a barrel. All we doing is keeping down they dynamite bill."

Creola shifted her weight in her chair. "Don't matter to me none," she said, undaunted. "Rufus done got scared and snuck out of town in the truck. I don't aim to die alone, and y'all's all I got."

"Rufus left you?" Sweet Pea asked.

"Never thought I see the day. Not if he had to get up out his chair to do it." Creola managed a weak laugh. "He was some scared. But he be back when things ease up. Or he gets hungry first."

"Y'all, maybe they ain't even after us," Vida said, trying to sound upbeat. "After I finally got Miss Hazel's car to the hospital, they acted like they believed what I told them. That she been out visiting the poor and sickly when she got shot. I even had the turkey birds to prove it."

Sweet Pea gave out a harsh laugh. "Who in they right mind believe that story? Fishier than a Friday night in a fry house." She dabbed her neck with a handkerchief. "He know about us. He know everything. He'll make his move in his own sweet time, when it best suits him. Our gooses is cooked."

"If that what you thinking, then how come us be sitting around on our hands for?" Vida snapped. "We just going to wait till he come for us?"

"We could get out of the county!" Creola blurted. "Might even leave the state. Get a train up to Memphis and never look back."

"Leave?" Vida was surprised that Creola had suggested it. "What happens if Miss Hazel dies? What if she can never speak for herself? Answer me that." The maids could hear the sadness rising in her throat. "No, I ain't going to leave her here all wrapped in lies. About how she done finally learned to behave herself and do what she was told. About how she got broke to saddle like ever woman oughta. And Daddy," she continued, "who's going to finish the story he started? I can't go off and let him be one more crazy nigger who killed a white woman."

The maids dropped their heads and studied their hands. They were too ashamed to look at Vida now.

"Y'all go on if you want, but I'm sure about my place. Somebody got to stay behind and tell the story." Vida searched for their eyes, her voice trembling. "Don't y'all see, if we don't tell it, the white folks will. And it ain't theirs to tell. It ain't..." She couldn't finish, her voice was so choked with tears.

Sweet Pea reached over and placed her hand on Vida's shoulder. "No. It ain't theirs to tell."

"Praise the Lamb," Maggie said softly, seeming especially peaceful tonight. For a moment everybody's eyes rested on her toadlike figure, as if trying to soak up some of her calm. They watched her as she rocked her ancient body gently to and fro, her leathery hands folded serenely in her lap.

After a while Vida looked up, still with tears in her eyes, yet in a clear, certain voice she said, "You know, we could go to the court-house and ask to take that voting test. We could do that."

Sweet Pea snatched her hand away from Vida's shoulder as if all her compassion had just drained through the cracks in the floor. "You gone crazy in the head?" she yelled. "I thought we was talking about how to stay alive! They put your name and address in the paper when a colored tries to vote. And since it be us, they might draw a map."

"Weren't that the plan?" Vida asked. "Ain't that what we was asking everybody else to do?"

"The plan was to get a hundred of us to march on the courthouse," Sweet Pea shot back. "Not four maids and a juker."

"But we the Rosie Parks League, remember?" Creola asked. "What would Rosie do?"

"In Hopalachie County? I don't know," Sweet Pea said. "Rosa had Luther King on her side in Montgomery."

"'Cept weren't on that bus with her, was he?" Vida reminded them. "She faced them down all by her lonesome. Besides, we got each other."

For a long time no one said another word as the idea hung heavy in the room. Maggie began to hum softly again. Vida smiled gently at her and asked, "What you think about it, Maggie?"

Maggie sighed heavily and began moving her gums in three-quarter time. Then she lifted her eye. "When I was a little girl, Momma Nell and me always come to town on Saditty." Maggie spoke in a low, quivery voice, like old people do when they're remembering in front of late-night fires. "I loved coming to town with my Momma Nell. We get all dressed up. Momma Nell'd iron my hair and put a ribbon in it. It was good as Santy Claus time."

Maggie stopped there, as if she were trying to remember the color of the ribbon. The maids silently watched her through the flickering of the lamplight, not knowing if she was finished with her story or not. For a long time she didn't move.

Then her chest heaved mightily, as if she had just remembered to breathe, and she said, "One Saditty we come up on a white man talking to a crowd about wanting they votes for guv'ner. This little sawed-off man say if he was to get elected he was going to put all the colored folks on a boat and send us back to Aferca. Then he see me standing there watching, and say, 'Hey there, little girl!' and I thought he was talking to me 'cause Momma Nell dressed me up so purty."

Maggie stopped again to remember, smiling.

"Then he say, 'Little girl, you going to like it over there in Aferca.' Say, 'Collard greens grow ten feet tall and they's a possum in every stalk.' He had a big laugh for a little sawed-off man. And everybody laugh right along with him. He petted me on my head and then reached in his pocket and give me a shiny new dime. Then he turns back to the peoples and say how much better Mississippi be without the niggers stanking up everything. Everybody clap and yell real loud."

Maggie stopped again for a moment and looked down at her hands, still folded in her lap. "All I knowed was I got me a dime out of it."

She raised her head and placed the back of her hand against the scarred flap of skin, like she might be shielding it from the sun. "I looked up at Momma Nell and big ol' tears was falling down her face. 'Why you crying for?' I asked her. Momma Nell told me, 'Girl, don't you go spending that dime.' She say, 'Keep it and let it 'mind you of today. Don't never forget who owns this here country. When you forget, you is dead.' She told me to hold on to that dime till the day I can come to town and spend it free and proud."

Maggie reached her stiffened fingers into the pocket of her dress. Out came a worn leather coin purse. She unsnapped it, reached into a little inside pocket, and brought out a tissue. Unfolding the paper in her hand, she held out a blackened coin in the lamplight. The maids all leaned in, staring wide-eyed, as if it were a hoodoo charm, pulsating in the dark.

"Many the time I got weak-willed and want to spend this here dime." Maggie chuckled at herself. "Wanting me some candy. Or the fair come to town. Or a pretty boy. Dime burned a hole in my pocket, but I didn't spend it," she said proudly. "No ma'am. I held on to it like Momma Nell told me to."

The maids were stone-silent, still studying the dime in Maggie's old hand.

"Y'all know something?" Maggie asked, her eye circling the little group. "Befo' I dies, I aim to spend this here dime."

⚭

The next day four maids plus a one-armed juke proprietor, with little ceremony, wearing their best dresses and, in Sweet Pea's case, a sassy red scarf, marched up the courthouse steps, through the vestibule, and past an oil portrait of the Senator looking as if he had everything under control. Not until they turned into the circuit clerk's office did anybody take heed. Nellie Grindle looked up from her desk behind the counter, smile at the ready. Then she saw who it was. "What y'all girls want?" she asked sharply.

Vida hauled back her shoulders and opened her mouth, but it was Maggie who said, "I here to reddish for the vote."

Nellie reached for her pointy-framed glasses that hung around her neck and studied the group for a moment before letting the glasses drop back to her chest. She managed to get herself to her feet. "Y'all wait right here!" she said, befuddled, and then fled the office.

"We in for it now," Creola whispered.

"She gone for the sheriff, I just knows it," Sweet Pea whispered back. "Our gooses is hanging on the spit and near about well done."

Hannah patted her bosoms. "I got my razor if he tries messing with me. I'll gut 'im like a catfish."

"It ain't too late," Sweet Pea offered. "We can hightail it out that door."

It was too late. Nellie had found Billy Dean across the hall in the chancery clerk's office, double-checking the tax rolls, and returned with him in tow. Billy Dean took a few moments to study the group. His eyes lit on a woman, then he would shake his head and move to the next.

"Now, ain't this a proud delegation from the colored community," he said. "We got the county whore. A one-armed bootlegger. Two tubs of lard with three eyes between them."

He glared at Vida. "And last but not least, the proud daughter of the local murdering reverend." He smirked at his own cleverness. "This all them Yankee Jew agitators could scrape up?" He paused as if he expected some kind of response, yet the women had no idea what he was talking about. He homed in on Vida again. "So, you want to follow in your daddy's footsteps, I see."

Vida tried her hardest to hold his stare. "I proud to. I ain't ashamed for my daddy." After the words left Vida's mouth, the sheriff's eyes bucked her off like a wild horse. She dropped her gaze and studied his star instead.

A world of silence was cram-packed into the next few moments. The sheriff stood there, his jaw muscles bulging and the forked vein in his forehead ready to pop. The hush was so complete and lasted so long that the women dared to shift their eyes questioningly to one another. What life-and-death matters were being considered here?

Deputy Butts walked into the office, and the tension snapped like a cable. Everybody jerked their heads in his direction. For a moment his eyes bobbled back and forth, trying to get a handle on things. He stammered, "What's going on here, Sheriff? You got trouble?"

Billy Dean heaved a breath. "No," he said wearily, reaching his thumb up to his temple. "Nothing more than usual. Bunch of niggers doing their damnedest to ruin my day."

Nellie was indignant. "It's a sight more than that! They say they want to register to vote. Sheriff, this is getting out of hand."

Billy Dean exploded. "Shut up, woman! I decide when things are out of hand or not. You understand that?"

Nellie couldn't answer. Scarlet-faced, with her mouth agape, she stood there frozen, humiliated in front of a bunch of coloreds.

Vida watched Billy Dean carefully, waiting with everybody else to see what he was going to do now, after yelling at a white woman. The sheriff's gaze fell on her. Again Vida looked directly into his eyes. She did not waver. For the first time in her life, Vida was holding a stare with a white man.

It was as if the world around her was hurtling out of control, yet she herself was balanced at its absolute center, enveloped in an eerie calm. Her thoughts were focused and sharp. Things were revealed to her. First she saw that the sheriff's eyes were the deep, dark blue of the night. Nothing at all like Nate's.

Then she saw another thing. Something she had never seen before in a white man's eyes, burrowing there in the corners and squirming under the lids. She understood why the colored were never supposed to look there in the first place, lest they see it, too. The sheriff was afraid, and she knew it had to do with her. The idea was so ludicrous Vida almost laughed right out loud. Her whole life she had been at this man's mercy, and now she saw that he was afraid of her. Why on earth?

In a flash, she understood deep in her bones what her father had meant. Even though she was a colored woman and maybe nobody would believe her, a story is made to be told and passed on. If it is picked up and touched and handled enough times, the truth will at last shine through the telling, and the world will finally see. What she was doing now, this very second, would set Nate and all those like him free. That's why those bad men in the Bible always tried to kill the story, no matter how lowly the teller. That's why her father put his faith in the story. And Vida knew this man's story. It was forever intertwined with her own. She could recite it loud and clear this very minute. Every jot and tittle. And he knew that she could.

The sheriff dropped his eyes. "Give them the test," he said.

"What?" Nellie gasped.

Billy Dean looked at the old woman again, yet the fury was gone. Only tired was left. "Just give it to them, Nellie. They ain't going to pass it no way."

She opened her mouth to speak, but Billie Dean wouldn't have it.

"Nellie," he said, his finger aimed at the woman, marking off his words. "Not. Another. God. Damned. Word." He spun around and left the office.

Nellie and Lampkin looked at each other in astonishment. As if the women were not there straining at every thought, spoken and unspoken, Nellie said indignantly, "Well, Lampkin, I reckon you're going to be in for a promotion soon."

The deputy grinned but didn't comment.

Nellie stared sullenly at the door. "Billy Dean Brister couldn't win another election if the Senator voted every dead man in the history of Hopalachie County."

∽

The women left the office and walked through the courthouse doors. They halted when they stepped out onto the gallery over-looking the square. All the town's colored had fled, and a small crowd of whites had gathered around the stone soldier, staring back at them.

The women, terrified, started down the steps. As they did, people began to line both sides of the walk. The crowd was eerily silent, like the woods after a shotgun blast. At first Vida thought it was because the women had taken the town by surprise and they hadn't had time to plan their courage.

Then the murmuring begin, "That's Hayes Alcorn's maid, ain't it?"

"And ain't that Floyd's girl with them?"

"And there's that old cripple gal that works for the Gooseberrys."

"You think they know?"

It struck Vida that what the crowd was seeing was not a group of women who had just risked their lives for the vote, but the personal property of Delphi's quality white folk. It was an odd blessing.

The women continued to move in a tight little knot across the square while the whites stared opened-mouthed. Though Vida didn't turn around to check, she figured they were still watching, trying to figure out what to do, as the women made the slow descent to Tarbottom.

Chapter Forty-Seven

SWEATING IT OUT IN
TARBOTTOM

"That's one test I done flunked," Creola grumbled as she came out of her kitchen carrying an iced tea in each hand. "How I supposed to know how to recite Article 3, Section 29, of the Mississippi Constitution?"

Sweet Pea took a jelly glass from Creola, adding, "And how about when she asked you how many bubbles in a bar of soap? What's that got to do with electing a sheriff?"

"Got a lot to do with it," Vida said. "You know they don't ask white folks them questions."

"Least we done it!" Creola said, deciding to be proud regardless. "And nobody can't say we didn't. Ain't that right, Maggie?"

Her eye shining in the dark, Maggie sang out, "Yes, Jesus!"

Creola walked out onto the porch where Hannah was sitting with her sawed-off shotgun slung across her lap and offered her the other glass of tea. Hannah shook her head and then nodded toward the pint of Ezra Brooks at her feet. "I'm fixed up fine, Creola. A nip or two ever now and then keeps my trigger finger warm."

Inside, Sweet Pea was talking. "Well, before y'all go pinning flowers on yourselves, if we do make it alive through this night, come tomorrow we going to have to decide what to do. Y'all know quick as our white ladies get wind of this, we good as lost our jobs. And they ain't going to protect us no more."

Creola eased herself down on her chair. "And that'll be the least of it," she said. "You done forgot who my boss is? If I shows up for work or don't, either way Mr. Hayes be chasing me around town with a rope." Realizing what she had said, Creola gave Vida a pained look of regret.

"Guess we could all move in together and live like them nuns I heard about in New Orleans," Sweet Pea said with a disgusted face. "I don't reckon they's a man in this county wants my company bad enough to get blowed up for it."

"How be ever," Creola said hopefully, "I bet when the word gets out, they be people all over the state come in and help us." She raised up her glass like she was making a toast. "Maybe even Martin Luther King show up in Delphi. Law! Won't that be something!"

"Maybe so," Vida said doubtfully. "But in case he don't, Willie say he give us some money to get away." So many things were still unclear to Vida, with her father in jail and no word yet if Hazel was dead or alive. She said firmly, "I'm staying, but y'all can go."

"Hannah say she can hide us out at her place if we wants," Creola reminded them. "But I reckon it ain't no safer there. Hannah says the sheriff'll probably shut her down."

"Or burn her down," Sweet Pea added darkly.

They talked continuously through the night, the mood shifting between giddy disbelief at what they had done and abject terror of the consequences. Hannah joined them near dawn. When at last they believed they had made it through the long night, there came a sound from off the front porch. Footsteps, slow and heavy, like a man's. Everybody held her breath as the steps drew nearer. Vida reached out for Creola's hand. A whimper rose from Sweet Pea. Maggie rocked her body gently.

Hannah raised her gun with her good arm and aimed at the door. "You better hurry up and state yo' business, whoever you is. While you still got a head to state it out of."

When there came a firm knock, it was accompanied by a shared sigh of relief. Night riders didn't knock.

"Y'all in there?" The voice was familiar. "Vida?"

"It's Mr. Floyd!" Vida said in a loud whisper.

Creola was still holding both hands over her bosom, like she was trying to keep her heart in her chest. "Nearly give me the thumps."

"What he want, I wonder?" Sweet Pea asked. "Think he'll bless us out 'cause of Miss Hazel?"

Creola hoisted herself out of her chair and scuffed her feet across the bare floor. After lifting up the crossbar and pulling back the door, she saw Floyd Graham, looking little and lost. "Come on in, Mr. Floyd," Creola said gently. "Don't mind the dark. Let me show you to someplace to sit down."

Creola led Floyd into the house. He stopped after a few steps. "No, I'll stand if it's the same with you."

"Everhow it feels right for you to do. You sure welcome to stand there long as you wants." Still, Creola left her chair vacant and remained standing herself.

Floyd appeared exhausted. He slowly looked around Creola's cabin until he was able to make out his maid through the dark. "Hello, Vida."

"Mr. Floyd," Vida answered sheepishly.

"I went over to your place first. I been walking from house to house. Y'all was the first one that answered."

"Yessuh. I ain't surprised. I 'spect everybody up under their beds this night."

"Well, I guess," Floyd said, not understanding. "I know it's late, and I'm sorry for it. But Hazel wanted me to be sure and find you."

All around the room a chorus of voices went up. "Miss Hazel?"

Floyd took a step back. "That's right. Hazel," he said, baffled at the intensity of the response. "She wanted you to know she's going to be all right. Bullet went clean through her neck. Only thing is, it took her voice for a while. Writes everthing down."

Vida reached out for Sweet Pea's hand. "She going to be all right!"

Maggie sang out, "Praise God!"

Floyd watched the maids, bewildered. "Didn't know you all felt that strong about Hazel," was all he could say.

"Yessuh, we do!" Creole cried. "That we do."

Floyd stood silent for a moment considering the maids' joy, not understanding much in his world tonight. He sighed heavily, his shoulders drooping, as if under some invisible weight. "Vida?" he said in a little boy's voice.

"Yessuh, Mr. Floyd."

"Was that really where she was? Delivering a Thanksgiving turkey to poor folks?"

The smile dropped from Vida's face. "Why you ask, Mr. Floyd?"

"I don't know. I hope that's where she was and all," he said uncertainly.

Considerable time passed without Vida answering his question. Floyd, clearly embarrassed, averted his eyes and began rubbing his fingers. He looked up carefully, "Can I ask you another question? Personal?"

"Yessuh," she said carefully. "What is it you wanting to know?"

"Hazel wasn't. . .I mean. . ." Floyd glanced up quickly at Vida, his eyes pleading with her, and then looked down at his hand again. "What I'm asking is, she didn't get hurt doing something she shouldn't of been doing, did she?"

Nervously, Vida ran her finger along the rim of her glass and without answering took a sip. When she looked back up at Floyd, he was still worrying his hand, rubbing his fingers, tying his best to get at those purple scars.

"I mean," Floyd said, struggling with his words, "what I'm asking is, she wasn't seeing another fella, was she?"

With a mouthful of tea, Vida let go a loud, gurgling "Haaah?"

Floyd glanced up from his hand with a wounded look but said

nothing. Having worked so hard to get the question out, he decided to endure the ridicule silently until he had his answer.

Vida coughed and wiped her mouth with the back of her hand. Floyd still thought he heard her giggling. The other maids hid their expressions behind their hands, and nobody would look at him.

Finally, having gathered herself together, Vida said with studied sympathy, "That what you thinking, Mr. Floyd?" She shook her head adamantly. "No sir! Ain't no other man 'ceptin you. I swear to it. You the one she loves. One of the last things she said to me."

On hearing that, he drew up his shoulders again. "Course she does," he said, yet his restored self-assurance couldn't hide the relief in his voice.

Smiling at him, Vida said, "I 'spect when she gets her voice back, she'll have some stories to tell us, won't she, Mr. Floyd?"

Floyd nodded. "I reckon. It's been a long time since we swapped stories."

He dropped his hands to his sides and looked around the room at the maids again, his face serious once more. "I hear y'all had quite a big day."

"Yessuh," they all mumbled.

"Can't of helped your daddy much, Vida."

"Nosuh, I reckon not. Doubt if it hurt him much neither."

"Maybe you right. Like I always say. . ."

"Yessuh, Mr. Floyd?

He smiled. "Funny, I forgot what it is I always say. Must be tired. Ain't been to bed for a couple of nights."

"You best get on back and get you some sleep, Mr. Floyd. You can rest easy now."

Almost out the door, Floyd turned back around and stood for a moment in the doorway. "Vida," he said, "I'm sorry, I mean real sorry, if anything I done caused you or yours any harm."

"Yessuh, Mr. Floyd. I believes you."

"And I'll talk to Hayes myself about Levi. See if we can't get things calmed down a bit." Floyd nodded his head, seconding his own motion.

"And Vida," he said again, "I know tomorrow's Thanksgiving and all, but if you can, try and come on early. The boy's been asking for you. And with his momma in the hospital again and all…"

"Yessuh, Mr. Floyd," Vida said. "I'd be proud to."

Chapter Forty-Eight

THE HOSPITALITY STATE

The Trois Arts League had just wrapped up its annual awards meeting and members were filing out the door in high spirits when Hayes Alcorn scuttled by them, displaying the requisite charm and courtesies but at the same time making a beeline for the liquor cabinet. After Pearl had said her last good-bye, she joined Hayes in the library, where she found him muttering to himself as he paced before the fireplace, consuming a portion of bourbon that would have put a stagger into the step of a normal-sized man.

"My people are dropping like flies all around me," he said when his wife entered the room. "Floyd Graham—that hillbilly—flat-out told me I was being too hard on Levi Snow. Then in the very next breath he had the nerve to ask for a business loan." Hayes crinkled up his brow and shook his head incredulously. "And get this!" he cried. "He came libelously close to accusing the sheriff of planting evidence."

Pearl, in high heels, stooped a little so Hayes could interrupt his tirade and give her a welcome-home peck on the cheek.

"Where *was* I? Oh, yeah. Imagine! Too hard on Levi Snow. That damned murdering nigruh sitting up in that jail as pretty as you please. And Hopalachie County catering to his every need! Well, that's it. Time to put a stop to it."Pearl took a seat on the sofa, knowing how Hayes hated for her to look down on him when he was working up steam. Touching her handkerchief to the dimple in her chin, she said, "I'm sorry, Hayes. What does all this mean? Will you explain it to me?"

"Gladly. Means I finally found me some boys willing to do what's got to be done." After taking a greedy swallow from his glass, Hayes continued. "Levi Snow's been sitting in that cell, paid for by the taxpayers, laughing at us while he's got his people carrying out acts of insurrection. If *your* brother hadn't run the Klan out of the county, this wouldn't be happening."

Hayes smiled a satisfied little smile and swirled the bourbon in his glass. "Well, by tomorrow night that situation will be remedied. There's going to be an example set. People will see Hayes Alcorn as a man of action."

Pearl frowned. "What are these boys going to do for you, Hayes?"

"I'll tell you what!" He was close to snarling now. "They going to take care of that nigruh once and for all. Before he provokes any more public acts of defiance." Hayes took another gulp and then shook his head. "That must have been a sight. A vicious mob of nigruh women storming the courthouse." A hint of a smile crossed his face as he noted the political bounce to the words.

He started his pacing again. "I swear! With Billy Dean Brister as sheriff, that gang of coloreds might be in charge of the county jail soon. Turn it into a juke joint and dance the Sassy Wiggle." He threw back the rest of his drink, leaving Pearl to wonder how he knew about such a thing as the Sassy Wiggle.

"And quite frankly, I'm surprised at you, Pearl. That you aren't any more concerned." Hayes put out his arm to the mantel, which was about shoulder-high, and leaned against it.

"Concerned, dear?"

"Can't you see what's been going on under your nose? Your very own maid tried to vote." His hand was now patting around on the mantel for something, but he kept an eye on his wife. "The fact that every maid in the neighborhood all at once got a wild hair to participate in the democratic process? All on the same day? Ain't that the least bit suspicious? Even to you, Pearl?"

"Well, yes," Pearl said, "now that you mention it, Hayes. I am concerned."

"Yes, I thought you might be when I explained it to you."

"About these 'boys' you mentioned," Pearl continued. "Are you saying you have a plan to harm Levi?" The handkerchief traveled to her throat.

"That's the idea, dear," Hayes said sarcastically. He began to sidle along the mantel, groping among the figurines and picture frames adorning the shelf behind him.

"Hayes, dear, I really believe you should reconsider this idea of yours," Pearl suggested, still smiling pleasantly.

"I don't need any more advice, thank you, *dear*. Action is what's needed." He finally retrieved a silver cigar case that had been pushed up behind a photograph of the Senator and Pearl as children. For the first time it hit him that the colored boy in the background of the photograph must be Levi.

Pearl waited until Hayes had selected one of the Havanas before she raised the handkerchief to her nose. "Please, Hayes, don't smoke in the house. I've asked you before."

Testily, Hayes flung the cigar back in the box and snapped the lid shut. As he stood there, sullen, he noticed the handkerchiefed hand had stopped flitting about and had finally lighted on the arm of the sofa. From where he stood, it reminded him of a prehistoric reptilian claw.

"Now, about Levi," Pearl said. "This is what I want to see you do, dear. I want you to leave him alone and stop stirring up all these disagreeable feelings toward him."

"He killed Delia!" he exclaimed. "Your own niece!"

"Pooh," she said. "Levi wouldn't hurt a fly, and anybody with a modicum of sense would know that. That's why no one has touched him. Goodness, Hayes, I'm surprised at you."

"But—"

"I've known Levi since he and I were children. The gentlest of God's creatures. And he adored Delia. I know. I saw it."

"But the Senator—"

"Isn't himself," she said. "Hayes, he doesn't know what to think now. My brother is crazy with grief. And for you to take advantage of his state...well, I don't think that's very considerate of you." Not able to muster the words to counter such lunacy, Hayes stood there blowing like a horse after a hard race.

"And what's more. About the maids. Creola has been with me for over twenty years. Don't you think I know everything she thinks and feels? She's no troublemaker, Hayes."

"She tried to vote, Pearl! The whole town saw it. You can't just dismiss. . ." He stopped and looked at his wife, dumbfounded. Her face hadn't changed, it was still pleasantly vacant, completely heedless of the desperateness of the situation.

"Pearl, listen, honey, let me explain. There was a gang of them. All out to overturn the system. A communist-backed insurrection."

"Hayes, really! I know every one of them. Creola? Well, that really is unthinkable. And Levi's daughter, she's overwrought from the way you've been treating her father. The colored do have feelings, Hayes."

Hayes slumped down into the fireplace armchair.

"Then there's Sweet Pea. Now, I myself have taken that poor wayward girl under my wing and turned her around with good literature. And Maggie. Really, Hayes, Maggie? Out to overthrow the system?" Pearl was taken by laughter so hysterical and unbecoming that Hayes had to shut his eyes against the ugly snorts. "Oh, dear!" she cried, laughter still coursing through her words. "Maggie! What could you have been thinking?" She started howling again.

Hayes sat through it all, seething.

"Now, dear," she said, drying her eyes with her handkerchief, "I want you to be governor as badly as you do. But believe me, this isn't the way to go about it." Pearl dismissed his silliness with a wave of lace.

"Listen to me, Hayes. If you want to win, I don't believe this race issue is going to serve you well. I think everyone is tired to death of it, myself. It's the nineteen fifties, for goodness' sakes. The colored question was settled in Mississippi long ago. It's old hat. We all know our places here. And if the only evidence you have to prove this conspiracy of yours is poor old Levi and a few colored maids, why. . .why. . ." she bit her lip, barely able to suppress another fit of hilarity, "why, I'm afraid you are certain to make a laughingstock of yourself. And," she said, unable to stifle a tiny, leftover giggle, "it's going to be hard enough for you."

"Yes, Pearl," Hayes said, now in a deep sulk.

"Oh, Hayes, you never understood how it was with us, did you?"

"Us?"

"Yes, us. My family. The Columns. The land. Everything and everybody on it. *That* 'us.' We are all part of that whole. Don't you see? You can't, never could, touch Levi, because he is part of us, too. He's been a part of us for three hundred years."

Hayes looked up at the picture on the mantel of Pearl, the Senator, and Levi as children. He was repulsed. "You talking blood?"

"Blood?" Pearl scoffed. "Blood, indeed! Hayes, blood is the least of it."

"What do you mean? Blood is everything."

"Blood is mostly incidental," she said, dismissing Hayes with a flourish of her handkerchief. "History is everything. Through the years his people have schemed to kill us in our sleep. Our people have sold, hung, and bred his people. Levi's great-grandmother burned down the house on the Virginia plantation. We hung his grandfather for trying to start a slave uprising. Levi's father died saving the Senator from drowning in the river when he was only a three-year-old child. Hayes, we have hated and loved and killed and saved each other for three centuries."

"Blood!" Pearl went on with a laugh. "For all that time we've taken care of each other. Looked to each other. Not to the government, not to the community, not to the church. You can't divide us any more than you can divide air. The Senator may not be talking to Levi, but they will never be able to separate themselves. They—we—all breathe through one another's history. Levi as good as raised Delia and Hertha. He was a second brother to me. The Senator was in love with Levi's wife before Levi was. That's the way it is. And it will never change. It's not about the weak loyalty of blood. It's fiercer and more stubborn than that. We are grafted to each other through our histories. We are fated to one another, for good or for evil. We may kill each other, we may save each other, but it is up to *us* to do it."

Pearl gave Hayes a stern look. "Nobody—and I mean nobody—better try doing it for us. Can you understand that, Hayes?"

Hayes looked at her like a pouting child.

"I thought not," Pearl said with a sigh.

She rose up from the sofa and walked over to him. Putting her hand gently on his shoulder, she said, "Hayes, I've been giving your future a lot of thought. If I'm going to finance your campaign, I would prefer that you focus on something pleasant and uplifting. Perhaps a statewide beautification program. Or tourism. That would be wonderful, wouldn't it? Get out the true story about Mississippi. The Hospitality State."

"Yes. Wonderful."

"Oh, Hayes, don't be so morose! I'm sure I'm right. I've always been good with my hunches. Like when I told my brother to name you president of the bank. That's worked out well, hasn't it?

"Yes, Pearl. I'm sure I will never be able to thank you enough."

The handkerchief flew into the air. "Hayes! I've had another inspiration. I think you should get down on your knees and beg that Hazel Graham to campaign for you. Why, I can probably get the Trois Arts League to nominate her as the Hopalachie County Woman of the Year."

Pearl touched the handkerchief to her heart and breathed deeply.

"She's a saint, Hayes," she said, her words deeply felt. "A genuine saint has been living in our midst all this time. I knew there was something special about that woman."

Chapter Forty-Nine

THE RESURRECTION

The sheriff pulled out from the old bootlegger's lair set deep in a hollow. His police radio was all static, exploding like fireworks in his head. Not helping matters, the sun was out again, sending the temperature up into the eighties even though it was November.

Billy Dean rolled up his window and turned the air conditioner on high. He'd had it put in just last week, special. Cold was the only thing that seemed to make his migraines ease off some, that and keeping the radio quiet. The only dispatches he ever got were the constant updates on the four-month-old countywide search for Delia's body, which was now the longest in Mississippi history. He could guaran-damn-tee there wouldn't be any news breaking on that front. Not by a long sight.

Why should he care? Today was the first day of his retirement from the honorable profession of law enforcement. He reached down and clicked off the radio.

He stopped the car before he hit the blacktop and dug into his jacket for the wad of cash. After counting it a second time, he crammed it in the car pocket with the rest of the day's receipts. He stomped on the gas, tires squealing onto the pavement. In spite of his headache, Billy Dean felt pleased with himself. Nice day for collections so far. It was to be his final one. As promised, Delia had sent word. Tomorrow, December 1, he was to drive up to Memphis and meet her at the Peabody. This nightmare was coming to an end.

And not a minute too soon. While he was cleaning out his desk drawer at the house that morning, he discovered it unlocked. He could have sworn there'd been a letter from Delia in there, one he hadn't got around to burning. Hertha was bound to be the one to have found it. Or Missouri. Either way, that meant his wife was onto him—he had no idea for how long, but knowing her, she was probably setting some kind of trap. Probably had already told the Senator. Anyway, after one last collection he was on his way out of the state for good. He'd worry about a divorce later.

The sky was beginning to cloud up again. It had been doing this all day. Big black clouds, fat with rain, would roll in on a cold wind, darkening everything around. Then they would move out again without shedding a drop, temperatures shooting immediately to almost summertime levels. Maybe he and Delia could live someplace where it stayed cold all the time. Snowed even. That would suit him fine. By now Billy Dean had pretty much talked himself into looking forward to a new life with Delia. After all, she was a good-looking woman. Probably meant the child would be good-looking, too. That would be a nice change. Wouldn't feel as if he were part of a circus act every time he took the family out in public. And them treating him like *he* was the freak.

His old uncle once told him that Brister blood always won out when it came to looks. He had been wrong. The Bristers had lost a couple of rounds bad, in Hertha's case. Besides being unsightly, his daughters were turning out as cold and calculating as the rest of their women kin. There was something mighty scary that came in on that side of the family.

Twenty minutes later, the sun shining in his face, Billy Dean crested Redeemer's Hill. He cut on his siren and floored it, careening down into the Delta for old times' sake. He remembered being a kid and taking the hill with his uncle Furman. Back when all he wanted was a Stetson and a pair of hand-tooled cowboy boots.

There was no turning back now. Soon certain things were about to show up missing. Such as the county tax receipts he had embezzled and the contents of Hertha's safe deposit box, the one that held a small fortune in heirloom jewelry. Then there were her family bonds he had cashed in. If by some miracle he could stay out of prison, he still wouldn't be able to keep his job, the only thing he loved besides Delia. Not with the coloreds trying to vote and Levi sitting up in jail, still alive and uncharged. There was already strong talk of impeachment. What a joke! Billy Dean Brister would be thrown out of office for being soft on the colored. His daddy would roll in his grave. No, he had burnt all his bridges. It was now Delia or nothing.

About a mile before Hannah's the rain began to fall, pelting the windshield with small, hard drops. He had to make one more collection before the day was done, and he figured that would push his private pension fund up to about fifty-five thousand.

Billy Dean cut off his siren and swung onto the dirt path that led up to Hannah's. His plan had held together so far. Barely. Hazel Graham had been one close call. Jesus, those idiots! Taking that fool woman for some kind of Yankee civil rights ringleader. And then shooting her while she was delivering food to the goddamned poor, for Christ's sake.

"God almighty!," he had told them boys, "Helen Keller lives just over the state line in Alabama. Y'all can probably go knock her off and be back by suppertime." Right there was another high-profile crime that would have to go unsolved by Billy Dean Brister. Just add it to the bill of impeachment.

⁓

The sheriff got out of the cruiser, leaving the door wide open, and eased up the plank steps without a creak. He didn't surprise anybody. Willie and Hannah had been waiting for him ever since Willie returned from Delphi with the news. For the first time ever, they were delighted to see the sheriff. His showing up at Hannah's instead of heading straight out to the Columns meant he *hadn't* heard the news. Finally they had something on Billy Dean Brister.

When Billy Dean stalked through the door, he found the two standing behind the bar, side by side, exactly as they'd rehearsed it. The sheriff asked for his whiskey as he always did.

Hannah reached under the bar and pulled out the fifth of Evan Williams she kept for the sheriff and set it down before him. He drank right out of the bottle, refusing as always to use one of her glasses. As the rain pecked at the tin roof, neither Willie nor Hannah spoke. They were biding their time.

"You know why I'm here, Hannah," the sheriff said. "Let's have it."

"Sheriff, this is your third run this week. I ain't got no more to give. Can't get blood outa no turnip."

"Then don't bother taking out my cut. Hand me the whole damned tin."

"That's a good idea," she said. "I'll show you what nothing looks like."

As Hannah reached behind her, she nodded at Willie.

"Sheriff, if you stop by this way when you get back from the Columns, I 'spect we'll have a little something for you then." Willie smiled his smoothest smile.

The sheriff narrowed his eyes at him. "What makes you think I'm going out that way? I never said."

"Nosuh! I reckon you didn't. I figured with all the commotion and all, you be heading out that way first thing."

"Commotion," the sheriff repeated almost to himself. He studied Willie closely.

Setting the cash box down on the counter, Hannah jumped in. "Don't mind him none, Sheriff. He ain't meaning to be telling you your business. Why, you was probably the first one to know about it, a big thing like that."

Billy Dean's eyes kept shifting between the two, desperately trying to snag the piece he was missing.

"Nosuh!" Hannah exclaimed. "I bet you knew before she hit the state line." Hannah smiled brightly at him. "Something as big as Miss Delia coming home alive."

"What'd you say?" he sputtered, gaping at Hannah.

But it was Willie's turn to go. "I sorry for misspeaking like that, Sheriff, suh. Hannah's sure right. Nobody knows the goins-on in this county as good as you. Nosuh!"

Hannah went next. "So when we heard what she brung back with her, well, we figured you'd surely head on out there first thing."

Hannah flipped the cash box in her hand and shook it. "That's why we ain't got nothing here for you yet. Thought we had a little time to scrape something together."

"What she brought back with her?" Billy Dean was sick at his stomach. She couldn't have had the baby already, could she? No, not for a couple of months. At least that's what she said.

"Yessuh," Willie said with a laugh. "What she brung this time sure beat them Yankee husbands to hell and back." Willie looked up at the sheriff with an innocent grin. "I hope you don't mind me saying so, Sheriff."

"Why should I—I mean—no." The sheriff was so tangled in what he was supposed to know and what he wasn't, his tongue knotted on him. Damn, how could Delia ever keep it all straight? At last he could only shout, "Mind your own goddamned business" and, almost as an afterthought, "you nigger!" Then he fled through the door.

As the sheriff tore away in his car, Hannah and Willie turned to each other and said simultaneously, "Nigger?" So that was the best shot the big bad Billy Dean Brister had left! Then they fell out laughing.

⁓

Billy Dean figured there was only one thing to do. He had to go straight out there and get into the middle of it. Shoot his way out if he had to.

When he pulled into the circular drive, everything seemed peaceful enough, the only disturbing detail being the little foreign car with the New Jersey tag. However, as he climbed the steps up to the gallery, he could hear shouting loud enough to pierce the cypress door. It was the Senator's voice. "I'm going to kill that sumbitch! Gimme my gun. Where the hell is my gun!"

The sheriff unsnapped his holster, eased the door open, and stuck his head inside. The first thing he saw was the Senator, jabbing wildly toward the top of the stairs with his favorite hickory cane, the one with the Confederate flag burned into the handle. From somewhere in the house he heard Delia crying, "Leave him alone, Daddy. I love him. If you kill him, you're going to have to kill me, too."

With his head still poked through the doorframe, Billy Dean wondered if this was the right time to be there after all. Maybe after things cooled down a bit. As he pulled the door to, the hinge creaked and the Senator whipped around and saw him.

"There you are!" The Senator came at him still waving the cane. Billy Dean drew his gun and aimed it.

"It's about time you done something right," the Senator said.

"Wha—?

"Billy Dean, take that gun and shoot the both of them. I'll take full responsibility."

Shoot Delia and my baby? Billy Dean thought, trying to reason this out fast. That don't make any sense. And why in the hell is he acting so glad to see me, now that he knows about Delia and me?

"Billy Dean!" came a cry from upstairs, "Is that Billy Dean Brister?"

Delia came down the stairs carefully, one hand on the railing and the other holding her very prominent belly. "Oh, Billy Dean! You've got to help us. Daddy's gone berserk." Once down the stairs, she scurried over to his side.

"Help. . .us?" Billy Dean asked, confused. He motioned with his gun to Delia's belly and asked haltingly, "You mean. . .us?"

She quickly turned her face away from her father. "No, Billy Dean," she said in a low, scolding whisper, "not *that* us." Then her face went all soft and innocent, and she cried out, "Oh, Billy Dean, I'm so sorry for not writing, but it happened so fast."

"Why should you be writing him?" the Senator asked, scowling. "What's going on here?"

Delia gave Billy Dean a quick little wink. Yep, he thought, she's enjoying the shit out of this. Whatever it is.

"No, Daddy, all I meant was, I should have at least sent the sheriff proof that I was still alive so he wouldn't go to all the trouble of searching."

The Senator laughed bitterly. "That would have been most considerate of the sheriff's feelings." He stamped his cane on the floor. "What about the feelings of your goddamned father?"

Delia gave her golden hair a sulky toss. "Well, you can probably deduce from this recent display of insanity why I might have had my hesitations."

God, she's smooth, thought Billy Dean. She had everything so off-kilter, he didn't even know where he fit into her little play.

The Senator aimed his cane at Delia. "Arrest her, Sheriff. Right now. Don't listen to any of her fancy talk. I want her taken to jail and then hung. That's what I want. Give her Levi's cell. Looks like he won't be needing it now that my daughter's been resurrected."

The sheriff grinned at the Senator, feeling a little relief that it was Delia he was furious with and not him. Whatever game she was playing, Billy Dean seemed to be totally in the clear. He watched her with growing admiration. She was a better schemer than he had ever dreamed. More beautiful than he remembered. He wanted her now more than ever.

"What's the charge?" the sheriff said, playing along with the Senator.

"Miscegenation!"

The sheriff hesitated, trying to recollect the word. "Ain't that...?"

"Yep, Delia got herself engaged to a nigger!"

"Daddy!" Delia whispered angrily, cutting her eyes upstairs. "I told you not to call him that."

The Senator jabbed his cane toward the stairs again. "Drove him right through Delphi in broad daylight in a foreign convertible. And a *Yankee* nigger at that. Delia, you've really gone and done it this time."

Delia poked her bottom lip out. "Jeffery's never going to come down now, Daddy."

"Jeffery?" Billy Dean said weakly. "Delia, you've gone and got engaged to a...and the baby, but I—"

Once more Delia shot Billy Dean a severe look of warning, and then, seeing that it had been received, immediately brightened, singing out sweetly, "Yes, the baby!" She laid her hand on her stomach. "You noticed! It must be impossible to miss now. How precious of you to concern yourself."

"Concern myself?" he stammered. "But..."

"Now, don't you worry, neither of you. Jeffery will be a wonderful father. Daddy, did I tell you he owns twelve filling stations in New Jersey alone?" Delia raised her voice to the top of the stairs. "Don't you, honey?"

There was only silence from upstairs. "See there, Daddy? Are you happy now? Jeffrey's too scared to even speak."

"He oughta be. I'm gonna to shoot his black ass the minute he hauls it down those stairs. Better yet, you go shoot him, Billy Dean. You already got your gun out. Go do it for me, son, as a personal favor."

Billy Dean didn't move. Things were happening too fast. He desperately needed time to regroup.

"You still going to have to resign being sheriff for bankrupting the county searching for a girl that ain't even dead. And for the voting mess. But if you do this little thing for me, I promise I'll find something for you. Go on and shoot 'im."

All Billy Dean knew was that he had better find a place to sit down, fast. His head was about to bust and his stomach was going queasy. Collapsing on the settee against the entryway wall, Billy Dean took off his Stetson and dropped it on the floor. He sat hunched with his head in his hands, the room spinning and the gun pointing at the ceiling.

"I'm hearing some pretty brave talk down there," came a booming Yankee voice from up above. "Who's got the guts to back it up?"

Billy Dean raised his eyes to see a giant of a man, barrel-chested and immaculately dressed in a New York–tailored suit, come stomping down the stairs. He was carrying a .45 of his own.

"There he is, Billy Dean!" The Senator was almost squealing. "You got a clean shot! What you waiting for, boy?"

Delia ran to Jeffery and flung her arms around him. "Leave him alone, Daddy. You're talking about the man who's going to be the father of your grandchild."

The Senator looked down at the sheriff. "I changed my mind. After you shoot him and lock Delia away, put Levi in the cell with my daughter. He's the only one that could ever talk any sense into that girl. Where is he when you need him, anyway?"

Billy Dean's head was swaying in his hands, his gun pointing over his head at nothing in particular as he desperately tried to figure his next move. Maybe I should go ahead and shoot the nig—Jeffery— he thought. No, then I'd probably have to shoot Delia, too. Maybe I could yell out, "That's *my* baby we talking about here!," but then I'd have to shoot the Senator.

No, she's got me. She's got me good. There ain't a thing I can say. Not a thing I can do. He cast a longing eye toward Delia, who stood there looking pure as the driven snow. Unwed, nearly seven months pregnant, and her arms around a—Jeffery.

Billy Dean had embezzled, perjured, defrauded, plundered, extorted, connived, and outright sold his pride for that woman. Probably doomed himself to a prison cell before the week was out.

Still, the craziest thing was, Billy Dean thought, I can't hate her for it. How does she *do* that? he wondered. Hell, he thought as he watched them there, holding each other, I can't even hate Jeffery for it.

"Boy," the Senator said, "are you all right? You don't look too good."

Billy Dean didn't say a word. There wasn't a word he could say. Not a move he could make. Delia had outcheckered him good. Jumped all his men and wiped the board clean.

Chapter Fifty

LOSS FOR WORDS

The bell rang from upstairs for the third time in twenty minutes, and again Vida, who was busy at the sink, sent Johnny up to see what she wanted. Two minutes later he had returned. "She wrote, *'I want Vida.'* I think she's lonely again and needs you to tell her a story."

Vida shook her head. "Your momma is the beatin'est white woman alive. Didn't you tell her your stories?"

"I told her all my good ones twice. I can't think of no more."

"Two hours before Mr. Floyd gets home, and I ain't had the first thought about supper." Vida wiped her hands on the dish towel and then flung it down on the countertop. "I knows what it is she's wanting. Might as well go give it to her."

She unplugged the coffeepot and placed it on the tray along with two cups, a glass of grape Kool-Aid, and a slice of fruitcake. Then she stomped up the stairs as loud as she could, trying to stave off any more bell ringing. Before she got to the door it started again. "Put that thing down before I hang it around your neck like a cowbell!" Vida yelled. "We here already!"

Johnny got the door, and Vida entered the room where Hazel was propped up on a bank of pillows, her neck wrapped in bandages, scribbling furiously on one of Johnny's tablets. She handed it to him, and he in turn held it out to Vida.

Vida dropped the tray on the foot of the bed and snatched the pad. "News flash," Vida said, not looking down at the paper but at Hazel. "They's a spoiled-rotten white woman in this very room who starting to take 'vantage of her piteous situation."

Thinking her not funny, Hazel pointed her finger at the pad.

Vida read the note and frowned. "Well, I tell you why I ain't been up sooner. I been cleaning up after my friends, as you know good and well. Can't we have our coffee and fruitcake and swap Santy Claus without you getting your tail bent?"

Hazel took the pad from Vida and wrote, "WELL?"

"Weeellll," Vida said as she poured the coffee, "well is a mighty deep subject." Both she and Johnny laughed at that, but Hazel flicked the pencil impatiently against the tablet like a drumstick.

"Sure was easier when you hid behind the corner and eavesdropped."

After handing Hazel a cup and taking away her pencil, Vida sat down on the edge of the bed, took a deep breath, and began to recount the day's gossip. "Creola say she done changed her mind about Miss Pearl. Creola done decided that Miss Pearl ain't so much nice as she is stupid."

Hazel narrowed her eyes and looked at Vida scornfully.

"Just because you done switched your mind on Miss Pearl, don't mean I can't have my own thoughts on the matter."

Hazel shrugged.

"Well, Creola say Miss Pearl told her next time she gets the fool idea to go vote, she should come talk it out with her first. Miss Pearl say she been doing some reading on the nature of colored people and how they can't think too good for theyselves 'cause they backed up with feelings left over from Africa and slave times. Miss Pearl say she'll do a better job of looking out for Creola, so she don't get herself in any more trouble." Vida and Hazel both shook their heads at that.

"Well, you know Creola was fit to be tied. She say next time she was going to pass that test, just to show Miss Pearl who was backed up and with what."

Vida handed Hazel Maggie's fruitcake. "Course, when Creola said that about voting, Sweet Pea right away reared back and say..." Vida looked down at Johnny, who was sitting on the floor taking in every word. "Cover your ears, child."

Johnny did as he was told. Carefully he watched Vida's lips.

"Sweet Pea say, 'Next time, hell! If I go 'round trying to vote every week, I ain't never going to get no damn man through my door.' "

Hazel rolled her eyes and smiled.

When Vida handed Johnny his Kool-Aid, he dropped his hands from his ears. He had heard it all the first time anyway.

"I don't know who she be fooling. It's my daddy Sweet Pea got her sights on." Vida grumbled. "Merciful Jesus, that's one woman I ain't never calling Momma. Course, Sweet Pea has a swolled-up head now, gettin' that big reward like she did. I tell you how that come about?"

Hazel shook her head, though she had heard it twice. "She say she was listening to Miss Hertha being real ugly to Deputy Butts. Carrying on about her priceless rings and cameos and things. Say if they can drag ever mudhole in Mississippi looking for her sister who ain't even dead yet, then they sure nuff can sic one blessed hound dog on Billy Dean." Vida laughed.

"That's when Sweet Pea took them to a place in the woods where she thought he was probably hiding. Caught him red-handed. 'Speck he's busy as a man can be, hashing over old times with his friends up at the state prison."

Hazel shook her head sadly. She had had such high hopes for the sheriff turning himself around.

"I thought for sure, spite of the roadblocks, he would have got clear up to Chicargo, or some such place." Vida was quiet for a moment, nodding, thinking. Chicago, for her, had come to symbolize the very heart of the unknown world.

"Anyway, that where he was, all right. He kind of give up. I reckon I can see why he went back there. One time I figured it had to be his praying ground. The last place he seen the face of God. I know for a fact that's the last place he seen his momma. I guess for Billy Dean Brister, God disappeared that day, too." She smiled sadly. "Boys and they momma, huh, Miss Hazel?"

Hazel looked over at Johnny, understanding what she meant.

"Said he was drunk as Cooter Brown. Crying like a baby."

Then Vida laughed. "Course he'll be safer locked up than on the loose. I heard some low-count agitator dropped Miss Delia's purple letter in Miss Hertha's mailbox. Should be some fine fireworks by New Year's Day. I swear, if that family was in a circus, I'd follow them town to town!"

Hazel waved her fork with satisfaction, hoping she got to see Hertha and Delia tear each other's hair out.

"And now we got us a Sheriff Butts to fret about. Course, we don't know much about him yet. We ain't got nobody in his house, but the League is working on it. Creola got a cousin." Vida winked at Hazel and they both smiled.

"And that ol' Misery! Well, you know how she be. She say, 'All that trouble y'all got into and didn't change nothing. Still can't vote yet.'" Vida grinned. "You hear that? Even got ol' Misery saying *'yet.'* Now that be a mighty change right there. A mountain done moved. Like Daddy said, 'You can't turn back a step once it's been took.' He say you might can turn back the person what took it. Kill him even. But that step is out there for good, waiting on the next person to come along."

Hazel nodded appreciatively, as if that were a really good saying. Seeing that Hazel liked it, Vida repeated it proudly, "Yep, that's exactly what he said, 'You can't turn back a step once it's been took.'"

Vida paused for a moment and then said, "I know it's crazy, but my daddy done won me over. We been talking to the folks who run that Montgomery boycott. I guess he and me going to become a couple of civil righters, right here in Mississippi. They's a lot to do.

They's a lot of little boys same as Nate going to grow up second-class citizens less somebody does something. 'Cept you can't tell nobody."

Hazel crossed her heart.

Vida went on for another several minutes, keeping an eye on Hazel, whose lids got heavier and heavier until she finally drifted off to sleep. Johnny and Vida quietly loaded up the tray. Vida turned out the lights, and the boy carefully pulled the door closed.

Downstairs in the kitchen, as Vida set the tray on the counter, Johnny said, "Santa Claus coming tonight. Ain't he, Vida?"

"Sure is, and don't say ain't."

"He coming to your house, too?"

"I 'speck he'll drop in. Along with all my other friends. And Willie and Daddy."

Vida ran a little more hot water into the sink and then swished the dishwater with her hand to build a few suds. "And tomorrow," she said, "I be back here. Me and you can show off our presents."

Vida placed the last dishes in the sink, and as she washed, she began to sing. This time the tune she put the words to sounded more like a carol. It was always changing. As she sang, she thought about Nate. What would he be getting for Christmas? He was ten tonight. Clothes, maybe? A football? Books? He could probably read real good by now.

She looked up out of the window. The weak December sun was nearly done for the day. Did he remember? she wondered, as she did every day.

After she repeated the two lines several more times, Johnny said, "You always singing them same words, Vida. Ain't you got no more?"

"Don't say ain't. Them's the only ones I know of." She continued singing what she knew.

Thinking Vida had sounded sad about that, Johnny said, "I'll make you some more for your Christmas present."

She smiled into her dishwater. "That would make me proud."

As Vida washed and Johnny hunched over his tablet at the table, they sang the words together.

Drivin' a big black car
For a big white man.

EPILOGUE

He stood at the window, watching the snow. It fell in a lacy curtain across the skyline, its folds covering the streets and gathering up over the sidewalk. Headlights and taillights and streetlights and traffic lights and neon winked and blinked and flashed through the snowy screen and reminded him of decorations on an immense tree.

The man never tired of watching the snow, seeing the seasons change with such force. Maybe because in this place, like the seasons, a man could make himself over, too. Here he could change into something more than anybody had ever told him was possible.

"One more time," the boy called out, bouncing on the bed behind him. "I want to watch your fingers. I bet I can learn to play as good as you."

He turned away from the window and the snow. "It's past your bedtime. They going to be back any minute."

"Just once more. Please? It's Christmas Eve." The boy looked at him expectantly, knowing that in the end he would get exactly what he wanted.

Even as he asked, the man was returning to the chair by the bed. He gently lifted the guitar from its case. The boy leaned in as the man showed him how to make the chord. He began the song once more, slowly this time, so the boy could study the fingering:

Vida, wear your white dress to the station,

Bring your parasol too.
I got me a real meal ticket,
A solid gold plan.
Drivin' a big black car
For a big white man.

༄

"I want you to teach me that one first."

The man laughed. "That right?" He plucked a high C and then bent the string, making the note rise up like a question. "Why you suppose that is?"

"Because you put my father in it. He's the big white man in a big black car."

"Yep. You right about that." The man strummed the final chord of the song. "And him and your momma are going to be back anytime. They'll be all over me if you still up."

"Tell me the story one more time."

Sitting down by the boy's bed again, he said, "OK, a quick version. I wrote that song because your daddy found a way to get me out of trouble when nobody else would bother with a Mississippi hick, cotton lint still in his hair. But he did. Imagine, a big-shot lawyer, standing up for a eighteen-year-old punk."

"You!" the boy laughed. "A Mississippi hick!"

"Yeah. Me," he said, laughing also.

"That's when Daddy asked you to come live with us."

"Yep. When he got me out of jail. I started driving for him."

"How old was I?"

"When I got out you were near about four. You know that for yourself. You trying to stretch this out."

"And now you're going to be a lawyer like him."

"One day. If he's a good enough teacher. End of story. Get to sleep now."

The boy yawned. "Are you ever going to write one about me?"

"When you can carry a tune to sing it with. Time for you to go to bed. Let's cut the light out."

The boy smiled, but his eyes were heavy. Reaching for the light chain again, the man said, "Time to cut off the lights. This time for true."

"Just one more."

"No."

"The story about the hands," he said and yawned again.

"Don't ring a bell."

"You know. When I was little. The one you told about the golden hands on a golden thread." The boy rubbed an eye with the back of his fist. "I heard it somewhere. Must have been you."

The man thought for a moment. Could the boy really be remembering?

"No, I never told it," said the man finally. "You must have imagined that one on your own. Maybe you got your own song to write."

How many more pieces would come to the boy before he would need to know the whole truth? How do you tell somebody a thing like that? How wide does a boy's shoulders need to be to carry that much sorrow?

"Thanks for the guitar."

"You're welcome." He clicked off the light. "Merry Christmas."

The boy, on his way to sleep, said softly, "I want to go there one day. Go see the big river and the alligator swamps. Cotton fields. That woman all dressed in white."

The man pulled the covers up over the boy's shoulders. No, he thought, there was more than sorrow that got left behind. There was love, as well. He'll need that one day. Everybody does.

"They just songs," he lied. "Believe me, you got everything worth wanting right here. For now."

He stood over the bed, studying the boy, his face illuminated by a wedge of light from the doorway. He reached down, intending to stroke him lightly on the cheek, but drew his hand back. He was growing up. Soon he would be too old for bedtime stories and lullabies. It would be time for the truth. Truth was already creeping up on the boy.

As the man stood there watching, having his thoughts, the boy began to snore softly. Still, he decided, only little-boy snores. He had his whole life in front of him with no past to fret over. Let him have that for tonight. There would time for grown-up truths later.

He was about to pull the door shut when he noticed the boy's fist. It was clenched on the pillow next to his head, as if holding on tightly to something as he slumbered.

Finally he whispered, "Good-night, little man," and carefully closed the door on the boy's dreaming.

† † †

ABOUT ROSA PARKS AND THE
MAIDS OF MISSISSIPPI

As a child growing up in 1950s Mississippi, I thought we had the worst television reception in the world. Nearly every night, broadcasters from our local channel interrupted the news to announce that they were experiencing technical difficulties. Little did I know at the time, the technical difficulties had nothing to do with broadcast signals, antennas, or any of the little doohickeys that made on-air programming possible. No, local stations in Mississippi purposely went dark whenever the national news was reporting something positive about Civil Rights. The technical difficulties were people like Mrs. Rosa Parks.

In 1955, Mississippi was waging an all-out war against integration, and the news out of Montgomery only strengthened its resolve to keep up the fight. That year, the Mississippi legislature established and funded the Sovereignty Commission, a state agency whose charge was to preserve segregation. It was authorized to employ any means necessary, including tapping phones, monitoring mail, planting spies, and paying informers, to gather intelligence on private citizens suspected of working for Civil Rights. The Commission passed along surveillance files to law enforcement, the White Citizens Councils, and the Klan. They were also charged with ensuring that the state's stand on segregation was always portrayed in a "positive light." State media outlets were already controlled by archsegregationists, so local reporting on Montgomery conformed to the Commission's standards. If national networks aired anything that was deemed favorable to Civil Rights, the local station interrupted the broadcast.

And there was one story developing next door in Alabama that terrified them.

On December 1, 1955, at 5:00 p.m., Mrs. Rosa Parks left her job as assistant tailor at a downtown Montgomery department store. She had a lot on her mind. It was Thursday, and on Saturday she was presenting an NAACP workshop for college girls. Would anyone come? Montgomery's black community was not known for its activism and especially not for its unity. Getting them to make a concerted stand was nearly impossible. Earlier that summer a daughter of an old friend had been manhandled by a bus driver and then beaten and arrested by the police. And Claudette was only fifteen. For a while there was talk of a boycott, but the community could not come together even to protest on behalf one of their most vulnerable. So much more groundwork needed to be laid.

Of course, Mrs. Parks had had her own experiences with Montgomery city buses. Twelve years earlier, she had paid her fare at the front of the bus and was expected to get off and reenter through the back door so as not to pass through the white section. That winter's day was rainy and cold, and she refused. The burly, red-faced bus driver lunged at her and threw her from his bus. Humiliated, she walked home five miles in the rain. She memorized his face and swore never to get on his bus again.

That driver could have done worse. There were plenty of instances of white drivers slapping, beating, and purposely catching black women in the doors and dragging them along the pavement. It could have been *much* worse if the driver had called the police, as one had with Claudette. Officers were known not only to brutally beat black riders with billy clubs but also to shoot them right there on the sidewalk for showing the least resistance. If a woman was put into a patrol car, sexual assault was a real possibility before she even got to the jail.

But that day, Mrs. Parks didn't expect any trouble. It was only a fifteen-minute ride home to where her husband, Raymond, was preparing dinner. To be extra cautious, she waited for a less crowded bus so there would not be as much potential for confrontation. Absorbed in thought, she paid her ten-cent fare and took a seat in the middle of the bus, where the colored section began. Her seat-mate was a black man. Two black women sat across the aisle. As the bus rattled along the avenue, Mrs. Parks could see the stores lit up with holiday decorations. Christmas was coming up fast. She began thinking about how she and Raymond were going to make this holiday special.

At the third stop, the white section of the bus filled. One white man was left standing. The driver shouted out, "Let me have those front seats." He wanted not only Rosa's seat but the entire row. She, the man next to her, and the women across the aisle would need to go to the back of the bus and stand, so one white man could sit down.

With a shock Rosa recognized the driver. He was the same one who had humiliated her twelve years before. She had sworn she would never allow another white man to belittle her like that again.

Rosa watched as the man next to her and the women across the aisle relinquished their seats.

In this moment, it all came down to Rosa Parks.

She had no way of knowing that this was not simply any moment, but *the* moment so many like her had worked for, the moment so many had planned for, prayed for. So many had died for. She had no way of knowing that her decision would determine whether there would be a boycott; whether the world would ever hear of Martin Luther King Jr.; whether for the first time in history a black community as large as Montgomery's could stay unified for even one day, not to mention the *382* days the black community eventually boycotted the bus system, crippling a major city's bus company. Indeed, she did not know whether a flame would be ignited that would inspire countless activists to launch their own Civil Rights campaigns, transforming the South and the nation forever.

What she did know was that only a few months before, Emmett Till, a fourteen- year-old boy, had been brutally tortured and killed in Mississippi, only to have his confessed murderers congratulated and acquitted. She thought of her proud grandfather, who protected his family from whites by keeping a loaded shotgun in the house. And how as a child, she had learned to sleep with her clothes on in case the Klan came during the night.

The driver now hovered over her, threatening. Not only did he have a gun, he had the police authority to use it. There was no end to the trouble he could cause her.

And Rosa Parks knew what trouble could look like. She had spent the past eleven years documenting racial brutality and sexual violence against blacks for the NAACP. She knew what whites were capable of. Yet now, in this moment, she wasn't a passive interviewer or note taker. She was the potential victim.

"Are you going to stand up?" the driver asked Rosa Parks.

Rosa looked him in the eye and gave the answer that changed everything. "No," she said.

"Well, I'm going to have you arrested."

"You may do that," she replied evenly.

She watched as black men on the bus found reasons to flee. She knew some of the women on the bus. No one spoke up for her, even though she prayed they would. No one said, "If you arrest her, then you'll have to take me, too."

She was alone now. She later said it was one of the worst days of her life.

Before I began researching *Miss Hazel and the Rosa Parks League*, I was certain that black ministers and other men led the Civil Rights Movement. I was taught that the successes resulted from black male leaders negotiating with white male leaders. Yes, there was Rosa Parks, a silent symbol of black victimhood, a potent reminder of the endurance of the meek and downtrodden. But she was more of a symbol than a flesh-and- blood person.

Then I began interviewing African American women in Mississippi who had worked in the movement. They told stories of escaping the Klan in hearses, hiding in caskets; of facing down armed whites when trying to get their children through the door of a whites-only school; of being beaten when trying to register to vote. Many of the ministers I thought of as movement leaders had actually been shamed into taking stands by these fearless women. Fannie Lou Hamer, a Mississippi fieldworker and Civil Rights force of nature, referred to those timid reverends as "chicken eatin' preachers," and did so to their faces! Even worse, some of the most respected black preachers were actually on the payroll of the Sovereignty Commission, turning members of their own congregations over to the Klan. And last but not least, the publisher of the state's only black newspaper was also an informant for the Commission.

I found that often the heroes and leaders were black women. And not just any black women, but usually domestics and fieldworkers, as opposed to middle-class blacks. And I learned that these heroes' heroes, those on whose shoulders they stood, were not necessarily men but other women. People like Ella Baker and Septima Clark, like Jo Anne Robinson and, yes, Rosa Parks.

So it was no surprise, as I dug deeper into the history of the Montgomery bus boycott, that the same pattern emerged. Men at the podium, women on their feet.

Mrs. Parks said that when she was arrested and taken to jail, she didn't believe anything would come of it. Three other black women had been jailed that year for challenging bus operators. Why should this time be any different?

But on the street, the rest of black Montgomery was learning that this time it was going to be different. An African American women's group that had been pushing black leaders for years to do something about the shameful city bus situation decided to act unilaterally. They were not going to wait to get permission from Mrs. Parks or the ministers. By the next day, they had printed and delivered 52,500 handbills.

"Another Negro Woman has been arrested....Next time it could be your daughter or mother!" the flyer threatened. A one-day boycott was announced for the following Monday. The message was clear. Black domestic workers, who made up most of the ridership, were getting the brunt of the abuse. Black men could not defend them, and whites were unwilling to. Black women had to do it for themselves.

By Friday night, the day after Mrs. Parks's arrest, every black woman, man, and child knew the plan for the boycott. It set off a firestorm among the 70 percent of black women who worked as domestics. Mrs. Parks was the straw that broke the camel's back. As one maid explained, "Miss Rosie Parks, one of our nice respectable ladies was put in jail, and folks got full and jest wouldn't take no more..." Another witness said, "Not only was Mrs. Parks arrested, but every Negro in Montgomery felt arrested."

The day was rainy and bone-cold, not good weather for staying off a bus. Mrs. Parks remembered looking out her window to see the sidewalks choked with maids, cooks, and washerwomen walking to work under a cloud of black umbrellas. All the buses passed empty.

Later that day, when she left the court building after her trial, Mrs. Parks found five hundred supporters, mostly women, chanting from the steps "They've messed with the wrong one now!"

A mass rally was planned that night to cap off the one-day boycott, and the preachers had to get their act together and select a leader to press on with the boycott. It was obvious that these women were of no mind to stop now. No one really wanted the job. It looked too doubtful and, considering the past, was bound to be short-lived, a humiliation for those out front. The new preacher in town, Martin Luther King Jr., surprised everyone and took up the challenge.

When the ministers arrived at the rally that evening, they found no timid souls. Five thousand people, mostly female domestic workers, had filled the sanctuary of the Holt Street Baptist Church to capacity. Outside, another ten thousand crammed the steps, packed the sidewalks, and stopped traffic for six blocks. No one had ever seen this many Montgomery blacks in one place. The police were helpless to contain it.

Emboldened, the ministers gave their fiery speeches. People sat, stood, clapped, and held hands while tears streamed down their faces. The crowd called out for Mrs. Parks. When she asked if she should speak, she was told by one of the ministers, "No. You have said enough."

The powers that be decided that Mrs. Parks would be more useful as a public symbol. The spotlight belonged to the men, but it was left to Mrs. Parks and the other women to do everything else: strategize, organize, administer car pools, raise money, do the walking, and absorb the brunt of the retaliation. They didn't complain. The movement was more important than anything else.

But the presence of these women could not be denied, and it relentlessly drove the movement and its leaders forward. When one woman was asked in court who the movement's leaders were, she replied, "Our leaders is just we ourself."

In their solidarity, black domestics had discovered what King called their "somebodyness." They stood up to their white employers and were fired from their jobs. As they walked, white segregationists threw balloons filled with urine from passing cars, hit them with rocks, and pelted them with rotten vegetables. When they had to pass by armed and jeering whites stationed on the street, they would not be cowed. One maid said, "Look at them red bastards over there watching us. They got them guns, but us ain't skeered." Another said, "When they find out you ain't scared of 'em, they leave you alone. The son of bitches."

In March, Mrs. Parks was arrested once more, along with 181

others, on a charge of conspiracy. This time, scores of female domestics descended on the courthouse. They wore bandannas and men's hats and had their dresses rolled up. The police tried to restore order, but the women responded by surging forward. When a policeman reached for his gun, one domestic shouted, "If you hit one of us, you'll not leave here alive!"

That defiance didn't stop with Montgomery.

Despite the national media being slow to catch on to the momentousness of the boycott and the local press deliberately downplaying the significance or censoring it outright, word got out. News of the heroic boycotters even into trickled into Mississippi, where racism was even more virulent, organized, and institutionalized.

In Alabama, law enforcement was known to cooperate with the Klan; in Mississippi, law enforcement *was* the Klan. County sheriffs were seen as complicit either in carrying out or covering up three murders in 1955 alone. One of course was Emmett Till, killed for "whistling at a white woman." Lamar Smith was shot in broad daylight on the courthouse lawn for trying to register to vote. George W. Lee, a preacher, businessman, and outspoken Civil Rights activist was killed by a shotgun blast from a passing car just before midnight.

In spite of state censorship laws banning the transportation of antisegregationist literature across state lines, random issues of African American newspapers like the *Chicago Defender* and the *New York Amsterdam News* found their way into the state. A single tattered copy was often passed from hand to hand, discussed in black churches, pool halls, barbershops, juke joints, and all other gathering places outside the white man's line of vision. Yes, they knew about Rosa Parks in Mississippi.

And then there were the maids.

The maids of Mississippi, like the ones in Alabama, saw themselves reflected in Mrs. Parks's experience. If the Mississippi Sovereignty Commission had a surveillance counterpart in the black community, it would have been the network of domestic help who spent their days cooking, washing, tending children, and cleaning their white employers' homes, all the while listening to the most intimate details of their lives.

Ostensibly, the work of maids was to perform the physical tasks involved in taking care of the white home and its inhabitants. Yet a critical, never mentioned, part of the job description was tending to the emotional needs of the family. Domestic help was there to shepherd white folks through their most private moments. They were also expected to affirm the opinions white folks had of themselves of being benevolent, fair, wise, and, of course, socially, intellectually, and morally superior.

When I look back at this era, the best analogy I can offer to describe the black presence in the white home is this: the maid turned herself into a one-way mirror. She became adept at hiding her true self while at the same time reflecting an image of her white employers that pleased, flattered, cajoled, and never threatened.

We white Southerners loved how we looked in the eyes of our maids and never doubted their loyalty. We talked as openly in their presence as if they were merely furniture.

Yet that one-way mirror of Jim Crow allowed domestic servants to pool privileged information in order to better resist oppression. One woman I interviewed had been the maid to a prominent white preacher in my hometown of Laurel. He also happened to be an active member of the local Klan, which had been terrorizing the county's freedom workers. Like most white employers he talked freely in front of his maid, putting his trust in that mirrored reflection. All the while she ran information back to Civil Rights activists, warning them where and when the Klan would strike next. And in 1956, one of the topics at every white dinner table in Mississippi was that "uppity colored girl" over in Alabama.

Many black domestic workers, inspired by the likes of Rosa Parks, became invaluable in the fight for the rights of their people. Rosa Parks taught them that when they, the least of the least, came together, nothing could stop them.

The editor of the *Christian Century* saw that as well. This is what he wrote about that evening in March when the unruly mob of domestic workers in Montgomery stood down the police at the court building: *"That night black women served notice that they were no longer going to be violated by or pushed around by white police officers. They put their bodies on the line in defense of their humanity, something anyone watching could see. The standoff marked the first fateful assertion of their full dignity as human beings."* The day the U.S. Supreme Court handed down its decision declaring segregation on the buses unconstitutional, after 382 consecutive days of solidarity, the Klan decided to remind working-class blacks that things would never really change. Over forty cars of white-hooded goons drove slowly through the quarters to invoke the old terror. The inhabitants hooted and shook their fists. Deflated, the Klan retreated.

A domestic worker put it more succinctly. "They bit the lump off and us making 'em chew it. Colored folks ain't like they used to be. They ain't scared no more."

Given all the mass demonstrations and organized marches that followed, it's sobering to remember how alone Mrs. Parks was that day on the bus when she had to make her decision. To take that first step to a place no one has ever gone is perhaps the most courageous thing a person can do. It's certainly got to be loneliest. But once taken, it can't be reversed. It's out there for everyone to see. That one step of courage sent ripples through the universe, and emboldened the unlikeliest of heroes to take their own next steps. It still does, sixty years later.

☙

After the boycott, Mrs. Parks was asked if it were true that she didn't move that day on the bus because she was tired. She replied, "People always say that I didn't give up my seat because I was tired, but that isn't true. I was not tired physically, or no more tired than I usually was at the end of a working day…no, the only tired I was,

was tired of giving in."

That is what her simple "No," meant to millions of black women, who existed on the bottom rung of the ladder of power. These people knew about giving in. Black working women saw themselves and their lives in Mrs. Parks's action.

As Nikki Giovanni said in her poem "Harvest":

...Something needs to be said...about Rosa Parks...
other than her feet...were tired...
...Lots of people...on that bus...and many before...
and since...had tired feet...lots of people...still do...
they just don't know...where to plant them...

Mrs. Parks's "No" showed a million women where to plant their feet.

A DISCUSSION GUIDE

1. Both Floyd and Hazel are driven to leave their homes in the hills. What is it they are in such a rush to escape? How realistic are their dreams?

2. The novel centers on two young mothers, one white, the other black. When Hazel and Vida meet, they are both grieving. How do their losses affect them as women?

3. Discuss Hazel's inability to belong. Would she have had the same difficulty had she stayed on the farm? How do these difficulties take shape when she encounters the other wives of her new class and neighborhood?

4. Hazel's quest for beauty becomes a singular goal when, as a child, she realizes she is unattractive. What role does physical beauty play in this novel?

5. How does Vida come to terms with the hostility she faces from Hazel's son Johnny? What do you imagine will become of him? Is it easier today for boys who do not conform to traditional ideas of what it means to be a boy?

6. What do you imagine for Nate's future? Will he ever learn the truth, and how might that change him if he does?

7. Consider the ways Hazel and Vida find freedom as well as the times they each require rescuing. What transformation do they

undergo throughout the course of this novel? How does the balance of power between these two characters change?

8. Rosa Parks never appears in the novel and yet her influence seems essential to the outcome of the story. What other acts of courage did you find in this novel?

9. The wives of Delphi society in the 1950s are vividly portrayed by Odell. What characterized their concept of the ideal woman? Where does Hazel fit into this ideal? What, if any, elements of the stereotypical 1950s woman remain today?

10. Why is Hazel so attracted to the maids? Why is Vida so repulsed by the white women? Hazel sees Vida as a friend, yet Vida has a very different attitude toward Hazel. What brings them together in the end?

11. Can you identify any instances of "internalized" racism (beliefs that have been accepted as true by the victims themselves) on the part of Odell's black characters?

12. Odell believes that one reason racism is so difficult to cure is that it is passed on as a gift of love, meaning it is often given to us by family members or those close to us, not by people we see as evil, but by those who love us and want to make us feel special at someone else's expense. Can you identify a scene in the novel where Odell's point is most clearly made?

13. In the current novel, which is a new rendering of Odell's decade old debut novel, *A View from Delphi,* and in *The Healing,* an historical novel set in the pre-Civil War South about an enslaved healing woman on a plantation, Odell tries to offer readers a deeper understanding of the history of slavery and the Civil Rights Movement in our country. What role do you think art can play in influencing the way we see our world? Can you

identify a book or film that was particularly important to your understanding of another race, religion or people?

————

Jonathan very much enjoys connecting with book groups. To check on Jonathan's availability please go to JonathanOdell.net to email an inquiry.

ACKNOWLEDGEMENTS

I want to thank Marly Rusoff, my agent who, after successfully placing my novel, *The Healing*, before the public, championed the idea of giving my first-born a second chance. *The View from Delphi* was released in 2004 by a small press to warm reviews but little exposure. Marly believed the subject matter to be even more relevant today and deserving of a larger reading audience. Her unshakable faith in the story gave me the confidence to structurally refashion the book, while keeping its soul intact.

The keen editorial insights of Julie Mosow and the enthusiastic support of Michael Radulescu at Maiden Lane Press were invaluable. I must also thank authors Julie Landsman and Mary Logue, as well as Chris Jerome, and Harriet Moore, who each contributed to making this novel a more gratifying read.

My dear friend, UC law professor Michele B. Goodwin, used our weekly breakfasts at times to lovingly challenge my white man's thinking on the constructs of race, class and gender.

I met Jim Kuether just as *The View from Delphi* was being released. In the ten years since, he has become not only my best friend, but also my most trusted editor. His artist's eye can pierce the heart of the story. One of the greatest rewards of this retelling is to bring Jim's talent and vision to the process.

And mostly I'm grateful to the African American witnesses to that age, those unlikely memoirists—sharecroppers, maids, midwives, yardmen, preachers, teachers, schoolchildren, and Saturday night brawlers—who shared their precious recollections to help this author discover the true measure of heroism.

Civil Rights activist Dorothy Cotton sums it up beautifully.

"The civil rights movement that rearranged the social order of this country did not emanate from the halls of the Harvards and the Princetons or the Cornells. It came from simple unlettered people who learned they had the right to stand tall and that nobody can ride a back that isn't bent."

JONATHAN ODELL ON
HAZEL AND VIDA

Many readers have asked me if my characters, Hazel and Vida in particular, are based on real people, as is so often the case with debut fiction.

The answer is yes. Much of the book is drawn from my early life experience, much to my family's horror. Actually, when I began the book, it was as an attempt to get even with everyone who had ever done me wrong—teachers, schoolyard bullies, my preacher, and, of course, my parents. Vida and Hazel began as absolute villains in my first draft. They represented people in my life I wanted to settle a score with. Vida represented Velner, a black lady my parents hired to take care of me and my brothers when my mother took a job. I hated Velner and Velner hated me.

Hazel is definitely my mother. When I began the book, I was going through therapy and beginning to understand my family's dysfunction. I was in my "angry truth-telling stage," so I "fictionalized" every wrong my mother had ever perpetrated upon me. In essence it was a poorly disguised hit piece. I even named the little boy Johnny so my mother would not miss the point.

When I finally let go of my agenda of trying to justify my resentments, I fell in love with both women. Now, even today, when I see my mother, she is so much bigger and grander than the box I had placed her in. By letting go of the need to explain my mother, I discovered her. Writing the book served as an avenue for reconciliation with my family. It transformed me, and instead of a condemnation, the book became a tribute to those who raised me.

PRAISE FOR THE HEALING BY JONATHAN ODELL

"A remarkable rite-of-passage novel with an unforgettable character.... *The Healing* transcends any clichés of the genre with its captivating, at times almost lyrical, prose."
—*Associated Press*

"A storytelling tour de force."—*Atlanta Journal-Constitution*

"Compelling, tragic, comic, tender and mystical....
It combines the historical significance of Kathryn Stockett's *The Help* with the wisdom of Toni Morrison's *Beloved*."
—*Minneapolis Star Tribune*

"Wonderful! Polly Shine is a character for the ages."
—**PAT CONROY**, author of *The Prince of Tides*

"A must-read for fans of historical fiction."
—**KATHLEEN GRISSOM**, author of *The Kitchen House*

"Jonathan Odell won me over with his fresh take
on the connective power of story to heal body, mind, and
community.... I'm still marveling about Polly Shine."

—**LALITA TADEMY**, author of *Cane River*,
An Oprah's Book Club selection

"*The Healing* is a lyrical parable, rich with historical detail and unflinching in the face of disturbing facts."
—**VALERIE MARTIN,** author of the
Orange-Prize-winning novel *Property*

"A haunting tale of Southern fiction peopled with vivid and inspiring personalities. . . . Polly Shine is an unforgettable character who shows how the power and determination of one woman can inspire and transform the lives of those around her."
—*Bookreporter*

"Jonathan Odell finds the right words, using the language of the day, its idiom and its music to great advantage in a compelling work that can stand up to *The Help* in the pantheon of Southern literature." —*Shelf Awareness*

"Odell has written one of those beautiful Southern tales with unforgettable characters. Required reading."
—*New York Post*

"Engrossing. . . . This historical novel probes complex issues of freedom and slavery."
—*Library Journal* (starred review)